I0819653

make me better

MORE BOOKS BY SARAH GAILEY

Magic for Liars
The Echo Wife
Just Like Home

American Hippo
Upright Women Wanted
Spread Me

When We Were Magic

make me better

sarah gailey

TOR PUBLISHING GROUP
NEW YORK

This is a work of fiction. All of the names, characters, organizations, places, and events portrayed in this work are either products of the author's imagination or used fictitiously.

MAKE ME BETTER

Interior art by Shutterstock

A Tor Book
Published by Tom Doherty Associates / Tor Publishing Group
120 Broadway
New York, NY 10271

www.torpublishinggroup.com

EU Representative: Macmillan Publishers Ireland Ltd, 1st Floor, The Liffey Trust Centre, 117–126 Sheriff Street Upper, Dublin 1, D01 YC43

The Library of Congress Cataloging-in-Publication Data is available upon request.

ISBN 978-1-250-85175-8 (hardcover)
ISBN 978-1-250-85176-5 (ebook)

First Edition: 2026

Printed in the United States of America

10 9 8 7 6 5 4 3 2 1

To love is to accept a future that contains grief. The grief may be ours, or it may belong to those we leave behind. To love a child or a partner or a dream or a community is to enter into a contract with the inevitable pain of loss.

This is a book about what pain we will accept and inflict on others to avoid the contract. It is about the paths we take to try to evade the inevitable.

This is for everyone who has ever tried to be saved.

PART ONE

you were pure once

SALT FESTIVAL

day one | afternoon

Celia tried as hard as she could to see nothing but Kindred Cove. The little boat beneath her felt like a tin can cut in half. Her fellow passengers blurred in her peripheral vision. Her hands trembled at the sight of the crowd amassing on the shore of the island.

The people seeped out through the trees and sluiced down toward the waterline. There were two hundred of them up there, maybe two hundred and fifty. Some of the children of the island hoisted tall branches with bright scraps of fluttery cloth tied to the ends. Unsmiling adults touched the children on the shoulders without looking down at them. Behind the gathering crowd, near the trees, a high banner read Welcome Salt Festival Visitors in uneven letters.

Celia chewed the already-raw inside of her cheek. She was nearly there.

As the water taxi approached the land, a man stepped out of the crowd on the shore. His skin had a leathery quality that spoke to frequent sun. His bright, penetrating eyes were pinned to Celia. She felt like a spider in the shadow of a housecat. But then his gaze shifted to the woman next to her, and Celia found herself able to draw breath again.

"Welcome to Kindred Cove." The man sounded neither hostile nor friendly, as though they were expected but not invited. *He doesn't want us here*, Celia thought. Then she checked herself: That was negative thinking, toxic thinking, making assumptions and ascribing intent. She reminded herself not to let her anxiety control her. She fixed her eyes on the banner and made herself focus on the first word: *welcome.*

"Where should I tie up now the dock's gone?" The stringy kid who had piloted the water taxi across the lake was chewing his gum at a volume that could not be accidental. He wore a sweat-stained white polo shirt with *Vetiver Tours* embroidered over the breast pocket. A small goiter on his neck moved in time with the rhythmic working of his jaw.

He couldn't have been older than fourteen. Celia couldn't remember if that was too young for a goiter. She couldn't even remember what caused them—something that was supposed to be in tap water, she thought, or in table salt. Too much of it, or not enough. She wondered what the kid wasn't getting in his diet, and immediately felt overwhelmed by the idea of trying to find a way to fix it.

She looked away from him, and the feeling of overwhelm faded. She was embarrassed at her own relief.

"You can tie up in a minute," the man on the shore said. He wasn't looking at the kid either. "Before we welcome all of you onto our shore, I want to be sure everyone's in the right place."

"I made 'em check in, just like you said," the kid replied. "They all—"

"I want to make sure," the man continued, louder now, more theatrical, "that everyone here is ready to step into an experience that will change their lives. The next four days will transform you forever. The Salt Festival is about connection, purification, cleansing, and community. It's about releasing yourself from the anchors that hold you back from the life you could be living. But more than any of that—it's about celebration."

His face opened into a wide, warm smile. Celia wanted to learn how to smile like that.

"It's about celebration," he repeated. "Are you ready to celebrate with us?"

A lukewarm shout rose up from the group on the boat. There were twenty of them, packed onto the tiny water taxi too tightly for anyone to yell without it landing in someone else's ear. Celia worried that the man on the shore would do one of those *you can do better than that* routines, trying to get them to shout louder. She hated those—hated the faux-chastising tone, hated knowing that it didn't matter how loud the first yell was because whoever was running things was always going to ask for a second one anyway. She hated the hard seed inside of her that choked off her ability to perform bright wet excitement on demand.

But he didn't try to extract another display of enthusiasm from the visitors. Instead, he strode forward into the water, his movements quick and efficient, his response so immediate that Celia tipped backward. The tall, tobacco-smelling guy standing just behind her caught her by the shoulders with a murmured *whoa there*.

Even though the sun-worn man was moving farther into the lake, coming at her fast, he didn't sink any deeper than his knees. He raised an arm and yelled the name *Caleb*, and a second man jogged out of the crowd to join him. Caleb had short brown hair, deep brown skin, and wide wet eyes fringed with thick dark lashes. He didn't look at the water taxi at all. Just kept his eyes on the water, picking his steps carefully.

Celia realized they were both walking on some kind of structure just below the surface. It was a structure that led straight to the water taxi.

"Want me to swim down to one of the cleats, William?" Caleb's voice came out in a soft baritone.

Celia repeated the name *William* to herself, as the man who seemed to be some kind of leader here made his way to the water taxi. "No," he said decisively, not looking back at Caleb. "We'll anchor to the black gum there." He made a gesture at the teenager who had piloted the boat across the lake. "Toss me your painter. That rope right there."

The kid looked back through the tight cluster of people on the water taxi. He let out a heavy sigh. "Okay. Can y'all try to make room for me to get through, or." There didn't seem to be anything lined up to come after the *or*.

Celia followed the path of the kid's gaze and realized it led to her. Her heart stuttered in her chest. She looked down and saw a coil of rope hanging off a cleat on the edge of the boat, right where she was standing. She pointed at the rope, looked from the kid to William and back again. "Is it this?"

"That's the one I need," he answered.

"I've got it." She wasn't sure who she was telling. Celia grabbed the coil. It was heavier than she'd expected, the wet rope scratchy in her palms. She tossed it clumsily to William, who caught it with ease. He gave an experimental tug and then pointed again. "There should be another one on the other side." Someone she couldn't see got that one too, and then William and Caleb were pulling the water taxi toward the shore, a rope over each of their shoulders, their torsos canted forward as they sloshed through the water.

Celia was uncannily reminded of pulling her car forward onto the track of a carwash, then putting it into neutral—drifting into the hellish pummeling of the mitter curtains with no control over her own movement. Still, she liked the way it had felt to throw William the rope. The practicality of it, the way she'd gotten to be helpful.

Things were moving forward because of her. That had to be good.

The boat was heavy, and their progress was slow enough for her to scan the crowd on the shore a few more times. Everyone watched the boat. She would have expected the people waiting for them to get bored, split into smaller groups, talk amongst themselves. The few children she could see should have been restless by now. A crowd of that size, in Celia's experience, couldn't be silent—they necessarily rustled, coughed, breathed, fidgeted. But all she could hear was the splash of the men's legs in the water, the restless shifting of the people on the boat with her, and her own heartbeat.

"Cleansing," the woman next to Celia muttered under her breath. "I'm so fucking sure."

Celia glanced down at her. "What did you say?"

"Hm?" The woman blinked up at her placidly. Her face was seamed with creases, her eyes enormous behind thick-lensed glasses. She spoke in a high, querulous voice that sounded nothing like the voice she'd used when she was muttering to herself. "What's that, dear?"

"Nothing. Nevermind." Celia pressed her lips together and looked away. Wasn't her business. She just needed to get to the island. She just needed this week to work.

This place would fix her. It would pull that hard seed out of her and seal the hole that would be left behind. It had to.

William was moving parallel to the shore, growing clumsy as he waded toward a slim black gum tree a couple of feet above the waterline. There was another boat—threadbare compared to the water taxi—in the shadow of the trees. Once they got close to it, he started to tie a series of knots in the rope she'd thrown him. She watched the deft movements of his hands as though she might learn to tie knots the way he tied them. As though she'd ever be the one doing it.

This would, she decided, be the beginning. She would take everything in while she was here. Everything. She would do the work.

She would get better.

"You're going to have to get a little wet," William said, stepping away from his knots, nearly losing his footing in the slippery silt. He sloshed his way closer to the water taxi, grabbed the low side of it. The water slapped against the side of the boat like a hundred tiny hands trying to find their way in. "You'll have an easier time wading from here than trying to feel your way along the dock. It's been tricky to navigate since it got submerged, and I don't want any of you falling off the side."

"Is it safe to touch the water?" That was the older woman next to Celia again. She asked the question in that same trembling voice, the one that made her sound ancient and fragile.

William looked down at his own feet, then back up at the group on the water taxi. "You're asking now?"

"I just thought—with the mine collapse, and all that—"

"Of course it's safe," Celia said. She tried to keep her voice light. "We've come this far. Might as well go the rest of the way, right?"

She reached down and rolled up her yoga pants—the lightning motif ones from last December, which she hadn't been able to sell and ended up buying from herself to keep her numbers up—then slipped off her shoes. She felt more than saw the shuffle of the other visitors as they copied her, taking off their shoes and preparing to enter the water.

"You can bring your shoes to shore with you," William said, reaching up to unlatch the gate in the rail on the side of the boat. "You'll see where to drop them." He offered his hand to each passenger that stepped off the boat, half-lifted the old woman down into the water. When it was Celia's turn, he kept her hand for a few seconds, holding her in place. She couldn't step down into the water unless he either bent his arm or let go of her, and he wasn't doing either. He just studied her face. "I'm glad you came," he said at last.

She pulled her hand back sharply. "What?"

"I'm glad you came," he repeated. "I can tell just by looking at you—you need it. You'll benefit so much from what we do here."

"Oh. Well." She felt a flush rising up over her neck. How had he seen inside her? Was it that obvious to everyone? "Yes, I do. Need it, I mean. I need to be here. Thank you."

She took his hand and legged her way carefully over the side of the boat. The water, when she stepped down into it, was colder than she expected it to be. It sank immediately into her flesh and yanked the warmth out of her.

Normally, such a shock of cold would make her recoil—but now, she was gripped by a powerful urge to dive in. To follow the path of her own body heat and find out where it had gone. Celia shivered, shaking off the sudden impulse. Reminded herself of what was in the lake, and how little she wanted to encounter it.

William saw her shiver. He winked. "The water's only cold compared to how hot you were from the trip here. I promise it's warmer when you're walking in from the land side of things."

She followed William, and the rest of the visitor group followed her. The silt was spongy beneath her feet, the saltwater of Lake Vetiver splashing with every step she took. Caleb worked at the knots on the rope that tethered the water taxi to the island. By the time they were on dry land, Celia's rolled-up yoga pants were soaked to the knee, and the boat was ready to depart.

The water taxi engine stuttered to life. It was loud and then it was gone.

"No way back," someone whispered, eliciting a giggle from whoever heard them. "Do you think we'll get to see the miracle tide?"

Celia didn't turn to see who'd spoken. She didn't want a way back. She only wanted a way forward.

The visitors stopped in front of the crowd of people on the shoreline. There were two tarps laid out, one with a pair of shoes in the middle and one that was held down by a duffel bag. A man in wire-rimmed glasses dropped his shoes and backpack next to the ones on the tarps. Celia followed suit. She stayed near the back of her group, watching the other visitors. A few couples, a few people older than her, a knot of very young women wearing matching crystal necklaces, a lost-looking pair of men with identical noses who she guessed were brothers. The old woman who'd been next to her on the boat.

Celia wondered why the others were here. She wondered if all of them were broken, too—if all of them had the same ache in their chests as she did. It felt as though someone had used a corkscrew to drill a slow hole in her breastbone. The hole never went away. The temptation to jam her finger into it and touch her own beating heart was with her every second of every day.

This will work, she reminded herself. *This will fix it. This will fix me.*

William clapped his hands once, sharply, looking over the visitors with an appraising eye. "So," he said. "You're here as our guests. What you might not realize is that you're the only new faces we'll see for the entire year. This festival—the Salt Festival," he added with a gesture toward the drooping banner, "is the one time each year that we welcome visitors. The other eleven months, nobody comes or goes without special permission."

Celia took a deep breath in through her nose, let it out through her mouth. She focused on gratitude for the opportunity this festival represented.

"While you're here," he continued, "you'll be living by the guidelines of our intentional community." One of the women in the crystal necklaces raised her hand. He ignored her. "I know you don't know the rules yet, don't worry about that. We'll help you. Each of you will be assigned a buddy to help you learn the ropes. Your buddy will also answer any questions you might have."

With this, he aimed a pointed look at the woman who had her arm in the air, staring her down until she lowered it.

Then he held a hand out, and a woman from the island stepped forward to give him a clipboard. She was half a head taller than William. A threadbare linen shirt, unbuttoned to the middle of her sternum, hung loose across her tentpole frame. She was pale, as if she didn't spend much time in the sun, but her nose and chest bore a stark scattering of dark freckles. Soft, bruiselike shadows drifted under her eyes and kissed the tops of her cheekbones. As Celia watched, the woman pushed her wild thicket of dark hair away from her face with one sweep of her long, slender fingers. She scanned the crowd and she must have seen something that amused her, because her wide, full mouth twitched like she was holding in a laugh.

William was still talking. Celia tore her eyes away from the woman, who she figured must be some kind of assistant to him. She told herself that she wouldn't get distracted while she was here. She reminded herself that she needed to focus.

"These assignments are not negotiable. You and your buddy will stick together at all times. Is that understood?"

The visitors nodded their agreement. Celia curled her toes in the dust. She had expected something of a charm offensive, but William was charmless, bordering on rude. It was nice, in a way—he wasn't meeting her pain with too much enthusiasm, too much kindness.

He started reading names aloud from the clipboard. Celia wondered if he'd split the couples or let them stay together, but she didn't get a chance to see, because while he was still assigning the crystal girls to their chaperones, a hand landed on her shoulder. She turned to see the tall woman who had handed William his clipboard.

"Hey," she whispered. "Sorry to distract you from this part, I know it's *sooo* interesting. I just need to grab a couple of things from you real quick."

Celia glanced down into the fraying basket in the woman's hands. It had several cell phones and wallets in it. She spotted a few wedding rings, too, and an expensive-looking compact with a faded monogram on the lid. There were several purses slung over the woman's shoulder, too. "Um. That's okay," she said. "I'll hang on to mine."

"Nah, you don't want to do that," the woman said agreeably. Up close, Celia could see that the freckles extended onto her arms, too. "It's no big deal, we'll just keep your stuff in the office during the festival. William has a safe in there. It's all normal, just your phone, wallet, keys, and any mirrors or photographs you might've brought with you." She gave the basket a little shake. "You can also just give me your whole bag if it's easier."

"What if I say no?"

The woman gestured to the scuffed-up boat in the shadowy patch where the treeline crept down close to the water. "You can go back if you want. It'll be a pain in the ass, but I'll take you. But I don't think you want that, do you? There's something . . . here," she said, lifting a hand and reaching out to touch Celia lightly on the temple. "Right around your eyes. I can see it. You belong here."

Something inside Celia surged forward at those words. *Yes*, it cried from inside her, *yes, you can see it, please take it away.* She shoved the feeling aside. "Fine," she said, "but if I don't get my things back at the end of the festival, I'll—"

"Oh, you should sue us," the woman finished for Celia, easing the purse strap off her shoulder. "For every penny we're worth."

"Celia?" William called. She looked up and realized she was the only person without a partner. William glanced at the woman with the basket and gave a nod. "I see you've already met your buddy for the week. You'll be spending your days with Easy."

"Nice to meet you, buddy," Easy said with a wink. "Want to come with me to drop this stuff off at the office?"

"Don't I need to stay and hear the rest of the orientation?"

"What orientation? Here." Easy handed Celia the basket. "Let's make like eggs and scramble."

Celia was on the verge of objecting until she realized that the other visitors were dispersing, following their assigned chaperones into the narrow gap in the treeline under the banner. The rest of the crowd dissolved like a spoonful of sugar in water, gone before she could think to look more closely at them. She hadn't seen any faces she recognized. "Wait, where is everyone going?"

"They're going where they go," Easy said.

William strode up to them. "Waiting for something? I doubt you two have time to spend standing here staring at each other. We've got an hour or so of daylight left. I suggest you use it well."

"Of course," Easy said. "I was just about to take her to the office to drop some things off."

"The office is off-limits to visitors." William looked Celia up and down. "Do you really think that's a good idea?"

"What a question." The temperature of Easy's voice dropped by a few degrees.

"I'm just asking," William replied. He raised his hands in a conciliatory gesture, and Celia wondered if she'd misunderstood who was in charge here at Kindred Cove.

Easy flashed William a grin. "Ah, William. You're such a worrywart. She gave me her word that she won't tell anyone else what she sees in there. Isn't that right, Celia?"

Celia looked at Easy, startled, only to catch a fleeting wink. "Um. Yes," she said. "Yes, you have my word."

Easy dropped a hand onto William's shoulder. "You see? I've got a good feeling about this one. We can trust her."

Celia glanced at William before she could catch herself. She wanted to see if he had a good feeling about her too. If he had any feeling about her at all.

When she looked at him, she felt panic flip inside her stomach. It was the same panic she'd felt back when her pregnancy-loss support group read *The Lonely City* together. During the second to last meeting she attended—the meeting where she said goodbye to Adelaide—they'd discussed a passage:

> *I felt like I was in danger of vanishing, though at the same time the feelings I had were so raw and overwhelming that I often wished I could find a way of losing myself altogether, perhaps for a few months, until the intensity diminished. If I could have put what I was feeling into words, the words would have been an infant's wail: I don't want to be alone. I want someone to want me. I'm lonely. I'm scared. I need to be loved, to be touched, to be held.*

Celia had read those final words to herself over and over again.

I'm lonely. I'm scared. I need to be loved, to be touched, to be held.

She'd felt rising terror at the words, but she'd been unable to look away from them.

Unable to look away, because for as long as she could remember, Celia had felt there was a voice inside her screaming *help me*, and that her duty to the world was to hold her hand hard over the small screaming mouth so no one would ever have to hear it. And rising terror, because reading that passage made her feel certain that she'd failed to smother the scream tightly enough.

The knowing tilt of William's head made it seem as if he could hear it. It also made Celia think William might know how to silence that scream for good.

"You can trust me," Celia said. William nodded. Celia took the nod and tucked it into the hole in her breastbone. The scream was still there, but it was muffled just a little.

She could already feel herself getting better.

Celia followed Easy into the shadow of the trees that covered the tiny island of Kindred Cove. She could feel William's eyes on the small of her back as they walked. It took all her willpower to keep from looking over her shoulder.

"What about our bags? Do we go back for those?"

"You won't need them, we have everything ready for you. But they'll get delivered just in case."

"Delivered? To where?"

Easy didn't answer. She was already well ahead on the path. She moved with a slow, loping grace, her long legs devouring the road, and Celia couldn't keep up without jogging. Easy didn't look back to see if Celia was following her; she kept striding up the curving dirt road, her arms swinging loose at her sides, the collection of purses slapping rhythmically against her hip.

"Hey, can you wait a second?" Celia called, walking as fast as she could without breaking into a jog. "I need to—ow, fuck." She grimaced as the ball of her foot landed on a small sharp stone. "I need to go back and grab my shoes."

"Nope," Easy answered, not slowing down. "We don't do that here."

"Don't do what?" Celia slowed once they were side by side, although not by much.

"Shoes." She reached out a steadying hand as Celia stumbled over another rock.

Celia glanced down at Easy's feet. No shoes. She thought back to the crowd, trying to remember if any of the residents of the island had been wearing shoes—but she'd mostly been staring at their faces, trying to spot Adelaide. She remembered William and Caleb walking confidently into the water, not pausing, not slipping off sandals or sneakers.

"Wearing those things separates you from the ground beneath you," Easy continued. "They're an artificial means of preventing yourself from having a real experience. How many times have you really let your skin come into contact with the earth?"

"Lots of times," Celia answered immediately. "I garden. I touch dirt all the time."

Easy's laugh was surprisingly loud. A few birds startled out of a nearby hickory at the sudden sound. "That doesn't count. You control your garden, right? You're the one who put all the dirt there, all the plants." She snapped a stalk off a tall fennel plant by the side of the road, stuck it between her molars, and talked around it like she was chewing on a cigar. "I bet you have a little stone path that cuts through it. I bet you treat your garden like a big potted plant that just happens to go outside. Look out," she added suddenly, pointing into the shadows of the trees ahead. "Tom is going to try to get your ankles. He's just playing, but his claws don't always know that."

Celia gave the patch of shadows a wide berth. A pair of wide yellow eyes glinted out at her as she passed. "Where are all the kids?" she asked, squinting to try to see more of what she hoped was just a cat. The sun was shining low through the trees, sending a cascade of dappled golden light across the path, and squinting didn't do her much good.

"What?"

"The children. I saw them down at the shore, but then they just—"

"Right." Easy sounded somewhere between confused and annoyed. "We don't invite them to spend a lot of time with visitors. It would disrupt their routine. Structure is important for a child's growth and development. Don't you agree? Well—I suppose you might not understand that," she added lightly, "since you're not a parent."

Celia told herself that Easy couldn't know how much her thoughtless words hurt. She couldn't know about the wound she'd just poked a questing finger into. *It's not her fault,* Celia chastised herself. *It's no one's fault but your own.* "Of course. Structure, routine. You grew up here, right? You're not one of the Salt Festival visitors that stayed?"

"What do you mean? Salt Festival visitors don't stay."

Celia paused. "I heard that sometimes the visitors end up deciding to live here."

"Maybe you heard wrong."

Easy's tone was cool enough to make Celia drop it. "Well, anyway. You grew up here, so you must have experienced the same structure the kids get now. Continuity is—"

"It was different back then. We've developed a stronger rhythm for the children in the past few years."

Celia could feel Easy closing off. It made her feel a hot flash of panic. "Were you here when the mines collapsed?"

"Course I was here. Worst day of my life," Easy said.

"Oh? Did anyone—I mean, did you lose someone?" Celia bit her lip. She could hear the hunger in her own voice. She wanted Easy to talk about death. To talk about how much she still ached, how open and weeping the old wound might be. Then maybe she could introduce her pain to Easy's pain, like forcing two snappish dogs to socialize, and Easy would feel understood, and then she'd stay open and welcoming. It was wrong to want someone else's pain this much. Celia knew it was wrong, but that didn't mean she could stop herself.

"Oh, Celia. You have so much to learn here," Easy said, her voice loose with disappointment. "No one is ever lost."

Then, without warning, she turned off the road and walked into the trees. Celia pulled up short. She wondered if she'd offended Easy so much that she'd—what? Wandered into the wilderness to escape the conversation? The moment she realized the absurdity of her thinking, Celia saw the narrow footpath through the undergrowth. Easy had stepped onto it, and now that she knew where to look, Celia could see where they were headed: a squat single-wide trailer with a couple of wooden steps leading up to the door and a faded sign hanging out front.

As she jogged to catch up, dry grass prickling the soles of her feet, she caught the word *administration*. "That's the office?"

Easy opened the door and held it ajar with her foot while she waited for Celia to catch up. "Come on, we have to drop this stuff off and then get you settled before dinner."

The inside of William's office was as bland a place as Celia could have imagined. There was a desk, a couple bookshelves lined with binders, a stack of bins against one wall. The only unusual thing in the office was a tall wooden barrel in one corner, the slats held together by rusted wooden rings.

Easy dropped the purses onto the desk and motioned for Celia to do the same with the basket. Celia hesitated. "I thought you said these were going to go into a safe?"

"I said they'd *be* safe," Easy replied patiently. "Don't worry, I'll lock the door after us. Nobody here steals, anyway. We trust each other."

Celia frowned. "I'm pretty sure you said William had a safe—"

"Can I ask you something?" Easy gently took the basket from Celia's hands, her eyes wide with concern. "I don't mean to be rude. I'm just wondering if maybe . . . do you come from a bad area?"

"What?"

She set the basket on the desk, then stepped forward until Celia couldn't see the basket anymore. All she could see was Easy's worried face. "I won't tell anyone. It's just that, I don't know. It seems like you actually think someone would just take something that belongs to you. Is it just the place you came from? Or is the whole world like that, out there?"

Celia hadn't thought about it that way before. Her neighborhood in Belleville was comfortable. She'd lived there her whole life, had inherited her parents' three-story townhouse when they'd died in the Poplar Street Bridge collapse. There were parts of St. Louis she wouldn't go to—the city itself always scared her a little—but her suburb was different. She was sure she was safe there.

"I guess the whole world is like that," she said. "It's just. You know. People take things."

Easy let out a low whistle and shook her head. "Not here. We have what we need and we share the rest. But I'll tell you what—William's got a locking drawer in his desk. I'll ask him to put the basket in there. He's the only one with the key, so your things will be safe and sound. Good compromise?"

"That works," Celia replied.

She felt the slightest glow of satisfaction. *I am braver than I think* was a mantra she'd picked up in the fitness club she'd joined a few years back, the one where they called the gym a *hang* and everyone did the same workout together every morning. She'd had to leave after a year, when she couldn't afford to purchase the Platinum Membership Package, but she'd kept the mantras. She repeated this one to herself now. It felt true. She and Easy had worked together to solve the problem. She'd spoken up for everyone's things, and now they'd all be safe because she hadn't let the issue drop. She *was* braver than she thought.

Soon the two of them were walking away from the office, empty-handed, up the same road that led to the dock. Easy pointed into the trees again, this time in the opposite direction from the office. "That's the canteen. I'll bring you back down to it after I show you your house."

Celia had already spotted this building. It was on the larger side, with a steeply pitched roof and flaking red paint, exposed beams underneath a wide overhang, low benches against the exterior walls. Something about it rang familiar, but Celia couldn't put her finger on why. She noted with gratitude that garden lanterns like the ones she had in her own backyard were staked into the dirt on either side of the path leading to it. She was willing to bet that, like her own, they had tiny solar panels on top and would flicker out after a few hours of darkness. She wouldn't end up in the dark down here, then, trying to feel her way through the trees. She'd be able to find her way.

Just when she was about to turn her attention away from the canteen, a flicker of movement caught her eye—a ribbon of strawberry blond hair, vanishing into the shadowy doorway. "Wait," she said, stopping. "Who was that?"

"Hm?" Easy was already ahead, her brisk stride carrying her quickly up the road.

Celia took a few halting steps toward the canteen and cupped a hand around her mouth, calling out. "Adelaide?"

Easy froze. "What did you say?"

Celia didn't answer. She stared hard at the building, willing a familiar face to emerge.

"Hey. Hey!" Easy was right next to her now, her hand on Celia's upper arm. "Did you just say—"

"Nothing," Celia replied quickly, tearing her eyes away from the building. "I just—I thought I saw someone I knew. An old friend from back home."

Easy searched Celia's face, her expression guarded. "Well, you didn't. Nobody who lives here is from St. Louis, and you're the only one in your visitor group who's from there. I'd know," she added, lifting her eyebrows. "I was in charge of vetting folks for this year's Salt Festival."

"I'm actually from Belleville. It's outside St. Louis." Celia didn't let herself glance back at the canteen. "You really picked everyone?"

"I made sure there wasn't overlap," she said, gently tugging Celia back toward the road. "No neighbors."

"But those girls with the crystals—"

"Aren't from Belleville. Come on, I want to show you where you'll be sleeping before it's time to come back down for dinner."

The incline of the road increased as they walked. Easy didn't say much more, except to point out what she called houses. To Celia's eye they looked more like sheds. The little buildings were raised on cinderblocks, each with a set of two wooden steps leading up to the entrance. Some of them had windows; most didn't seem to. Each roof was canted in one direction, a single steep slant that went from one broad side to the other, overhanging the front door. All of the sheds were coffin-small, no bigger than the nursery Celia had painted shell pink back home. They sat at odd angles to the road, scattered like handfuls of seed.

Each one was painted a different color. Yellow, orange, blue—shades that looked like they'd been vibrant once, but were now faded and peeling. There were signs hanging in front of each one, too, the letters burned into the wood just like the sign that hung outside the main office. The labels identified the colors of the houses. *Yellow House. Orange House. Blue House.*

Celia was out of breath by the time they made it to Grey House. Easy flung the door open with proprietary pride. "Here we are. You and I will be staying here for the week."

Celia poked her head into the cabin. It was unfinished inside—the thick, treated wood of the walls seemed to be the full extent of the material that stood between her and the outside world. There was a bunk bed shoved against one wall, a small writing desk opposite. A braided rug in shades of gray sat in the middle of the floor. On the back wall, a set of shelves were affixed to the inside of the wood. A single empty walnut shell rested in the middle of one shelf.

There was no toilet, no chair, no window. The room was dustless and immaculate.

"Do you normally live in here?" Celia asked, her eyes falling on the soft-looking quilt that was laid over the thin mattress on the bottom bunk. She could make out letters on some of the patches; after a moment she realized that they were scraps of old slogan tees.

"No, I'm usually in the Old House at the top of the island. But this week, I get to be your buddy, so we'll be hanging out in here. Nice, right? Oh, your bag is under the bed, by the way."

"Under—how?"

"I told you, they got delivered. This was fast, though, I didn't think that would happen until after dinner. Anyway, it's underneath because we don't put them on top of the covers in case of bedbugs."

"I don't have bedbugs," Celia said, reaching under the bed to fish her bag out. Whoever put it there had shoved it all the way back into a corner.

"Oh, sure. But the person whose bag was next to yours on the water taxi might. It's just a precaution. Here, let me." Easy knelt beside her and reached one long arm under the bed to retrieve the duffel. The faded pink denim didn't look as out of place in the cabin as Celia would have imagined.

Her eyes fell on the zipper. She always put the tabs to one far side, so they tucked under the lip of fabric on the corner of the bag and would be less likely to accidentally come undone. Now, the tabs were squarely centered, a finger-width gap between them.

She didn't want to ask Easy if someone had gone through her things. Not after what had happened at the canteen. But she wanted to know if there was still a sonogram tucked into the bottom of her bag. She should have given it up when Easy had first approached her with the basket, but that hard emptiness in her chest hadn't let her do it.

She realized that if someone had gone through her bag—if someone had rummaged through her underwear and toothbrush and now-useless socks—she wanted them to have found the sonogram. She wanted them to have taken it from her. She couldn't give it up on her own, but maybe if someone here made her give it up, she'd finally be able to get better.

She didn't ask Easy about it. She just shoved the duffel back under her bed with her foot, pushing it in as far as it would go. As it vanished, a thought struck her, and she twisted to look over her shoulder. "You said you were in charge of vetting everyone? All the visitors?"

"Yep." Easy was slouched against the doorframe, inspecting her fingernails.

"Including me?"

Easy glanced up at Celia then, one brow lifting lightly. "Dunno. Are you part of *everyone*?"

Celia turned slowly to face Easy. "Did you read my letter?"

A slow nod, a faint pinch of pity around the corners of her mouth.

That nod dropped a stone into Celia's stomach. Because that meant Easy already knew what was wrong with Celia. When she brought up the fact that Celia wasn't a parent—she'd known exactly what she was saying. She'd known about the pain that lived in Celia's chest, she'd known about the scream inside Celia's soul, and she'd known about the relentless grief that had come to define Celia to herself.

Celia cleared her throat, trying to dislodge the lump that had stuck itself there. "I think I can find my own way back to the canteen, you don't have to show me. There's just one road, right?"

With three long strides, Easy crossed from the doorway to the bed, until she was standing nearly on top of Celia. "You're scared that you're going to be all alone here," she said softly.

"I'm—"

"You are. Don't pretend you're not." She gazed down into Celia's face, the pity gone, something bright and inviting entering her eyes. "You never have to be all alone again, Celia. I've got you. I'll show you everything."

"Everything?" Celia repeated, and the word felt new in her mouth.

Easy straightened and gave a brisk nod. "C'mon. Let's go. Before it gets dark. The first dinner for visitors is always amazing. You'll see."

Celia followed. She felt sun-dazzled. She hurried to keep up with Easy's quick pace. The road felt softer beneath her feet than it had before.

As they made their way back down the hill, Celia stared at the cabins, wondering if they were all like Grey House inside. They looked so strange, and so familiar—small and sturdy, the texture of the wood aggressively rustic, the woodburned signs amateurish in a way that filled her with strange affection. It wasn't until they reached the canteen—where she saw the desiccated old corkboard next to the open double doors, and heard the familiar sound of many voices gathered inside for dinner—that it clicked.

"Easy," she asked tentatively. "Did this used to be some kind of . . . camp?"

Easy paused. "What?"

"This place. It looks so much like the summer camp I went to as a kid." Celia nodded to herself, her certainty growing. It had been a friend's sleepaway Bible camp. She wasn't religious as a child, but she'd wanted to go with her friend for the summer, and so the church that ran the camp had given her a Seeker Scholarship, hoping to convert her. Celia's father had used those summers to pick up double shifts at the package-processing warehouse. Before dropping her off at the start of June each year, he'd warned her not to let anyone make her feel embarrassed about her scholarship. But he shouldn't have worried. Everyone had gone out of their way to become her friend, to explain things to her, to sit by her. They'd wanted her to become part of their world. She didn't have the scream in her soul yet, not then.

Maybe it could be the same way here.

Easy's response was distant, bordering on irritated. "This place has always been Kindred Cove, even if people used it for something else before. Come on, I think we're the last ones."

Easy placed a hand at the small of Celia's back—gentle pressure, encouraging her to cross the threshold of the canteen. Celia leaned back into her palm.

I need to be touched. She lingered for just a moment, looking at the corkboard, imagining the sign-up sheets and bulletins and notices that used to hang there. *I need to be held.* She could feel the ghosts of a thousand dinner lines snaking out these same double doors. Easy's hand was warm at the base of her spine. The voices of a hundred people carried on the warm evening air. *I don't want to be alone.* Celia felt the tips of her toes hanging out over that unappeasable abyss. The pain behind her sternum was overwhelming, ribcage-buckling, smothering.

I'm lonely.

For years, she had been unable to imagine being loved and touched and seen enough to mend the broken thing inside of her that created such pain.

I'm scared.

Even now, as she remembered the long-past time of her life when her parents had still been alive enough to send her off to camp, emptiness yawned open all around her.

Help me.

Celia leaned back into the pressure of Easy's palm for just one more heartbeat, and then she stepped forward into the canteen.

Sixteen Years Ago

Edith walks from house to house as the sky grows dark overhead. There's nowhere on the island where she can't hear the roar of the lake.

She saw it happen early that afternoon. The huge machine toppling and sinking, the open dark hole in the lakebed, the sudden strange churn of the water. For all that she's seen in her life—all the pain and hunger and uncertainty—she's never seen anything like what she saw today. Now, she knocks on doors, one by one, gathering her people to her.

She is the one who calls the hundred residents of Kindred Cove up to the chapel for a headcount.

She is the one who makes sure they are safe.

Everyone has questions. Everyone is upset, afraid. The community at Kindred Cove has never discussed the end of the world before. They've talked about war and starvation, climate collapse and religious oppression. They know to fear catastrophic storms and government raids and doubt. But none of them ever knew to fear this.

Many of them share what it was like to see the water in the lake vanish. Many of them share what it was like to see it come flooding back. None of them share what Edith is hoping to hear. None of them seem to have seen what happened to him.

None of them know where Dad is.

William and Leona are the last to arrive at the chapel. Both of them are disheveled, sweat stained and wild-eyed. "We looked everywhere," William says. "We've been looking for hours. We can't find him."

It is nearly full dark by now. If he's not at the chapel, he's not coming to the chapel. Everyone knows this, but Edith insists that they wait. She sends Leona to gather up the beeswax candles she's been making, and she puts everyone else to work tidying the chapel, collecting quilts and laying them on the floor and front steps, readying the place for a night in which all of them will stay here, together.

There's a tug on her elbow. It's Adelaide, eleven years old and officious, always prepared to remind whoever might be listening that there are rules and the rules should be followed. She doesn't look so self-assured now, though. Her eyes are enormous, her lips pale. Edith looks down at her hopelessly. "I'm sorry, kiddo," she says, too overwhelmed to catch herself before using the nickname Adelaide has recently begun to hate. "I don't know where he is."

"It's not him," Adelaide says. "It's Easy. She's at the cliff. She won't come away from it."

Edith runs outside, down the steps and up the road. Easy is standing at the cliff, just like Adelaide said. She's staring down into the white foam of the current below. The wildflowers that grow on the cliff face have been mostly torn away, and there's just bare dirt crumbling into the water a few meters down.

Edith pulls Easy back. "Come away from there," she says urgently. "You'll fall. There could be a landslide. It's not safe."

"But—"

Edith turns and looks over her shoulder and sees Leona hurrying up the road, her skirt acting as a hammock for all the candles she could find. "Come to the chapel, now. We're going to light candles so Dad can find us if he doesn't know where we are."

Easy looks up, her small face streaked with tears, her eyes wide with fear. For as much as she acts like eleven years old is as good as grown, Edith thinks, this one is still just a baby. "Are we going to die?"

Edith crouches down and looks into those panicked eyes. "Take a deep breath in," she says. When Easy obeys, Edith claps a hand over her nose and mouth. "That breath inside you? That's got the world in it, doesn't it?" She nods. Edith can feel the twitch of Easy's nostrils, pressed flat under her palm. "You're transforming the world just by taking it into yourself. Now breathe out." She pulls her hand away and Easy exhales in a rush, bending forward a little with the suddenness of it. "You just put yourself into the world. That breath was part of you, and now it's not. Isn't that so?"

She nods slowly.

"We're all changing all the time," Edith says. "If we all change today, so be it. Now come on, you're holding things up. Everyone's waiting."

As she pulls the child toward the chapel, she can see the flicker of the first candle being lit.

SIX MONTHS AGO

1

Adelaide could still remember the freshwater days of Kindred Cove, when the work of the children was to listen. She would sit at Dad's feet and eat overripe honeydew until her throat closed up. She'd gaze up at him as she sank her teeth into the too-soft green flesh of the melon wedge she was supposed to share with Easy, wheezing as quietly as she could so as not to interrupt Dad's teaching.

Easy would watch her sister, reproachful and hungry, willing her own stomach not to growl loudly enough for anyone else to hear. But it always did. Dad would look down at the noise and notice that one of his children was glaring at the other, and he'd send Easy to sit in quiet solitude until she could purify her intentions enough to participate in the community.

Adelaide would stay there with her gnawed-to-pulp melon rind, her hands tacky with juice and her eyes puffed nearly shut, Dad's rough fingers nested in the strawberry blond tangles of her hair, glowing with the knowledge that she was the good one.

She left Kindred Cove right when she was supposed to leave. She'd stayed gone for too long—but when she was sent for, she came back. And now, William's patched-up little boat was on its way from the mainland, racing the miracle tide to bring Adelaide home.

The wide stretch of saltwater between the mainland and Kindred Cove had been swelling all day thanks to new growth on the reef. When the late September sun struck the surface of the water, the lake glittered with blinding light. William's speedboat skated across the water just ahead of that rolling wave, with Adelaide as a figurehead. The light bouncing off the water landed a spotlight on her. The small pink swell of her mouth was half puckered, like she had something to say but didn't want to say it. Her free hand rested lightly on the taut rise of her big-and-getting-bigger belly.

Her wide eyes were fixed on the Cove.

The two of them reached the dock a minute and a half ahead of the final wave of the miracle tide. William told her the reef had been fed at dawn that day, and that meant the last, largest wave of growth would come around sundown—they were lucky to beat it. William and Adelaide jumped off the boat and quickstepped to shore, his bare feet and her taped-up shoes both touching soil seconds before the dock vanished under a rush of cold saltwater.

Below the water's surface, the reef bloomed into marvels that defied explanation. The water rose and it stayed risen, cinching in tighter and tighter around the Cove even as the reef built a bridge between the island and the mainland.

Back before he disappeared into the water, Dad liked to say that a miracle didn't always feel like a blessing. Sometimes it could feel like a cause for worry. But, Dad would say, that worry didn't mean a miracle wasn't happening. The world might feel smaller, but maybe that was because something incredible was being built all around you. Something divine.

The day Adelaide came home felt like that. A miracle, even if everyone wondered what she'd have to say for herself. Even if some of them worried about what she might bring back with her. She'd been gone for so long, but it didn't matter because it couldn't matter: The return of a prodigal was an occasion to be cherished and celebrated. Time to slaughter the fatted calf, break open the comb and let the honey run into the milk, sink your teeth deep into the soft sweet flesh of the ripest plums. Nothing should be held back; nothing should be reserved. There was no room for the reservation of complete faith.

As Adelaide approached the crowd with the miraculously risen water of Lake Vetiver erasing the footprints behind her, the air hummed with a held-back question: *Where have you been?*

The people of Kindred Cove watched Adelaide scan their faces, her brow tight. It wasn't hard to guess who she was looking for.

"Easy's at the Old House," William muttered. "Waiting."

"Not for long," Adelaide replied. She moved with the same determination and certainty she'd always had. She cut through the crowd and started making her way up the long twisting trachea of dirt that started at the dock and ended at the Old House. The people parted for her easily as she walked up the road, their hands twitching with the urge to reach for her, to touch her arms, her face, her hair, her ripe stomach. Their eyes touched her everywhere their hands couldn't.

It had been so long since Adelaide's community had tasted the salt of her sweat on the air. As she passed them, she angled her chin to let the sunlight catch her cheekbone, so they could see her better.

She wanted them to remember her like this.

2

Easy was sitting on the front steps of the Old House. She was a weary smile of a person, long limbs always heavy, eyes that cast shadows. There was an upside-down mug next to her, dripping a dark ring of moisture onto a section of wood that was already stained from thirty-something years of upside-down mugs. A gangly gray tabby napped at her elbow.

Adelaide probably hadn't planned on greeting Easy with a frown, but the sight of the stained front steps pulled one out of her anyway.

"You came back," Easy said, her expression mirroring Adelaide's.

"You must have thought I wouldn't."

"I hoped you would," Easy replied, answering the question by dodging it. "Prayed, even." She nodded to the falling-apart shoes clutched in Adelaide's hand. "Those things look done for. Want to toss them into the lake?"

Adelaide tilted her head, her toes curling into the dust. "I'll need them for the trip back. Your letter said—"

Easy stood suddenly, startling the tabby awake. It bolted off into the grass. "Let's not talk about that now. I missed you, Del."

The old nickname—one nobody else had ever used or would ever use—put a fishhook into Adelaide's middle and reeled her up the stairs into Easy's embrace. Easy's arms looped around Adelaide and held on tight, her shoulders spasming with what might have been a laugh or might have been a sob. She smelled like beeswax and peppermint oil. It was impossible to tell what her face was doing because she had it buried in the soft fall of Adelaide's hair. She always used to hide her feelings in that hair, back in the freshwater days of the Cove.

"Missed you too," Adelaide breathed.

The two of them settled into their old places on the steps. Easy sprawled out from the top step like someone had tripped and spilled her down the front steps of the Old House; Adelaide perched on the bottom step and leaned forward, the bulk of her belly parked between her spread knees. They talked on that porch for a long time as people bustled around at the chapel next door.

The sisters sat out where everyone could see them, and nobody interrupted because Easy and Adelaide coming back together was important. So important. Still, not-interrupting didn't mean people didn't hear things. It was a quiet little island, the Cove, and so many things needed to get done to prepare for the party.

Edith, for example, found that she needed some wildflowers from the cliffs just behind the Old House. She needed them right away, to fill little jars and decorate the chapel. She passed by a few times to gather the right ones and make sure the bouquets were perfectly balanced. She collected blue toadflax and tall bellflower and bloodroot, too much bloodroot, even though it wasn't the best for bouquets by a mile. And so, by coincidence, Edith happened to hear Adelaide's proposition.

"Together. The two of us. It's the best way to do it."

"I can't think of anyone, anywhere, who would agree with you," Easy replied. "This is not a good idea. A child needs more than we can offer on our own. We can't—"

"I know one person who would agree with me. *My sister.* Where'd *she* go?"

"I'm right where you fucking left me." Easy said it fast and quiet like whipping a tablecloth out from under a plate.

Edith ripped out more bloodroot, red sap oozing around her hands. She couldn't help thinking it shouldn't be growing here at the Cove. It should have been torn out already, replaced with something more productive.

Later on, from his vantage point on the ladder, Caleb was the one who heard the real meat of the argument. He'd noticed that the apple tree between the chapel and the Old House had some problematic branches. They were blocking the sunlight through the western windows, and Caleb needed something to keep himself busy before the big party—two problems that could solve each other. He brought out the tall ladder and climbed it with a pair of handheld shears, and he took his time trimming the stems off the troublesome branches. By going slowly, he reasoned, he could collect the stems and give them to Edith for the chapel.

"But your letter—you asked me to come back. I waited for you. I came back for you. You can't tell me that's not what you wanted?" That was Adelaide, a plea in her voice like a cat asking for dinner. "You're not okay here, Easy. I can smell that mug from here. Where did you even get—"

"Made it," Easy replied, a smirk creasing the edges of her voice. "In the kitchen sink."

"You did not!" A smiling rebuke. The sisters could always slip into laughter mid-fight. "That would be so gross."

"What can I say? I like my gin with just a whisper of drain hair in it."

The honk of Adelaide's laugh cut clear across the island. "You're disgusting."

"See? I told you I'm no good on my own."

"Don't say that." The laugh vanished, and the smile too. "Easy, please. I know you think—"

"You think you know what I think," Easy interrupted again, her voice growing hard. "But it's been a long time, Del."

"Five years isn't that long."

"You don't even sound like you believe that. Five years is forever. And I've grown. You don't understand as much as you think you do."

"I know you've made some mistakes," Adelaide tried again. "But they don't have to define you. I know your heart. I know you can be . . ." She trailed off, searching for words, her hands idly stroking the sides of her belly.

"Better? I wonder if you do know." Easy waved a hand at herself, gesturing to the long loose spill of her body before sweeping her wild profusion of dark hair away from her face. "I wonder if you think I'm permanently broken. Maybe you still think I ought to find a way to fix myself. Maybe you think you need to be the one who fixes me."

"I don't think you need to fix yourself, Easy. I just think—your letter. You asked me to come. You must have had a reason for that." Adelaide sounded more than a little frustrated. She looked at Easy sidelong before switching tactics. "The baby is coming soon enough. I don't want to be on my own with it. I need your help with everything that comes after."

"Do you know what I see when I look at you?" Easy asked, her voice tender.

"Don't."

"C'mon. You need—"

"I said, don't."

Easy paused for a long time then.

Long enough that Caleb finished with the apple tree and cleaned up all the twigs that had fallen beneath it, and couldn't come up with any more reasons to linger.

Leona barely glanced at him as she made her way toward the Old House. The road to the chapel needed to be swept so people could pass safely. If they'd had time to plan for Adelaide's return, the children would have handled it, but there hadn't been time and nobody was thinking about the details, so Leona knew that if she didn't handle the job, no one would. While she was at it, she figured she might as well sweep the dust and pebbles all the way to the end of the road and off the cliffs, into the water.

Leona was still sweeping when Easy spoke again.

"How far along are you?"

"I'm not sure," Adelaide answered. "At least five months."

"You're awful big for five months."

"I said *at least*."

Another long pause, cut only by the sounds of distant voices inside the chapel and Leona's broom scraping the dirt of the road.

"So you have, what, four months to figure out your plan? Five?"

Leona glanced up just long enough to see Easy sitting forward beside Adelaide, her hands clasped, her head bowed. The collar of her shirt hung open and the edge of an old scar peeked out, shining in the late-afternoon sun.

"Maybe less," Adelaide said, tracing the old brown rings on the wood. "But I don't need to figure out a plan. I have a plan already. I just need you to come with me, and then everything will be okay."

Easy snorted. "Of course you already have a plan. You always do." Then, softly: "We can talk about this more after the party. Okay?"

Adelaide replied even softer, so soft that Leona had to stop sweeping for a moment to hear. "You asked me to come. I don't see what *more* there is to talk about."

"You really want to miss your homecoming party? Everyone's been working so hard to make things nice for you, Del."

Leona held her breath to make sure she didn't miss anything.

"Okay," Adelaide finally said. "It'd be hard to get back home tonight, anyway. But I'm leaving tomorrow. And I hope you're coming with me."

When Leona stopped moving dust from one side of the road to another and looked up, she saw Easy lifting one long lock of strawberry blond hair from her sister's shoulder.

"We should cut this. I've never seen you with it short before."

"I like it long."

"You might like it short."

Adelaide didn't answer. Leona left them sitting there, and she clung to the grim relief she felt knowing that the girl was home.

That was all that mattered. The rest would take care of itself.

3

There had been celebrations in the chapel at Kindred Cove since the night Adelaide left, but none of them had felt quite like this one. None of them had felt right without Adelaide at their center.

The children had spent half the day scrubbing out the chapel. The windows were thrown open wide, so the living smell of Lake Vetiver could permeate the air inside. Beeswax candles sat in the windowsills, the flames guttering every time a breeze came off the lake, which was often. The late-afternoon sun provided more than enough light—the candles were really just for atmosphere, to provide a sense of abundance. So said Leona, who kept the bees and made the candles, and who loved to dominate a party by defining *abundance* with an emphasis on the products of her hives.

Harvey and Caleb, who kept chickens on the south end of the Cove, intermittently glared at the candles and smirked at the cluster of folding tables in the middle of the room, where a huge dripping slab of honeycomb was going ignored. Harvey and Caleb had provided devilled eggs because everyone loves devilled eggs. Nobody was eating the honeycomb, because no one ever ate the honeycomb, but the devilled eggs were already nearly gone.

The two men weren't enjoying their triumph, though, because while everyone had been down at the dock making plans for this party, Edith had asked them to give her a chicken. She'd insisted that a sense of abundance (she'd nodded to Leona there) necessitated a chicken. Nevermind that Harvey and Caleb didn't have a spare chicken to kill, and certainly didn't feel like going to the trouble of scalding and plucking and gutting one just so Edith could boil the color out of it.

In the end, Adelaide's arrival had stopped the argument without a resolution having been reached. Edith, before they all parted ways, had expressed her sincere disappointment, and her hope that Harvey and Caleb might develop a stronger sense of connection to the gifts of the land.

She wasn't too disappointed in them to eat eight devilled eggs all on her own, Harvey noticed. A sense of connection to the gifts of the land, indeed.

Adelaide sat in a chair on the low stage at the front of the chapel, watching Harvey mutter into Caleb's ear. The chair was the same carved wooden one Dad used to sit in, worn smooth from years and years of use. A pile of old shirts was folded up and tied with twine as a makeshift cushion. Easy stood nearby, her mouth a tense checkmark, her fists forming twin bulges in the pockets of her trousers. Her eyes kept darting between Adelaide and whatever Adelaide was looking at—the candles, the eggs, the flowers, Harvey. And now Jessie, young at seventeen and forever the beloved baby of the island, who was sauntering toward them with a mean glint in her eye.

"Easy. Guess your letter made it to the mainland," she said with a sticky grin. She held a half-eaten peach in her hand, the exposed pit glistening in the golden light of the early dusk. "Adelaide, why'd you come back? Did you have enough of the wide world?"

Easy pulled out an old folding pocketknife—also Dad's, once upon a time—and took the peach from Jessie, using her blade to dig out the pit. "Jessie, you're glowing. What'd you bring us tonight that's got you so proud? Fig preserves, I'm guessing?"

Adelaide's eyes stuck on Dad's old knife for a few seconds before she managed to meet Jessie's appraising stare. "Are you doing the preserves now? That's lovely," she said. "You're working with Marco, then? Where is he? I'd love to say hello."

"Maybe you don't want to ask about that," Easy murmured.

"It doesn't matter," Jessie snapped at Easy, her wide eyes going narrow, her lip lifting to show the tip of one dull tooth.

"What do you mean? Where's Marco?" Adelaide asked, her fingers drumming against her thighs.

Jessie's gaze slid to one side. "He's not lost," she said, and that was all, because this was the Cove, and that meant there was nothing more to say.

Easy held out the peach half. The pit was at her feet. "Go tell Harvey that the kids are on cleanup duty once the party's over, will you?"

Jessie snatched her newly pitted peach half out of Easy's hand. "Whatever, Dad." She turned on her heel and stalked away without another word.

Adelaide stared after her. "What'd she call you?"

Easy licked peach juice from the inside of her wrist. "She's still struggling with what happened to Marco," she murmured into the heel of her own hand.

"She's young," Adelaide said. "But why did she call you—"

"Hmm. I keep hoping she'll grow out of holding on to things. She knows better than to still be so pissy about Marco. We spoiled her, maybe, by letting her move into the adult group so quickly."

Adelaide blinked rapidly. "She's with the adult group?"

"Not anymore. That happened while you were gone. She's back with the kids now, though, because of shit like this. Should kick her back down to road maintenance with the three-through-eights if she doesn't shape up."

Adelaide stared up at Easy with naked bewilderment. "Wh—"

"That girl is spoiled rotten." Edith's voice was rich with laughter as she approached. Easy stepped aside automatically, as everyone did for Edith. "But how could we not spoil her? She was the next best thing to you while you were gone, Adelaide." She crouched next to the chair and rested a palm on Adelaide's stomach. Edith didn't look up, her eyes trained on the shadow of Adelaide's navel where it dimpled beneath her cream-colored sundress. "Do you mind if I . . . ?"

She didn't finish the sentence before slipping both of her hands under the hem of Adelaide's dress. The eyelets on the fabric rippled with the sudden movement, the hill of her hand creating a rolling wave just like the one that had chased Adelaide home earlier that day. The skirt pooled in the crooks of Edith's elbows until the flickering candlelight caught the milk-white skin of Adelaide's thighs.

The room went quiet as Edith's hands rose up under Adelaide's dress and settled on either side of her belly.

"Easy," Adelaide whispered, her voice breaking under the weight of the word. "I don't want—"

Easy shot her a quick sidelong glare, a look that said *no more from you* without needing words. Adelaide recoiled from the sharp glance, looked around the room to see if anyone else had noticed. It was the first time she could ever remember Easy chastising her, even if the rebuke had been subtle.

She didn't see anyone watching Easy. Every eye was on her belly. All of them were on her belly.

Edith let her eyes drift shut as the heat of Adelaide's skin sank deep into her palms. Her hands were rough with calluses, but they were warm, too, and she had the kind of certain, gentle touch that Kindred Cove required. She could gauge the ripeness of a fig with the gentlest pressure, could tell when mushrooms were about to come up just by rubbing soil between her thumb and middle finger. She knew the feel of everyone and everything that lived at the Cove, and now, she would know this baby.

Edith flexed her fingers, digging them into the soft surface of Adelaide's flesh until they met resistance. She inhaled a deep breath through her nose, then parted her lips and breathed in again through her mouth. The tang of sweat and saltwater gave way to earthy sweetness. Adelaide had always had a sweetness to her, but the earthiness was new.

"It's healthy," Edith said, "and it's still high."

"Good," Easy said. She dropped into a low crouch beside Edith, her attention fixed. "That's good. Thank you, Edith. I'll take it from here." Edith stepped away, and Easy laid her hands over Adelaide's belly, her spidery fingers light on the taut fabric of Adelaide's dress. Then she let her voice drop into the rich timbre of public proclamation. "I am so thankful from the depth of my soul for this great gift of life." The walls of the chapel hummed with whispered echoes of *thankful* and *gift of life*. "We will welcome this child into our family with profound love and abundance." A loud *yes* from Leona. Easy ignored them all and let her head fall back, pressing her hands harder against Adelaide's belly. "Our daughter has come back to us, and she has brought sweetness with her. Together we will be grateful every day for the marvel of conception. We will manifest health and tireless diligence in this and every other child born to the paradise we create here at Kindred Cove."

The room echoed her, the word *tireless* layering over the word *paradise* until finally everyone who wasn't Adelaide had agreed with Easy's statement of gratitude.

Easy looked up at Adelaide, radiating patience and certainty.

Adelaide looked down at the rise of her stomach. She'd never heard Easy speak in that voice before; she'd never seen her sister looking so sure of herself. It reminded Adelaide so powerfully of Dad that she felt the sick heat of old longing rising up the back of her neck.

Easy raised her eyebrows, prompting. *Go on.*

Adelaide cleared her throat and nodded. "Together," she said, as though learning a word in a new language for the first time.

Easy's face split into a smile so bright it shoved the last of the sunlight down past the horizon. "Together," she agreed.

Edith stepped forward, pressing her lips to Adelaide's forehead. "Come to the garden tomorrow morning," she murmured. "You have a lot of work to catch up on."

The party resumed with fresh life and heat in it. The light outside was fading from dusk to dark, and the room was mostly lit by Leona's abundant candles now, casting everyone in strange, flickering shadows. Easy grinned down at Adelaide, affectionate and a little wild.

"Seems like you've got some things to fill me in on," Adelaide said.

"Tomorrow," Easy replied. "For tonight, let's just enjoy being together again. Didn't you miss me?"

"I missed the hell out of you."

"Well, put it back where you found it," Easy replied with a laugh. "I worked hard on growing that hell and I want it handy."

"Okay, but—"

Before Adelaide could finish, Caleb interrupted them. He brought a knotted handkerchief and a mischievous smile with him.

"Adelaide," he said, his gaze sliding over her as though he was ignoring a stain on an otherwise pristine tablecloth. "Easy, I wanted to make sure you didn't miss this. It's the last of the season. Good thing you came when you did—I was going to eat it after dinner tonight."

Easy gazed at the knotted cloth with frank interest. "What is it?"

"Yes, show us," Adelaide said, a little too loud, trying too hard to catch Caleb's eye.

He still wouldn't look right at her. He unknotted the fabric with slow, hesitant movements of his fingers. "Spent all day moving the chicken pen around the garden, my damn hands are so tired I can barely—there!" Triumphant, he opened the handkerchief to show Easy his prize: a glistening wedge of bright green melon.

"Oh!" Easy gasped at the fug of sweet fragrance that rose up to meet her. "Wow! It's gorgeous, Caleb. Well done."

Caleb glowed with pride. "The last of the honeydew. All yours. Don't tell Jessie I saved it back, she'll get righteous with me."

Easy took the kerchief tenderly, leaning forward to kiss Caleb on the cheek. "Thank you," she said. "You've done well."

After Caleb had walked away—ostensibly to check on something or other, more likely to quietly boast about the sweetness of the melon—Easy's smile died away. "Don't worry about Caleb," she murmured, folding the handkerchief around the fruit carefully. "He's just nervous about falling off the wagon, now that you're home. He'll relax once he's sure he can handle having you here." She tried to hand Adelaide the bundled-up melon. "Take it. He was only giving it to me so you could have it. Everyone knows it's your favorite."

"No, that's okay. You should have it," Adelaide replied.

"Are you sure?" Easy's forehead creased.

Adelaide nodded. "Oh, absolutely positive." She waved a hand as though to indicate that the issue was more than settled. Her eyes glowed with reflected candlelight. "I've never actually liked honeydew. It's all yours."

Easy stared at the slice of melon all night. After the party was over, before she took the long road down to the shoreline, she walked to the cliffs behind the Old House. She unfolded the handkerchief, breathed in the too-sweet smell of a melon she'd never actually gotten the chance to try. She'd always thought of the melon as Adelaide's, even when Adelaide was gone. She'd never let herself have any.

This whole time, not even a taste.

The wind tugged at the handkerchief in her grip. She licked her lips and tasted salt. Adelaide was home now. Everything would be made right, at long last. She'd make sure of it.

Easy crushed the too-soft flesh of the melon into her mouth. A flood of juice filled her mouth and throat so fast that she nearly choked on it. The already-damp handkerchief in her hand was all she had to wipe away the sticky liquid that ran down her chin and across the long expanse of her throat. It wound up saturated, and she dropped the sodden fabric over the edge of the cliff rather than bother with trying to clean it. The lake could have what it wanted.

"Do you know what I see when I look at you?" she whispered to herself. The words tasted like sweet melon.

It was exactly as good as she'd always imagined it could be.

One Year Ago

Celia has been staring at the same email for an hour and a half. She can't figure out how to end it. It's an email to Carolyn, who is the Vice Sapphire VP of the luxury athleisure company Celia works for. Or, no, she corrects herself, doesn't work for—represents. She is a representative of the company. A Brand Ambassador, as Carolyn likes to say, is the smiling face of comfort and style.

The last line of Celia's email, as it's currently written, says, *Thank you for understanding, and I look forward to coordinating a time for me to drop off the unsold inventory!* It's a sentence structure that she learned from a book about Owning Your Power as a Female Business Leader. First, gratitude; then, confirmation of assumed agreement, paired with a logistical demand. *I appreciate you making time for our conversation about my new role at the company—let me know when you'd like to chat!* was the example given in the book, modeling the best way to end a job interview.

Celia thinks she's done a pretty good job in her email. She is Owning Her Power by asking Carolyn if she can return unsold inventory for a refund. No, she corrects herself, she's *telling* Carolyn that she's *going* to return unsold inventory for a refund. She flips the book open, scans a page, and corrects herself again: She's *confirming* with Carolyn. This is confirmed.

But the book doesn't say anything about how to end the email. Should she say thank you again? Leave it there and sign off? Add a comment about the new line of lightning-bolt-print yoga pants? That last option is encouraged by the company sales handbook. *Every email you send should mention the product at least once.* But she's mentioned the product already, by asking to—no, by *confirming* that she's *going* to return it.

She wonders if she can ask Adelaide how to finish the email. Adelaide doesn't seem to know much about technology, but she always seems so relaxed about the things that make Celia anxious. She'll probably have some easy answer that will make this message feel effortless.

Celia has just decided to ask Adelaide for advice after the next time they see each other at grief group—when she hits send by mistake.

She slams her laptop shut hard and goes directly to the Apple Store. At the service counter, she asks how to un-send an email. They tell her it's not possible. She tells them that she turned the computer off before it could finish sending—less than a second after she hit the button, honestly, the email has to still be in her outbox.

But when she opens the laptop to show them, she discovers that shutting it didn't turn it off. It's been on this whole time. The email sent, and there's a reply from Carolyn in her inbox already.

She doesn't want to open it. She can't imagine wanting to open it. She does not feel the power that, according to the books, she is supposed to own. Hot fearful shame burns through her at the thought of what Carolyn's email will say.

She finds herself weeping at the counter. The service technician's eyes shoot across the sales floor, searching for his manager. After a couple of minutes he pats Celia on the shoulder and slides her laptop back to her.

"You should try to get some help," he says, his palm on her closed laptop. "You should talk to someone."

Celia doesn't know who she could possibly talk to about this. Not Adelaide. Not her grief group. She doesn't want them to see her this way. She doesn't want anyone to see her this way.

She is, as always, alone.

SALT FESTIVAL

day one | evening

The sun that poured in through the high windows of the canteen painted the room in streaks of hazy light. Celia couldn't tell what the sunlight was catching on—dust or smoke or the exhalations of the hundred or so people in the room, rising to commingle in a shared mist.

The residents of the Cove sat on benches pulled up to long wooden tables. Three rows of three, each made from thick planks of wood worn smooth and dark with time and use. Celia had expected a cafeteria, but each twelve-person table was set up for family-style dining. The visitors and residents who had arrived before her reached across each other for tiny dishes of flaky salt, passed large wooden bowls of dark greens counterclockwise. They handed sweating pitchers of water to each other, some with cucumber slices or lemon wedges floating inside. They laughed softly in the way of strangers who were determined to become friends.

Easy wound her way between the tables. Celia followed. As she looked for faces she recognized, she realized that there were just two guests from the water taxi at each table. They each stood out in a dozen small ways—the too-bright dye in their clothes, the city-styled haircuts, the hesitant smiles they offered their hosts.

"Is someone missing? There were more of us than this on the boat, I thought. I could have sworn I saw an older couple . . . ?"

"Hm?" Easy waved down a compact teen girl with long hair and a general air of irritation. "Celia, this is Jessie. She's in charge of the kids. If there's anything you want from the kitchen that's not on the table already, you ask her for it, and she'll have one of them go and get it for you. Okay?"

"Okay. Thanks, Jessie," she said, although Jessie was already walking away, and Celia privately thought the girl would not appreciate being asked for much of anything. "When does she get to eat dinner?"

"The kids eat dinner later, after we finish. They're on service duty while the grown-ups eat," Easy said. She pointed around the edge of the room, where children lined the walls. Celia was startled—there were so many of them, and she couldn't think of how she'd missed them at first glance. But the children stood so still, watching the diners, occasionally stepping soundlessly forward to clear a plate or pour water from a sweating pitcher into a half-full glass. They were so quiet that the moment Celia looked away from them, they seemed to vanish.

Easy sank down into the chair at the end of one table. She gestured to a seat at the end of a bench, next to the older woman from the boat—the one who had asked if the water was safe. As Celia sat, the woman leaned in close to Easy. "Where are the missing people?" The frail voice she'd put on for William was gone, and her eyes were sharp behind her thick glasses.

Easy reached toward the center of the table to snag a pitcher of lemon water. "Missing? I'm not sure what you mean, Audrey."

"There are only twelve of us at each table," the woman replied. "Where are the other people who live here?"

"Some of them are working in the kitchen." Easy poured water into Celia's cup, then into her own. "And we're only the first dinner shift. Did you really think you were seeing the whole population of the Cove in here, right now?"

"There's definitely a couple of visitors missing, too, though," Celia ventured. "An older couple. And that lady's . . . husband, I think?" She turned in her seat to look at a rail-thin, auburn-haired woman. She remembered standing in line behind the woman when they were all filing onto the water taxi, because the woman had spent the entire time clinging to a stone-faced man in a yellow shirt that said TREAD LIGHTLY on the back in huge block letters. Celia had stared at the words on his shirt, debating whether or not to ask him to explain the reference. The woman sat alone now, in the middle of her bench, speaking to no one. She took small, nervous sips of water, her eyes darting constantly around the room, her plate untouched.

Easy shrugged. "Rinna's husband? No idea. Maybe he volunteered to help out in the kitchen. It's nice when people do that on the first day, you know? Really shows that they're not just here to take."

Celia looked down at her empty plate, stung. She'd only been on the island for an hour, an hour and a half at the most, and it hadn't occurred to her to offer to do anything. She hadn't realized that might put her into a category of people marked as selfish. She thought maybe she should apologize.

Before she could say anything, though, Jessie appeared beside her with two steaming bowls of food. "It's just grits tonight," she said. "No complaining."

"Jessie," Easy said, a gentle scold in her voice.

"What? Some people complained."

"Service should be silent," Easy singsonged, earning a scowl from the girl.

Celia peered down into the bowl Jessie handed to her and couldn't see anything to complain about. The bowl contained much more than "just grits." There was a fried egg on top with a velvety orange yolk, tiny tomatoes with blistered skins, corn that glistened with butter and fat flakes of what looked like sea salt. At the sight of it, Celia felt her middle split open with need.

She couldn't remember the last time she'd felt hunger like this. The past few years of her life had no space for it—there was always something else in the way, either nausea or cramping or grief striking her in the belly like a cannonball. She'd become an expert in the different brands of meal replacement smoothies, had almost learned to ignore the way the chalky sludge of protein slurry slipped over the back of her tongue each day.

But Celia found that she actually wanted this meal. The hunger was so demanding that it felt like panic, and she nearly flung the bowl away—but no. She was determined to accept everything the Cove had to offer. So she sank down into the hunger instead, letting it nip at her ribs with blunt teeth.

She turned to thank Jessie, but the girl was already back against the wall, silently fuming between two children who were half her height. "This smells delicious," Celia said to Easy instead.

Easy grinned at her. "Wait'll you taste it. Have you ever had goat butter before?"

Celia had never eaten a meal like this one. The butter was tangy and grassy. The egg yolk was custardy and rich. The tomatoes were sweet and summery, with a deeper flavor than she could ever remember tomatoes having. The salt flakes on the corn crunched between her molars. It was the first time she could remember feeling the flavor of food throughout her entire body.

"I remember when my daughter was that age," Audrey said, glancing over at Jessie. Her bowl was already empty, and she was adding greens to her plate for what looked like the second time. "Every second of the day she was inventing a new problem to have."

"She's just cranky," Easy said around a mouthful of grits. "Jessie loves wrangling the kids, but she hates standing with them."

Across the table, a stern-faced woman with a long black braid draped over one shoulder wiped her mouth with a napkin, then leaned forward. "You still haven't told us why she got moved back down to work with the kids all those years ago."

"Let's not spoil our appetites, Leona. I promise I'll give you all the gossip later." She winked at Leona, then turned toward Celia and Audrey. "I'd rather know what made you two decide to apply for a visit to Kindred Cove. I already know why you're here, from your applications—but how did you hear about us?"

"I bought your salt from my chiropractor. They had a pamphlet," Audrey said. It was a thin explanation, like she was holding back everything that mattered. She shifted her attention to Celia again, deftly moving the conversation away from herself. "What about you?"

Celia stirred a yellow runnel of yolk into her grits. She debated how honestly to answer the question. "A friend told me about this place. She said you heal people here, and I figured—couldn't hurt to try, right?"

Maybe it wasn't right to call Adelaide "a friend." Celia just didn't know how to refer to people from her grief support group. They were her colleagues in suffering, and accomplices in her most searingly selfish moments, and witnesses to her most fundamental flaws. She knew their pain and their yearning and their emptiness—but she didn't know their last names. Should she count them as friends?

Leona nodded encouragingly at Celia. "What did your friend tell you about us? There are no wrong answers. It's just good to know what people come here expecting."

"Oh, not much. Just . . . she said that you do things differently here. That you know how to let things go. She was dealing with a loss, and said you all would have known how to help with it. I need that." Her eyes got that tired feeling that had replaced the burn of tears so long ago. "I need help letting things go."

"You're here to heal," Easy said, laying one of her hands across Celia's wrist. "Your friend must have seen that you needed it."

Celia didn't volunteer the rest of what she knew about Kindred Cove. She'd learned plenty while she was tracking the place down based on Adelaide's descriptions of her childhood home.

The search had given her something to cling to. Something to hope for. A future.

"I heard," Audrey said from beside Celia, "that this place nearly got sucked right down to hell a few years ago."

Leona rolled her eyes wearily. "I wouldn't go that far. But yes, we had an . . . event." She went on to explain the story of the lake's transformation. It was the same thing Celia had heard in all the videos she'd watched online. Videos with titles like "Ten Spookiest Lakes You've Never Heard Of" and "Science Can't Explain This." Celia had been scanning each one for any clues as to how to reach the place that had shaped Adelaide.

It was a man-made disaster that had transformed Lake Vetiver all those years ago. Most of the videos told the same general story: how a rig searching for oil deposits beneath the lakebed accidentally drilled into a massive salt mine, causing the ceiling of the mine to collapse. The lakewater flooded into the mines fast, filling them and temporarily draining the lake. But the lake didn't stay empty. The pull of that huge new drain tugged at the outlet where the lake met the nearby bay, reversing the flow of the water and yanking thousands of gallons of seawater down into the caverns below the lakebed.

The videos claimed that the massive whirlpools and waterfalls resulting from the collapsing mines had lasted for two full days. They often added visual effects of celebrities being sucked down into the water.

At the end of each video was the same present-day photograph: a drone capture of a cluster of children on a tiny island, standing on a cliff covered in candles, throwing flowers into the water at the annual festival commemorating the collapse.

Celia had watched all the videos at least a few times over, searching for details that would bring her to Adelaide. She'd heard this story before. But hearing it from Leona was different, because she'd been there.

"All that water poured down into the dark, and the mine just drank it down," she said, her eyes huge, her gaze unfocused, as though she was still staring down into the depths of the old salt mines. "I didn't know that the earth could open its mouth like that. I've never seen anything hungrier in my whole life."

"It's amazing that nobody died," Audrey said.

Leona looked at her sharply. "Sorry," she said, "who are you, again?"

"You know perfectly well that this is Audrey," Easy said. Her eyes were on the greens she was spooning onto Celia's plate, but her voice had a warning in it. "And you know perfectly well that she doesn't mean it like that."

Audrey scraped her fork hard against her own plate. "How don't I mean it?"

"One person fell into the water that day and was never seen again," Leona said tonelessly. "But we don't say that he died. He became part of something greater than himself."

"Was he—" Celia started to ask—but then, under the table, Easy tapped a fist against her knee. Next to Celia's leg, out of sight, Easy extended one long finger and gave it a single shake. *Don't.* So Celia didn't.

"He became part of something greater than himself, and now he's with us always," Leona continued, either ignoring Celia or unaware that she'd spoken at all. "His transformation showed us our calling. The Salt Festival is our annual reminder to pursue that calling. We become greater than the sum of our parts, and we grow something beautiful."

Audrey made a skeptical, cranky noise.

Celia cleared her throat to cover it, not wanting Audrey to step on whatever Easy'd warned her away from. "When do we get to start? The . . . process, I mean?"

Easy raised an eyebrow. "What process?"

"The healing," Celia said, embarrassed by the shape of the word in her mouth. It felt naive to speak the idea aloud. "Becoming greater than the sum of our parts." That felt even sillier. The way she said it didn't carry the same weight as the way Leona said it. She supposed that must be because she didn't really know what it meant.

Easy let out a low, breathy laugh. "What makes you think you haven't started it already?"

The steady hum of voices in the canteen was broken by a loud crash from the kitchen.

Celia turned automatically. Her gaze skipped across all the other people who were looking in the same direction as her, past the children who were flooding toward the kitchen. Jessie pushed by, muttering to herself, and Celia caught the edge of a sentence.

—I told Adelaide it would fall—

Celia rose from her chair involuntarily. She needed to follow Jessie, to catch up with Adelaide, to look into her eyes and see that she'd had her baby. To confirm that this place had kept Adelaide safe and whole and protected her from loss.

Or, the hard seed inside Celia whispered.

Or to confirm that it hadn't.

She watched Jessie vanish through the swinging kitchen doors—toward Adelaide, maybe.

Toward her joy, or toward her pain, which would be the mirror of Celia's pain. The abyss that Celia had spent so much time staring into, looking at the contours of a suffering that mapped onto her own. The reflection that Celia had been missing for six long lonely months.

She didn't want her own pain, and she didn't want to yearn for Adelaide's pain. This place would make her better than all that. But it hadn't made her better yet, and she wasn't yet strong enough to resist the pull and promise of Adelaide.

She had only followed a few steps when she felt a hand on her wrist.

"Let the kids handle it," Easy said, her lips close enough to Celia's ear that she could feel the heat of her breath. "Someone probably just dropped the forks. It's fine. But it's their responsibility, and that means you have to let them be responsible for it."

"I heard . . ." Celia stopped herself, swallowed the name *Adelaide*. "I thought I heard someone saying somebody got hurt," she finished. It didn't come out convincing.

"Then you definitely shouldn't go back there. The last thing you want to do is get between help and someone who needs it, right?"

Audrey was suddenly behind them. "Well, if someone got hurt, we can't leave it up to the children, can we? Maybe this woman can help," she said, gesturing vaguely toward Celia. "Maybe she's a doctor." She was wearing the same expression of bland kindness as the one she'd affected when they were on the boat, right after she'd said, *I'm so fucking sure.*

"She's not a doctor. She's self-employed," Easy said, nudging Celia back toward her chair. She sat reluctantly.

Audrey followed suit, regarding Celia with frank interest. "You own your own business?"

"Run my own business," Celia replied, glancing over her shoulder toward the kitchen. "I'm a Senior Brand Ambassador."

Leona rapped on the table, pulling Celia's attention back to the conversation. "That's a very impressive title. What are you an ambassador for?"

"I distribute luxury sportswear." She didn't mention the debt she'd incurred for her title. There were two thousand dollars' worth of yoga pants in her garage, boxed up and stored between cartons of perfume and eyeshadow and essential oils. Her garage was dedicated to all the up-front purchases she'd made from different outfits that promised she could set her own hours, be her own boss, make thousands of dollars a month from the comfort of her home.

She knew she could move all that inventory once she was better. The woman who'd recruited her for the yoga pants sales job sent weekly emails to the team, filled with advice and mantras, reminding her that she was the master of her own destiny. Celia knew she could make those words become true. She just had to fix herself. Learn to focus on the right things. Become—how had Leona put it? Something greater than herself?

And getting better meant ignoring what she'd heard Jessie say, ignoring the crash from the kitchen. Letting things here at Kindred Cove operate the way they were supposed to, so this place could heal her the way it was supposed to.

"The island really is fascinating," Celia said, determined to do better. To *be* better. "Will we get to see more of it?"

"Sure, I can give you a whole tour," Easy replied, a languid smile pooling across her face. "What do you want to see?"

"I don't know," Celia replied. "Everything. Are there any cool buildings around? Is there a lighthouse?"

Leona laughed. "Why in the world would we have a lighthouse?" she asked with naked incredulity.

"I don't know," Celia said again. She rooted around in her mind for explanations, forethought, anything she could offer that didn't start with the words *I just assumed.* "It's an island. I guess I figured you'd want to warn people about it." She took a sip of water. It tasted like lemon, but under that was something strangely metallic. "Oh, this is off."

"It's not," Easy said. "We use a mild form of thermal distillation to collect salt from the lake during the rainy season, when the flats can't evaporate. We use the same system to purify the rainwater we catch. It's safe to drink."

"So this is lake water?"

"Probably safer than what you have at home," Leona replied tartly. "No natural gas contamination, no lead pipes. Just what nature gives us. And we have no reason to warn people away," she added. "If they come, then they belong here."

Celia eyed the little bowl of salt on the table. She remembered how those fat flakes of salt had crunched between her back teeth, how bright they'd tasted. The lemon slices in the pitcher in front of her were yellower than the lemons back home. The cucumbers in the other pitcher were greener. Everyone here was drinking the water and it was fine, they were fine. Why wouldn't it be fine?

She took a sip from her glass. The flat, metallic taste was still there, but it wasn't so bad now that she knew to expect it.

After dinner, they left the room without clearing their plates. It felt strange, decadent, like being in a restaurant instead of being at a campground. Out of the corner of her eye, she saw Jessie pushing a small girl by the shoulders, steering her toward the table. The girl looked no older than seven. She held a wicker basket in her hands just like the one that had held the visitors' phones and purses. The basket was already heavy with plates and cups, but she added more to it without hesitation.

Celia tried to catch Jessie's eye, wanting to ask her about Adelaide—but then Easy was guiding her out of the canteen, and Jessie and the little girl were vanishing into the kitchen, and it was too late.

Outside, Leona flagged Easy down, asking to chat for a moment about the next days' festival plans. As soon as Easy's focus was on Leona, Audrey bustled out of the shadow of the canteen. She beelined for Celia. "I need to talk to you. I saw what you saw," she whispered.

Celia followed her a few steps away. "Where's your chaperone?"

"Inside. I told him I needed to get some air. You heard someone, right? A person, in the kitchen? Tell me what you heard."

Celia looked back at Easy. She was deep in conversation with Leona. Neither of them looked happy. "Why?"

Audrey clasped one of Celia's hands between hers. Her fingers were cool and dry. The skin over her bones felt thin. "Just tell me. Tell me who you're looking for. Tell me who you lost."

Celia shook her head and repeated herself. "Why?"

"Because I lost someone, too. My daughter. Mackenzie. She came here a few years ago when she was pregnant, and that was the last time I saw her. She must still be here, her and her baby—he'd be four now."

Celia hesitated. "Is she one of the Salt Festival visitors that decided to stay?"

"That's what I thought," Audrey replied. "But I asked that man William about her, and he said they don't accept new members from the Salt Festival. He said that whoever told me they do that must have been mistaken." Her grip on Celia's hands was vise-tight. "We can help each other. You help me look for my daughter, I'll help you look for whoever you're missing."

"I'm sorry, but—I don't know how I'd help you look for your daughter, Audrey. I don't even know what she looks like."

"She's your height. Little older than you. Tell me if you see her. Or a child who might be hers. Please," she added, her eyes filling with tears. "Please. I know she's still here. I know she is. I'm not leaving without her and my grandchild."

Audrey was squeezing her hands tight, so Celia squeezed back. "I'll tell you if I see anyone. I promise."

"What about you? Who are you looking for? Who did you lose?"

Celia's dinner was suddenly heavy inside of her. How could she answer that question? She thought of the bridge collapse on the news, her parents there and then gone; she thought of blood in the toilet and on her underwear and swirling down the shower drain; she thought of the stirrups at the obstetrician's office, the way they'd cupped her heels like cold sucking mouths as her body forced out a small dead thing that should have been alive.

She had lost all of them. She was looking for all of them.

She was looking for a way to *stop* looking for all of them.

Movement behind Audrey caught her eye—a flash, a face, the edge of a familiar laugh. "There," Celia breathed, letting go of the question and all its possible answers. She tugged her hand out of Audrey's grip and pushed past her, back toward the canteen. "Hey!"

She took off toward the canteen, running. She'd seen Adelaide. It had been her—her face, a little of her hair, peeking around the corner of the building. Celia would know that laugh anywhere. She sprinted toward the canteen and didn't stop, not even when her foot landed on something that bent one of her toes painfully to the side—she could deal with the pain later because she was going to catch up before Adelaide managed to get to the other side of the building—

She was flat on her back before she understood what had happened.

There was no breath in her lungs, no earth beneath her feet. Pain came a few seconds after impact, a full-body shiver of it. She felt like a slammed door. The pain rose around her, closed over her head. She sucked it into her throat and it went down thicker than air. A noise came out of her that was too deflated to be a groan. All she could see was an expanse of darkening sky broken by gently shifting leaves.

Jessie's face appeared between Celia and that sky.

"Fuck," Jessie breathed. "Sorry, are you okay? You came out of nowhere, I was chasing Nona down, and—"

"Oh goddamnit, Jessie, what did you do?" Easy came running. Celia could feel her footfalls reverberating through the earth, through Celia's spine, into her skull. "Celia? Can you hear me?"

"Nnnh," Celia said. She'd meant to say *yes, of course, I'm fine*, but the words wouldn't come out. She rolled gingerly onto her side, coughed a few times, sucked a breath in. Tears rolled down her cheeks. She wasn't crying, not really—the tears had just been knocked loose of her somehow.

Still. They were the first tears she'd shed in months. She touched them and looked at her wet fingers in wonder.

"I'm so so sorry," Easy said, crouching beside her, one hand on her shoulder. "You were moving so fast you must not have seen Jessie, huh? She just—" She pantomimed something that didn't really translate into human movement. "And then you were down. You all right? Nothing broken?"

Celia shook her head. "Nothing broken."

"Good. Jessie, you cannot—I mean absolutely cannot, what were you thinking? This is how you end up on duties again. Celia is a guest here, and—"

"You don't get to speak to me that way, Easy," Jessie snapped. "Just because you hiked Dad's britches up around your belly doesn't mean the rest of us have forgotten how you used to—"

"Children." Audrey stepped close, touched Jessie's arm, rested a palm on Easy's back. "Everyone's fine. Jessie made a mistake. Let's go our ways." At their startled faces, she laughed. "Sorry. My grandmothering instincts are too strong for me to let two kids like you get into a fight over something as small as Celia falling down."

Easy stood and extended a hand to Jessie. "Audrey's right. I'm sorry I spoke to you in unkindness, Jessie."

"Maybe you should take some time to reflect on yourself," the younger girl spat. "Seems like it's been a while."

Celia took Easy's hand, since Jessie was ignoring it. She hauled herself to her feet and brushed the dirt off her backside. "That was embarrassing. I'm so sorry to have made a scene."

"What were you running for?" Easy asked.

"I thought I saw . . . um, that cat from before," Celia answered, forcing a laugh. She didn't know why she wasn't just naming Adelaide. She didn't want to have to explain what she was looking for, she supposed. Didn't want to have to expose her worst yearnings to the people who were supposed to repair her. "I love cats. Just wanted to go say hi. Sorry."

Leona walked over, frowning. "Everyone okay?"

"Everyone's fine," Easy answered, her gaze lingering on Celia. "But Celia's covered in dirt. I'm gonna take her to get cleaned up. See you at Candle Hour."

"I'll walk with you, if you don't mind," Audrey said as Leona and Jessie wandered back to their business. "I seem to have lost my . . . buddy. Maybe we'll run into him."

Easy glanced back into the canteen. "No, I see him inside. You're with Caleb, right? Sorry, he's distractible lately. I'll grab him for you."

As they jogged inside, Audrey gripped Celia's arm, yanking her down until their heads were level. "That girl did not run into you by accident," she hissed into Celia's ear. "She saw you running, stepped out, and clotheslined you. Her arm hit right across your chest," she added, tapping Celia's sternum. There was an ache there, like a bruise about to form. Celia pressed on it herself, savoring the way the pain in her chest was on the outside instead of the inside for once.

"She's just a kid," Celia whispered.

Audrey shook her head. "Be careful in this place."

Celia straightened just in time to see Easy returning. She was towing the soft-eyed man who had helped William tie up the boat. Easy delivered him to Audrey, then linked arms with Celia. "Sorry about that," she said, leading Celia away from the canteen at a brisk pace without letting her say goodbye to Audrey. "And seriously, I'm sorry about Jessie. She should know better than to be so careless, especially when we have visitors. Are you sure you're okay? All in one piece?"

"All in one piece," she confirmed.

Easy looked at her sidelong. "I'll make it up to you," she said firmly, leading them both back up the path toward Grey House.

"Oh, that's okay."

Celia's mind wasn't on the conversation. She was thinking of how it had felt when the air left her lungs. It had been like falling into a whirlpool, into the great open mouth of the earth, into a cavern that had been filling with salt since the birth of the world. In that moment, her body had been entirely out of her control. She'd turned into an animal. It had felt like dying.

Easy was still talking. "You're going to have the best days of your life here. We're going to help you, Celia." She sounded determined. "And—hey. You remember earlier, when you asked about the healing process? About when it would begin?"

Celia nodded, mortified. She should never have asked that question.

But then Easy tilted her head back, the sun catching the long line of her slender throat, and she grinned up at the sky like she'd never seen anything so beautiful. "This is part of it," she breathed. "You fell, and then you got back up, and now look at you. Walking on your own two feet. I'll bet that five minutes ago, when you were flat on your back, you thought you'd never be moving forward again. Do you know what I see when I look at you now?"

"No—what?"

"You'll figure it out. I know you will."

Celia looked up at the sky too, trying to see whatever Easy could see up there. She thought about the way the darkening sky had looked when she was gazing up at it from the ground. Easy was right—part of her had thought she could never get back up again. Part of her hadn't wanted to. Part of her had believed that she was right where she belonged. Every thought, every feeling, every worry and hope had left her mind. There had been no past or future, no loss or regret. No grief. She'd been, for a moment, a being of pure unfettered existence. It had been terrible and beautiful.

She never wanted to feel that way again, and at the same time, she wanted to feel that way forever.

Celia kept her eyes fixed on the sky as Easy led her up the road. She believed that there was something up there worth looking at.

She was determined to keep looking until she could figure out what it might be.

Nine Years Ago

Una is on all fours in the center of the chapel. Her community stands around her as she rides out wave after wave of pain. They chant her name—the name she took when she came to the island, not the one she was baptized with as a baby. Dorothea Chen isn't on this island and never has been. There is only Una now, Una and her community, Una and these people who love her more than anyone else ever has.

There are no candles—it's too close to the Salt Festival, and they can't afford to waste the wax—but Edith has brought some of the little solar lights that surround the canteen, and there's a fire burning in the center of the road. The ashes will be swept away by morning.

By morning, Una knows, this will all be over. Labor can only last for so long. At one point, as the grip of a contraction threatens to break her in half, she thinks that perhaps she will die. If she dies, at least she won't be in labor anymore. That wouldn't be so terrible.

She can't help screaming when the pain comes. The sound tears out of her. It's not connected to her mind—it's a sound that comes from her pelvis, from her flesh. It is not the sound of Una screaming; it is the sound of Una's body screaming.

When she screams, her community screams with her. In front of her, William tilts his head back and howls; behind her, Edith keens shrilly. All around her, they call out, giving voice to her pain as though it's their own. She can't hear her own cries, not over theirs. This, she knows, is how it should be. Everyone hurting together.

There are voices from outside, too. From beyond the chapel steps, beyond the Old House, beyond the cliff.

There are voices from the water.

When she screams, they scream with her.

When the pain ebbs, she drops to her elbows and rests her forehead on the wood of the chapel floor, panting. A long string of saliva hangs from her bottom lip. She is too exhausted to wipe it away.

Outside, she can hear the sound of the children playing. They're running after each other, yelling, throwing sticks and leaves into the fire.

Soon, her baby will join them. *No*, she corrects herself, *not mine. Not my baby. Ours. Our baby.*

"Our baby," she says slowly. She doesn't realize she's speaking aloud until those who are gathered around her—the family that has taken her in, the community that has loved and shaped her, the people she trusts most in all the world—start to echo her.

"Ours," they say. "Our baby. Ours."

"We're having our baby," she calls out.

"We," they repeat.

"We're doing this," she says, and her voice rises, breaking into another scream as the great fist of her abdomen clenches shut again. "Together."

"Together. Together. Together."

FIVE AND A HALF MONTHS AGO

1

Only one truly bad thing had ever happened to Jessie.

She knew this was unusual. Her whole life, she'd been hearing about the bad things that were possible in the world. But those bad things had missed her entirely. She'd never broken a bone. She'd never been in the crowd during a mass shooting. She'd never doubted her purpose—not even when Marco went under. Because, as she reminded herself every single day, Marco going under wasn't a bad thing.

He'd transformed, that was all. And now, he was all around her, always. There was nothing bad about that.

Only one bad thing had ever happened to her.

"What are you doing out so late?" Adelaide called from the front step of the Old House.

"Could ask the same of you," Jessie replied from where she stood on the road. She wasn't about to admit that she frequently snuck out of the canteen, where the children slept, to pace the cliff behind the Old House. She wasn't about to admit how frequently she fantasized about the edge crumbling away beneath her. "Aren't you worn out? I thought being pregnant was supposed to make you tired."

Adelaide shrugged, idly tracing the stains on the front step with one finger. She was already so much bigger than she had been when she got home. Jessie couldn't believe she was supposed to have weeks and weeks left before the baby came. "I'm just waiting for Easy."

Jessie frowned. "She's not home?"

"She's off meeting with William to find out what's going on with the boat. He keeps saying it's broken, so we're getting it fixed. So I can go back to the mainland."

"Oh. I thought you were staying longer. It's only been, what, a week since you got here?"

"Two."

Jessie toed the splintery edge of the front step. "What's your hurry?"

Adelaide scooted over on the step. "Wait with me?" It was an invitation instead of an answer.

The sight of Adelaide's belly sparked envy inside of Jessie. She swallowed down the words before they could get loose: *It should have been me.* She knew her jealousy was an evil that would poison her from the inside out if she let it. She reminded herself to smile, to gentle her voice, to extend patience and kindness. "I'm surprised you never got in touch. While you were gone, I mean."

Adelaide gave her a long, searching look. "How would I have done that?"

"Oh, I don't know," Jessie replied. "You could have written a letter, or—"

"To what address?"

"You were gone for nearly five years. Some people were worried about you."

Adelaide nodded as though they were in agreement. "You grew up a lot while I was away," she said.

A white flash of anger consumed Jessie as suddenly as the despair she'd felt when William first jumped into his boat to pick up Adelaide from the opposite shore. She let the feeling take her. "You could tell Easy that," she snapped. "You have no idea what it's been like. What she's been like while you've been gone—"

"Tell me." Adelaide said it so gently that Jessie felt herself deflate just as fast as she'd puffed up. The sudden flush of certainty it'd given her drained away as Adelaide continued. "You're right that I don't know what it's been like. Tell me what I missed."

Jessie combed her hair back away from her face with one hand. She didn't want to tell Adelaide any of it. She wanted to tell Adelaide all of it. She wanted to run off the cliff and fall into the water.

Jessie couldn't bear to fill Adelaide in. She decided to take a risk instead. She decided to make a confession.

"I didn't think you'd come back." When Adelaide didn't reply, Jessie continued. "I didn't think you were worthy of a Salt Year. I thought you'd left us behind for no reason, and I thought you took my Salt Year with you." She cleared her throat. "So. After you left . . .

I went to William and Easy, and I asked them to let me try to do my Salt Year here instead of out there. Me and Marco."

Adelaide blinked hard at the sound of Marco's name. "You would have been, what, thirteen?" Adelaide asked.

"I was thirteen when you left. Thirteen and a half when I asked them. William said I was too young, but then Easy said they should give me a chance to prove myself. That they could promise me to Marco if we waited until my sixteenth birthday. She said it would give me time to prepare myself, to prove myself. To decide if I really wanted to give up my chance at a real Salt Year. Honestly, I think she just wanted to buy time for you to come home."

"But then I didn't come home." Adelaide had her head tilted back. She was looking at the stars. Jessie watched as a fly climbed the length of her throat, its feet sticking to the sweat-tack of her skin. "What happened to her while I was gone? She's so different now."

"Is she? Or were you just seeing her wrong, before?"

Adelaide didn't answer for a long time. Her brow was furrowed, her eyes still fixed on the sky. It was a habit she and Easy shared, Jessie realized—looking up when they didn't know what to say. After a while, Adelaide glanced back down. "Did you end up trying? You and . . . anyone?"

Angry tears blurred Jessie's vision. "We didn't get a chance."

Adelaide's hand was in hers, squeezing just a little too hard, looking for a squeeze back. "I'm so sorry," she said. She sounded sincere.

Jessie couldn't take that. She didn't want Adelaide to be sorry. She didn't want Adelaide to understand and comfort. She changed the subject as hard as she knew how. "What's it like out there? In the world?"

"Hm."

Jessie waited, figuring that Adelaide was just considering her answer, but after a while she prodded again. "Is it really as bad as everyone says?"

"That's a good question." Then, very quietly, she said, "Worse. It's worse. And better."

Jessie's heart sank. "How much worse?"

Adelaide shook her head. "It's bad everywhere, Jess. Police. Cameras. Plastic. Religion. There's broken glass in the street so you have to wear shoes wherever you go, sometimes even indoors. People don't look at each other. There are huge fires and huge floods and everything, everywhere, costs money." She passed a palm over the curve of her belly, shaking her head. "Even clean water. Even clean air."

Jessie let out a low whistle. "You must have missed it here."

"Course I did. But, here's the thing." She paused for an excruciating stretch, seeming to chew on each word she was about to say. "What nobody tells you is, out there? If you have a baby? You get to keep it."

Jessie surprised herself by laughing. "What does that mean? We keep our babies. Unless they go under, but even then, they're still—"

"Still with us, I know. That's not what I mean, though. If you have a baby out there, you get to keep it all to yourself. It's just yours. Like—you know your coin? The one you hide under your shelf?"

That stole the laughter right out of Jessie. She didn't think anyone knew about that—the tiny circle of silver that lived beneath the little shelf in the back of the pantry tucked between the wood and the metal bracket that held it in place.

"I don't know about a coin," she whispered.

"The whole outside world is like that. You get things and you keep them. Coins, books, clothes. And you don't have to keep any of it secret. Imagine if this dress," she said, reaching out and plucking at the faded linen of Jessie's skirt, "was only ever yours."

Jessie suppressed a shudder. She couldn't tell if it was a shiver of disgust or of desire. Maybe both. "What about it?"

"It's like that out there with people, too. You marry someone, and they become yours. You have a baby, and it belongs to you. When I have this baby, out there on the mainland, it will be all mine. No community standards. No work groups. I'll decide what it eats and what its hair looks like, what words it learns, what songs it sings. I'll teach it what love means. It'll look to me for everything. Every idea. Every feeling." Her voice stretched thin with yearning.

"That can't be right," Jessie started—but Adelaide wasn't listening anymore. The conversation was between her and an idea now.

"It'll have to love me, no matter what. It won't be able to punish me or tell me I'm not good enough. Because I'll be the one it belongs to. That's how it works out there. That's what I'm going to have."

The idea was like a hot pan on the range in the canteen. Jessie didn't know quite how to pick it up without burning herself. "Easy missed you," she said at last.

Adelaide snorted. "I don't know who the hell Easy is anymore. But that's fine. She'll get back to normal soon. When we're on the mainland again, everything will be okay." Worry drifted across her features. "She'll be okay."

This time, Jessie did squeeze her hand. "Easy's doing better than okay, though. She's doing great. You should really give her more credit. She worked hard while you were gone. Stopped being such a shitshow all the time."

Adelaide gave her a sidelong glance. "I thought you were mad at her?"

Jessie sucked in a deep breath and held it until her vision began to tunnel. The truth was, she'd never stopped liking Easy. Even when she realized that Easy was a disaster, back before the years of transformation that had turned Easy into the thing she was now—even then, she'd liked Adelaide's wayward sister.

But then Easy'd caught Jessie on the day Marco went under. She never threatened to tell anyone what Jessie had done. She'd just gone to William and said that it seemed like Jessie wasn't ready to be an adult after all, and she'd trapped Jessie where she was—working alongside the children, sweeping the road and cleaning out the kitchen and sleeping on those long wooden tables in the canteen every night. Easy had done this to her. And now she didn't know if she'd ever get her Salt Year.

Jessie could never forgive her for that.

"You didn't always think Easy was a shitshow, you know," Adelaide said, filling the silence Jessie had created with her held breath. "When you were tiny, you used to follow her around all over the place. Her little shadow."

"That was before I grew up." Jessie tucked her feet up underneath her. She glanced down at Adelaide's feet, trying to see if they looked any different than they had two years before. She couldn't imagine a life spent walking around in places that weren't safe enough for a person's feet to touch the ground. How untended the world must be, to have gotten so dangerous. "Anyway," she said with conviction, "it's good that you came back. It sounds awful out there."

"The bad parts are worth it. You'll see. It'll be your turn to go, soon. I'll be waiting for you out there, and I bet you'll end up telling me some things you like about the world, once you've seen it." Adelaide was not quite smiling. She lifted her hair in one hand, fanning the back of her neck with the other. The fly on her collarbone lifted off her in a slow, lazy flight. "Can you keep a secret? About life out there in the world?"

Jessie's stomach clenched. "No."

Adelaide leaned toward her anyway, her eyebrows raised, conspiratorial. "Sometimes," she whispered, "I even kind of liked wearing the shoes."

Jessie was on her feet before she could stop herself. She stared down at Adelaide. She felt like her heart was trying to carve its way out of her body through her stomach. A distant splash sounded from somewhere beyond the cliffs.

Adelaide knew. Somehow, Adelaide knew. Easy had told. She must have.

"Jessie? What's the matter?"

Was Adelaide's concern sincere, or was this a trap? Had Jessie somehow laid out a snare for herself with her questions about Adelaide's time on the mainland? She felt so stupid, so obvious. Asking about the world in the first place. What had she been thinking?

She already knew the answer. She'd been thinking about Marco. She couldn't ever seem to *stop* thinking about Marco, and what his transformation had taken from her. And now she couldn't tell if Adelaide knew what she'd done, and the island was sinking out from underneath her feet, and her hands were in fists and she couldn't seem to catch her breath.

"Hey." Adelaide slowly stood, reaching for Jessie. "Seriously, are you okay? Maybe you should sit down—"

Jessie flinched away from her. "Sorry. I have to go. I was never here. Okay? I was never here at all."

She ran.

2

Jessie let the soles of her feet slap the dirt of the road that wound through Kindred Cove without thinking about where she was going. That was one of the beautiful things about the island: She never had to plan her destination. The road was one long branching corridor that led from everywhere to the pier. All Jessie had to do was follow it.

She didn't stop until her feet were wet.

Jessie could remember when the miracle tide had swallowed up the first dock. The original one. She'd known, back then and all her life, that she'd end up being promised to Marco. It was a foregone conclusion, an inevitability. Marco had helped build a new dock right on top of the old one. While he worked, Jessie brought cool water down to him, a jimsonweed flower tucked clumsily into her braid, and she watched the sweat stream down his temples.

He'd been standing calf-deep in the newly risen lake, drinking the water she brought, when the miracle tide had come in. The reef had fed that morning, and it was blooming, expanding, enormous. You could almost see the shadow of it moving, if you looked at the water at the right angle. They'd both run up the incline, fleeing the rising water, her with her skirt clutched in her hands to keep the hem from getting soaked, and then they'd turned around to watch the water rush up toward them.

Marco's hand was a warm weight on her shoulder. "That's the second onc this week," he'd muttered. He would never have admitted to being nervous about the fate of the Cove, but Jessie could feel it in the grip he had on her.

That worry in him was what had made her go to William, to ask about trying to fix things. Easy's two-and-a-half-year compromise rankled her at the time—it didn't seem fair to have to put off the work she was clearly meant for. She wanted to get pregnant and stay pregnant, to push out a hundred healthy babies who would keep the road clean and the salt flats raked. It was her destiny, and she didn't want to have to wait for it.

Still, she'd obeyed William, and she'd made good use of the time. She'd spent it honing herself, making herself perfect for Marco and the holy work they'd do together. She kept herself balanced, faithful, industrious, clean. She did everything Harvey told her to do, without complaint or hesitation. She helped with the other children, keeping them on task, flicking their ears hard when they whined about being tired or sick or hurt. William had even asked her to help him in the office, sorting the donations past years' Salt Festival visitors left behind.

That was what got her into trouble. Sorting the donations. At first it felt like a disgusting chore, something she was glad to help William with in order to lessen his load, the same way she was glad to help Caleb muck out the chicken coop. She was proud to be trusted with the work, pleased at the opportunity to participate in something so important.

And she liked feeling needed. William simply couldn't do the work alone anymore. Back then, Easy hadn't been involved at all—she'd been too busy fucking everything up all the time, making gin and talking about people like they were dead and sleeping late and swimming down to the reef at midnight.

Things were different now, but back then, it had all been on William's shoulders. He was so busy managing the business that kept Kindred Cove alive. He handled all the sales and distribution and shipping, ferrying purified and packaged salt from the island to the mainland once a month and figuring out how to turn that salt into money. He was also busy making plans for the day the reef was finished growing, bridging the Cove and the mainland. He never told Jessie what the plans were, but they seemed to consume most of his time and patience. She worried for him. It must have been hard, carrying so much.

With all that on his shoulders, it made sense that William needed her help. Especially with researchers from the mainland nosing around, trying to get answers about the unprecedented growth of the reef, sticking their instruments into everyone's business. Every time

William was contacted by someone from the mainland to report that a researcher was trying to rent a boat and come visit the Cove, he had to drop everything to handle it. He'd take his boat all the way across the water to track down the interloper and convince them it wasn't appropriate to interfere in the Cove's business, and then he'd come back exhausted. It took half a day at a minimum every time, and so much courage. He was good at it, though. Sometimes he convinced them to offer donations, too—clothes, cash, entire wallets. She couldn't imagine how much finesse and faith it took to turn a skeptic into an ally like that.

The sheer burden of people from the world being able to reach him, of having to travel away from the safety and certainty of the Cove—Jessie just couldn't imagine it. She'd been eager to help however she could, eager to prove her usefulness in the time leading up to her and Marco finally getting the opportunity to make the Cove a better place.

No one seemed to remember that Jessie was the one who stepped up to help, long before Easy got her shit together.

While she waited for Marco, Jessie spent regular evenings in William's office. She put labels on thumb-sized bottles of salt. The labels said *Kindred Cove Medicinals*. She might put two hundred labels on bottles of *Abundance* or *Balance* or *Vitality* or *Forgiveness*. It was all the same salt inside, harvested from the lake year-round by the littlest hands the island had—but William said people liked the different labels. She never opened the bottles. The caps were sealed plastic and she didn't want to touch them, even if William said it was okay because it was work she was doing on behalf of the community.

She dropped the bottles into their boxes, one by one, and then she sealed the boxes and stacked them by the door, and every time she added a box to the stack she knew she was that much closer to becoming the person she was meant to be.

When she ran out of boxes, she usually sorted donations from the Salt Festival visitors. There was a big backlog. When she started working in William's office, the whole back half of it was a snowdrift, nearly ten years' worth of detritus that nobody had really known what to do with. Jessie was the one who got a system in place to sort it all, to figure out what was useful and what wasn't.

Clothes and handkerchiefs went into a big bin to be washed and divided among the residents of the Cove. Watches and jewelry went into an old shoebox for William to deal with. Medication went onto the big first-aid shelf that nobody ever touched. Cash went into a drawer in William's desk. Wallets, credit cards, driver's licenses, photographs, and shoes went into a large barrel. Jessie didn't know what happened to the contents of the barrel—that was William's business.

She wasn't supposed to touch electronics. She left those where she found them and William handled them for her, because he cared about her. Because he supported her. Because he wanted her and Marco to be able to build the future of the Cove.

She'd been careful about handling the donations at first, the same way she was careful when she pruned the blackberry canes in the garden. She knew how dangerous some of these items were. For the first couple of weeks, at the end of an hour's work, she'd run down to the waterline to scrub her hands, imagining that she could feel the slick filth of the world bleeding off her hands and into the blessed waters of the Vetiver.

But over time, without really noticing she was doing it, Jessie grew accustomed to the things she saw and touched. She'd find herself looking at photographs of complete strangers, people with tattoos and piercings and headphones, people who had never once felt the kiss of a good loving correction from an entire island's worth of family—and she wouldn't feel afraid or disgusted or even surprised. She took to staring at the photos until she could find something to shake her: a police drone on the skyline, a child in a VR headset, a piece of food wrapped in plastic.

After a little while, those things stopped shaking her, too.

At first she couldn't tell if her acclimation to the donations was right or wrong. She was doing important work for the Cove. She was preventing William from taking on another burden. Surely her comfort with the work meant she was developing something like expertise.

But then she started to linger over other items, things worse than photographs. A pack of cigarettes that she raised to her nose briefly before tossing it into the barrel. A stick of chewing gum that she touched to the tip of her tongue. A cell phone in an inside jacket pocket that William had missed—it was turned off, but she depressed the single button on the side of it over and over, just to feel the smooth click under her thumb.

She told herself that she was just getting to know the work. Developing an intimate understanding of the materials, just as Edith had told her to develop an intimate understanding of her own body in preparation for the moment she and Marco were committed to each other. It was, she thought, not so different.

Even then, some part of her had recognized this as a lie she was telling herself. She found herself keeping her eyes on the door as she touched and tasted, startling at small noises, flushing with guilt when William returned to check on her progress. This office was the only place on the entire island with no peepholes, no gaps in the walls. Pure privacy. She admitted to herself eventually that she *liked* it that way. She wanted to be alone in the office. She wanted to be alone with the donations.

It was the first time she'd ever had a secret.

She tried to fix it. She fasted and she meditated and she reflected and she journaled and she punished her own flesh until it broke and bled. She did every single mindful thing she could think of to try to return herself to a sense of balance. She even risked opening a bottle of salt, pure and undiluted by the water of the Vetiver. She piled the broad, flat flakes onto her tongue and forced herself to swallow until she retched.

None of it worked. So she compromised by giving herself a deadline. She would be given to Marco on her sixteenth birthday. She told herself that she had until then to get this wretched curiosity out of her system.

She could handle that. It was like everyone told her Dad used to say: *Love without sacrifice is as good as indifference.* She was more than prepared to make sacrifices for the good of the community.

Once she made that agreement with herself, none of it felt nearly so awful. Curiosity was natural. Everyone said so. Chickens were curious. Babies were curious. Dad's teachings called curiosity *the sign of a mind that was ready to learn.*

She convinced herself that what she was doing wasn't wrong. And it was Marco who suffered for it.

3

It happened so easily that she could almost convince herself it had been inevitable. It was the day before her sixteenth birthday. Easy had sent William to come find Jessie at Edith's. Jessie remembered wondering when, exactly, Easy had started sending William places. She remembered trying to figure out when the island's pet disaster had turned into its golden child.

When William found her, she'd been trying on the dress for the next day's Salt Ceremony. Normally it would happen at the Salt Festival, but since Jessie wasn't going to get to leave for a Salt Year, Edith and William had decided this was the way to mark the occasion. The dress was made of white silk that clung to her like a kiss. William had smiled down at her, told her that she was a vision. Then he'd asked if she could come help him at the office.

She'd felt a thrill of illicit excitement. It was her last day. The last day before she had to redirect her curiosity into effort, the last day before Marco would take her and turn her into a vessel to serve the community's needs—and here William was, presenting her with one last opportunity to indulge.

William took her down to his office and left her in there with a huge tote full of donations. It was packed with clothes and wallets, the last of the most recent batch of mainlander donations. Jessie looked at the tote and felt a curious twist of guilt for not having attended to it sooner. She almost found it funny, in hindsight, that she'd known guilt over her absence from this task even as she transgressed while performing it.

That evening, she did more than just transgress. She indulged. She lingered over every single item—tracing the faces of the people in the photographs, rubbing the soft leather of a wallet against her cheek, slipping coins into her mouth so she could suck the strange tang of them down into her throat. She'd found her coin, the tiny silver one, and tucked it into her armpit to sneak home with her. She'd found a compact with pressed powder in it and she'd stolen a glance at herself in the tiny mirror inside before snapping it shut. And then she'd gotten to the bottom of the bag, and there they'd been.

A pair of shoes.

The bottoms were perfectly flat, made of some lightweight foam that smelled faintly of greenwood smoke. A thin strip of plastic was anchored to the foam and split from there into two straps. The material was stained heavily with blood. Lots of the shoes donated by mainland researchers were like that. William said it was a natural consequence of confining oneself to deviant separation from contact with the earth. With the open sides on this pair, Jessie imagined they must have left a trail of dark footprints leading up to the edge of the Vetiver.

The shoes were both unattractive and hypnotizing. Jessie held them in her hands, feeling the worn-smooth undersides of the soles. They were the last thing she needed to deal with on the last day she'd have this job. She wanted her curiosity to have been sated by the work she'd already done, but it wasn't. It wasn't enough.

She needed something more.

She looked at the door. She had no way of knowing when William would return. She should drop these shoes into the big barrel, run down to the pier Marco had built nearly two and a half years earlier, wash her hands, and go home to prepare. Her whole life was about to begin, she knew, and she should begin it well. *Start as you mean to go on.* Everyone said that.

But she wanted. She *needed*.

Slowly, so slowly that she could almost convince herself it wasn't happening at all, she bent down and slid the shoe onto her foot.

The anchor of the forked strap slid between her first and second toes. It was a little sticky with old blood, but it fit into the notch between those toes easily, as though her feet had been made for this. Her breath caught at the feeling of the foam beneath her heel. It was like stepping into Edith's cupped hands to get a boost up into a tree that needed trimming.

She stood on one foot, staring down at the contrast between the mottled, bloodstained strap and her own pale skin, consumed by the sight. For the first time in her whole life, she felt sated.

And then the door to the office opened.

Jessie's head jerked up so sharply that she lost her balance. She could tell that she'd made a sound but she didn't know what the sound was, how loud it had been. She stumbled backward into her chair. The compact flew off the edge of William's desk, landing with a clatter and flying open, little crumbs of pressed powder flying everywhere. The shoe flew off the end of her foot and landed on the floor a meter away with a loud *smack*.

Easy stood in the open doorway, staring at her.

"I was just—I wasn't—I was sorting it," Jessie stammered, heat climbing up around her ears like the lake climbing up around the island. "What are you doing here?"

Easy slid into the office, closing the door behind her. "I was looking for you," she said softly. Then she walked to the middle of the room, crouched down, and picked up the shoe.

"Don't touch that," Jessie snapped. "It's bad for you."

Easy looked up, still crouching, and hefted the shoe as if weighing it in her hand. "Don't worry," she said.

Jessie shrank back in William's chair. "I don't know what you mean." The words came out of her small and weak. She was caught and she knew it.

But Easy had just given her that lopsided smile. "I mean, don't worry. It's okay to try things. If it was just a mistake, you can learn from it. That's how a person grows. I know that better than anyone, right?"

Jessie knew that wasn't true, the part about learning from mistakes. She knew she'd done something wrong, something so wrong that there was no way to even begin explaining it. She'd used material from the world to separate herself from reality. She'd gazed at herself in admiration. She'd been tempted and succumbed.

She'd betrayed the Cove. She'd betrayed Dad's memory, which mattered even if she couldn't remember him.

"You don't know what you're talking about," she snapped. "You should go."

Easy tossed the shoe into the barrel. "I just wanted to say . . ." Wiped her hands on her pants and turned to Jessie. "I just wanted to say that you don't have to do any of this."

There was sweat blooming across the back of Jessie's neck. "Any of what?"

"The whole Salt Year thing. You don't have to do it. You don't have to try to get pregnant. I know you think you have to, but you don't. You can stay with the children as long as you want. You never have to have a baby if you don't want to."

Jessie recoiled. "What the fuck are you talking about? Of course I want to—"

"Not of course," Easy whispered, stepping forward and looking at Jessie with such painful earnestness that Jessie had to look away. "Everyone says it's what we have to do, but it's not. There are other paths. I never, ever wanted to do it. Never. The idea of getting pregnant and giving birth makes me want to swim down into the mines." She took another step forward, and Jessie took a small step back. "So I didn't. I opted out of all that. And it was hard for a while, but now it's not hard anymore. I swept the road for you, Jessie. There are other futures you can have here."

Jessie held her hands up, ready to push Easy away if she came any closer. "I don't want what you have," she said. Her voice was shaking. "I don't know what's wrong with you. But I don't want it to be wrong with me, too."

"Are you sure?" Easy whispered. "Because this is your chance. You can choose to stay in the children's group. You can choose not to lose anything."

"Don't come any closer. Don't touch me. I don't want anything you want. I don't want to be anything you are." Jessie was nearly spitting by the time she finished.

Easy's expression was grave now, and Jessie remembered thinking that she'd made a terrible mistake, because at some point in the prior year, Easy had turned into someone who sent William places, and that meant she could decide on consequences. Power meant punishment, and Jessie had spat on the fresh new power Easy seemed to hold. She looked at the stillness in Easy's eyes, and she braced herself for whatever was to come.

She could never have braced herself enough.

"Okay. That's your decision, and I respect it. But you'll need to come with me," Easy had said. "Something's happened."

4

Easy had spoken so carefully after that. As though Jessie was fragile, vulnerable. As though Jessie wasn't to blame. As though she hadn't kicked away Easy's attempt at mercy.

What had happened was all Jessie's fault, but Easy explained it to her as though there was nothing anyone could have done to prevent it.

Marco had been pacing the shoreline all day, Easy said, walking in and out of the water. Jessie knew that part already. Everyone, herself included, had assumed that Marco was just practicing mindful bathing, preparing himself for the next day. Preparing himself for her.

But a few minutes ago, Easy said, Marco had walked into the water and stayed there. He hadn't come back out. A moment later the miracle tide had appeared—heading away from Kindred Cove.

Marco had gone under. He'd gone under and his body had erupted, joining the reef that was slowly bridging the distance from the mainland to the island. He'd become something greater than himself. And he'd done it while Jessie had her foot inside of a shoe.

She knew that this couldn't be a coincidence—her chance to fulfill her life's purpose being taken from her on the day she chose to indulge herself in depravity.

Easy had agreed. She hadn't told anyone what she'd caught Jessie doing—she'd silently swept up the shattered disc of face powder as Jessie had sobbed under William's desk. She'd been patient. She'd been kind. But then, over the course of the following week she'd finished her transformation from human disaster to leader of the Cove by telling everyone that Jessie needed to continue working with the children. That something in her must not have been truly prepared for the work of adulthood, if Marco had journeyed so far away from her.

Easy had turned into the person who decided on consequences, and she'd made it so Jessie remained a child in the eyes of the island for the entire long stretch of years that Adelaide was gone. And the worst part was that Jessie couldn't disagree with her about any of it.

Now, Jessie stood with her bare feet in the lake, breathless from her sprint down the island, away from Adelaide and down to the shoreline. She stared at the dark surface of the water, trying to see the dock that Marco had built. The wood his hands had touched had been consumed by the Vetiver. The waters were rising more and more, and if the Salt Festival happened this year, they'd rise even higher.

If only she'd been worthy of the Salt, she knew, she could have stopped all this from happening. She could have patiently waited for Adelaide to return, and then she could have taken her own year away from the island. She could have found a way to get a baby in her belly to bring back to this place that trusted her to be good. She felt sure that if she'd just done everything right, then William would have stayed in charge, and Easy would have stayed broken, and everything would have been different somehow. Marco could have lived.

But she'd failed. She'd faltered in her faith, and she'd been punished for it. And now Marco was gone forever, and here forever, and would never touch her, and would never leave her, either.

She fell to her knees, shoved her face into the water, and screamed. She screamed hard enough that the sound might reach Marco, wherever he was now, whatever he'd become. She squeezed her eyes shut, but the salt stung them anyway and when she reared up, the brine of the lake streamed into her mouth. The salt burned in her throat as she choked on it.

She was thankful for the pain. She knew it was what she deserved.

Today

The Short Woman is worried that the Tall Woman will think she's cutting in line. She's not cutting in line, even though she's stepping into the line, in front of the Tall Woman. She just wants to grab the vial of Kindred Salt that's on the aisle display at the too-expensive grocery store where the Short Woman used to buy cream-top milk and eggs that, on the carton, promise the laying hens have a good life.

The Tall Woman has the same eggs in her basket. "Those are good eggs," the Short Woman says as she sidles past the end of the Tall Woman's shopping cart.

"Get to the back of the fucking line," the Tall Woman whispers. "Come on. We're all in a hurry."

"I just—" The Short Woman stands on her toes and reaches for the salt. It's packaged in a brown glass bottle with a paper label. The label's a little crooked. The ink on the label is blotched with water. That doesn't matter. She needs it.

The Tall Woman understands the situation quickly, forgives the Short Woman for the crime she hadn't been committing after all. She leans over her cart and plucks the brown glass bottle from the shelf, hands it over. Her heavy silver bracelet has the word *grateful* stamped into the metal. "I love that stuff," she whispers. "I use it every morning before going to my cycle group."

The Short Woman nods eagerly. She knows the cycle group the Tall Woman means. She had a membership until a month ago, when her husband got laid off and she could no longer afford the expensive membership to the gym where the stationary bikes sit in perfect rows and the music is louder than thought. She never went to the morning sessions, though. It's too hard for her to wake up that early. "I haven't tried it before, but the girl at the front desk? At the Piedmont location?" She sees the Tall Woman recognize a fellow cycle group member, which was the point of mentioning the Piedmont location. "She told me about it. She said it's amazing," she confesses.

The Tall Woman eyes the bottle in her hand. "Manifest," she says, nodding. "That's a good blend."

"Does it really help? With, um. With attracting the energy you desire?" The Short Woman feels herself flushing, her cheeks and temples burning. She's only just started reading about the law of attraction, has only taken a couple of online classes. She knows she sounds new and uninformed. She wants to be further along. She wants to be better.

The Tall Woman nudges her cart past the Short Woman as the line moves forward. She smiles, the kind of smile that belongs to someone with that heavy silver bracelet and two-hundred-dollar yoga pants and a cart full of groceries that the Short Woman can no longer afford. "You have no idea," she says. "You have no idea how much it will help."

SALT FESTIVAL

day one | evening

The first Candle Hour of the Salt Festival took place well after nightfall. Easy and Celia were among the first to arrive. The sky was full of stars, more stars than Celia had ever seen in one place, and the night air hummed with what sounded like the noise of every small creature that had ever existed. It was still humid, but when Celia lifted her hair off her neck, the evening breeze coming off the lake blew a cool breath across the fine hairs at her nape. The shoreline glowed with the light of a hundred tapers. The smell of beeswax met Celia before she passed the edge of the treeline, and by the time she and Easy made it down to the water, the perfume of the candles had wrapped itself around her, sweet and floral.

"This is beautiful," she murmured. "The candles are amazing."

Easy snorted. "Don't let Leona hear you say that, or it'll be all she talks about for the next six months. *Nobody appreciates my candles the way that one Salt Festival visitor did*," she added.

Celia laughed. "That was uncanny. Like she was standing right here in front of me."

Easy started to turn toward the water, then paused to look back at Celia. The candlelight made her eyes gleam yellow. "That's the first time I've seen you laugh since you got here. No, wait—don't get self-conscious. I just meant that I'm glad. Laughter looks good on you." Voices drifted down to the shore from the trees, and Easy's attention shifted to the guests who were coming down the road to join them at the shoreline. It was written across her whole body—the shift of her shoulders, the way she stood a bit taller, the set of her jaw. She was theirs now. "I'm going to have to do some official business. You won't mind standing on your own while I'm putting on the show, will you?"

"Of course," Celia answered quickly, wanting it to be true. She stood there as the rest of the Salt Festival visitors filtered down to the water's edge, moving around her and in front of her until she was at the back of the crowd.

Easy turned to face them all.

Celia wanted to feel trusted, independent—but she couldn't quite get there. She felt disconnected. Easy looked around at everyone and her eyes didn't touch Celia. The crowd had diluted the connection between the two of them so effortlessly, Celia thought, that she might very well have disappeared from Easy's mind altogether.

"Welcome to the first Candle Hour of this year's Salt Festival," Easy said. The candleflames around her fluttered in the gentle stir of the night air. Behind her, the lake shifted restlessly. "If you look around, you might notice that there aren't that many of us here tonight. That's because this first Candle Hour is just for our visitors, and for the residents who will be guiding you through your time here. Does everyone have their buddy? Except Celia over there, who I've abandoned for the moment," she added, raising her chin toward the back of the crowd.

People turned to look at Celia. She forced a smile, waved a little, wasn't sure if she was supposed to say anything. She wondered if Easy had somehow sensed her maudlin feeling of isolation. If she'd felt a need to offer the reassurance of acknowledgment.

"Okay, so everyone has a partner," Easy continued. "The reason this Candle Hour is just for you, new friends, is because you've come here to try to change something about yourselves. About your lives. You feel small and alone and insignificant. You feel like nobody sees you, not really. Not for who you truly are." She lifted her arms high. "You feel lost," she called up to the dizzying blanket of stars. "You're hurting and scared and sad and you want to feel"—she looked back out at the crowd, her eyes locking immediately onto Celia's—"better."

Celia's skin flushed with heat. The dusty soil beneath her feet seemed to sway like the deck of the water taxi. Easy's eyes glowed with bright candlelight.

"We can make you feel better, friends. While you're here, you'll discover the greatest secret truth of life—that's right, I'm giving it away on day one," she added, drawing laughter from the crowd. "This truth can heal you. This truth can make everything okay. There is no grief or fear or loss or death if you know this truth: that nothing is ever lost."

She paused then, her hands in fists, the breeze running saline fingers through her hair. Celia could hear someone in the crowd crying softly. No one spoke.

And then Easy's posture shifted—her shoulders dropped, her hands unclenched, her face opened into a relaxed, warm, understanding smile. "Don't worry," she said. "I know it sounds nuts right now. But by the end of this week it'll make sense to you. I promise!" More laughter, a loud sniff from the direction of whoever had been crying. "Tonight, we're just going to set some intentions. Not for this week—trust me, we have more than enough planned for all of you, you'll have plenty on your plate if you just come along for the ride. No, the intentions we set tonight will be for something much, much more important. The intentions we set tonight," she said, rocking forward on her toes, looking for all the world like she was about to lift off the ground and float into the crowd, "are for you. Your life. Your soul. Your purpose.

"Everyone, face your buddy. Look them in the eyes."

All around Celia, people rotated like clockwork figurines. She spotted Audrey toward the front of the crowd, turning toward Caleb, their faces indistinct in the muted light of the candles. Firelight flickered off the crystal necklace around one girl's throat just a couple of feet away from Celia; she was looking up at a tall, broad-shouldered man with an eager smile.

Celia chewed on the inside of her cheek, unsure of what to do with herself. Easy didn't look in her direction.

"Now, think about what it is that you want. Take your time. It's okay to think out loud. And listen—no cop-outs, okay? You don't get to say that you want the tumor to go away, or for your marriage to work out, or whatever." A few nervous chuckles. Celia looked down at her feet in the dust, twisted her fingers together. *Alone*, she thought, the word as familiar to her brain as her own name. *Alone, I'm alone, I'm alone.* Easy continued. "All that shit is just another way of saying you want your problems to go away. But what about when your problems are gone? When every obstacle is out of your way? What then? When you know you can have whatever you want, and nothing is stopping you—what will you pursue? Who do you want to *become*?"

She said *become* with a weight and power that struck Celia in the solar plexus. Celia felt her eyes flood with tears and she felt her mind flood with the same words over and over again: *I'm alone, I'm alone, I'm alone.*

But then Easy cut a path through the crowd, moving toward her with that long, loping stride. She touched a shoulder here and there, weaving behind whoever was in her way—until she was standing in front of Celia, her hands outstretched, her eyes soft.

"Figure out what it is that you want," she said, her gaze fixed on Celia, her voice carrying loud enough for everyone to hear, "and then tell it to your partner." She took Celia's hands in hers and leaned in close, her voice dropping to a near whisper. "What do you want, Celia?"

Celia blinked hard, her lashes damp. Easy's hands were cool and dry in hers. The lake lapped at the shore in a whooshing heartbeat-rhythm. The reflected light in Easy's eyes flickered as she watched Celia's face.

"I want to be loved," Celia whispered.

"That's not it," Easy replied at once. Her voice was soft, but insistent.

Celia tried again. "I don't want to hurt anymore."

Easy shook her head wryly. "You're not even trying. You could have those things any time, Celia. Tell me the real shit."

Celia hesitated. "The real shit?"

"Yeah. The real shit."

Celia knew what the real shit was, and she didn't want to share it. Not out loud. "I put it in my letter," she ventured. "Isn't that enough?"

"You tell me," Easy answered. "Is it?"

Of course it wasn't, because she hadn't put everything in the letter. She hadn't put in the fact that she hadn't been in a romantic relationship in eight years. Not because she didn't want to—but because when she met someone she wanted, someone she felt a real connection with, a strange, dangerous thing would happen to her. Her mind would turn into a tongue, poking over and over into the bloody missing-tooth cavity of her attraction. She would find herself thinking as if they were already with her. *Andrea will be so proud of me* or *What will Marc say when I tell him?* or *Ren won't think this pillow sham goes with the bedspread.* She would walk around her house differently, leaving curtains open, imagining that the person she wanted might be just outside, watching her, aroused by the way she stirred her coffee. She would dream about them. She would become fixated.

And then, over time, as reality continued not to map onto the fantasy of her involvement with the person she wanted, she'd find herself bitter. Resentful. Once, she'd gotten halfway through composing an angry message—*you're so distant lately, it makes me wonder if we can even make this work long-distance*—before catching herself.

There was another time when she hadn't caught herself. The outcome had been far less disastrous than she'd deserved. The person she confronted, a friend of a friend who she'd met once at a brunch and developed an immediate crush on, seemed to believe her when she said the email had been sent by mistake. Still, it was a close enough call that she'd decided to cut herself off: If she knew that the blanket rule was *no dating*, she wouldn't be at risk of getting wrapped up in a fantasy dating life with someone who barely even knew she existed. It worked well enough—no more almost-disasters. Still, she could feel something inside herself grasping, longing for the delicious oblivion of obsession.

That was how she had ended up deciding to have a baby.

Being obsessed with a stranger, an acquaintance, a mutual social media connection—that was, she knew, unhealthy. But being obsessed with a baby? Being obsessed with *her own* baby? That was to be expected. That was virtuous. That was *good mothering.* She could pin her brain to a child, could endlessly imagine and fantasize and fixate, and the result would be something to celebrate. She'd never be alone again. She'd never have to hurt again.

There would be someone there to share the endless screaming pain of being alive.

It had been a good plan. Except that it hadn't worked. And that was the real shit. That was the thing she didn't want to share.

It hadn't worked, but she still wanted it.

She looked down at her hands, at Easy's hands, at the place where their fingers met. She swallowed hard, hoping her words would be too quiet for Easy to hear.

"I want to be a mother."

Easy's reply came from right next to Celia's ear. "You want to be a mother."

Celia nodded.

"Say it," Easy murmured, leaning back to regard Celia. "Say it again."

"I want to be a mother," Celia said, her voice barely above a whisper.

"Again."

"I want." Celia choked on the words.

"You can do it."

"I want to be a mother," she said, and this time, her voice was just loud enough to reach her own ears.

From the other side of the crowd, a woman's voice rose in a shout. "I want to love my husband!"

Celia looked up, startled. Easy rolled her eyes, shook her head. She squeezed Celia's hands, sudden and hard. "Again," Easy said, her gaze intent. "Ignore her. She's not giving us the real shit."

Before Celia could speak, Audrey's voice rose from the front of the crowd, hard and demanding. "I want to see my daughter again."

More voices followed hers, all of them crying out with shrill, jubilant certainty.

"I want to see my son's wedding!"

"I want to believe in God, for real!"

"I want to see the world!"

Easy yanked on Celia's hands, capturing her attention and then keeping it. "Ignore them," she whispered harshly. "That's all garbage, and you know it. Meaningless. None of them are digging as deep as you are, Celia. None of them are sharing the real shit. They're afraid to do the work. Say it again. Say it like you mean it. Do you mean it?"

Celia nodded. Easy nodded back, her eyes wide, her grip on Celia's hands painfully tight now, and Celia yelled without meaning to yell, her voice rising up in her like a sudden tide—

"I want to be a mother!"

Her voice was the last to call out a desire. The shoreline fell silent. Celia was breathing hard, her heart pounding. Easy tilted forward and kissed her on the forehead, a light, dry brush of lips on skin—and then she was gone, moving once more toward the front of the crowd.

"Good job, friends," she said, her voice low but still carrying. "You dug deep. You found your true purpose, and you shared it with all of us. I'm proud of you."

Celia bit back a smile. She looked around and saw others smiling, too, and she knew that they were fooled—they thought Easy was talking to them. But Celia knew that those final words could only be for her.

"Now, we don't go into the water at night," Easy said. "It's too dangerous to let visitors swim in the dark." The air hummed around her voice. Celia felt eminently alive. "But you've done well tonight, and you deserve a preview of the week to come. Whoever *really* wants what they want—whoever truly means what they just said to all of us," she added with a glance at the faces around her, her eyes flickering with hot intensity, "come past the candles. Stand with your feet in the Vetiver, and taste your future."

She turned away from them and walked past the glow of the candlelight. Celia squinted to watch the shadow of Easy's body. She bent and scooped something up out of the surf: a cup.

Easy held the cup high, the long line of her body a shadow against the glittering surface of the lake. "I want everything," she cried, and then she tipped the cup and poured the water over her face, her throat, her chest, her hair. She gasped and spread her arms wide. "Now tell me, friends! What do you want?!"

PART TWO

even the very worst of us are within reach

SALT FESTIVAL

day two | morning

Celia dreamed of the water all night. She dreamed of being lost in the depths, of huge shadows looming all around her. In the dream, she could breathe underwater, although it took effort. With every lungful of cool brine, she felt the constant ache in her chest dim a little more. Just before dawn, she swam to the surface of the lake, toward the thin light of a distant moon, and when she broke out of the water and into the chill morning air, she found herself in the bottom bunk at Grey House, still dressed in her clothes from the day before.

She silently thanked her internal clock as she slid out of the bottom bunk. At home, she was an early riser, a sunrise-jogger, a pre-breakfast reader, and she was thankful to find that years of habit hadn't abandoned her here. She didn't like the idea of waking up late here. She thought it might seem ungrateful, somehow.

A peek at the top bunk revealed Easy, still fast asleep in a tangle of bedclothes. She faced the wall.

Celia watched her ribcage rise and fall for a few seconds before padding out of the little cabin. Her bladder was so full that she felt the weight of it shift as she slid through the door. She walked in what she thought was the direction of the outhouse. It took effort not to sprint—every step jostled her bladder, and she felt a kindergartenish terror that she might not make it. But she did make it, sprinting past a patch of scrunched-up jimsonweed buds and up the narrow steps to the door with the crescent-moon cutout. She kicked the door shut and tugged her pants down in one jerky motion.

A guttural sigh came out of her unbidden as she unburdened her bladder. She tipped her head back and closed her eyes, feeling the animal relief of release. She pressed her bare foot to the door to make sure it stayed shut, vaguely remembering the night before when it'd swung open on her thanks to a stiff breeze coming in off the lake. She was tired, her legs aching from hours spent standing on the boat, on the shoreline, at Candle Hour. Her back throbbed where it'd hit the ground outside the canteen. Her hair was still sticky with saltwater from Easy's cup. The day was going to be long, she could feel it.

She opened her eyes—and realized she wasn't alone.

Through the moon-shaped cutout in the door, one wide green eye was staring directly at her.

Celia yelled, jumped, tripped over her lowered yoga pants. By the time she righted herself and burst out of the outhouse, no one was there. She ran a few steps up the road and spotted a figure running away from her—wide hips, slim shoulders, long coltish legs.

Strawberry blond hair. A familiar laugh.

Adelaide.

The previous night, before the visitors to Kindred Cove had been sent off to bed, there had been a brief review of the rules. Easy had emphasized the importance of sticking together—visitors and buddies, she'd said, should be inseparable during their time here—and of respecting the privacy of the community that lived at Kindred Cove.

But by Celia's math, people who watched her pee didn't get to ask for privacy.

She raced up the road, her feet slapping the dirt hard. The figure rounded a corner and Celia followed, the chase heating something deep and animal in her, the sound of her own increasingly labored breathing ragged in her ears. She sucked down the damp green early-morning air of the Cove.

The effort of breathing felt familiar, reminded her of looming shadows—the cool water of her dream slicking down the raw ache in her lungs, making her every breath slow and heavy—but the memory slipped away at the next bend in the road. The incline was difficult in places, the road twisting and looping back on itself, tightening into narrower and narrower switchbacks as they made their way up the shallow rise of the land. Her quarry kept slipping out of sight.

She passed a fenced-in yard filled with chickens. The entrance to a dirt trail, marked by a wooden stake with a bumblebee carved into the front. An orchard, the trees in full bloom, the air sweet with the heavy fragrance of orange blossoms, nectar-drunk bees weaving lazily from flower to flower. A massive garden, one that stretched well out of sight, bounded on one side by a wall of sunflowers.

It was at the garden that she lost track of the person she was pursuing. She slowed to a stop, her lungs searing, her heart beating so hard that she thought she might be sick. She bent forward to brace her hands on her thighs. Her head swam. Had they outrun her? Or had they slipped into the garden, or maybe into the trees?

Had it been Adelaide? Or had she only imagined that it could be?

Part of her wondered if there had ever been anyone ahead of her at all. Maybe she'd imagined that wide green eye staring in at her. She walked up the road a little farther, resting her hands on top of her head, moving slowly, trying to get her breath back. The sun peeked over the horizon as she made her way. Her feet stung. Once she got past the orchard, the trees vanished.

There were two buildings in front of her. The closest was a chapel. It was easily the most well-tended building she'd seen since arriving on the island, white-painted and many-windowed, the front doors thrown wide to reveal a plain interior. A pile of candles sat haphazardly in the middle of the floor. She didn't look closely enough to see if they were the ones from the previous night's gathering down at the shoreline, but from a distance they looked like the same butter-white pillars that had lit the edge of the water.

Just beyond the chapel was a house. Not a one-room cabin or a single-wide trailer—a house, one that might have been plucked out of her old neighborhood and dropped here. The house was one story tall, longer than it was wide, shingled and frilled with lacy gables that looked plucked from a towering Victorian manse. It was skirted by a wraparound porch with dry, half-collapsed rails. A house like that could have looked squat and bizarre anywhere else, but here, it simply looked . . . open. Like it was waiting to receive guests.

Just past the house, the road continued for a short distance before ending abruptly. There were no trees beyond the end of that road—only a sharp drop into the water.

She walked around the back of the house, her breath still coming hard. She remembered Easy saying something the day before, something about living in *the Old House*. She wondered if this was it. She stood on her toes to peer into the windows. The inside of the house was all white. White walls, white floors, white ceiling, everything high gloss. She remembered being small and painting a bathroom like that, asking her mother why they needed such thick, shiny paint. Her mother had winked at her and said, *It's the easiest kind to wipe clean.*

At the back of the house she found a wide, windowless expanse of wall. In the center of the wall, just above Celia's eye level, there was a peeling patch of paint. As she watched, a soft breeze swept across the island, catching the edge of that patch of paint and lifting it.

It flapped gently. There was something dark underneath.

She crept closer, took the patch of paint between her thumb and forefinger. As gently as she possibly could, she lifted it. It felt thicker than peeling paint should. Beneath the white paint, she realized, a piece of heavy canvas was fixed to the wall. It was a cover for whatever that darkness on the wall was. She peered under the flap of painted canvas, careful not to tear it.

The dark something turned out to be a hole.

She looked around. No one was nearby, not that she could see. Whoever had looked in on her in the outhouse was long gone.

There was no one to see her looking. She wondered if that was the thought that had been behind the staring eye she'd seen from inside the outhouse: *There's no reason not to look.*

So she looked.

She pressed her eye to the hole. And then she jerked her head away, swallowing a scream—because someone was looking back out at her.

Celia darted away from the wall, her heart pounding again. She waited to hear footsteps, someone running through the house, someone coming out to see who had been looking in at them the same way she'd emerged from the outhouse—but there was no sound. There was nothing.

She looked again. There it was, just like before—an eye, staring back at her. She blinked, and the person inside blinked, too.

Celia cleared her throat. "Hello?"

They didn't reply.

"Are you . . . are you okay in there?"

Still no answer. Still, they blinked back at her. Their eye was deep brown just like hers, and fringed with light, sparse lashes. They looked back at her with just as much concerned curiosity as she felt.

"What's your name?" she tried.

From inside, a small voice whispered back. "Nona."

"Nona? Are you okay in there?"

Hesitation. Then a sigh. "Not yet. But I will be soon."

Unease twisted in Celia's chest. "Do . . . do you need help?"

Celia thought she heard the word *yes*—but Nona's voice was barely audible over the sudden crunch of footsteps.

"Now, that's a funny question to be asking a wall."

Celia stumbled backward, away from the house, tripping over her own heels and landing on her ass. Easy looked down, bemused, her mouth twisted to one side, her arms folded loosely across her chest.

"Easy," Celia panted. "What are you—I mean, you're—"

"Awake? Yeah, we have that in common," she said, offering Celia a hand to help her up. "What are you doing up here? Chasing down another cat?"

"I went for a run." The lie preceded thought. It slipped out of her like a spat cherry pit as she took Easy's hand and pulled herself to her feet. "I didn't want to wake you."

She saw Easy believe her. "You're not supposed to be up here by yourself. I mean, you're not supposed to be up here at all, but you're *really* not supposed to be on your own."

"Sorry, I didn't realize. Who lives in this house?"

"I do, usually. Me and my sister. Listen—I was going to bring you up here later today anyway, I've got something planned. To make up for last night. But you can't be here right now." Her eyes darted toward the house. "Please don't tell anyone you slipped away from me like that? It would cause so much headache, you have no idea."

Celia hesitated, then nodded. "Sure. Do you want to grab breakfast?"

Easy led the two of them back to the road, her stride brisk. Celia tried to look over her shoulder at the house, but it was already vanishing behind a bend in the road.

"Not yet," Easy replied. "You've got an appointment to keep first. We're almost late already, but it's fine, just tell them I took a long time getting out of bed. Everyone will believe that." There was the slightest edge of bitterness to the words. "Watch out," she added, nodding to the road in front of them.

Celia stumbled when she saw what Easy was warning her about.

Her bare foot had nearly landed on a huge insect with a hunched, shining back and spindly legs. She let out a yelp. "What *is* that?"

"Camel cricket," Easy replied, already ahead of her. "The kittens love chasing them. You don't have them in St. Louis?"

Celia stared down at the creature. It was the size of her thumb. "Belleville. And I—I don't know. There aren't many bugs at all in my part of town."

"Thought you had a garden," Easy called over her shoulder.

Celia abandoned the bug, jogging to catch up with Easy as she led the way back down the road. "I spray for bugs. I've never seen a cricket that big before. Hey—where does everyone else live? I only saw a few cabins on my way up the road, but there must have been two hundred people at the dock when I got here."

"Oh, no, you haven't seen nearly all the houses," Easy replied. She glanced at Celia, slowed her pace. "There's a lot of island that's not visible from the road, you know. The trees are deceptive. I know they seem spread out, but if you really look?" She lifted her chin. "You can't see that far past them."

Celia looked around at the black locust, mockernut hickories, and clusters of prickly ash that crowded right up to the edge of the road. They did look spaced apart, without much underbrush between them—but Easy was right. The trees were dense enough to block her view. Anyone could have been back there among the trees and she wouldn't know it. She couldn't imagine ever finding her way through all that growth.

"So people just live back there?"

"People live everywhere, Celia." Easy sounded a little exasperated.

"I guess so." They walked in silence for a few minutes, Celia nursing a snappish, retaliatory indignation. "You couldn't have warned me about the outhouse?"

"What about it?"

"The outhouse. It's—you can see right into it."

Easy squinted at her. "So?"

"So, maybe I don't want anyone watching me pee?" She didn't know how to explain why this mattered. She didn't know how to explain *that* it mattered.

"Why not? It's not like it's a secret that you pee. Someone probably just wanted to know who was taking so long in there," Easy replied.

"Honestly, half the time I don't even bother with the outhouse. It gets so hot in there. It's faster if you just go by a tree."

Celia stared at her, feeling indignant and foolish all at once. She felt certain that she had a good reason for wanting to piss in private, but she couldn't figure out how to say *why*.

Easy shrugged, stepping nimbly around another enormous cricket. "If it's important to you, I can ask William for a tarp to hang up over the outhouse door. That way people will know you're using it, and they won't look."

Celia didn't want a tarp to hang up. She didn't want people to know when she was in the outhouse. But she didn't know how to explain why, and everything she could think of felt flimsy and useless. "That's not what I want, though," she started, her voice losing strength with each word.

Easy stopped and turned to regard Celia. She looked deep into Celia's eyes, then stepped forward and took her hands. "I know." Her hands were cool on Celia's, her fingers rough but delicate, her grip firm but gentle. She leaned in close enough that Celia could smell the faintest hint of fennel on her breath. "What you want is for nobody to ever see how much you're hurting. What you want is to hang on to your hurt and keep it for yourself, because you think it's all you really have. But I can't help you with that, can I? So I'm trying to help with this. Now, am I asking William for a tarp or not?"

Celia took a shuddering breath, fennel ghosting over her tongue. "No," she said. "No. Let's get wherever you said we need to be. The outhouse is fine how it is."

Easy smiled. "Good. Let's get moving. Everyone's waiting on you."

William jogged up the road to meet them. There was a crowd of visitors behind him, gathered at the shore where Candle Hour had taken place the night before. All of them looked impatient.

William glared at Easy. "Where have you been?"

"Sorry," Celia said. "I had a hard time getting up. Easy had to pry me out of bed with a crowbar."

Easy glanced at her, clearly startled. "Yeah. But we're here now."

As William went back to the gathered crowd of visitors and their chaperones, Easy leaned in to whisper in Celia's ear. "You didn't have to do that."

"I know," she whispered back. "But now you owe me one."

Easy bumped Celia's shoulder with her own. "Thanks."

William was standing calf-deep in the water, his feet planted on the submerged dock, his arms wide as though he was waiting for someone to run up and embrace him. "I hope everyone got enough sleep," he said, glancing at Celia. She felt a twitch of shame, even though she hadn't actually slept in. "Today marks the first full day of the Salt Festival. All of us here at Kindred Cove share a set of values. We believe in community, intention, honesty, and accountability. And today, you're invited to join us in those values. Don't worry—you don't have to commit to them forever," he added with a wink. It drew a bigger laugh from the crowd than Celia thought it deserved. "But all of you came here to grow and heal, and I think you'll find an opportunity for that healing here, this morning, in Lake Vetiver."

He went on for a little while, explaining the history of the lake—the shallow freshwater puddle it had been before the mine collapse, the depth and complexity that had been introduced to it after the disaster, the rich diversity of life that had sprung up in the aftermath of what should have been a tragedy.

Celia glanced around at the group. Audrey was there, looking from face to face, her glasses flashing in the early-morning light. The two men Celia thought were brothers were there, too, and about half of the young women with crystal necklaces. The thin auburn-haired woman—Celia thought she remembered Easy calling her Rinna—stood near William, attentive to his every word. Celia couldn't see her TREAD LIGHTLY husband anywhere.

"Where's everyone else?" she whispered to Easy.

"Hm?"

"We're not all here. The visitors, I mean. At least . . ." She counted briefly. "Five of us are missing. They were here last night. Two couples and—"

"They're in the other group," Easy whispered back. "Pay attention, this is important."

"What other group?" she asked—but then William looked sharply in her direction, and she pressed her lips together tight.

"Which is why we enter the waters of the Vetiver this morning, before we break our fast," William was saying. "To recognize that life can spring up out of suffering. To affirm that we are one with the rich diversity that comes from hardship."

The thin woman near William covered her mouth. Her wedding band caught the sunlight and flung it into Celia's eyes.

"To anoint ourselves with life, so that we might live a little brighter every day," William finished. "Here, your healing begins."

And then, without warning, he jumped off the edge of the dock and into the water.

Someone gasped—one of the girls with the crystal necklaces. Celia watched with wide eyes as the ripples where William had entered the water died away. After several seconds, the surface of the water was still again.

"You ready?" Easy murmured.

"But—is he—" She watched the water, waiting for William to surface.

"He's fine. This part's to build suspense," Easy whispered. "It seems like he's under there longer than he is. Trust me, when someone gets taken by the lake . . ." She cleared her throat. "It feels different. Here, hold your breath, you'll see."

Celia sucked in a deep breath and held it. Before her lungs started to protest, William erupted from the water a hundred feet away from the shore, bellowing. "Life!" He held his arms up over his head, spraying water high into the air. "Why hesitate? Why hold back? Life is waiting for you! Come seize it!"

The crying woman went first. She ran in, slowing as the water and silt dragged at her legs, high-stepping until she was deep enough to swim. After she went into the water, one of the brothers whipped his shirt off over his head and ran after her. The girls with the crystal necklaces followed in their underwear, and then all their chaperones went, too.

The visitors entered the water in various states of undress. The residents left all their clothes on the shore in a single, undifferentiated heap.

Easy looked like she was about to encourage Celia into the water, but she was interrupted by a voice calling out from the road behind her. "Easy, hang on a second." Jessie came running down the road, her skirt clutched in one hand to let her legs move more freely. There was fresh blood on one skinned knee. A short, gray-haired woman followed behind her, moving quite a bit slower. "Edith needs you."

"Sure thing. Where are the kids?"

"They're raking the flats, they're fine. Everyone's keeping in line after what happened with Nona yesterday. Want me to keep an eye on that one while you two chat?" Jessie pointed her chin at Celia when she said *that one*.

"Wait, no, she hates me," Celia hissed to Easy.

Easy squeezed Celia's shoulder and answered at full volume. "She doesn't hate you. We don't hate people here. You got this." She jogged over to Edith.

"Easy's right. I don't hate you," Jessie said, tripping down the sloping road and passing Celia on her way to the lake. The bottoms of the girl's feet looked as dark and tough as a dog's paws. "And either way, she'll be back for you soon enough."

"What's Edith need her for?" Celia had to hurry to keep up with Jessie, who was moving fast toward the water, her heels barely touching the ground.

Jessie looked over her shoulder, her expression rich with uncut condescension. "They're just checking in about stuff. I heard you're looking for Adelaide, is that true?"

Celia broke into a jog to catch up. "Adelaide? You know Adelaide? Do you know where Adelaide is right now?"

Jessie didn't answer. She was half running now, an unstudied canter that quickly left Celia behind. The girl pulled her dress over her head as she ran. She dropped it onto the pile and ran into the water.

A cry left Celia's mouth as Jessie splashed along the submerged dock, the word *no* slipping out of her before she could form a thought to stop it. She took a few halting steps forward—an instinct to run after Jessie, to try to save her from the unsafe structure beneath the surface. And then Jessie must have reached the end of the dock because she was in the water, her head slipping below the surface.

Celia did not breathe again until Jessie's head burst back up out of the water, her hair plastered to her face. "Come in," she called, her voice high and cheerful. "Life is waiting for you!"

When Celia had been doing her research on the Cove, she'd found some videos that focused more on the reef that surrounded the island than on the collapse of the mine. These videos tended to revel in the fact that millions of dollars had been spent researching the unlikely biome at Lake Vetiver. They crowed over the waste of time and money, claiming that all the king's horses and all the king's men couldn't seem to agree on an explanation for the rapid expansion of the massive reef that threatened to connect the island of Kindred Cove to the mainland. They skated past the unusual structure of the reef and the unprecedented cycles of coral growth to focus on the uselessness of scientific inquiry.

And in the comments below those videos, Celia had found her lifeline. Hundreds of people discussing the benefits of the salt that was harvested from the lake, talking about the reef and how it changed the water into something miraculous. The salt, commenters insisted, could do everything from replacing vaccines to curing infertility.

Celia purchased a vial of that salt at a farmer's market near her house, just like Audrey had. Then she hassled the person who sold it to her until they gave her the name of the researcher who'd sold it to them, and then she harried that exhausted-looking researcher for weeks on the mainland. She had followed him from his research site to his lab to his tiny apartment, refusing to leave him alone until he told her precisely how to get to Kindred Cove.

The researcher had tried hard to warn her away from the water. Then, when it was clear she wasn't going to heed his warning, he tried harder to get her to wear protective equipment. *I never get within a hundred meters of that water without hip waders, double gloves, and a respirator*, he'd insisted, pressing a box of nitrile gloves into her hands. *We don't know enough about what was down in those mines. It's not safe.*

And then he confirmed that the island held an annual festival to heal outsiders, and that they were still accepting applicants, and he promised to pass her letter to the right person. She hadn't thought he'd do it—but a few weeks later, she'd gotten a phone call from the researcher. *You're in*, he said. *Never contact me again.*

"Are you sure it's safe?" Celia said weakly.

"Course it is! We all go in the water all the time. Except Edith," she amended. "But that's different." Jessie vanished again, surfacing much closer to shore this time. "It's perfectly safe."

"But," Celia protested, remembering the box of gloves that the researcher had pressed into her hands. The way he'd said *we don't know what was in that mine.*

"Trust me," Jessie said, as though she truly couldn't think of a reason why Celia wouldn't trust her. She looked over her shoulder at the other visitors and residents, all of them swimming and ducking their heads under the water, all of them perfectly alive. "It's safe."

Celia was going to say no. She was going to say that she didn't want to get into the lake, that she didn't want that water slipping into her ears and between her lips. She was going to stay on the shore. But then she felt the cool kiss of water on the very tips of her toes, and she realized that, without thinking, she'd taken just enough of a step forward to meet the water's edge.

It didn't feel unsafe. It didn't feel any different from regular water. Something inside her took on a dangerously reasonable tone, reminding her that she'd waded through the water yesterday when she'd arrived at the Cove. She'd let Easy pour the water over her head and body, along with the rest of the visitors, after Candle Hour. She'd eaten the salt at dinner. Nothing bad had happened to her.

And then there was the dream she'd had. It was coming back to her in little pieces, the memory stronger with every moment that she stood with her toes touching the water. She'd dreamed of the water embracing her, taking her into its arms, swaying her back and forth. It had felt like being rocked by a calm and loving mother.

Almost without choosing to do it, she walked into the water. At first she told herself she'd just go in up to her ankles, to soothe her sore feet. Then she thought it couldn't really hurt to go in up to her knees, since she'd gone in about that far already yesterday anyway. It wasn't like more harm could be done by duplicating the exact same amount of risk.

But some part of her knew all along that she would end up in the lake. That part of her was very nearly patronizing in its patience—*Take your time*, it seemed to say, *we have all day*. And when she finally did strip off her filthy yoga pants and her sweat-crusted shirt, she knew the overwhelming relief of having succumbed to the inevitable.

The comments under all those videos had insisted that Kindred Cove was something special. Adelaide had agreed. She'd said that this place could heal people. She'd said that it was a place of miracles. She'd said she was never going to return here—but then she'd told Celia she was going home after all. So Celia knew, deep in her heart, that this place must have some power in it.

The lake was alive. The island was beautiful. And this place could fix her. She knew it could.

Jessie was floating on her back, her eyes closed.

"Wish I could wash my hair," Celia said. It was a nothing-thought, words that were coming out of her just to fill the air.

The girl grinned. "So do it. Just dunk your head in. The water is perfect." Then her expression changed, her smile faltering, her eyes opening to slide sideways toward Celia. "Why were you asking about Adelaide?"

Celia treaded water, her arms moving easily below the surface. She glanced up at the shore, where Easy was still deep in conversation with Edith. "You mentioned that Edith wanted to talk to Easy about her," Celia said, even though the girl had said no such thing. "Are they friends?"

"It's just that we're not supposed to talk about Adelaide with visitors," Jessie said tentatively.

"What does that mean?"

Jessie seemed not to have heard the question. She twisted a long, wet lock of hair around one finger. "I shouldn't have mentioned her, except that Edith was talking about her the whole time we were walking from the garden, so I kind of forgot. I probably shouldn't even tell you that I'm not supposed to talk about her. Why do you want to know about her?"

Celia couldn't figure out the purpose of Jessie's doe-eyed act. The girl was playing at naivete, but her eyes flashed with sharp intelligence. Celia remembered the feeling of her back slamming into hard earth the night before.

"Just curious," she said at last. And then she turned toward the sound of William's voice, and she swam toward the waiting group, away from Jessie's questions and her own.

As she combed her way through the water, following William's voice, Celia's fear and doubt and grief began to ebb. She couldn't believe that she'd been afraid to enter the water. Now that she was in it, she wanted to dive down. She wanted to go deep. She wanted to let it have her. She wanted to find her way to that open wound in what had once been the lakebed and slip inside of it, to sink into the dark and open her eyes and look at what there was to see, to spread her teeth wide and let the cool damp salt into her mouth where it could lick at the insides of her cheeks—

Celia flailed up out of the water, splashing with sudden desperation. She thought she was the one screaming at first, until she realized her mouth was full of saltwater. She spat it out and spun in the water, searching for the source of the noise.

It was Audrey. She was screaming and swimming for shore at the same time, choking on water as she went. Her scream resonated all the way down to Celia's solar plexus. It sounded so familiar.

Celia swam toward her, catching up in the shallows. She intercepted Audrey, standing in front of her, helping her find her footing where the water was only chest-deep. "What's wrong?" she gasped, holding the older woman by the shoulders. "What is it?"

Easy came running along the submerged dock next to them. "Hey, what's up? What's going on?"

Audrey was sobbing, breathless, shaking her head. "I saw her," she wailed. "I saw my Mackenzie, she was—she was down there. Under the water, just around the side of the island. I swam off away from the group to look and I found her, I saw her face. I have to go back, I have to get her—"

"Okay. Okay, that's okay," Easy said in a steady tone, wrapping Audrey in a tight embrace. She caught Celia's eye over the top of Audrey's head. "This happens every year," she said. Her gaze was heavy with authority. "Some people have an intense reaction to the lake. I'll handle it."

"But—"

"Enjoy your swim," Easy interrupted. She rubbed Audrey's shoulder with one hand. "Seriously, I've got this. Jessie, can you let Caleb know I'm walking Audrey to the office? He really should be the one taking care of her right now," she added, looking out toward the water with her brow furrowed. "But tell him I've got it."

Jessie walked out of the water beside Celia. "Sure. Do you want to keep swimming, Celia?"

"Not really." Celia watched as Easy and Audrey walked away. Easy had a hand on Audrey's back, just between her shoulderblades. She guided Audrey along the path, toward the road, toward the office, toward whatever comfort waited for her there.

"Don't worry about her. She's just getting ready to grow," Jessie said. "She'll be fine. Easy will handle her. Besides, I heard that last night at Candle Hour, she said she wanted to see her daughter again. Shouldn't she be happy? She got what she asked for." She took Celia's hand and tugged her toward the water—but Celia couldn't stop staring at Easy and Audrey. Their heads were tilted close together. The two of them looked deep in conversation already.

Celia felt a strange hum of jealousy. She wanted to be the target of such intent attention. She wanted to be thought of and fussed over. She wanted to be important to everyone.

And then they melted away through the gap in the trees, and the jealousy vanished just as suddenly as it had arrived. Celia ran her hands through her hair, pushing it off her face, lifting it away from her neck. Streams of water ran down her arms.

She didn't feel like herself. She felt strange, mercurial, overbalanced. Every emotion ran through her like a hot current through wire. She wanted to cry, she wanted to scream, she wanted to drown.

Celia looked back into the water, where all the swimmers had gathered around William. She could see the flare of his shoulders going pink in the sun. She could almost make out what he was saying—something about *the water touches everything we are* and *you can find the truth inside yourself, if you have a good community to help you recognize when you've found it.* She couldn't hear everything, though, which meant that she was missing it. William was sharing something important with everyone else, and she was standing here, feeling jealous of a woman whose grief and fear were turning her inside out.

She didn't want Audrey's pain, which was the exact thing Celia was trying to excise from herself. She didn't want to be jealous of Audrey, or of anyone ever again. She didn't want to feel sad or scared or alone or embarrassed.

So she walked past Jessie and into the water and swam once more toward the crowd. As she swam, she stopped being able to hear William's words. All she could hear was the water, flooding into her ears and echoing the sound of her own heartbeat back to her.

She listened as closely as shc could.

Twenty-Two Years Ago

In Des Plaines, Illinois, there's an abandoned cathedral. Caleb is eleven years old when he asks his mom about it. He's fascinated by the sight of plywood lidding the massive stained glass windows that used to point St. Isidore's dismayed face toward the sidewalk. Caleb's mom tells him that the diocese withdrew funding from that church in order to build a new one, over in Palatine. Palatine, she says bitterly, hardly needs the money, but that's just how things go, isn't it? The people of Des Plaines losing the nice things they have, so Palatine can add to the pile. Caleb doesn't think Palatine seems to be all that different from Des Plaines, but then again, they have a new cathedral so what does he know.

Caleb's mom also tells him to stay away from the old cathedral, because she knows her son just well enough to know he's drawn to it. She tells him that it's dangerous and probably full of old left-behind crap. The warning backfires spectacularly, because she knows him a little but not quite enough. The sound of danger pulls him to the place like water sluicing down a storm drain.

He drags Sadie along with him because even though she's younger, he always feels safer with her around. She looks up to him, follows him, trusts him. Her presence transforms him into someone who can be followed and trusted. They get into the place by knocking loose plywood out of a window—not the window with St. Isidore, but a side window with no glass in it. They hop over the bug-corpsed sill and land in a crunch of broken glass. The two of them walk around for a while in the empty, echoing space, looking at the dust and the old pews and the mouse droppings, scaring each other by knocking things over.

Just when the place starts to go from interesting to boring, Sadie spots a door. On the front of the door is a little plastic sign with two words on it in white text: BELL TOWER

They look at each other and no words are necessary for them to agree that they are going to the top of the tower. Getting there is surprisingly complicated—where Caleb would have expected a hollow cylinder with a single staircase going up, up, up like the inside of a lighthouse, there are instead three rooms stacked on top of each other, connected by oddly placed stairwells. The bottom rooms seem to be abandoned storage, stacked-up chairs and slumping cardboard boxes. Caleb and Sadie run fast as they can through the second level, a dark, damp-smelling room with long padded ropes dangling from the ceiling like a circle of nooses.

The room above that one is the payoff. Daylight falls through holes in the roof, sending bright streaks across the floor and onto the bells, some of which have fallen from their rotting frame. The sky Caleb can see through the holes above is churning with the kind of clouds that usually send them running inside to check for extreme weather warnings. But they're already inside, technically, and it doesn't occur to either of them to run anywhere.

As he stares up at the dark roil of the sky, one of the bells rings. The sound it makes is sharp and high and Caleb's entire body hums in response. In the next instant, the bell adjacent to it rings, too, and then the next one. Caleb looks down at Sadie, who is already staring back at him, fear and wonder shining out of her face as her chest heaves with every labored breath. He doesn't hear her wheezing yet, though, so he doesn't worry.

Then the hail starts falling in earnest, striking not just one bell at a time but all of them, all at once. The noise is unbearable. They race back down into the nave to wait out the storm, listening to hail strike the roof as the bells chime under the assault of falling ice.

Caleb will never forget the ring of that first bell. Neither will Sadie, not for the duration of her short life. Later, after she's come to the Cove, she'll tell her brother about how Harvey makes her feel like she's back there. Like she's at the abandoned cathedral, unaware that the bell has simply been struck by falling ice, every inch of her attuned to the pure sweet sound that has come out of nowhere to surround her.

He'll tell her that it feels the same way for him, and he'll ask her if she wants to move to Kindred Cove for good. And he'll be deeply, truly joyful when she says yes.

FIVE MONTHS AGO

1

Harvey pushed his way between the children. They stood in slack-limbed rows at the edge of the trees near the salt flats, and the sight of all their small heads turned in the same direction, of all their slim shoulders rigid with attention, was enough to tell him that something was wrong. A collection of fifty children should have been made of noise, but they were unusually silent and watchful.

The too-clear sound of soft breathy grunts and flesh thudding into flesh propelled him forward. His hands floated out from his body to find backs and elbows, moving the children aside with as much gentleness as he could find within himself.

He'd been practicing gentleness for a long time.

These days, it almost came naturally.

Harvey saw what the children were watching long before he was able to stick himself in the middle of it. Nona and Tristan were on the ground. Nona—nine, pale, graceless—wasn't fighting back at all. She lay limp beneath Tristan, whose hands rhythmically pounded at her small, still body. His fists landed in a different place with every strike. Tristan was two years younger than Nona and small for his age. He shouldn't have had an advantage over her, which made Harvey think at first that the girl was unconscious. But then her head rolled toward him, and he saw her open, red-rimmed eyes, and he understood that she was choosing not to fight back.

He felt his limbs grow heavy with fatigue. He couldn't believe they were doing this again.

"Enough," he called. Tristan didn't stop, though, not until Harvey hauled him off Nona by the collar. "I said that's enough, Tristan. Time to stop."

"Fine," Tristan said, wiping his always-damp nose with the back of one salt-white hand. His hair was down to his shoulders, thin and dark and stringy. "But she asked me to."

"I know she did." He sighed as Tristan stood, leaving Nona to lie on her back in the dirt. It was hard for him to take his eyes off the sight of the girl's glassy brown eyes, her colorless hair spread out behind her head, the fan-shaped pattern she and Tristan had left in the dust as they'd found their way into the rhythm of her beating. "I told you all to quit doing this. Didn't I? Didn't I tell you to stop it?"

A soft shuffling of feet. The children were silent.

Harvey crouched next to Nona. "Do you remember what I told you last time?"

She shook her head, the back of her skull rolling against the dirt.

"I said that when you hurt each other this way," he said, kindly but loud enough to carry, "when you do this, that's something called a punishment. Do you remember what *punishment* is?"

More silence. Nona blinked, and small pearly tears slid down to her temples, darkening the dust that powdered her face.

"Punishment is when you hurt someone to try to fix them. Imagine that. What if you had a broken cup, and you decided to smash it until it was better? Do you think that would work?"

Nona shook her head again.

"Of course it wouldn't," Harvey said. "And it doesn't work with people, either, does it?" He reached down a hand to Nona, and she took it, pulling herself up to meet him. "No. It doesn't. We have to love each other into being better." He brushed the dirt from her shoulders. They were so, so small under his hands, and he thought—as he always did in moments like this one—of his own shoulders at her age. Of how he'd been just this size once, and how often large adult hands had seen fit to hurt his small body in order to try to fix him. This thought was what made the gentleness come to him, even when he didn't want it to come.

"But I was late," Nona said. It came out in a half whine. "Again."

Harvey turned to look at the gathered children. The littler ones met his eyes. The bigger ones did not.

Jessie, the oldest by far, stood at the back of the group. Her eyes were pointed out over the lake, her arms across her chest. Her thick brown braid was draped over her collarbone. She chewed on a fennel stalk, an affectation she'd stolen from Easy. "Is that true?" Harvey asked. "Was she late again?" He saw Jessie's eyes flick to him, saw her know that the question was intended for her rather than for the group.

After a long moment of silence, she rolled her eyes. "No. She wasn't late. Because you weren't here yet, so we couldn't start anyway. So nobody was late."

"And did anyone here tell her that? Did you all let her know that she didn't need to take on all that guilt?" More silence. "You're Nona's community. It's your job to tell her if she's done something wrong or not." He scanned the gathered faces, sighed. "Fine. Do better next time," he said.

The children took it as the dismissal it was, breaking away to gather buckets and rakes, then trudging down the slope toward the salt flats at the waterline. Soon, only Tristan, Nona, and Jessie remained with him.

"I would have been late if you'd been here," Nona insisted quietly. Her gaze was fixed on his kneecaps.

Harvey tapped sharply on the top of her head, and her chin snapped up, her eyes wide. He looked down at her and tried to make his expression into one that she would remember. "That's not for you to decide," he said. "You don't know if you're late or early until your community tells you. Do you understand? It's up to them to tell you what you are, and it's up to you to believe them."

"But—"

"Do you know what I see when I look at you?" Harvey asked. Nona shook her head slowly. "I see a nine-year-old who is right on time. And do you know what the rest of your community sees?" He glanced over his shoulder at Jessie, his eyebrows high, his lips tight, beaming *hurry the fuck up* at her.

Jessie twirled her half-chewed fennel stalk between her fingers. "I see a nine-year-old who is right on time," she said flatly.

"Tristan?" Harvey glanced down at the smaller boy. "What do you see when you look at Nona?"

Tristan looked up at Jessie uncertainly, his small red-knuckled hands twisting together in front of his stomach. "Um." Jessie bent down to whisper in his ear until he recited the words. "I see a nine-year-old who is right on time."

"Hear that?" Harvey said. "We all see the same thing. What are you?"

Nona whispered the words. "I am a nine-year-old who is right on time."

Harvey rested a hand on her head, felt her neck tense to take on the weight of it. "That's right. Now, do you want to tell me what made you think you were late?"

Nona sighed, the kind of great shuddering chest-heaving shoulder-dropping sigh of a child whose body is made of pure emotion. "I was in the garden. I wanted to see the chickens come in," she said. "And Caleb caught me sneaking, but then he let me hold one of the babies, so I forgot to come down here until after I normally would."

Harvey hesitated. If he hadn't just talked the girl into forgiving herself for her imagined transgression, he'd be scolding her for sneaking around in the garden. But at her age, she'd get confused if he turned the conversation back to consequences again. She knew she shouldn't have done it, he could see that well enough. She'd taken a beating for it. What would his scolding add to the impact of Tristan's fists?

"Go do your work," he said at last. "You too, Tristan." The two of them darted away to join the other children, their pain and guilt and power and violence falling away from them like dust off a snapped shirtsleeve.

"What about me?" Jessie drawled.

Harvey turned slowly to face her. He turned slowly because the slowness would stop him from wheeling on her. He reminded himself that Jessie was, by decision of the community, a child. He needed to be gentle with the children. "You," he said as calmly as possible, "should have stopped that from happening. You know better than they do."

Jessie gave a tart sniff. She seemed determined to remind him, at every turn, that she didn't respect his role in the community. That he might be in charge of the children, but he was not in charge of her. "You shouldn't have let her get away with the chicken thing. Makes it look like you're getting attached. Like maybe you think you have a claim to her."

Harvey imagined himself wrapping a rope tight around his own heart, a rope that he clenched in one fist. He told himself that he'd yank it right out of his chest if he moved too suddenly. That kept him still. That kept him calm. "I'm not getting attached. I'm teaching.

That's my work on this island. I thought you were mature enough to understand that distinction by now." He saw the sting of his words hit Jessie just hard enough. Now he needed to offer her a balm, so he would be the one serving up both the rebuke and the relief. *That's leadership*, he heard Dad whisper in a distant pocket of memory. "Listen. I need your help."

"My help?"

"Yeah. You're right that this chicken thing needs to be addressed. It's getting to be a problem. I should talk to Caleb about it. Can you manage this group while I go speak with him?"

Her posture shifted, her shoulders easing back, her chin rising. "Of course. I can be in charge as long as you need."

"I won't be more than an hour."

"I could—"

"Thank you, Jessie," he interrupted. Then, without giving her a chance to say more, he walked past her, into the trees, away from the sound of the kids working at the salt flats.

He needed to figure out what to do about Jessie. She clearly wanted to be free of the children's group, to be treated as an adult. But after what had happened with Marco, she had a lot to prove to the community. He needed to find ways to let her prove herself, without seeming to make allowances.

Once he was out of sight of the flats, he let his pace slow. The trees were close together on this part of the island, and he wound between them with his hands held slightly out from his sides, brushing the trunks as he went. His days were spent moving from confrontation to confrontation; from problem to problem; from solution to solution to solution. He was tired of dealing with Jessie's bitterness. He was tired of telling the children not to beat each other. But he loved his life at Kindred Cove. He reminded himself of that with every tree he touched and every leaf that bent beneath his feet.

By the time he arrived at the road, he didn't feel so tired anymore. He didn't feel anything.

2

The question of who the garden belonged to—Edith or Caleb—was a question that was both hotly contested and never discussed.

Edith had been the first to understand the soil all those years ago, when the lake was still freshwater and the Cove was new. She'd been the first to till the earth and pound stakes down into it, the first to yank up fistfuls of dollarweed and goosegrass. She'd been the one to see the first two seasons' worth of crops die, since nobody knew, at the start, how to amend the soil, and because Dad didn't want anyone using the internet to look up the right way to plant things. It was Edith who came to him with a swollen belly—both pregnant and starving—and a mountain of courage to demand special dispensation for a trip to a mainland library, so they wouldn't starve on this island they'd decided to transform into a paradise.

It could have been her garden for keeps.

But Caleb was the one who really *lived* in the garden. He was the one who rigged up a mobile chicken pen, so the flock could eat fat caterpillars off the tomato vines without wandering off and digging up the freshly planted onions. He governed the goat, Agnes, to help clear old growth and make room for new planting. He hauled gray water up from the kitchen after every meal. He walked through every inch of the garden every day, and he was the one who told the kitchen what kind of harvest to plan for. In his heart, that garden was his.

Before coming to Kindred Cove, Caleb'd never had anything that felt like it was *his*. He'd spent his childhood in Des Plaines roaming around half-vacant office parks with a group of kids roughly his age, none of whom liked each other all that much. Their days were largely dedicated to searching out grass medians to sit on, and hucking rocks at scraggly little ginkgo saplings until the warning whistle of approaching security drones chased them off.

He could remember being freshly thirteen years old, lying on his back on the top bunk, listening to his younger sister Sadie wheezing in her sleep on the bunk below. Their mother said Sadie had a demon in her lung. Caleb was pretty sure, even back then, that Sadie had asthma, and that the diffused essential oils their mom made her inhale were making that asthma worse. But him saying so hadn't done him nor Sadie any favors. He could remember lying on that top bunk with the backs of his thighs stinging from the wooden cooking spoon his mother never used for cooking. Back then, he would stare up at the brown bulge on the ceiling from where the roof had a leak, and he'd think, *If I could start over, I wouldn't keep any of this.*

Now, he lived in a completely different world. He had a little patch of land to tend, thirty-six chickens to care for, Edith to argue with. He slept beneath a roof that kept the rain out. He never needed to worry that anyone would find anything to punish him for, because he wasn't trying to conceal anything. He had the freedom to be his fullest self without hiding.

And through it all, he had Harvey to keep him on the right path.

He didn't know what had become of his mother. As for Sadie—demon or not, her lungs didn't bother her anymore. She was part of something bigger than herself. He was fiercely unsad about it.

He liked his life. He liked the person Kindred Cove had helped him become. He liked knowing exactly what every day would bring. Maybe that was why, four weeks earlier, he'd watched Adelaide's return to the Cove with some trepidation.

Newcomers and visitors made him nervous. Adelaide wasn't a newcomer, and she certainly wasn't a visitor, but she'd spent years off the island. She moved strangely now that she was home, picking her way along the dirt road with careful, slow steps. He'd noticed other things, too, at her welcome party and in the time since—the way she sat with her legs crossed at the knee instead of the ankle, the way she touched people with the tips of her fingers instead of her whole hand. The way she took small, unhurried bites, letting food linger on her tongue for a long time before swallowing it.

The world had settled on her like a layer of dust and he couldn't seem to stop noticing. But he believed that she could shake it off, go back to being herself. He had to believe that.

Caleb adjusted the mobile pen around the scraggly, half-dead sunflowers as Edith poured last night's dishwater over the mounded soil of the potato patch, careful not to let any of the water touch her. Dew was steaming off the leaves of the potato plants in the slanting light of the dawn sun. Edith was smiling.

"Do you see that?"

Caleb nodded, even though he wasn't sure what she was asking about. It was easiest just to nod when Edith talked, he found.

"Look how the leaves strain up toward the sky, strong and full. That's exactly how a potato plant is supposed to look. That's the future we're manifesting."

"Mm. Yeah, they look great." Caleb wrestled with a section of wire fencing. The ground around the sunflowers was uneven, and the chicken pen wasn't sitting right. The girls'd knock the fence over if he didn't fix it. He was sure that if he just shoved hard enough, it would sink into the ground and stay put.

"And who do we have here?" Edith said loudly.

Caleb didn't look up. He wasn't interested in seeing whatever bug Edith felt like celebrating. He just wanted to fix the pen so he could wheel the coop-wagon over and get on with his day.

But then, a voice that made his hands freeze.

"It's just me, as demanded."

Edith did not meet the laugh in Adelaide's words. "Demanded? What, did your time away make you forget how to do honest work? I expected you here twenty minutes ago."

"Sorry. I ran into someone."

Caleb tried to hurry his hands. He shoved at the edges of the mobile pen hard, willing it to sink into the ground so it would be straight enough to connect to the next section over. He did not want to see Adelaide's streaming strawberry blond hair or her small pink mouth or her slim hands resting over her swollen belly.

But then Harvey's voice joined hers, deep and resonant, and Caleb's panic began to drain away. "Blame me for holding her up, Edith. I was being distracting."

"I'm sure I slowed you down," Adelaide said teasingly. "I'm moving a little slower than I used to. Still getting my calluses back."

Caleb looked up just in time to see Edith frowning down at Adelaide's bare feet. "How can your feet still be so tender when you've been back home all this time? Although, goodness knows what you were walking on out there. When I was a little girl," she continued, lowering her voice to a conspiratorial hush, "they'd pour fresh blacktop in the summer, and it would sink under your feet like cooling taffy." She made her broad shoulders shake in a performance of a shiver. "Grab a bucket, you can help me water the sunflowers. Get that dipper, too."

Caleb caught Harvey's eyes with his own. The two of them shared a silent, condensed conversation within the space of a few seconds and the twitch of an eyebrow: The sunflowers didn't need watering. They were mostly dead, the seeds from their enormous heads long-since harvested. That's why Caleb was putting the pen up around them—the chickens would have the time of their lives scratching around the base of each massive stem, hunting for seeds, turning fallen leaves down into the soil. The next day, he'd stake Agnes in this same spot so she could eat the stalks. Edith knew the plan. Why would she waste water over here? There was only one explanation. It was intentional. The waste, the interference—she was reminding Caleb who the garden belonged to. And there was nothing either of them could say about it.

Harvey took a deep, slow, obvious breath. Caleb mirrored him. Harvey was right: no getting upset. No point.

Keep breathing. Keep working.

Adelaide, ignorant of their unspoken exchange, stooped to heft a bucket of gray water, wincing at the weight of it.

"It'll do you good to get strong before the baby comes," Edith said, lifting a bucket of her own in each blunt-fingered hand. "Have you thought about letting Easy cut your hair? You'll want it out of your way."

"Mm." Adelaide's eyes slid away from Edith. "Caleb, Harvey, we won't be in your way, will we?"

Caleb kept his eyes on his work. "Of course not. Just don't knock anything over."

Harvey nodded. "Oh, and Edith, be careful you don't spill—you wouldn't want to get any water on you."

Edith gave him a poisonous glare, holding the buckets far from her body. "Thank you for reminding me."

"I wanted to ask you all," Adelaide huffed, clumsily lugging her bucket with both hands, "if you've seen Easy this morning?"

"Not this morning, no. I've had my mind on my work," Edith said primly.

Adelaide's eyes were on the ground as she walked. She was stepping carefully, avoiding rocks. She seemed to be struggling with the weight and unpredictable movement of the water in her second bucket. "She wasn't in her room when I woke up. We were supposed to discuss something important."

"What's so important that you have to talk to her right this second?" Edith stopped to set one of her buckets down a third of the way along the rows of dead sunflowers, and then the second one two-thirds in. "You and your young arms can carry that last bucket to the end of the row. We'll work our way back."

Harvey stepped closer to Caleb, close enough that Caleb could smell the salt of the flats on him. "I need to talk to you," he murmured.

Caleb nodded. "Sure. In a minute? I'm almost done here."

Adelaide had stopped walking to look up at the sunflowers. They were seven feet tall, studded with dead heads. The few leaves that still clung to the brown stalks were the size of her face. "I didn't say I had to talk to her right this second," she said with a frown. "It'll wait. It's just that I never heard her leave this morning, which means she must have gotten up way before I did. When did she start waking up so early?"

"She's got a lot of responsibilities. You remember responsibilities, don't you? Or do they not have those, wherever you've been all this time? In the land of wearing shoes and sleeping in?"

"It's—Easy told me to sleep in Dad's old bedroom, instead of in the room we used to share. Because I wake up a lot in the night right now. The bed in there is so soft," Adelaide stammered. Even after all that time away, Caleb could see, she was still intimidated by Edith.

She sloshed her bucket clumsily, splashing water on the base of a sunflower. A bolt of gray shot out from the sunflower patch with a yowl—that tabby kitten that liked to follow Easy around must have been hunting in the sunflower patch, and it had gotten a nasty, soaking-wet surprise for its trouble. Caleb glanced up at the sound and caught sight of a deep red flush climbing Adelaide's neck as she sighed and rubbed her hands on her damp skirt. The fabric rucked up with the movement, exposing her thighs.

Caleb gripped the fencing harder.

"Caleb. We need to talk now, not later. It's important," Harvey said.

"Yeah, I heard you. I'm almost done."

Edith and Adelaide stepped from flower to flower. Edith wielded the dipper expertly. It was a long-handled soup ladle Caleb had snatched, along with a host of other supplies, on his last day of work at a casino kitchen. It had the casino's logo stamped into the metal, two interlocking capital *W*'s. Edith ran her thumb over the logos as she scooped up water with the dipper, depositing it at the base of each sunflower stalk.

"That a tool of the world could be used to build paradise," she said. "What a strange gift."

Caleb bristled. She said that shit every time she used the ladle. "If you don't like it," he said tartly, "use your hands to scoop the water. Oh, wait, you can't use your hands for that, can you?"

"I didn't say I don't like it. It's a wonderful gift you brought here with you," she replied, the words starch-stiff.

"Hey." Harvey put his hands over Caleb's on the fence. He leaned in close. "I need you. Now."

Those words were enough to move Caleb. They always had been.

It had been this way between them since their shared first day on the job at the casino. Both fifteen, both pretending to be older. Both pretending not to be interested in talking about where they'd been or why they needed work. When they met, waiting to meet the kitchen hiring manager, Caleb had still been nursing a blistering sunburn from his walk through the desert and into the city. Harvey had still been nursing a blistering hangover from a weekend spent mourning-slash-celebrating the loss of his old job slapping escort cards at tourists on the Strip.

"How do you get fired from a job like that?" Caleb had asked, incredulous.

Harvey had shrugged in reply. "Missed a couple of days."

The hiring manager at the restaurant kitchen hadn't asked any questions beyond their availability, which was infinite. He'd nodded at them without so much as getting their names. After that nod, Caleb and Harvey were parked in front of the huge industrial sink for ten hours a day, six days a week, listening to whatever music the sous chef picked and scrubbing plant-based proteins off heavily carbonized pans.

They'd seen something in each other back then. They weren't kindred spirits—Harvey had calluses everywhere Caleb was soft, and Caleb's sense of humor had elbows everywhere Harvey's spirit was bruised. But they clung to each other like stumbling drunks, each one's weaving momentum helping to prop up the other, and they made their way together.

They'd moved into a rathole apartment with no air conditioning, no refrigerator, and no lease agreement. They shared a mattress on the floor and a single bottle of three-in-one shampoo-conditioner-bodywash. They never precisely dated, but they screwed around every so often, when it felt especially right or especially wrong. They fought when they were hungry or exhausted or bored. They slapped bedbugs off each other and they loved each other, simply and wholly, for precisely who they were.

And then William and Dad came through town, and their lives changed forever. Together.

Caleb would walk away from anything if Harvey needed him. Anything at all.

"I heard you had a visit from Nona today," Harvey said as they walked toward the fallow beds at the north end of the garden.

Caleb watched the ground ahead of his feet. "Nona? Which one is that?"

"The only one who was in your garden this morning. She said you let her hold a chicken."

"Ah. That one. Well." He stepped deliberately onto a sharp-looking stone, let the point of it dig into the soft arch of his foot. "She was already going to get in trouble. So I figured, why not let her have a good part of her day too, you know? She's a sweet kid."

"She's only nine, Caleb."

Harvey stepped in front of him then, forcing him to pull up short. When Caleb looked up into the eyes of his oldest and closest friend, he felt no fear. "So? What's that have to do with anything? It's not like she slaughtered the chick. She just held her, that's all."

"She's young. She needs guidance." Harvey ran a hand through his thick dark hair, his shoulders loose with exasperation. "You can't just give her a treat to make up for the fact that she's going to feel guilty for having done something bad. It made her feel even more guilty, because she knew she shouldn't have gotten the treat, and then she—"

"Okay. I'm sorry," Caleb said. "I get it. I won't let it happen again."

Harvey's gaze tightened. "I mean it. You didn't see what she did with that guilt. If you're ever going to be allowed to get more involved with the kids, you have to—"

"I said, I heard you." Caleb saw Harvey's irritation at being interrupted again. He saw Harvey decide to let the irritation go. Then, to his surprise, he saw Harvey reel the irritation back in, pulling it closer, choosing to hang on to it.

"We'll talk about this more tonight. I have to go keep an eye on things, make sure nobody else is doing anything stupid." He started to walk past Caleb, his face clenched in a dark frown.

Caleb caught him by the elbow. "Hey. Don't leave in a shitty mood. I really am sorry, okay? I wasn't thinking. I'm not used to being responsible for the kids, that's all. I won't let it happen again. Promise."

Harvey paused, then bumped his shoulder against Caleb's, his eyes softening. Just like they always did. Just like Caleb knew they always would. "I know you won't. I believe in you," he added. "You've done so good with the other thing. You can figure out how to do good with the kids, too."

"I'll do better," Caleb whispered. It was mostly to himself—Harvey was already walking away, waving to Edith and Adelaide, turning onto the road to head back down to his day's work.

Caleb watched him go, and he wanted to keep his promise. Not just regarding Nona and the chickens but regarding everything—all his faults, all his flaws, all his struggles.

But then Adelaide called him back across the garden, and he saw the way her skirt clung to her legs, and he felt it: the way his weakness was constantly closing in on him from all sides. The way a promise to do better could only carry him so far. He wanted to run down the road, into the water, where he'd never be able to let anybody down again.

But the fence still needed to be set up. So he pointed himself back toward the sunflower patch, and he walked, step after step, toward the failure that was waiting for him there.

Eleven Years Ago

Sadie is standing in the canteen kitchen with her arms crossed. She's glaring down at the range. The burners stare back at her, cold and unmoving.

"I don't understand," she says. Her brother's best friend, Harvey, is next to her with a basket of eggs. "How am I supposed to boil the water without contaminating the eggs?"

Harvey sighs, shifting the basket. The eggs make a heavy noise. "I'm telling you, it won't contaminate anything."

"I'm not even allowed to wear shoes here," Sadie snaps. She hates snapping at Harvey. He's too sweet to snap at. His soft eyes immediately drop to the floor. But he's not making any fucking sense. "How are shoes evil but propane isn't?"

Harvey hoists the basket onto one of the stainless steel countertops and rests it there. He rubs his face with both hands. "Because it's natural. It's—maybe you should ask Adelaide to explain. She always does a good job explaining stuff."

"Oooh, does she?" Sadie swishes across the kitchen to her brother's friend, twirling the long linen skirt of her borrowed dress. "Does Aaah-delaide explain things sooo good? Is that what she's doing all night long with Caleb in his little shack? What do you think she's explaining to him in there?" Her irritation is forgotten. The chance to make Harvey blush is too good to pass up.

He obliges by turning a deep crimson. "It's not like that. They're—okay, you have to stop," he laughs, swatting Sadie away as she swishes her dress at him. "Quit it!"

"I never figured Caleb would go for . . . you know. A girl. But she's nice. They're cute together." Sadie peers sidelong at Harvey's still-pink ears. "Do you think they're cute together?"

"They're not really 'together,'" Harvey says, not meeting her gaze. "It's more like . . . they're coworkers, kind of. It's hard to explain."

"Hm. Seems like lots of things around here are hard to explain." She pokes a finger through the eggs. "These are all really different sizes. Won't some of them cook faster?"

Harvey sidles past her, brushing close against her hip. He grabs a long kitchen match. "That's the idea. Some people don't like runny yolks. This way, everyone gets what they want." As he bends to light one of the burners, his shirt rides up, revealing a well-muscled lower back.

Sadie licks her lower lip. "I don't know if I like runny yolks or not. I don't think I've ever had one."

"Today's your day, then." He rises, grinning down at the flame he's made for a moment before moving the big pot of water onto it. The metal scrapes against the tops of the burners.

Sadie twirls out of his way. She's not making fun of Adelaide anymore, but it's fun, tossing this ridiculous skirt around. "Why do you like it here?"

He doesn't answer right away. He's so like Caleb, Sadie thinks—always thinking for a minute instead of just coming out and saying things.

She remembers how quiet her brother was when they were kids, until the moment the bedroom lights went out. Then he'd lie on the top bunk of the bed in the room they shared, and he'd tell her everything he was afraid to say by daylight: the rock that had struck a real police drone and sent him and his friends scattering, the fear he had that their mother might be losing her mind, the boy in his class who had touched his arm and let his fingertips linger for just a little longer than usual. He always used to ask her the same thing: What did it all mean?

She wonders what Harvey's like in the dark, in his little shack here on this strange island. After the sun's gone down, what might he reveal?

When he finally speaks, his voice is low and close-by. He's watching her like he really cares what she thinks of his answer. "I like it here," he says, "because Caleb's here. He's . . . he matters so much to me, and this place makes him happy. And I like that here, I don't have any questions. On the Cove, everything has an answer. I know exactly who I am and what I'm supposed to be doing. I don't worry that I'm missing anything. I have purpose here. They tell me what my purpose is, and I get to fulfill it." And then he asks Sadie a question that's never occurred to her before. "Do you have purpose?"

"Me? You mean like, in coming to visit Caleb . . . ?"

"No." The first few, small, slow bubbles rise to the surface of the water in the pot. "In your life, Sadie. In your soul. Do you feel like you know why you're alive?"

The question pinches at something deep inside of her. She drops the skirt and tongues the backs of her front teeth. "Not really," she says. It comes out of her as weak as the bubbles breaking the surface of the water.

Harvey gives her a hopeful half smile. The sight of that smile makes a few small, slow bubbles rise up in her chest.

"Well," he says, taking a step toward her. "Maybe that can change."

SALT FESTIVAL

day two | afternoon

Celia still had water dripping down the backs of her legs as she and Easy walked back up the road from the lake. She'd stayed in the water as long as she could, soaking in everything William had to say.

He had explained how a community could support a person through anything. He'd told them that no person who was surrounded and supported, who was adequately loved and known by the people around them, could continue to feel pain.

Celia heard this and thought of her big empty house. It had a guest bedroom that had never been used; she changed the bedsheets once every six months out of the simple fear that she might turn back the covers one day to find a family of mice nesting in the mattress. She thought of birthdays spent working, and unbought merchandise, and social media posts with no replies, and she thought: *How can I make a baby when I can't even seem to make a friend?*

The whole point of the baby had, in the first place, been to eliminate the pain of being alone. There would be no loneliness ever again, she'd thought, once she had made herself a friend who couldn't leave her. But then she'd lost the first baby, and the second, and all the ones after that too, and she'd discovered that the loneliness and grief and hurt could compound.

Every time her solution failed, the problem expanded.

By the time she left the water, the salt of the lake settling into her bones, Celia felt the hollow spaces in her soul ringing like struck bells.

"I like your dress," Easy said, giving her a sidelong once-over.

Celia looked down at herself. Everything the visitors had cast off before entering the water had been taken away for washing; there'd been dresses and shirts laid out for them on the shore when they'd emerged. Celia's dress was linen, loose fitting, a dusty pink that might once have been red. "I like it too," she said, surprised to find that she meant it. "Where's Audrey? Is she okay?"

"She's fine. Resting. You hungry? Want to grab something to eat before we head up for your surprise?" Easy asked, glancing at her as they approached the canteen.

It must have been close to noon. Celia had been swimming for hours, and before that, she'd run nearly the full breadth of the island. Her last meal had been dinner the night before. "To be honest, if you come too close to me, I can't guarantee I won't take a bite out of you."

Easy laughed. She had a good laugh, clear and bright. "We can't hang out or anything, but run inside and grab something from the kitchen to take with us. There'll be stuff sitting out for visitors to take, you'll see it. I'll wait for you out here."

Celia hurried into the empty canteen, leaving Easy in the middle of the road under the dazzling sun. It was cool and dark inside. There was a stillness to the air. It was a feeling that Celia had only ever encountered in places that people used but did not inhabit—school campuses after hours, grocery stores past closing time, empty theaters. She felt distinctly intrusive as she rounded the long service counter and walked into the kitchen.

The kitchen itself was precisely what she expected from a place like this. Industrial, all stainless steel counters and wire racks, a huge eight-burner stove, serving spoons and spatulas hanging from hooks. She caught a distorted glimpse of her reflection in the bowl of a hanging ladle. It was the first time she'd seen her own face since the previous morning, when she'd glanced at her reflection in the rearview mirror on the bus that took her and the other visitors to the boat.

She remembered something William had said that morning, about people being hypnotized by their own reflections. He'd said that a person's community was a truer mirror than any glass could be. She thought of the time she'd spent across the grief group circle, staring at Adelaide and the others, transfixed by the kaleidoscopic view of her own pain.

She looked away from the ladle.

A large, heavy door revealed a pantry the size of the cabin Celia had slept in the night before. She grabbed two dense pucks of oats off a long sheet pan and made her way back out, resisting the desire to linger and snoop, the urge to press her palms to every scratched-up surface.

Easy was right where Celia had left her. She was talking to Jessie. Celia drew near and caught the tail end of something Easy was saying—*you'll move up when you're ready to move up*—but before she could make out anything further, Jessie turned and gave her a scalding glance. Then the girl was gone, dashing up the road on light feet.

"Where's she headed?" Celia asked.

"Chores," Easy answered. "Oh, nice, Edith made oat cakes. Is there one for me?"

They continued up the road, passing the scattered cabins, retracing the steps she'd taken on her run that morning. The oat cake was sweet and moist, softer than she'd expected. She finished it fast and wished she had another. Her legs burned. "Where are we going?"

"Back to where you were snooping around this morning," Easy said around a mouthful of oats.

"I wasn't snooping," Celia lied. "I was just—"

"You saw the chapel, right?" Easy interrupted. "We're going there. You're gonna help me prep for tonight's Candle Hour. We only do the first one down by the lake, after that we're up the hill every evening."

Celia was grateful to have the conversation so deftly steered away from her transgression that morning. "So Candle Hour isn't a thing you guys do here all the time?"

"Seriously? How much beeswax do you think we have? Candle Hour is for the visitors. You'll understand the longer you're here." She stepped around a large loose stone in the road, and then the two of them were rounding the final bend beyond the orchard. The chapel appeared before them like a landing bird. "You ready to get to work?"

The chapel was spacious and welcoming, painted in bright white. There were a few buckets of water inside, a pile of folded rags. "So this is my big surprise? Chores?"

"This is the best part of living here," Easy said. She seemed to mean it sincerely. "The work. What do you do back home?"

"For work?"

Easy's shoulders twisted as she pulled off her worn button-down, stripping to a thin undershirt. "For satisfaction."

The question froze in Celia's mind. No one had ever asked her that before. She knew how to answer the question of what she did for work—*I run my own business, I'm a proud Brand Ambassador, would you like to hear more about how you could maximize your earning potential from the comfort of your home?* But she couldn't think of anything that she did for satisfaction. "I guess I don't," she said.

Easy's face shone with excitement. "Let's see if we can change that."

They worked for hours. Celia's hair dried as she helped scrub and rinse the floors and walls of the chapel. She fetched new buckets of water from down the hill, she wrung out rags in the middle of the dusty road. When all that was done, she simply sat in the center of the floor, breathing in the salt smell of the lakewater-washed walls, searching herself to see if she was, indeed, satisfied.

If she closed her eyes, she almost felt like she was still in the lake. Under the water, where all the noise and movement of the world disappeared. Where she could let herself be unpersoned, if only for a short time. Where she could let go of gravity and breath and the solidity of her own skin. The air of the chapel gently shifted in a light breeze just as the currents and eddies of the lake would, and Celia gave herself over to both. Here in the chapel, she could let all her thoughts sink down to the bottom of her skull until she was left with nothing but peace.

She had been at Kindred Cove for just twenty-four hours. And already, she could feel herself changing.

"You're thinking some awfully big thoughts, huh?"

Celia opened her eyes to find Easy looking down at her, a candle in each hand. She'd been hanging up the last of the rags to dry when Celia sat down. That could have been minutes ago, or hours ago. Celia's head swam a little as she looked up at Easy's wild dark hair and flashing eyes.

"I don't think I'm having any thoughts at all," she said. Her mind felt wonderfully empty and still.

"Perfect. That means you're ready." Easy held up two candles, taken from the big pile in the middle of the floor. The smell of saltwater inside the chapel was softened by the perfume of the beeswax. She handed Celia one of the candles. It was roughly the width and length of Celia's forearm. Easy pulled a folding knife out of one pocket and opened it to reveal a small, very sharp blade.

"Watch what I do, yeah? I'll show you on one, and then you can try it yourself. Just don't copy the parts where I mess up. We're doing waves." She used the knife to slowly carve a rippling wave pattern all the way around the candle. It was jerky in places, occasionally jagged. Easy buffed the wax with her thumb to smooth the lines out. She extended the waves down the length of the candle, spacing them out at the top and bringing them closer together at the bottom, until Celia could barely make out the difference between one line and the next. When Easy was done, she handed Celia the knife, her fingers loose on the blade. "You ready to try?"

Celia looked at the unblemished candle in her hand. She could picture herself carving it well, but when she lifted the tip of the knife to the wax, she froze. "I don't think I know what I'm doing," she said.

"Sure you do." Easy rested a hand on the back of Celia's neck.

"Just think of it like drawing. If you fuck it up, we have more," she added, nodding toward the pile of uncarved candles.

Celia pressed the blade into the wax. It was harder than she expected it to be. Slowly, so slowly, she carved a wobbly line around the top of the candle.

"See?" Easy gave her a lopsided smile, guiding her hands over the undulating lines. "It's not so hard. This time, try to make it a little more wavy."

Celia watched as the pattern she was making went from disjointed and jagged to rolling and fluid. "Why waves? The lake doesn't really have waves, does it?"

Easy picked her own candle back up, continuing the motif. "Only little ones, when there are big storms. And the miracle tide. It's not really about the lake," she said before Celia could ask any questions about the miracle tide. "I remember Dad and William carving waves into candles way back before everything happened. Maybe they just liked it."

"Or maybe it was the only thing they knew how to carve," Celia responded drily, rubbing the rough edge of a wave with the pad of her thumb until the line was a little gentler. "If it's simple enough that even I can do it."

She followed the movements of the waves she was carving, followed them with her eyes and with her hands. Her tongue traced figure-eights on the roof of her mouth. Her breathing slowed. She caught herself rocking back and forth in a slow, steady rhythm, her shoulders and hips counterbalancing each other, and she closed her eyes to lean into that rhythm, inhaling island dust, exhaling damp salt air, moving with the waves, moving with the water—

Heat bloomed in her thumb. She opened her eyes and saw the knife pressed against the candle, a chunk of something red pressed between the blade and the wax, and then a fat rivulet of blood snaked its way down the heel of her hand, across her wrist, dripping onto the stairs.

"Fuck!" Celia jumped to her feet, dropping her knife, dropping the candle.

"What happened? Are you okay?" Easy suddenly sounded very far away.

Celia couldn't answer. There was some instinct in her screaming that she needed to *move*, but as soon as she tripped down the chapel steps, she realized that the instinct didn't have a direction to it. The cleaning rags they'd used to wash down the chapel walls were hanging off the branches of the apple tree between the house and the chapel. She ran to the tree and snatched one down, wrapped it around her thumb, squeezed tight. The fabric was immediately saturated with red. She took another rag and wrapped it right over the top of the first, then stood for a moment, frozen, unable to come up with a next step.

Her heart pounded in her temples. Out of the corner of her eye she could see Easy standing on the chapel steps, staring after her, calling something out. She couldn't feel her thumb. She couldn't feel anything. She took a slow, shaky breath, trying to steady herself.

Salt air ghosted over her tongue.

Her eyes focused, her gaze snapping to the cliffs just past the Old House.

She ran.

Celia was already past the front steps of the Old House by the time she heard Easy's footfalls behind her, but she didn't turn around. She raced down the road, her bare feet gripping the dirt and pushing off it again easily. She didn't slow down. She didn't hesitate.

Her legs were still pumping long after her feet left the ground. For one beautiful moment, she was completely free—free from gravity, free from soil, free from herself. There was no Celia; Celia was left behind on the cliff's edge. She hung in the sky like an early-evening star.

She didn't experience the sensation of falling. There was no plummet into the water, not for her. Instead, there was freedom followed by immersion with seemingly no division in between. One moment, she was dissolving into the open air, her skin a mere suggestion, her entire self given over to the irreversible inevitability of having jumped. The next moment, she was solid, every side of her held in place by the gentle hands of the Vetiver, a yolk perfectly contained inside the warm wet white of an egg.

There was nothing, and then there was everything.

The salt didn't even sting.

She kept her eyes closed, lost in the way the water cupped her skin and combed its million fingers through her hair. It was just like her half-remembered dream from the night before. She was in the lake, safe and quiet, perfectly surrounded, enveloped on all sides. The water was warm as blood. The water was her blood, her blood was the water. Just a few hours earlier, she'd been afraid of getting into this water. She couldn't remember why. She couldn't remember anything.

When Celia started to run out of air, she wanted more than anything to simply open her mouth and inhale. She could remember how it had felt in her dream, so natural, like a dance from her childhood. She could let the lake breathe for her, let the water cool the burning in her lungs—but then there was a tug on her arm, and she returned to the surface, slipping herself up into the afternoon air with barely a sound.

The tug on her arm was Easy.

She was in the water with Celia, breathless, her hair hanging in her face, her thin undershirt stuck tight to the ridges of her ribs. "Are you okay?" she asked urgently, like she already knew the answer would be no.

"I'm better than okay," Celia answered. "I feel amazing." It was true. She felt powerful. She felt loved. She felt like she really could have breathed underwater if she wanted to.

Easy blinked at her. "What the fuck, Celia? There's blood everywhere. There's a trail of it that goes all the way back to the chapel. What just happened?"

There were little waves coming off Easy's arms as she treaded water. The ripples rolled toward Celia like exhalations, and she moved with them, felt the rhythm deep in the small of her back. Celia held up her hand. The rags were gone, lost to the water. A neat wedge was missing from the pad of her thumb. The wound was still bleeding, but the blood oozed slowly rather than pouring freely as it had before. "I got distracted," she said. "I cut myself. But it's fine now. See?"

"I wouldn't use the word *fine*," Easy said, her eyes lingering on the wound. "You jumped off the cliff."

"Did I?" She tried to remember jumping, but there was nothing in her mind between the moment the knife had sunk into her flesh and the moment Easy had tugged her to the surface. "Well. Seems like you did too."

Easy studied Celia, water dripping off her eyelashes and beading on her lower lip. "Did you see anything down there?"

"No, I don't usually open my eyes in the water."

"You can. It doesn't sting or anything."

"Should I?" She didn't wait to find out what Easy would say in response. She dove back under the surface of the water. After a moment of hesitation, she forced herself to open her eyes.

She didn't see anything at first. Just water, and light cutting through it, and the vast shadow of the depths in her periphery. She spun around, trying to see everything at once, and then, there—a flash of color. She spun back, trying to find the rich dazzling pink—

A flutter, like a dress caught in a breeze, below her. She tried to swim down toward it, but the water resisted her. She exhaled a little, trying to deflate herself, wanting to sink down and see it closer. She reached a hand in front of her, stretching her arm far as she could.

As she watched, the flutter in the water seemed to grow. Seemed to be reaching back toward her.

She couldn't swim down far enough to get close to it. When she returned to the surface again, her lungs aching, her only thought was to catch her breath and then try again. "I saw something," she gasped, turning to look for Easy.

But Easy wasn't paying attention to Celia anymore. She was looking up at the cliff.

Standing at the top of the cliff, looking down at them, was a figure. A small woman with a round face and long strawberry blond hair, one foot tucked behind the opposite ankle, her arms wrapped around her waist. The weight of recognition crushed the breath out of Celia's body.

She'd know that figure anywhere.

It was Adelaide.

Eleven Years Ago

Jessie is sneaking.

She's incredibly good at sneaking. When she and the other kids play hiding games, she loves to be the seeker best, because she can move around so quietly that people don't even know they're about to be found. They don't hear her coming, so they don't know to go perfectly still and silent, and they give themselves away with little twitches and sighs. That's her favorite part—the moment when she gets to observe someone who thinks they're alone. Knowing that soon, they'll be wondering how long they were being watched.

Jessie is only seven, but she's the champion of hiding games, so much so that even the older kids don't want to let her play the seeker anymore. She has to find her victories in other places. Today, her target is Easy.

Jessie has been following Easy for most of the day. She has the day free for sneaking because she threw up a lot last night. Normally throwing up doesn't merit a sick day, but this time William and Edith and Leona were all sick too, so they said that whoever ate the bad salad in the canteen should take a day of rest. Jessie doesn't need a day of rest, though—she feels fine now, and so she's using the free, unsupervised hours to follow Easy wherever she goes.

It should be boring. Easy is hauling water today. It's the task William gave her last time she messed something up. Jessie can't remember what Easy did wrong this time—crying at the dinner table, maybe. She gets punished for that a lot. Or maybe she's being blamed for the bad salad. Either way, William's got her hauling water until she can learn how to be better. It's good, Jessie thinks, that he loves Easy enough to want to fix her.

Following Easy around the island while she does her corrective task should be boring. It's not boring, though, because it's a huge challenge to follow Easy as she works without being seen by anyone. The trick is to avoid not just Easy's attention, but the attention of everyone on the island.

First, Easy walks down to the dock, which is in the middle of the bare shoreline, exposed. Jessie has to move through the trees near Easy's path, unnoticed. (Once, a few weeks ago, she managed to get all the way down to the water. She thought about slipping into it so she could swim silently up and spy on Easy as she retrieved a green bottle from below the dock, but then Easy looked up just when Jessie was about to dart out of the treeline and into the lake, so she's given up on that idea.)

Next, once Easy has filled the two large metal buckets with water, Jessie has to follow her up the road. Easy's not allowed to take any shortcuts through the trees in the places where the road loops around on itself, even though that would save a lot of time. Or, Jessie supposes, because it would save a lot of time. So she has to make her way all the way around the outside of the loop of road—which, for Jessie, means running through the treeline next to her, all without tripping or making noise.

The top part is hardest, because the chapel and the Old House stand on a pretty clear patch of land. There are trees across the road from them, but that's not the side Jessie's on, and crossing over would break the oblique cloud of Rules that come with this particular game. She has to dash silently from one building to the other as Easy passes. If Easy looks over her shoulder even once, Jessie will be caught.

Finally, she has to crouch in the brush next to the cliffs as Easy dumps the water in the buckets off the edge and into the lake. It's windy by the cliff, and she's afraid of falling in—they're not supposed to swim off this side of the island, since it's so much deeper and the cliff is so steep. Jessie's not afraid of drowning, but she is afraid of being caught. Plus, it would ruin the sneak if Easy saw her fall.

It's a fine way to pass the time. Each trip up the road, which is steep in places and uphill the entire way, takes Easy about thirty grueling minutes with full, sloshing buckets. Each trip back down takes twenty, with empty buckets. Jessie sneaks all the way up and back down the road with her every hour, including Easy's breaks to drink from the hidden bottle and wrap fresh rags around her bleeding palms.

Easy is going to be hauling water all day to make up for whatever she's done this time. Jessie's not bored yet, but she will be eventually. There's only so many times she can fool Easy before it gets old.

FIVE MONTHS AGO

1

"Caleb, help me out here," Adelaide said as Caleb returned to the fencing. It was still loose. Adelaide was out of breath. Caleb gripped the section of pen hard enough to hurt his palms. It didn't matter to him that she was out of breath. It didn't. "You're sure you haven't seen Easy today?"

"Course not. I would have told you sooner if I had."

"It's too bad you missed the sunflowers when they were in full bloom. They're your favorite," Edith said, ignoring Caleb entirely, hauling the conversation with Adelaide onto a new subject with characteristic gracelessness.

"I actually prefer—"

"You should be glad we've already got the oil from the seeds," Edith continued as though Adelaide hadn't spoken. She ran her thumb over the logo on the ladle over and over. "You'll want a healthy amount to massage into your undercarriage toward the end."

"I'm already toward the end," Adelaide muttered. At a sharp glance from Edith, she added, "But thank you. I was using coconut oil back home—back where I was before, I mean. And I know the sunflower oil you make will be better."

The two of them emptied the second bucket, and then the third, in near silence. Edith was fuming over the mention of coconut oil, Caleb could tell. When they reached the end of the row, Adelaide paused, looking up at him. The bottom half of her dress was soaked through from the sloshing of the water she'd been carrying. "Does the goat actually like dead sunflowers? Or does she just eat them because she has to?"

Dead sunflowers, she'd said, which meant that she knew they didn't need to be watered.

That was fine, Caleb decided. He wasn't angry at Adelaide. He wasn't angry at Edith, either. He shoved the section of fencing hard, and the ground finally gave way to the metal. He wasn't angry at anyone. He was doing better already. "She likes the fiber," he replied. "The leaves are just right. We'll grind meal from the heads, too. Keeps the chickens happy."

"Happy chickens make good eggs, that's for sure." Adelaide's voice was bright. Her words were carefully empty. She was being cautious, Caleb could tell. There was a thought in that head of hers that wasn't coming to the surface.

Edith made a noise low in her throat. "You'll find out how happy those chickens are when Caleb gives you an extra egg today."

That made Caleb look up again. "What?"

"She needs it."

"I don't need it," Adelaide objected. The soft brown linen of her half-soaked dress was bunched up in her hands. There was a small brown bruise on one of her thighs, just above the inside of her knee.

Caleb forced a long breath out through his nostrils, let go of the wire he'd been using to affix the sections of the mobile pen to each other. "If you need an extra egg, you can have an extra egg. We have plenty. The girls have been hard at work."

Adelaide laughed her new laugh. It was too loud for the Cove. He wondered if she'd ever stood in front of a steaming industrial sink, trying not to let the degreaser touch her skin, laughing like that so a line cook would hear her and take notice. He wondered if that laugh had ever made anyone on the mainland look at her with desire. He wondered about the source of the bruise on her thigh.

"Fine," she was saying, "I'll take the extra egg. Only if it isn't too much trouble?"

"It isn't too much trouble," Edith answered for him. "In fact, you should go get those now. It'll get Caleb out of my way while I finish watering."

He stared at Edith hard. He wasn't in her way. She was in *his* way. They both knew it. They both knew that they both knew it. He chafed his sore palms against each other. "No trouble at all. I've got the coop-wagon just on the edge of the garden there."

They walked across the garden, past the dry cornstalks and the freshly pruned blackberries and the coffee trees that refused to fruit. Adelaide snagged a tomato as they passed the vines. It was one of the last ones still hanging on. It looked overripe, soft in her hands. She polished it gingerly with her thumb as they made their way toward the coop-wagon. Caleb did not watch the way the skin dented under the pressure of her touch.

When Caleb was a kid, he'd always lived in run-down apartments, and he hadn't known what "mobile homes" actually were. The coop-wagon was more or less what he'd pictured when he first heard the phrase: a little wooden house-like structure up on wheels. It had a miniature covered wire run hanging off the back so the girls could stretch their legs even when he was struggling to set up their pen. At night, he could take the coop-wagon back home, where he'd attach it to one side of the big run and let the girls have their space.

He'd built it all himself the year after Sadie came to Kindred Cove. He'd needed something to do with his hands after she didn't leave the Cove, the way so many people didn't leave the Cove. He'd needed something to take his mind off the way she hadn't left.

He'd done a good job.

The chickens in the covered run let out a chorus of distressed sounds as he and Adelaide approached. She still had her dress bunched up in one hand, the tomato in the other. "I'm still thinking about those devilled eggs you made for the welcome party, you know. They were great. Where did you learn the recipe?"

He paused, his mind snagging on the question. "Huh," he said after a moment. "Would you believe I don't know?"

She raised her eyebrows as she sank her teeth into the too-ripe tomato, the flesh resisting her for a moment before giving way. A spill of juice fell onto her bare collarbone and she made a questioning noise as she reached up a reflexive hand to wipe the juice and seeds from her skin.

Caleb looked away, aiming his attention at the big sliding door on the side of the coop-wagon. "Yeah, no, I never really learned. I guess I kind of just absorbed it as a kid. The air in the Midwest is pretty much permeated with the knowledge of how to devil an egg."

In truth he really *couldn't* remember a time before he knew how to make them. His mother had made two dozen every Sunday. They were destined to live in the refrigerator under a layer of plastic wrap tented over toothpicks, vanishing slowly over the course of the week.

He couldn't remember ever eating one, although he was aware that they'd probably made up about half the volume of his diet back then.

They were the first thing he'd made when Sadie came to visit him at the Cove—something to make her feel at home. She'd said they tasted different from Mom's. *Yellower*, she'd said, gesturing at the yolk piped into the center of each hard-boiled white. Caleb had grimaced, remembering the grayish yolks they had back in Des Plaines, wondering if she missed those. If maybe his were wrong, somehow. But then she'd asked to see what he fed his chickens to give them such bright yolks, and she'd asked to hold one of the new chicks, and she'd wanted to learn all their names. It was that moment that first gave Caleb hope for his baby sister.

He tried to feel that hope for Adelaide now. For Nona. For everyone on the island.

"Wow." Adelaide spoke through half a mouthful of tomato. "That's so impressive. I wonder what else you absorbed."

"Mmm. Mercury, probably, from the groundwater."

Adelaide laughed again, softer. This was her real laugh. It was the one he remembered, and it was just for him.

Caleb opened the sliding door to reveal one of the nesting boxes in the coop-wagon. There were three eggs in the nest and no broody hen to hold a grudge against him for taking them. Something simple, at long last. *Thank you*, he thought reflexively.

Adelaide took her time contemplating the eggs. The shells were an even, creamy brown. She rested a fingertip on one, tracing the contour of it. After a minute she took two eggs out of the nest. She lowered them gently into her bundled-up skirt. Caleb caught a flash of red another tomato, maybe—and then the fabric was in her fist again, hidden away tight.

With her skirt lifted like that, he could see so much of her skin. Her skirt brushed over that bruise like a lip touching a cheek. Caleb's tongue felt too big for his mouth.

Adelaide cleared her throat. "Caleb? Are you okay?"

"What? Of course. Sorry, just got lost in thought for a moment."

She eyed him. "Are you sure? That conversation with Harvey seemed intense. Are you in some kind of trouble?"

He gave himself a little shake. "No! No, everything's okay. I was just thinking about Easy. Where she might be. What did you need to talk to her about?"

The redirect worked. Adelaide looked away from him, shifted her weight from foot to foot. After a moment, she met his eyes again, her gaze furtive and urgent. "She's taking me to the mainland," she said, fast and low. "Today or tomorrow. She promised last night. I told her I'm not waiting around anymore while she ties up loose ends or whatever. We're leaving. We're going home."

Caleb stared at her, speechless. He couldn't believe what he was hearing. "We?"

"Me and Easy. I'm finally getting her out of here, Caleb. She thinks she doesn't want to go, but I've known her for her entire life, and—"

"You haven't known her the past few years," he interrupted. He couldn't feel his hands. His heart was beating frantically. "How can you talk to her now and think she's the same as the person you left behind? Do you even see her when you look at her?"

"She's my sister," Adelaide snapped. "Nobody sees her better than I do."

Caleb didn't say *don't go.* He didn't reach toward her, didn't tell her that she was making a mistake. He looked down at where her skirt was still bunched in her fist. "If you see her so well," he said softly, "then where is she right now?"

Adelaide's certainty melted away in front of him like candlewax under a flame.

After a too-long silence, she shook her head. "Thanks for the eggs," she whispered. And then she was gone, walking across the garden and out of sight.

Rather than watch her leave, he returned to his work. He did not think of Nona's delight at the chicken he'd placed into her arms. *Set up the pen, move the chickens into it.* He did not think of Adelaide's fingers twined into her skirt. *Clean the bedding in the coop-wagon.* He did not think of Sadie running into the lake, the water flying up around her, her laughter at the cold shock of it on her legs. *Gather the eggs.*

He did not think of anything at all.

2

That afternoon, after his work was done for the day, Caleb sat on the front steps of the house he shared with Harvey, waiting. It was so hot that he could hardly register his own sweat anymore. There was no part of his body that wasn't slick with it. A tickle at the nock of his throat turned out not to be an insect but a rivulet. He swept at it with the side of his hand and then stopped, remembering the gleam of spilled tomato on Adelaide's collarbone.

He wanted to be better. He really, truly wanted it.

"Phew," Harvey said when he finally came up the road. "You don't look so good." He studied Caleb with an air of detached evaluation, the same way Caleb might look over a chicken that had stopped laying. "Have you been drinking enough water? It's hot as hell, you know you have to hydrate when it's like this."

Caleb snorted. "Look how much I'm sweating. The sheer volume. You think I could do this if I wasn't drinking enough water?" He sluiced a layer of sweat off his arm and flicked his hand to fling it to the dirt. His stomach gave a fearful flutter at the thought of what he needed to say to Harvey. "I need your help."

"You're still worried about this morning. Look, I overreacted, it was a stressful start to the day for me. It's not a big deal."

"It's not just about this morning." Caleb felt the air tighten around him like a drawstring. It was time to be brave. "I'm not doing great right now."

"Okay. What do you need?" Harvey crouched in front of him so their eyes were level. Sweat was beaded in the hair at his temples.

"Adelaide." Caleb tried not to let his expression betray the naked terror he felt at what he was about to admit. "I mean, no. I don't need Adelaide. But the problem is Adelaide. I had a setback. With her, I mean."

Harvey's expression shifted to one of grave concern. "You didn't. Tell me you didn't—"

"Not that bad, no. Even if I'd tried to, Adelaide wouldn't have gone for it. She's . . . different now."

"What, then? What happened?" Harvey's eyes flicked over Caleb's body again, as if he was looking for a wound.

Caleb swallowed hard. His throat was dry enough to click. Maybe he did need to drink more water. "Can we go inside to talk about it?" Seeing Harvey's hesitation, he lowered his voice to add, "Please. We can come back out if you think we need to go up and take a period of reflection together."

Harvey answered with a reluctant nod, and the two of them went inside.

Their house suited them both fine. It was big enough to fit both their beds, an open shelf with neat stacks of folded clothing, a sink and a long countertop, a few cupboards. There was a discolored patch on the wall where a mirror had been taken down ages and ages ago, when Dad first came to the Cove and transformed it.

He always used to say that people were too easily hypnotized by themselves. *Try looking for your reflection in your community*, he would say. *You'll be amazed by what you see.*

They didn't need a bathroom because the outhouse was just a little ways down the road, and they didn't need a living room because the front steps were right there for them to sit on, and they didn't need a mirror because they had each other to look at. It was, Caleb thought, the perfect way to live.

Still, it was staggeringly hot inside. A punishing, clarifying heat. Neither of them moved to open the window.

Harvey sat on the floor and rested his back against his bed, nodding to the patch of floor just across from him, then leveled his gaze at Caleb. "Okay. Tell me."

Caleb sat, crossing his legs in a mirror of Harvey's posture. Their knees nearly touched. "It's been getting worse, lately. I've been getting worse. I know you've noticed. Giving Nona the chicken today—I knew I shouldn't do it, but I did it anyway." His heart was pounding, his skull felt like it was sizzling inside. He didn't want to say it. He desperately needed to say it. "And then, this morning, Adelaide came to the garden to help Edith. Edith, by the way, can I just say—"

"Sure."

"She's always—"

"Like that, yeah. It's ridiculous. She's ridiculous."

"So anyway, after you left, Edith told Adelaide to ask me for eggs. I walked her over to the coop-wagon, and she had this brown dress on."

"Right," Harvey replied, drawing out the word as though to say *I know you don't think I'm going to believe that the dress is the important thing here.*

"She was using the skirt to hold up some vegetables from Edith, and I saw her knees and her legs."

"You've seen lots of knees and legs." Harvey's tone was flat with skepticism. "Hell, you've seen Adelaide's knees and legs. Plenty of times."

Caleb nodded emphatically as the stifling air pressed in around him. "Right. Yes. And I haven't broken my promise, not in seven years. I swear I haven't." He was being too defensive, he could feel it in his aching teeth and see it in Harvey's raised eyebrows, but he couldn't stop himself. "I mean, I've seen way more than what I saw today, and I haven't—I mean—I haven't."

Harvey gave him a sympathetic little frown. "But today?"

"Today." He could do this, he knew he could. "Today, I saw Adelaide's knees, and I was thinking about how she'd been out in the world, and how she seemed like someone totally different, you know? Someone new. Someone coming in from the outside, and who knows what she was doing out there and what she's going to do here now that she's back. And." He froze, his ribs crushing his lungs, his heart going flat.

"You have to say it," Harvey whispered. "I can't say it for you. Deep breath in." He inhaled slowly through his nose, his hands moving slowly and fluidly toward his face, and Caleb instinctively breathed with him. "Good. That's good. See, you can handle the world coming in. Now exhale all the parts of you that want to conceal and lie and hide." He opened his mouth wide and exhaled hard, the air coming out in a whispered roar, his hands shooting back down toward the floor.

Caleb knew this was the same thing Harvey did with the children. There was a relief in that—he let himself be a child, Harvey's child, just for a moment. Just for now. Taken care of and watched and governed by someone bigger and smarter and stronger. He forced the air out of his lungs as hard and fast as he could, trying to wring the urge to deceive out of himself. He slapped the floor at the same moment as Harvey did, leaving wet handprints behind.

There. That was better. Now he was strong enough to tell the truth.

"I wanted her."

He took a shaky breath. It was the kind of breath a person draws just after vomiting, sour and raw with the effort of getting the poison out.

"Just for a second?" Harvey asked as though he already knew the answer.

"No. Longer than that. A good fifteen minutes, I'd guess." The truth scoured him. Fifteen minutes. Long after she'd left. He knew that his mind should have been on his work, but no: He'd been thinking about Adelaide's fingertip on the eggshell, Adelaide's teeth breaking the tomato skin, Adelaide's dusty calves as she walked on down the road to the canteen. He'd closed his eyes and imagined the way her swollen ankles would feel in his grip.

Fifteen minutes.

Harvey chewed his lip, looked down at his palms. Caleb hated himself for putting them both through this. If he'd just been able to control himself better, the two of them could have been down at the canteen. Harvey should have been talking about the antics of the kids at the salt flats that day, but instead here he was, bracing himself for the kind of hard conversation they hadn't had in seven years.

When Harvey looked up again his expression was grave. "Between this and the thing with Nona—"

"I don't know how to fix both problems at the same time. How can I be doing so much wrong, all at once? I don't get how I can be ruining everything like this—I'm so fucked-up, Harv, it's like I can't get anything right and—"

Harvey held up a stern hand. "They're the same problem."

"What? No, it's—the thing with Nona and the thing with Adelaide aren't—"

"You didn't hold up your end of your agreements with this community, because you were being selfish. Which problem am I describing?"

Caleb hesitated. "Yes. Okay. Yes. I wanted to see Nona being happy about the chickens, even though I knew it was wrong. And then with Adelaide, I wanted—"

"Don't." Harvey shook his head tightly. "Don't say it. Saying it is just as bad as doing it." He lifted his shirt hem to mop his face. "Okay, so. I don't see any difference between these two problems. You breached the boundaries of our community agreements due to individual harmful desires. Do you understand that if you want to be part of this community, you need to respect the community rules and boundaries?"

Caleb winced, nodded. "I do. Yes. Should we . . ." He almost couldn't get the question out, wanted Harvey to say it for him. But Harvey didn't. "Should we go up to the Old House?"

Harvey closed his eyes for a moment, then shook his head. "No. No, you've been doing so good for so long, and if we go up there—look, you didn't *do* anything, right? You don't need everyone breathing down your neck. We can just handle it here."

The relief within Caleb was tidal. "Okay. Here."

Harvey gave him a small, encouraging smile. "So. Last time you breached the boundaries of the community, you made an agreement with the community regarding your own accountability. I'm proud of you for holding up your end of the bargain by telling me about this lapse. You also made an agreement with the community regarding your future actions."

He stopped talking and it took Caleb a beat too long to remember that he was supposed to respond. Seven years of good behavior had made him rusty. "I did. And in my, um—" He faltered.

"In your actions today," Harvey prompted in a whisper. "Look into my eyes. See yourself."

Caleb looked into Harvey's eyes, right into the black centers of them, where darkness sank as deep as the hole in the lakebed. He saw his own face looking back at him from that darkness, and he studied himself there. "Right. In my actions today, I demonstrated a lack of commitment to that agreement. In my heart and in my mind I demonstrated that I hold myself and my worldly desires over the needs of the community, and I am sorry."

Harvey blinked away the sweat that was beading in his eyelashes, glanced at the front door. "Fuck, it's hot," he muttered. Then he seemed to collect himself, returning his focus to Caleb's terrible admission, returning Caleb's reflection to him. "Right. You didn't succumb to the desire to further break your agreement with the community, did you? With Adelaide, or on your own?"

"No." Fast and emphatic again—he couldn't leave any room for doubt. "No, never. Not until Easy says—"

"Unless."

"Not *unless* Easy says I'm ready. Which I acknowledge and accept I may never be." Caleb clenched his hands into fists, dug his nails into his palms, tried to let the pain clarify his mind. He couldn't afford to make this worse.

Harvey reached out and, with terrible tenderness, without even looking down, he took Caleb's fists. He pried them open and rested his thumbs over the little dents Caleb's fingernails had left in the skin. That's how well they knew each other—Harvey could find the place where Caleb had been hurting himself, just by touch. "Do you know what I see when I look at you?"

Caleb hesitated, then shook his head.

"I see a man who can make this right."

"Really?"

"Come on. Say it."

Caleb froze. "I can't—"

Harvey shook his head. "You can. Look into my eyes. See yourself." He spoke in a low voice, the same one he used to help Caleb get back to sleep after a desert nightmare woke him up screaming. When he used that voice, it felt like the two of them were the only ones around for miles and miles. "You've been doing so good. And Adelaide coming back is a lot to deal with. It makes sense that you'd stumble a little. That doesn't mean you're not still *you*," he added with an encouraging half smile.

"But what I did to the community—"

"So make it right," Harvey insisted. "You've come such a long way. I know you can do this. And besides, it's so fucking hot—you don't really want to be in that room today, do you?" Harvey gave his hands a squeeze and then let them go. "Come on. Help yourself grow. Make yourself better. When I look at you, I see a man who can make this right. Now: What are you?"

He sounded like he was telling the truth. He sounded like he really believed it. Caleb blinked away the sweat that was trying to drip into his eyes and tried to will himself to believe it just as much. He stared at the version of him that Harvey saw, and he stitched his every hope to the idea that Harvey could see him better than he could see himself.

"I am a man who can make this right," Caleb whispered.

Harvey grinned. "When I look at you, I see a man who was pure once. What are you?"

"I am a man who was pure once," Caleb answered. It came out easy, familiar. He could do this. If Harvey believed in him, he had to believe in himself, too.

"Keep going," Harvey whispered.

"I was pure once," Caleb repeated, "and I can be made pure again. By allowing myself to experience the desire to transgress, I have transgressed," he continued in a fuller voice, gaining momentum now. "The Cove requires my absolute celibacy until I've demonstrated my commitment to the community adequately, and I disrespected that boundary today by allowing myself to falter. The Cove requires my absolute support of the rules governing the children, and I disrespected that boundary today by indulging a child's disobedience. In the interest of growing and bettering myself so as to better participate in intentional community, I will . . ." He hesitated, not wanting to let himself off too light. "I will fast for the remainder of the week."

Harvey pointed at him sternly. "Not including water. You still have to hydrate."

"Not including water," Caleb agreed, and the weight of his failure fell away from his shoulders, leaving him lighter than air.

They stood and Harvey wrapped Caleb in a close hug. Both of them rained sweat, their hair dripping, their shirts plastered to their bodies. "It's Wednesday," Harvey whispered. "Just hold out until Friday. You can do that with your eyes closed."

Caleb laughed. The laugh got away from him, the relief of having come clean and the promise of forgiveness rushing through him like lightning. He found that he couldn't stop laughing, and then Harvey was laughing too, and their foreheads were pressed together and their sweat was in each other's eyes and all of it was just right.

"Together," Harvey said.

"Together," Caleb answered.

"It's gotta be like, a hundred and twenty degrees in here," Harvey said with a grin. "Let's get the fuck outside, huh? I bet there's still salad down at the canteen. Well, for me, anyway. And hey, Caleb?"

"Yeah?"

"Don't let any of my kids get attached to any of your chickens. I'm the one who has to explain what happens to those things after they die."

Caleb grinned. "They get transformed. Nothing is ever lost, haven't you heard?"

Harvey rolled his eyes. "You tell that to a sobbing eight-year-old."

They headed out into the early-evening air, which was still hot but which felt as cool as the kiss of the Vetiver compared to the inside of the cabin. Caleb felt renewed by relief.

He'd fixed the problem. He was still on his way to becoming the man he was meant to be. He was still at Kindred Cove, far from the Vegas Strip and the desert reform camp and the top bunk of that old Des Plaines apartment.

Soon, he would be perfect.

He would learn not to want anything—not Adelaide's mouth on his throat, not a hot meal at the end of a long day, not the smile of a little girl who'd gotten her heart's wish. Not even Sadie, back where he could see and touch and talk to her. Nothing—except the knowledge that he was doing what Kindred Cove needed him to do. That was all Caleb would want.

Once he was made perfect, that would be enough for him.

Two Years Ago

The water taxi's motor is struggling. Langdon tells himself he isn't worried. The motor's always struggling. Doesn't matter if he's hauling a single tourist across Lake Vetiver—or if he's delivering two truckbeds' worth of propane, rice, oats, matches, vinegar, and bulk-packed glass bottles to Kindred Cove. The motor coughs just the same either way, like it's not meant to go in the water.

He feels the same way the motor sounds. Tired to his teeth. Langdon is twelve, and at night, lying on the pull-out couch in the living room of the apartment he shares with his grandmother, he swears he can feel his bones growing. Like bubbles stretching and popping inside his arms and legs. His grandmother keeps asking him if his shoes hurt his feet, and he doesn't know how to tell her that everything hurts, so how should he know if his feet hurt more than they're supposed to?

The little boat drags toward the dock at the Cove, where William is waiting. Langdon cuts the engine a ways out like he's supposed to, and lets the boat drift slowly and silently toward the island.

"You're early," William grumbles as Langdon tosses him the first line from the side of the boat. Langdon's arms feel sluggish, heavy. "You're not supposed to get here until everyone's all wrapped up in their celebration up there."

"What celebration?" Langdon asks, getting the second line ready. "It's not the Salt Festival for another month yet."

"We celebrate other things," William says. "Next time, come when I tell you."

Langdon knows, from growing up in his grandmother's house, that there's no point arguing with William, who does not wear a watch and really has no way of knowing that Langdon is right on time. He just keeps his head down and wills his body to unload the boat. The quicker he unloads, the quicker he and the boat will be able to limp back to the mainland, and the quicker he gets back, the less chance his boss at the water taxi company will notice he's got the boat out late.

"Did you bring everything I asked for?" William asks once most of Langdon's deliveries are on the shore. Behind him, a small knot of young children are gathered in the trees, waiting. They won't come get the cargo, Langdon knows, until he's pulling away from the island. They're not supposed to talk to strangers, he supposes.

"Sure did," he replies. He retrieves a heavy plastic carrier from beneath his seat on the boat. "But . . ." He trails off, not sure how to approach this next part.

After a moment, William raps the side of the boat with one heavy knuckle. "But what? I don't have all night, kid."

"What do you need him for?" Langdon asks. He doesn't usually negotiate with adults. His experiences of them haven't led him to expect honest answers or rational demands, so he can't usually see any cause to bother treating them like they can be reasoned with.

This is different, though. This is worth the risk of whatever might come out of William as the result of having a kid question him.

William surprises Langdon with an answer he never would have predicted: a broad, warm grin. "Hah! Should have known you'd be curious. You an animal lover?"

Langdon is, in the secret heart he never shows to anyone, profoundly fond of all animals. His grandmother hasn't noticed yet, but he stopped eating meat a month ago, secreting away all his portions to sneak to feral neighborhood cats like the one in the carrier he holds now.

He shrugs. "Guess so. Wouldn't want to give him to someone who—" He hesitates, but he's too far into the sentence to go back now, and too tired to come up with a different ending. "Someone who's gonna hurt him, or. I don't know. Sacrifice him, or something."

William laughs. It's a rich, kind laugh that makes Langdon feel like he's in on the joke, even though he doesn't know what's funny. Langdon wipes his damp palms on his pants one at a time, passing the carrier from hand to hand.

"I'm not gonna sacrifice him. We don't do that kind of thing here. Hell, we don't even eat meat most of the time," he adds. He doesn't reach for the carrier. The moon glints off one of his eyes as he watches Langdon. "He's gonna have the best life there is, kid. See, our tomcat just passed away. Old age. That means we only have female cats on the island right now, and we need this young gentleman"—he gestures at the carrier—"to help breed up the next generation."

"Why?" Langdon asks. He's not sure why that counts as "the best life there is," although from William's tone he's pretty sure it's something he's supposed to understand.

"Mice," William replies simply. "They get into everything if you let 'em. We need a good healthy supply of kittens to chase them down. That tomcat you've got in there? He's about to spend his days napping in sunbeams, eating all the mice he can catch, and tangoing with lady cats. Now," he says, nodding to the carrier, still not reaching for it. "Does that sound okay to you?"

Langdon hands over the carrier. Inside, the fat gray tomcat's eyes flash, noctilucent in the moonlight. He and William don't look so different to Langdon, not in the dark. "That sounds okay. Just take good care of him. He's nice. He doesn't scratch you unless you mess with his tail."

"I feel just the same way," William says. He takes the carrier with one hand and with the other, withdraws a fat roll of bills from his front pocket. It's tied up with a length of twine. Langdon won't count it until he gets home. No need—William never shorts him.

"One last thing," Langdon says. "My nana asked if I can get some more of that salt y'all make here? She doesn't trust the salt from the store. Says they put iodine in there to . . ." He blushes, but again, he can't find his way out of what he's started saying. "To make young men sterile."

William laughs again, the same warm laugh. "Can't have that, can we? Here you go, tomcat." He reaches across his hips into the other pocket, the one that didn't have money in it a moment ago, and pulls out a decent-sized bottle of Kindred Salt. "Was planning to give it to you as a tip anyhow. When you bring the Salt Festival visitors next month, I can bring you more. Sound good?"

"Sounds good." Langdon takes the salt and tidies the boat while William unties the bowlines. He's going to be able to cover his share of rent for the next few months out of that roll of cash, and his grandmother will be glad for the salt. And maybe, after a couple more years of ferrying cargo to Kindred Cove at night, he'll be able to afford a water taxi of his own. Then he'll be able to stop giving seventy percent of his fares to his boss. Maybe get a place of his own someday. Maybe sleep in a bed, wake up feeling rested for a change.

He finally gets the motor to wheeze to life, and he steers toward that bright future.

SALT FESTIVAL

day two | afternoon

Celia swam hard for the cliff where she'd seen Adelaide. It seemed impossibly far, and then all at once it was there in front of her, a flat palm of stone rising up out of the water. She scrambled onto the little ledge of rock that stuck out into the lake. It scraped her knees and her hands, but she hauled herself up onto it and then she saw the narrow goat path that traced a zigzag all the way to the ledge high above.

"Celia! What are you doing?" Easy called from the water. She sounded worried, edging on angry.

Celia looked back to see Easy already swimming toward her. She started up the path—it was barely as wide as her shoulders, and she couldn't keep herself from clinging to the rock face as she went. She didn't want to have to wait. Behind her, she could hear Easy growing closer—light splashes in the water, a grunt of effort, wet feet slapping against stone.

"Celia. Will you stop?" Easy's voice was still taut. "Celia—"

"I just want to talk to her," Celia said without meaning to. "You saw her too, right?"

Easy's footsteps were close behind her now. "Talk to who?"

The last switchback hairpinned up to the top of the cliff and Celia looked out hungrily: There was the chapel, there was the Old House, there was the edge of the orchard.

She stopped short. Easy's foot bumped up against the back of her heel. Celia felt the hope draining out of her. "Adelaide," she said at last. "She was up here. I know she was."

Easy caught Celia by the elbow and pulled her toward the Old House. Her strides were long enough that Celia had to jog to keep up. When Celia looked down, she could see the dark brown spatters of the blood that had fallen when she ran to the cliff in the first place;

the water that flew from her hair and her legs landed in the dust and re-wet the blood, making it new again.

"Inside," Easy said, tugging Celia up the steps and into the Old House. It was small inside, and dim. Afternoon light filtered in from the windows in the kitchen. The hall was filled with the perfume of melted beeswax. A single long hallway extended from the front door to the back of the house. Everything was white inside, except for the door at the end of the hallway, which was dark wood.

Easy led Celia toward that dark door, then pivoted and pulled her into the kitchen. They stood there, surrounded by white-painted cabinets, the water running off them and making puddles on the white wood floor.

"You're going to tell me how you know Adelaide," Easy said. "And where you saw her." Celia hadn't realized before how dark Easy's eyes could be, how flat her mouth could become. But then Easy reached out and took Celia's hand, traced her thumb across the backs of Celia's knuckles, and she said, "Please," and Celia felt that she wasn't in trouble after all—that she was being invited into something, that a door had opened between the two of them. She wanted to pass through that door more than anything.

So she explained. She told Easy about how she'd decided to have a baby. She'd tried so many times, in so many different ways. She'd lied to a dozen hookups about birth control. She'd paid a friend of an acquaintance a hundred and fifty dollars to hand over a turkey baster's worth of semen, sealed up in a Tupperware container that still had a *bouillabaisse dec 15* label stuck on top. She'd gone to an expensive doctor, and then an even more expensive doctor. She'd injected herself with hormones, mottling her belly with deep purple bruises, and she'd swallowed down supplements and she'd swallowed down herbal teas and she'd swallowed down everything she could find—and, in the end, she'd nearly succeeded five different times.

But the "nearly" was killing her. Four miscarriages, each one a little further along than the last, and a stillbirth. She'd been twenty-one weeks along for the last one, and she'd thought, truly, that it would pass the same as the rest, but it wasn't the same at all. It had torn her life in half. She hadn't wanted to see it, but she had seen it anyway. The soft parenthetic curve of the back of a head, smaller than she ever would have thought a small thing could be, there and then gone.

She told Easy all of this and Easy listened. The two of them, at some point, sank to the kitchen floor, sitting in the puddled cool water they'd brought in on their bodies. They faced each other with their legs touching and Easy didn't interrupt, didn't ask questions, didn't offer insight; her face remained still and somber as the day waned, as the light in the room cooled and dimmed, as Celia shared the fullness of her grief.

And then Celia got to the part where she'd met Adelaide.

"I started attending this support group," she said slowly. "And Adelaide was there."

"In a support group?" It was the first time Easy had spoken since Celia had begun her confession.

Celia nodded. "She came, but it didn't really seem like she needed the support. She never talked about grief or loss or feeling like a failure or—any of the stuff the rest of us were talking about, you know? But she talked about this place." With her thumbnail, she traced a line in the painted wood of the floor. "She talked about missing it. Feeling an empty place in her life where it used to be. And then she showed up one meeting, and she told us all that she was pregnant, and that she was coming back here to get something she needed in order to raise the baby. And she looked so happy." The last word came out of her like a cough.

"So you came here to find her?"

Celia shook her head hard. "No. No, absolutely not. I came here for me. I came here to fix myself. But. I don't know. I'm sure it doesn't make any sense to you, me wanting to see her."

"Of course it makes sense to me." Easy's mouth buckled in a sad, soft smile. "You want to see someone who managed to do the thing you couldn't do. You want to know what she has that you don't have. Or you want to know that she didn't manage, and that you're not the only one who can't seem to do what everyone else can."

"No, no, not that," Celia said, much too fast to be convincing.

"No?"

"I just wanted to say hello. I wanted to ask if I could see her baby." It felt believable. It felt probable. It felt less pathetic than the reality that Easy had so effortlessly witnessed and called by name. "And when I saw her standing up there on the cliff—"

"On the cliff?"

Celia nodded. "You saw her up there too, right?"

"Not in the water?"

"No—why would she be in the water?"

Easy's eyes flicked across Celia's face. "Can I ask you something?"

For a wild moment, Celia thought about saying no. She nodded, not trusting herself to speak.

"What would you feel, if you saw that baby?"

"Hope. I'd feel like maybe—"

Easy lunged forward, her palms slapping the floor in front of Celia's lap. She stopped a breath away from Celia's face. Her eyes were bright as she gazed hard at Celia. "Don't lie," she whispered. "Don't. You need this, so tell the truth. What would you feel?"

Celia swallowed. Bitter salt ghosted across her soft palate. "I would be jealous," she whispered. "I would want to know why—why her and not me. I would—" She stopped, not wanting to say more.

But then Easy said it for her. "You would hate her. You would hate her for having what you don't have, and you'd know that it was wrong to hate her, so you'd force yourself to love her."

"Yes," Celia breathed.

"And the love would eat away the edges of you," Easy continued, "and some part of you thinks that if you let enough of your edges wear away, you'll end up with something good left over. You think that's how you're gonna fix yourself. By letting yourself be eaten."

Celia hadn't thought of it that way. But as Easy spoke the words, Celia felt the truth of them. It was there in the queasy clench of her belly, in the way she wanted to back away and shake her head and say *no no no none of that belongs to me.*

But of course it was true. She wanted to see Adelaide because she wanted to see proof that this place could work, sure—and yes, that hard, cruel part of her wanted to see that Adelaide was suffering. But wasn't there another piece, too? Didn't she also want the pain of seeing what she didn't have? She'd imagined it a hundred times. The way it would sting to see Adelaide glowing with motherly pride, the brave earnestness with which she would look Adelaide in the face and say *I'm so happy for you*, the way she'd mean it. The way she'd break down later, alone, with her head in her hands and her pain in her mouth.

The way she'd let her emptiness flood her.

Easy was still talking. "You want to own the way it hurts to think about Adelaide. You want to be able to take it on and battle it and defeat it. But Celia—come on, look at me. Will you look at me?" She ducked her head to catch Celia's eyes, gave a small encouraging smile. "There you are. Don't you think it's time to stop picking fights with your own hurt?"

She nodded. The movement of her head shook loose the tears she hadn't noticed building.

Easy brushed a tear away from Celia's cheek with one thumb. "You could be so much more than your pain, you know."

The next thing Celia knew she was in Easy's arms. Easy was stroking the back of her hair and making shushing noises like Celia was a child waking up from a nightmare. *Shhh, shhh, shhh,* Easy said, and the rocking of her arms and the sound of her breath passing between her lips felt and sounded just like the lake against the cliffs, knocking away the loosest stones and smoothing every rough edge into something soft.

Celia sobbed like the child she hadn't been in decades. She emptied herself into those arms until she felt hollow. Until she felt pure.

Until she felt ready to be filled up with something better than herself.

Candle Hour began at nightfall. This time, Celia was not late.

She and the other visitors walked up the hill from the canteen to the chapel after dinner. There were only nine of them now—the young women with the crystal necklaces, both brothers, Rinna whose husband was still missing, a few others. They were all still in their borrowed clothes.

Celia wore nothing underneath her linen dress, which was stiff and tough with air-dried saltwater. She didn't remember taking her bra or underwear off—had she left them on the shore after the morning's swim? Or had she slipped out of them sometime after she'd finished sobbing in Easy's arms? It shocked her how quickly she grew accustomed to the feeling of only being separated from the world by the thin, soft linen of this borrowed dress. She didn't want to pull her own clothes out of the duffel beneath her bunk, didn't want to push her legs into the cheap fabric of the leggings she'd brought with her.

She didn't want the day to end.

She caught up with one of the tall brothers and touched him on the arm. "Have you seen Audrey?"

He looked down at her blankly. "Who?"

"Audrey. The older lady who came with us on the boat. She's about this tall," she added, holding her hand at the height of her shoulder. "Wears big glasses?"

"Oh, the lady who freaked out while we were swimming today? I heard she's sleeping it off," he said. "Either that, or she's with the other group."

Celia frowned, looking at the other brother, the one who hadn't been at the lake earlier that day. "I keep hearing about this other group. Were you with them earlier today?"

"Nah, I just overslept," he said with a grin. "Stayed up a little late checking out the local wildlife. Speaking of which." He broke away from the group, jogging ahead, slowing when he reached a figure Celia thought might be Jessie. He rested a hand on the girl's shoulder; she looked up at him and laughed.

One of the girls in the crystal necklaces peered around Celia. "Isn't she like . . . sixteen?"

Celia thought Jessie was older than that, but she couldn't tell for sure. She wondered briefly what the other group was doing—but then she shook the question off, determined to focus on more important things. She was here, she reminded herself, to grow.

William was waiting for them on the chapel steps. He was surrounded by the candles that Easy and Celia had carved earlier that day. The inside of the chapel was full of candles, too. There were a few folding tables with food on them inside. Residents of the island surrounded the little building—more of them than Celia had seen in one place since her arrival on the island. Some leaned against trees across the road from the chapel. Others sat on blankets in twos and fours, leaning on each other, murmuring in close conversation. As the knot of visitors approached, William raised his arms; conversation ceased, and the residents of Kindred Cove began to applaud.

"Welcome to your second Candle Hour," William called out. He sounded excited. "Today, you learned about the sacred waters of Lake Vetiver. Be glad you're learning about them now, and not in September, when things get chilly," he added with a wink. It got a laugh out of the crowd. "You also got some free time to explore the island. Did anyone find themselves drawn to work?" A hand went up—Rinna, her wrist striped with a single winking gold bangle. Celia put her hand up too. "I hope you found the satisfaction you deserve," William intoned.

"I got to help beat the laundry clean. It was amazing!" Rinna called out. Her eyes glittered in the candlelight.

"Good, good," he replied. It sounded automatic. Then he raised his arms again, as though he was waiting for someone in the crowd to leap up and embrace him. "This afternoon, you listened to me talk. A lot." Another laugh from the crowd. "I told you a little bit about life here at Kindred Cove. I encouraged you to make the most of your time here, to leave the wide world behind you and let yourself become someone who is capable of the kind of growth and learning you can't find anywhere else. Those of you who were invited to enter the water today—you are the ones who took that call seriously. You had the courage to risk losing yourselves, in pursuit of finding something greater. Thank you."

The gathered residents clapped again. Celia tried to remember hearing William say any of that. She didn't think she'd left her old self behind, but she wanted to. She wanted it more than anything. Her thumb throbbed.

"Tonight is going to be a little different," he said. "Tonight, you'll hear from someone who understands better than any of us what it means to live with intention. Edith?"

More applause. The gray-haired woman who had come down to the water to chat with Easy walked up the chapel steps to stand beside William. He introduced her as a co-founder of the community at Kindred Cove, told some long and involved story about the garden and a potato crop and a library. Celia tuned out, scanning the crowd around her, looking for Easy. She accidentally made eye contact with the crystal-necklace girl who had asked about Jessie's age, earning a frown and a significant glance at the chapel steps.

"My commitment to Kindred Cove is in the land," Edith was saying. "Everything you've eaten while you've been here, I grew with the work of my own two hands. Well, except the eggs and the goat cheese," she said, nodding to a young man in the crowd. Celia recognized him—Caleb, the man who had been assigned to chaperone Audrey. She wondered how he could be here if Audrey was off somewhere else. "But all the vegetables and grains, all the fruit and beans—all of it comes from my garden."

Celia was still watching Caleb, wondering if he knew where Audrey was, and so she saw the look that flashed across his face. It was raw, animal anger. She only caught a glimpse of it before he turned and walked into the trees.

"That's my commitment to this community," Edith continued. "I nourish the people around me with my labor. Every morning when I wake up, I leap out of bed—well, no, I roll carefully," she amended with a laugh. "My knees aren't really up for leaping anymore. But in my heart, I leap. Because I'm excited to do work that I know will help people. Not just work that will help rich strangers earn more money, but work that will help the people I care about most, by filling their bellies and feeding their bodies. Who here can say the same? I know that everyone who lives at Kindred Cove full-time can, but what about our visitors?" She looked to the visitors, her eyes moving from face to face. Celia was sure they were difficult to see—it was nearly full dark, and Edith was looking out at them from her candlelit stage, right in the middle of all that flickering light.

But when her eyes landed on Celia's, it seemed like she could see everything. All Celia's questions and doubts and expectations. All her shortcomings. Celia felt suddenly sure that this woman knew she'd plunged into the water beyond the cliffs earlier in the day. Guilt pressed in on her. The wound in her thumb throbbed. She hadn't meant to. She hadn't known she wasn't supposed to. None of that made any of it right. She could never undo what she'd done—

Edith's eyes left her face, and Celia felt that she could breathe again.

"I've given up a lot to live here," Edith went on. "I've lost more than most people could ever imagine having in the first place. I've chosen this community, these people, over myself every day for the last twenty-eight years. And I wouldn't have it any other way. The opportunity to choose something beyond my own selfish impulses—to build something bigger than I could on my own—that's a more valuable gift than the wide world ever saw fit to grant me." She looked down at her hands, then up at the sky, a beatific smile spreading across her face. "I am part of something greater than myself. And I am grateful."

More applause. She went on to talk about the soil, the way it anchored her to the guarantees of growth and work. Celia couldn't concentrate. The sound of the water crashing against the cliffs kept distracting her. She could swear she heard her name on the breeze. A hand ghosted across the small of her back, but when she turned, no one was standing close enough to have touched her.

She wondered how old Jessie was. She wondered how old Easy was, for that matter. Neither of them could be as young as they seemed. Or maybe she just didn't want to feel old. She couldn't tell. The lake lapped against the cliffs and the candleflames surrounding Edith danced and the smells of salt and beeswax mingled in the night air. Celia felt dizzy.

A floating feeling overtook her. It was a feeling she'd often lost herself to in the year after the bridge collapse, when loss had flooded in around her from all sides, when there had been so much life to figure out and nobody to help her make sense of her future. She'd walk through the house she'd grown up in with a feeling like her head was drifting three feet above her body. She'd find herself in rooms she couldn't recall entering, halfway through sentences she couldn't recall starting. She'd looked down once to find a piece of buttered toast in her hand, half eaten, with no memory of how it got there.

It had been frightening then. She'd felt removed from herself, scooped out like an avocado pit. She'd wondered if her mind was still her own. But here, now, at the Cove, the floating feeling didn't seem so scary. It was safe, welcoming, like a hammock she could hang above her own consciousness. She didn't fight it. She let herself drift, like flotsam on the surface of the lake, trusting that eventually she'd wash back up onto the shore of herself.

Edith finished talking about the importance of the land and walked down off the chapel steps, greeted William with a warm embrace. He took her place again. "We have all been given an enormous gift here at Kindred Cove," he said. "The land provides for us and the water blesses us. You're all here with us to share in the gifts of this incredible place. You're here to heal, and to be healed." A whisper rippled through the gathered residents. "And by the end of this week, you will be different. It's starting for some of you already. I know you can feel it. You can feel yourselves growing. And just as the land of the Cove nourishes us, in our bodies and in our souls, it's up to you to feed that growth happening inside of you." He nodded, agreeing with himself, and Celia found herself nodding, too. "As we celebrate tonight," he continued, "try to find the land inside yourself. Search for what anchors you. What makes you want to leap out of bed in the morning? What does your work do to serve the people you care about most? Find the answer, and use it to nourish yourself. Together?"

All around Celia, the residents of the island responded. "Together!"

William grinned out at the crowd and said it again. "Together."

PART THREE

accountability is the love language of community

SALT FESTIVAL

day two | evening

Celia made her way slowly up the chapel steps. The chapel was warm, almost oppressively so, thanks to the abundance of candles. There was a huge hunk of dripping honeycomb on one folding table, and trays of devilled eggs, and piles of ripe plums staining the clean rags beneath them.

"Don't bother trying to eat the honeycomb," Easy said into her ear. "It's impossible to do without getting honey all over yourself."

Celia jumped. "Where have you been? You were missed at dinner." *I missed you*, she did not add.

"Taking care of some things. Figured you'd be busy soaking up Edith's wisdom. Was I right? Did she tell you about leaping out of bed? Did it change your life?" She plucked a plum off the pile and lifted it to her lips, her eyebrows raised, her eyes fixed on Celia's.

Celia didn't know how to answer that. She didn't have anything to leap out of bed for back home. She thought of the yoga pants and essential oils in her garage, the cases of lip dye and perfume and—and, she realized with a how-could-I-forget start, crystal necklaces. That was why she kept thinking those other young women looked familiar. It was because she'd once spent a month and a half trying to sell the exact necklaces they were all wearing. The stones were supposed to enhance something or align something, Celia couldn't remember. Nobody had wanted to buy them from her.

She wondered, now, if that was because she hadn't felt a sense of purpose in peddling them. She hadn't wanted to leap out of bed in the morning to tell people about the crystals and how they could help make people's lives better. How was she supposed to know what "better" even felt like?

She hadn't leapt out of bed to try to get pregnant either. Celia realized it, suddenly, remembering how she'd trudged through the dates and the medical appointments. How the sex she'd had, back when she was trying to make a baby for herself, hadn't felt distinct from the shove and pinch and ratchet of a speculum. She'd looked forward to both activities with the same level of grim determination. She'd thought of it as necessary—as a chore that stood between her and her perfect life, her forever-companion, her baby.

But maybe she'd been going about it all wrong. Maybe she'd been sabotaging herself by failing to find the joy in the work of conception.

Maybe that was the way in which she was to blame.

Celia wanted to know what Easy would say about that. She wanted to hear Easy say *you're right, it's all your fault.* "What did Adelaide tell you about me?" she asked, taking a plum between her thumb and forefinger.

Easy was engrossed in her own fingernails. "Hm?"

"I met her at grief group. Did she tell you about that? I found out about it from a flyer I got outside the Apple Store. Do you know what that is?"

"A grief group or an Apple Store?"

". . . Both, I suppose."

"I thought you called them grocery stores. Which I honestly don't understand, because—"

"No, sorry, no. It's a place where you buy computers." Celia faltered because Easy was staring at her, hard. "A computer is—"

"I know what a computer is," Easy said quietly. "Let's talk about this outside."

She gripped Celia by the wrist hard and dragged her out of the chapel, down the steps, walking so quickly that Celia stumbled and nearly fell a few times. When Easy finally stopped, in the shadow of the apple tree where they'd hung rags to dry earlier that day, Celia jerked her arm away.

Easy leaned in close, close enough that Celia had to take a step back, then another, until she felt the bark of the apple tree snagging on the fabric of the back of her dress. Easy braced a hand on the tree trunk just above her head, bending over her. "You don't want to talk about that kind of thing here," she murmured.

"What, computers?"

"Adelaide's Salt Year," she said. "People here won't engage if you bring up computers—it's not taboo or anything, it's just that nobody will know what the fuck you're talking about because we don't keep up with that stuff. But you can't talk about the time when you knew Adelaide. You didn't even—" She stopped short, sighed sharply through her teeth. "God, I didn't want to have to tell you this. Earlier today, you said you knew her out there. But you didn't. Okay? The version of her that you met wasn't real. It was Adelaide's Salt Year. She was doing her duty to this community. I know you might think that she was your friend but—"

"No, no. Not my friend," Celia said. It stung to say out loud, but hearing it felt true. Celia had thought they were friends. But then Adelaide left. "We were just supporting each other through a hard time. We both wanted to be mothers so badly. I was about to start another round of IVF, and she—"

"IVF?" Easy's front teeth rested against her full bottom lip when she said the letter *F.*

"In vitro fertilization. A doctor was helping me try to get pregnant—"

"I know what it means," Easy murmured. She ducked her head to catch Celia's eye. "Why were you getting IVF? After all those miscarriages, why didn't you think about some other way to become a mother?"

Celia hesitated. She wasn't sure if there was a trap waiting for her inside that question. Some people in the fertility-and-child-loss support group had been more than a little judgmental. One woman had accused Celia of making her body into a trash compactor for fetuses, a comment that had caused the group to end early and had sent Celia into a black fugue for a full week.

Easy didn't sound like that woman, though. Easy sounded like she wanted to know the answer.

"I had one embryo left," Celia said. "And I wanted a baby that was mine. Adelaide understood—she wanted that, too, you know? A baby that came from her eggs and her body. Someone who could be all hers. I gave her a referral to my—"

Easy pressed her hand over Celia's mouth. Her palm was warm and dry, her fingers sharp against Celia's cheek. "I don't want to talk about Adelaide." Easy pressed her forehead against Celia's, then slowly took her hand away. "I want to talk about you," she whispered. "Now. Why don't you tell me about how much you wanted a baby that felt like it was yours? I want to know more about that. Tell me, Celia."

She stayed there, right there, and Celia found herself saying it all. The words poured out of her hot and fast. At some point she started crying again, and when her chest shuddered with a sob, the rising motion brought her closer to Easy. Celia's tears slid down the side of Easy's nose as she talked about wanting to have the things mothers got to have. Being the things mothers got to be.

She talked about her own mother dying in the Poplar Street Bridge collapse. The way she'd suddenly become a new kind of alone—the only person in the world with this specific chin and these specific freckles and this one specific memory of what it had been like to lie on her back in the sun beside the woman who made her. She described lying on her mother's side of the bed, pressing her face into her mother's pillow every night until the scent of her mother's leave-in conditioner faded and the pillow just smelled like a pillow. And she talked about what it had been like to lose that last baby—to feel the sudden wrong weight of death inside of her, to sit with her heels in plastic stirrups and stare up at the ceiling and think, *I want my mom.*

"I'm sorry," she whispered. "I don't know where all this is coming from. I think it's just been a long day, and—"

"Don't do that," Easy interrupted. Her lips brushed the air in front of Celia's mouth. "Don't try to suck it all back in. You needed to say that. I bet it's the first time you've said it to anyone, right?"

Celia nodded, the movement making her forehead roll against Easy's forehead.

"You lost your mom, and you want to give someone else what you had with her. Because then maybe you can get a little bit of her back. Is that it?"

"Kind of. And—" The words stopped in her throat, but she forced them loose. "And if I have a baby, if I carry it and give birth to it, then it can never leave me. Not all the way, right? There's always going to be part of me inside part of them. Even when they grow up and move away and have a life of their own, I'll always be there."

"In the freckles," Easy whispered. "And the nose, and the memory of the day in the sun."

Celia let out a shaky breath. "Yes."

Easy blinked, her lashes brushing Celia's cheekbones, and then she pulled away. The sudden absence of her made Celia rock forward onto her toes. Easy caught her by the shoulders and pressed her lips to Celia's forehead. "This," she murmured into Celia's hairline. "This is power. What you just told me is power. You see yourself, Celia. Do you know how rare that is?"

Celia felt the heat of Easy's mouth on her skin. It sent spreading fingers down through the center of her. "It doesn't feel powerful," she admitted. "It feels like I'm just admitting that I want what I can't have."

Easy leaned back, her eyes sparkling. "Well, that's just not true."

"I know there are lots of kinds of—"

"Right, no, that's not what I mean." Easy bounced on the balls of her feet. "The thing you want. The kind of mother you want to be. You can have that, Celia. You can. You just have to pursue it. Come with me," she said, taking Celia by the hand and leading her behind the chapel. "Check this out. You see those kids?"

She pointed to a cluster of children, scrawny and tangle-haired. One of them was holding her skirt up to support a huge bundle of plums; the rest were purple-chinned and sticky with juice. They were taking turns holding their hands behind their backs and diving face-first into the pile of fruit, emerging with one or two plums clenched in their teeth. "Whose do you think those are?"

Celia looked up at Easy in alarm. "Are they all yours?"

"In a sense," she said. "I didn't push any of them out of my body, but all of them are my responsibility. Someone in my community gave birth to each one of them, and we're all part of raising them. Nona there, with the plums? She's all of ours."

Celia watched as one of the children bent to retrieve a plum, stumbled, and dove into the girl's skirt. The fabric slipped out of her hands and the plums went rolling across the path. Everyone dove for them, scooping them up and running, except for the kid who had fallen. He stayed down, his face pressed into the dirt, not crying, but not moving, either.

"Is he okay?" she asked, starting to move toward the boy—but Easy grabbed her gently by the arm, holding her back.

"He's fine. That's part of the game. It's something the kids made up late last year, don't worry about it." Easy pointed and Celia looked back to see who was striding over to the boy. Jessie approached, grinning, and crouched down next to him. She took him under the elbows and flipped him onto his back, and he scream-laughed as she dragged him away. "See? All good." She turned back to Celia, her eyes going serious. "Those are my children. They know it, and I know it. I get to shape them. I get to make them who they'll always be. No matter what happens to them in this life, they'll never, ever forget me, because I'm stamping myself into them forever. Isn't that what you just said motherhood is about?"

Celia looked around, searching out the scattered children. They were tucked in next to the chapel, under trees, beside bushes, gorging themselves on the plums they'd managed to grab. "I haven't seen this many kids before, only the ones at dinner. Where are they all day?"

"You'll see them more once you start looking. You know—hm." She hesitated, seemed to be questioning herself. "No, maybe I shouldn't ask."

Celia wrapped her arms around her middle. "Ask what?"

"It's a hard question. It's the kind I'd normally save for the last day you were here, but—I don't know," Easy said, shaking her head. "I think you're further along than the other people here. I think you're ready for a hard question."

The air felt thin in front of Celia's face. She sucked down a breath and wished it was warmer. She couldn't figure out what had made Easy stand so close to her while she was sharing her every secret. She couldn't think of how to make Easy come close again. "I'm ready."

Easy shoved her hands deep into her pockets, her shoulders rising. "Does some part of you think that having a baby will fix everything else?"

"Wh—no, what do you mean?" Her stomach twisted. She felt caught.

Easy frowned. "Maybe I was wrong. Maybe this is too much."

No, Celia thought desperately, *come back.* "It's not. I just didn't understand. Tell me again?"

Easy considered this for a moment, then shrugged, shook her head a little. It seemed like she was giving up.

But then she looked up at the dark sky, the same way she had on that first night, and she spoke again, her voice soft enough that Celia had to lean in closer to catch the words. "I wasn't born here. Did I tell you that? No? I didn't think so. I don't usually like to talk about it." Easy started walking back toward the apple tree, her pace slow. Celia followed. "The people who were my parents back then brought me here when I was little. I was furious. I don't even remember what I was mad about. I think I just didn't like that things were changing. I kept crying and yelling, and they kept explaining it to me over and over again—that we were going someplace better. They made me leave my tablet and my VR headset behind. I had one of the ones with puppy ears on it, did you ever have one of those?"

Celia couldn't help laughing a little at the memory. "Oh my god. Yeah. And the controllers were—"

"Little paws," Easy said, holding up her hands with her wrists bent and her fingers curled, mimicking the gesture that turned the headset on. "I was furious when they said I couldn't bring it with me. And I wanted my shoes. I remember that, too. I insisted on wearing my shoes all the way up until we stepped off the boat. But then, a month or so after we got here, Dad asked me this question. He said, *If you spend all your energy resisting what's good for you, how are you going to have any energy left to make the world around you a better place?*"

Celia had her back to the chapel. Easy had her back to the Old House. Celia watched over Easy's shoulder as a single flickering light traveled past one of the windows in the Old House. Someone was in there, avoiding the party. Audrey? Adelaide?

"That night," Easy continued, "he showed me the stars." She pointed at the sky. Celia looked up and felt something in her spin on its axis. "He said, *It's not the same here as it is where you're from. But it's not all bad, is it? I bet you haven't seen stars like this ever before in your whole life.* And he was right. Back where I was from, the sky was all smog. Horizon to horizon. I said I thought the stars were amazing, and you know what he said?"

Celia shook her head. A breeze was coming in off the lake, lifting her hair off her neck. The leaves of the apple tree rustled softly overhead. The flickering light in the window of the Old House had vanished. The party felt a hundred miles away. Celia had floated on the current of Easy's words, leaving herself far behind.

"He said, *You're just as amazing as a sky full of stars.* He said, *Here, you don't have to look at a mirror to see yourself. You just have to look up, look around. And when you look up at all those stars up there? Well. You're not even seeing a fraction of what's inside you.*"

Celia looked up at those stars. She tried to imagine any of the adults she'd known as a child caring enough about her inner life to even understand that she might be missing something. Even her parents, who'd tried their best right up until they'd died. Even they had never seen her quite so clearly. "That must have meant a lot to you," she said. The words felt inadequate.

"It meant everything to me. He meant everything to me. It was the first time I felt like anyone had really seen me. My moms left after a couple of years here, and I decided to stay. Because of him."

"How old were you?"

"Eight and a scrap," she said, looking up into the branches of the apple tree, reaching to touch a leaf. "I was really mad at them for leaving. I was mad at myself for staying. I was mad at Adelaide, because she was always doing everything right and I was always doing everything wrong. But even in the bad years, after Dad was gone, or when Adelaide was so far away, out in the world meeting you—even then, I would look up at that sky and remember the way Dad saw me when I was a sad little kid. And I would think, *Easy, you can be better than you are. If you just try. You can be good.*"

"Are you?" Celia asked. "Good?"

She looked down into Celia's eyes with a lopsided smile. "I'm getting there. Are you?"

For the second time that evening, Celia was at a loss. Was she good? Had she ever been good? How would she know how to even begin to answer? "I, um. I don't know." It felt like Easy was putting her eye right up to the hole in Celia's breastbone to peer at that awful hard seed behind it.

She rested a hand on Celia's shoulder. The reflection of distant candlelight flickered in her eyes. "I think you could be. I think you could be really, really good, Celia. If you wanted to. And I think you could help these kids be good, too. I think helping them could help you, if you could just admit to yourself—" She stopped short, bit her lip.

"What?"

"If you could just admit to yourself that everything hurts, all the time. And that the answer to all that pain isn't inside your body right now, waiting to grow into a solution. You can be good, and you can make everything better, if you just let yourself see that. I know you can."

There was weight to her words. That weight settled over Celia like all those stars in all that sky, settling into the lake at Kindred Cove, sinking down into the water to meet the reaching fingers of the reef. This was what Easy had been coming to all along. She'd asked Celia, before, if she thought having a baby would fix everything else, and this was what she'd meant. Not just that Celia thought the baby would solve the pain and the loneliness and the endless sadness. Not just that.

Something even deeper.

The question shook Celia and the answer stilled her.

Am I good?

You could be.

Heat spilled across her cheeks. She didn't know when she'd started crying again. She couldn't seem to stop, today. "I don't know how," she said at last.

"That's okay. Nobody does, not on their own," Easy said. She finally, finally folded Celia into her long arms. Celia breathed in the salt smell of Easy's skin and pressed herself into the warmth of Easy's body and sobbed out the knowledge that she'd never known if she was good or not. The dark windows of the Old House were forgotten, the open wound of her pain closed tight over the dark space where goodness could grow.

"I'm sorry," she whispered, her lips against the soft fabric of Easy's shirt. She didn't know what she was sorry for, but she knew that she meant it.

"It's okay. It's never too late to try," Easy said, pressing a palm to the back of her head. "What matters is, you're here. You're here now. And we'll figure out how to make you good. We'll figure it out together."

Celia felt the word push its way past her lips and fall out onto the crook of Easy's neck. "Together."

Fourteen Years Ago

Adelaide and Easy are alone in the Old House. They have been alone here a lot since Dad disappeared a year and a half ago.

As far as they know, nobody has thought to address the fact that they have never slept where the other kids sleep, on the tables and floor of the canteen. Nobody on the island gets assigned their own house until they leave the children's group and take on the adult work of growing the community—but Adelaide and Easy don't need to be assigned their own house, because all those years ago, Dad took them under his roof and kept them there. And now he's gone, and the two of them haven't stopped sleeping here. Which means that every night, they have the place to themselves.

"Do you want to see it?" Easy asks, whispering even though nobody else is in the pitch-dark house. She always whispers in here. "It's right down the hall."

Adelaide shivers. "No. I've never seen it before and I don't want to start now. Besides, you see it enough for both of us."

"William and Edith say I need it." Easy sounds more than a little sad. She's caught a lot of William's focus since Dad vanished, and the strain of his role—what he calls the "work of manifesting leadership"—has been landing on her hard. She can't seem to do anything right in his eyes or Edith's. "I just wish I knew why I need it so much, and you never do."

There is a secret between them. A closeness that isn't the closeness of community. They love each other in a way that is deeper than the love of the Cove, but not wholly separate from it, the same way a pit is buried within a plum. They are sisters, and their connection to each other—their trust in each other—is as deep as the new hole in the lakebed.

Adelaide's voice softens with pity. "Come on. It's not so bad, right? You can just close your eyes."

"It's worse if you close your eyes. You'd understand if you saw it."

Adelaide slides out of her own bed and crosses the room to Easy's. She yanks the covers off her sister by feel, then worms her pinky finger into Easy's fist. It is their secret signal. It means *you can break my finger if you want to*, and it also means *I trust that you won't*. "Fine. Show me."

Together, the two of them pad out into the hallway, Adelaide's pinky still clutched in Easy's damp, hot fist. They go to the door that Adelaide's never opened. There's more light out here from the moon shining through the kitchen window, enough that Adelaide can see Easy's hand shake when she reaches for the knob.

She opens the door, and together, they look inside.

Adelaide cries for the rest of the night, and the whole next day, too. So much that Edith takes Easy aside to find out what's wrong. Apparently Adelaide won't say what happened—*won't say what you did to her*, Edith says. Easy doesn't tell, either, because every time she's cried at the sight of the closet door in the past, William has doubled the duration of her punishment, which he refuses to call a punishment. Easy doesn't want Adelaide to be punished for crying.

The thing is that Adelaide has never had to take a period of reflection before. Easy wants her sister's first time in there—whenever it happens—to be a short one. She's already planning to be outside the door waiting, ready to help Adelaide recover. She wants to be there to help.

And, she admits to herself in the deepest corner of her secret heart—she wants to be there to watch.

In the end, neither of them gets punished, because William and Edith can't decide what they'd be getting punished for. Easy understands this to be a fluke. Actions have consequences, always. Sometimes consequences arrive unattached to actions—but there is never an absence of consequences.

Adelaide never tells anyone that Easy showed her the room. But when she does get invited to take her first period of reflection, she's not nearly as scared as she would be otherwise. Easy stands outside the back of the Old House, eye pressed close to the flake-painted wood, the entire time Adelaide is inside.

She'd never leave her sister alone. Not for this. Not for anything.

FIVE MONTHS AGO

1

Everyone needs a leader.

William believed those words with all his heart.

They were among the first words Dad had spoken to him, looking into his eyes on the curb outside the Dog and Sparrow after lighting up a cigarette he'd bummed from William's pack. William would never forget how his hangover had seemed to crystallize in that moment, his headache becoming sharp at the edges. Everything had suddenly become clear: The way he was living was about to become "before."

William knew Dad for over a decade before everything at the Cove got turned upside-down. It was enough time for him to start understanding what those words, the foundation of life at the Cove, truly meant. He'd spent his life trying to lead himself, which he now knew was why he'd felt lost for so long.

Dad had changed that. Dad had saved him, had instilled in him a sense of community and loyalty. That loyalty was why William stayed at Kindred Cove, even when everything felt impossible. It was why he took on the mantle of leadership after Dad's death, even though it didn't fit him at all.

And it was why, when Easy asked William and Harvey to come to the mainland with her, William said yes. Without hesitation, without getting frustrated at the way his work would have to wait.

Harvey didn't accept right away. That man needed a leader desperately, but wouldn't admit it. He insisted that he needed to be there for the children, that he needed to supervise them as they worked the salt flats. But then Easy had suggested leaving Jessie in charge—the girl needed to take on some adult responsibilities anyway—and Harvey's arguments had melted away.

"Do you know what I think?" William said as they splashed along the submerged pier toward the shabby little boat that kept them tethered to the rest of the world, the saltwater of the Vetiver coming up to their knees. "I think you hate the water."

"I work the salt flats with the kids, William. I can't hate the water."

William snorted, climbing into the boat. It rocked under his weight. "Then tell me why you're looking at it that way."

Harvey wasn't looking at the water any kind of way. He wasn't looking at the water at all. Still, he looked up at William with pure panic in his eyes. A vein throbbed in his throat. It was almost too easy to find the fear in this one, William thought—he was always so afraid of finding out that he'd done something wrong. That he was going to be sent away.

"You gonna get into the boat, or just hang on to the edge of it?" William decided to keep a loose, relaxed half-smile on his face. Decided to give away nothing. "I was thinking we'd ride together, but if you want me to drag you behind me until we get there, I'm happy to oblige."

Harvey scrambled into the boat. He looked, with noticeable effort, at the lake. "I don't hate the water," he said vehemently. "I just . . . respect it. For what it's capable of."

That was more like it. William rewarded Harvey with an understanding nod. "And what would you say that is? What is the Vetiver capable of?"

"It performs miracles."

That answer was too fast and too tidy. It was a test-taking answer. William darted a look at him as the boat's engine coughed to life. "It *reveals* miracles," he corrected. "Miracles aren't confined to the Vetiver. Miracles are larger than any of this."

A muscle in Harvey's jaw twitched. "Of course."

"When we say that there are miracles in the water, we aren't talking about the Loch Ness monster." William was smiling for real now. He loved this—shaping the conversation. His voice almost took on an accent when he was in this mood, somewhere between country and folksy. It was a bit of an indulgence. William was originally from Palo Alto. But nobody needed to know that.

Harvey sat down on the little bench at the rear of the boat, but the boat stayed put—they weren't starting across the water yet. "Of course," he repeated with a forced little laugh. "I misspoke. I respect the lake for revealing miracles."

"All I'm saying," William said, as though Harvey hadn't spoken at all, "is that the miracle and the Vetiver aren't the same thing. They're connected, but they aren't the same. So you hating the lake wouldn't be the same thing as you hating the miracle. I think anyone would understand that, actually. What with all you went through."

He darted another glance at Harvey, whose face had gone slack. He didn't have such tidy answers anymore, did he? Not when Sadie came into the conversation. He looked like a marionette with all the strings cut.

Before he could recover himself, Easy came loping down to the shoreline.

"There you are!" William called.

She made her way down the road, then stopped at the waterline to roll up each pant leg with quick movements of her spidery fingers. "Wouldn't miss it," she said. "Just needed to finish giving Adelaide her haircut."

William eyed her. "She still saying she wants to leave the Cove?"

"She's fine," Easy replied. It wasn't an answer.

Harvey glanced between them, startled. "She wants to leave?"

William gave Harvey a reproachful look, and he hoped it was clear to Harvey that the glance was all the answer he was going to get. The young man shouldn't have asked that question. It made him sound doubtful.

The boat rocked as William finally maneuvered them away from the dock. William loved this part of his life, too—his hand guiding the boat where it needed to go, the wind in his hair, his mind clean with certainty. He knew who he was, where he was going, what he was good for. Behind him, Harvey sat on the bench with his shoulder pressed to Easy's, his little heart probably jackrabbiting inside his chest with the question of what was about to happen.

That was what the young man needed to learn, William thought. It didn't matter what was going to happen. All that mattered was the knowledge that whatever happened would be what he deserved.

2

The sun struck the water, leaping up into William's eyes. His hand on the steering wheel guided the boat toward the shore like the tab of a zipper moving down the back of a dress. Behind him, Harvey was squinting out over the water. He hadn't said a word in the forty minutes since they'd left the shore.

He was thinking of her. William could tell. He'd stood just the other side of the wall a dozen times, maybe more, when Harvey was taking a period of reflection, and he knew what it looked like when Sadie was perched inside that young man's mind. He tended to ruminate on the first time he saw her, and the last.

William considered that perhaps it had been cruel to bring her up. But people had to grow somehow.

"What do you think, Easy?" William called over the cough of the boat's engine, picking up a thread of conversation as though it had never been dropped. "Does Harvey hate the water?"

Easy's voice rose up clear and bright, without even a hint of surprise at the question. "Do you, Harvey? Hate the water, I mean?"

"I've been blessed beyond measure," Harvey said at last. The breeze coming off the water tried to swallow his words. "We all have. The miracle tide doesn't change that."

William pointed to the distant shore. He wasn't pointing at anything, but he hoped Harvey would think he was—would try to figure out what William was seeing, that he couldn't. "The researchers from the mainland. What do you think they call the reef? Do you think they call it a blessing?"

"I wouldn't have any way of knowing what they call anything."

"Guess."

"Honestly, I wouldn't know where to start. They're from the world."

"Guess," William said again, and there was an edge on his voice this time. He glanced behind him to see if Easy had heard it. Her face was still, unreadable.

Harvey let out a nervous little laugh. "I suppose they'd call it . . . an anomaly? Something like that. Something inadequate."

William nodded slowly. "What do you think, Easy? What do they call the reef?"

"A phenomenon, maybe. Something to be studied." She glazed the word *studied* with disdain.

"They call it a miracle!" William looked over his shoulder, the wind blowing his hair across his face, and grinned at them both. "Same as us. Oh, not to everyone," he added when he saw Harvey's skeptical frown. "But to me. They call it a miracle when they talk to me. So you see? No one's out of reach. Even those people." He slapped the steering wheel, nodding into the wind. "Even those people."

The conversation was over after that.

Under William's guidance, the boat passed right over the dark eye in the bottom of the lake. The water wasn't clear enough today to see the coral that reached up out of that deep hole, but William could feel it beneath him, feeding and growing and incorporating everything it touched into its own perfect, unknowable structure. Each polyp was its own little leader. Each one told the whole rest of the reef where to go and what to do, and together, their voices formed the decision to grow and grow and grow.

A miracle.

Easy stayed put when they finally arrived at their destination. She didn't even stand up—just nodded to William, as though in confirmation. William wasn't sure what Easy was confirming, but he nodded back.

She wouldn't send him into a situation he couldn't handle. He was sure of that.

The contact who greeted them at the shore looked all wrong to William at first. It was how he always felt, off the island, looking at someone he hadn't seen before. The feeling of seeing a new face outside of the context of the Salt Festival was like seeing someone naked. It was like seeing someone's corpse.

Here was a face full of secrets, secrets that weren't even secret on purpose, secrets that sprouted naturally from the person's status as a stranger.

Strangers weren't supposed to exist. In a just world, everyone should know each other, should be connected like a network of polyps reaching toward the sunlight. And because of that, William didn't consider strangers from the mainland to be human, not really. They were like strange animals that visited in the night, making noises that were only for the other animals to understand, sniffing the ground to follow each other from place to place. They weren't for him to know.

The person raised a hand and waved. With their other hand, they pulled a tiny sphere out of their pocket and held it to their mouth for a moment before exhaling a thick white cloud.

The person on the shore finished tying the boat to the mooring post and climbed down into the water. It came all the way up to the knees of their squeaking waders. William smiled. The water was rising on the mainland, too. The reef was growing all over.

He waded to shore without once glancing back over his shoulder at Easy. She'd given him that nod. He could operate independently. His own man.

He looked up to see the stranger watching his and Harvey's progress with a queasy expression. William pushed out a deep, rich laugh. "How many times do I have to tell you not to worry?" A little folksy again, a little jovial. "You don't need to wear those silly overalls! The blessed waters of the Vetiver don't harm the faithful!"

He stole a peek at Harvey, who looked to be chewing on his own tongue. Was the young man thinking about Sadie? Was he thinking about the word *harm*?

This was Harvey's first time off the island in fourteen years. The young man had no idea what the world was like now. He was like a child here, and he'd have to look to William for everything he didn't know.

"I wish you'd wear waders, at least. There are contaminants," the stranger replied, gesturing down at the rubber coveralls they wore. "And we know so little about how this species of coral works."

"Yes! That's why I brought my friend here with me to talk to you." William hoped he was on the right track. Easy hadn't actually told him why he and Harvey had come to the mainland, but the combination of Harvey and the researcher implied that Easy wanted them to have a conversation. There was no way she was trying to bring Harvey in on any of the rest of it. "You folks have been so helpful to us. Least we can do is return the favor."

"Incredibly generous of you. And thank you for making time to talk to me today . . . ?" They peered around William, their entire body forming a question mark.

"Harvey. I'm Harvey. I supervise the children. Manage them, I mean. Or, I guess it's the same thing." A wild blush flooded his cheeks and ears.

The stranger didn't seem to notice. They walked right past William with a hand outstretched. "Billings. No relation."

Harvey looked to William, clearly not understanding the joke, afraid to accept the gesture. "It's not for you to understand," William whispered back, nodding at the outstretched hand, and Harvey hesitated for only a moment before taking it. He didn't let it go, or maybe the stranger didn't let him.

William stepped forward and rested a heavy hand on Harvey's shoulder. "No need to clarify, Billings. We don't participate in worldly politics at Kindred Cove," William said. "Harvey is at no risk of confusion."

"Ah. Of course." Billings kept their attention on Harvey. They were still holding on to his hand. He was trying hard to tug it away now, without much success. "Anyway. Harvey, who manages the kids."

"The children. And I guess it's more—"

"Supervision, right." They dropped his hand at last. "I've been so eager to talk to you. Come, let's sit. Can I offer either of you anything to drink? I don't have coffee, sorry. If it's not too early for it, I've got Coke. It's warm, but it's still—"

"No, thank you," William interrupted. "We treat our bodies with more kindness than all that."

They followed Billings to a little pop-up shade with three folding chairs under it. Everything was hot. Everything was plastic. One loose corner of the shade snapped in the breeze that came off the lake. The sound of it made William think of headlights illuminating fresh-dug holes in distant fields.

"Well." Billings gestured to the chairs and William sat. Harvey sat too. Billings reached into a pocket of their cargo vest and pulled out a slim black rectangle. "Do you mind if I record our conversation on my phone?"

Harvey stared at it, transfixed. Something even further from home than the offer of the Coke. William tried to think of the last time he would have seen one. A decade and a half ago, they were smaller and thicker and flat. Things had changed out here during Harvey's time on the island.

These days, the material was thin and flexible, gently curving. One side was matte, the other glass, both rimmed with the tiny circular flashes of a dozen lenses. William saw the sight of the phone send a shiver through Harvey. He wondered whether the young man was afraid or aroused, or both.

"It's just so I can transcribe our conversation accurately later. If I rely on my notes, I'll never be able to capture everything." Billings smiled as they tapped the center of the screen twice, bringing up an icon of a small red circle in the center of a white square.

The rest of the screen was still dark. Harvey leaned forward to peer at it, then flinched away at the reflection of his own face in the black glass.

William wanted to get this moving. He wanted to find out what Easy had sent them into this situation for. He waved a hand in a gesture of vague assent. "Of course."

Harvey looked at William with alarm. William saw the movement out of the corner of his eye, but he ignored it, kept his gaze locked on Billings. Harvey would have to be his own independent little polyp, moving with the group but handling himself. He could do it. William knew he could.

"Thank you so much," Billings said again. They were still bent over the device but they smiled up at Harvey, their eyes glittering with excitement. They tapped the red circle. It began a slow and steady rotation around the edges of the screen, like a prisoner pacing the perimeter of his cell. "We're recording now, Harvey. You can start whenever you'd like."

"Um. Right, well. My name is Harvey," he began. "I . . . I live at Kindred Cove." He looked to William after every couple of words. William didn't have a hint to give him, but he offered an encouraging nod. *Whatever you're going to do*, he thought, *do it right.*

Billings coughed, then sipped at their little sphere again. "Right. And just for posterity's sake, this is Tan Billings, grant ID number six-nine-one-eight-four-one." They added the date and a long string of geographical information before sitting back in their chair. "Take it away, Harvey who manages the children."

Harvey wiped his palms on his thighs. "Right. Well. I live in Blue House? With, um, with Caleb. I'm his accountability partner for his current correction. He's more in charge of the chickens, I help him out sometimes. I mostly manage the children, and I directly supervise when they're working on distillation processes. Solar and thermal. That means the process of separating salt from water so we have water to drink and salt to eat and um. Sell." He rubbed the back of his neck. He was uncomfortable with the idea of selling salt, William guessed. That was fine. It was good for him to be uncomfortable around the idea of money.

Billings glanced at William with the tiniest hint of a frown before recovering. "Okay, great," they said, in a tone that didn't quite rise to meet *great*. "And . . . how long have you been in 'Blue House'?"

"Always," Harvey replied promptly.

"So you were born on the island?"

Harvey's blush rose again. "Oh. No, that's—I moved into Blue House when I got to Kindred Cove, though. When I was sixteen. I've been there ever since."

Billings made a little *ah* sound. "And you and Caleb have lived there together the whole time? How did that work when it came to you and Sadie?"

The breath shot out of Harvey like he'd been punched. But then he gathered himself. William watched him closely, watched as he governed his emotions. Watched as he reminded himself that he hadn't lost anyone. That nothing is ever lost. It was good work, what Harvey was doing. It just wasn't quite good enough.

"It. Sorry, what do you want to know about? Distillation is a process of—"

"It's all right, Harvey," William interrupted, dipping the vowels deep into that country affect he was putting on. "Billings here wants to know all about what happened with Sadie. That can include the parts you aren't proud to bring up. It won't be anything I don't already know," he added, putting on a smile that made the skin at his temples crinkle up tight.

"So there *was* someone named Sadie?" Billings glanced between them. "Someone who passed away?"

William did not nod. Did not shake his head. Did not give Harvey any clues as to how he should proceed. He simply crossed his legs and said, "Go on."

Behind them, the waters of the Vetiver licked at the shoreline with tiny splashes.

"Sadie," Harvey said at last, his voice snagging on her name. "Well. It's—when Sadie arrived, Caleb was actually in Indigo House. Right next door."

William remembered. Dad had been in charge of things when Caleb and Harvey had come to the island, and he'd put them next door to each other, figuring they'd do better if they felt like they could support each other. *Just until we find out how to get them to stand on their own*, he'd said, and they never quite had. William wondered if he should talk to Easy about revisiting that.

Harvey continued. "Sadie was his sister, did I already say that? Um. She stayed with him when she visited."

"Was she one of the Salt Festival visitors? One of the ones that decided to stay?"

Harvey shook his head. "Salt Festival visitors don't—"

"No," William interrupted. "She wasn't a Salt Festival visitor."

"I didn't know anyone was allowed at Kindred Cove outside the festival," Billings said haltingly.

"They're not," William replied smoothly. "Sadie was an informed exception. And she did end up coming back the next year to stay for good. In Blue House," he added, nodding at Harvey. Handing the story back to him.

Billings reached under the chair to grab a red can. The color jolted William. He hadn't had a Coke in a long time, but he still remembered it perfectly—soda so sweet and cold he thought it might shock the fillings out of his teeth. The can cracked open under Billings's fingernail with a hiss and they took a long slug. "Right. So that's when you and Sadie were married?"

Harvey shook his head hard. "We don't—we weren't married. That's a legal institution. We don't participate in that sort of thing at the Cove. We believe in community, not government. William thought we should try pairing up, though, and she moved in with me so we could try to, you know. Fulfill her greater purpose."

"Did you?" Billings was looking down at that little red circle on their phone screen. "Get her, uh, 'fulfilled'?"

"We tried. And we thought, once, that maybe we'd managed to—but she lost it. Or maybe it was never there. It's hard to tell."

Billings made a small sound in their throat. "Is it true that children on the island are taken away from their parents at birth?"

William cut in. "That's not true, no. We don't take anyone away from anyone. We live a life of interconnectedness, where everyone helps and supports everyone else in all things. No one is ever alone, and no one is ever lost. Do you have that in your life on the mainland, Billings? Or is that unique to us?"

"Right," Billings said briskly, "nevermind, forget that last question. So what about the reef? I'm sorry, Harvey, I don't mean to be indelicate here, it's just—I was told that you saw the whole thing. I'd love to know more. We can only get so close to the reef when it's, you know, doing its thing. For safety reasons. You get it. And without funding for a submersible drone camera, it's hard to—"

"I don't want to talk about that." It came out of Harvey in a rush, like water breaking. He clapped a hand over his mouth, but it was too late. The words were already out there. William felt the weight of disappointment settling into his fists. Harvey had so much more growing to do. He needed so much more guidance. "I mean—it's—that's in the past. What happened to Sadie doesn't inhabit my heart because my heart is full. My focus now is on my work and my community."

"I don't understand." Billings leaned so far forward in their folding chair that the back legs lifted slightly off the ground. "A description of how people . . . change, around here—it would be invaluable. I was told you would describe it for our records. Has something happened?"

"Nothing's happened." William's voice was a little less jovial now. "Of course Harvey will share with you. Harvey, you wouldn't want to get in the way of these people's important research into the miracle of the reef, would you?"

"No," Harvey whispered.

"So. Tell Billings here what you saw. We don't have all morning."

Harvey's jaw trembled. He inhaled slowly through his nose, out again through his mouth. He shoved his hands between his knees, trying to hide the way they shook. "I saw her go under," he whispered.

When he didn't say more, William prompted him, even though

he shouldn't have needed prompting. "An honest person is never afraid of the truth. Tell the rest."

Harvey nodded for too long. He seemed unable to stop himself. "She'd been feeling funny," he said, almost ironing the tremor out of his voice. "We were hopeful that—we thought maybe she was pregnant. She was supposed to take a Salt Year, and neither of us wanted her to have to leave the island. She'd arrived so recently, and she was so happy at the Cove. So we were excited at the idea that maybe she wouldn't have to go."

Billings made an impatient gesture. "What do you mean by *funny*?"

"What?"

"You said she felt *funny*. What's that mean? We obviously haven't been able to talk to any of the victims—"

"There are no victims here," William corrected. "Nothing bad is happening to anyone."

Billings sighed. "Right. Still. Anything you can share would be helpful. Really, anything."

"She said she felt lightheaded that morning," Harvey ventured. He cleared his throat. "She was really happy. I mean, of course, she'd been happy ever since deciding to move to the Cove. But she was almost giddy, that last couple of days. She kept bringing me things—a ladybug, a feather, a perfect strawberry. To show me how beautiful they were."

"When did she start acting different?" Billings pressed.

Harvey sighed. "I guess . . . that day? She tossed and turned all night, and then she woke up restless. She, um. She smelled funny."

"Funny?" William asked, then wished he hadn't. He was supposed to know all of this already.

"Metallic, kind of. Sharp." Harvey twisted his fingers together in his lap. It wasn't like him to fidget, to hesitate, to struggle like this. William thought, for the second time since they'd come to shore, that Harvey looked like a child. "And then around mealtime, after her morning work, she stopped talking to me. She'd been helping me with the children, and she just stopped mid-sentence and turned away from me. I thought maybe she was upset about something. She put down the salt rake she'd been using and she wandered off, and I followed her."

William had seen part of it. He'd been coming out of his office when the two of them had passed by, Sadie walking down the road toward the water, Harvey trailing behind asking what was the matter. She'd been wearing a faded blue dress, the skirt swaying with her every step. William could remember the fluid movement of her calves as she strode past him, down the spiraling dirt track that led down to the water. Harvey had called after her but she hadn't turned back, not even as she shucked off her dress and then stepped into the water beside the old pier. Her long brown hair had spilled across the water, and then slowly vanished below the surface after her as Harvey splashed in to try to pull her free.

William often wondered, late at night and early in the morning, what he would have seen if she'd turned her face toward him as she went in. He wondered if Sadie would still have been somewhere in those eyes.

"And then," Harvey continued in a voice that he could not prevent from breaking, "she came back up. At first I thought she was playing a joke, but then she didn't move. I ran into the water to grab her." That was a lie, William knew—Harvey had already been in the water, had been trying to dive down to get Sadie out. But then the reef had surged the way it sometimes did, shooting a cloud of polyps toward the Cove. It had given her back, pushing her to the surface, and Harvey had stood in the water staring in horror for minutes before he'd dared to reach out and touch her. "It looked like she'd drowned. But when I flipped her over, it wasn't her anymore."

"What was it?"

Harvey spoke in a near whisper. "Long, soft fingers. That's what it looked like. Dozens of them." William had seen them, too, had stood at the water's edge with his arms crossed over his chest as half the island came and joined him. They'd all watched those fingers, deep pink like the underside of a tongue, erupting out of Sadie's chest and growing, growing, growing. Harvey had dropped her in horror, shouted, nearly fallen.

The fingers had swayed as Sadie's body dipped in and out of the water. They'd reached for Harvey, and then more had slid up out of her belly, her armpits, the fold of her groin. They'd expanded, the ends splitting and branching, again and again until Sadie was replaced by those fanned-out fingers. The massive structure they formed had bobbed gently with the motion of the water.

Harvey had backed away fast but not fast enough to prevent one from touching him on the wrist. He still had a small scar, the shape of a crescent moon, where it'd gotten him. William caught him scratching it all the time.

He was scratching it now. "I'd say it took a minute. Maybe less. And then there wasn't anything left of her anymore, really. I looked—I thought maybe the coral was just stuck on her, you know? Maybe I could take it off her. But then she flipped over in the water and I could see that it'd shredded right through her back, too. Couldn't see nearly any skin anymore," he added. "Just a little hair. Kind of caught at the top." He passed his hands over his face, blew out a hard, quick breath. "She sank fast. I guess you could call it more of a dive. And you know the rest of what comes after that part."

Billings nodded. They didn't need a description of how dead things in the water of the Vetiver made their way down to the reef and blossomed even further to join it. William figured the researchers probably saw more than he could guess at. Fish and deer and who knew what else, dying in the water and becoming part of something greater than themselves.

Billings did ask a few clarifying questions, though. Details about the shape and size of the fronds that Sadie had become. They wanted to know how much she'd been eating and drinking in the days leading up to her transformation. They wanted to know what her last words to Harvey had been.

"She said she felt wholly and supremely happy at the Cove," Harvey replied firmly. Billings's eyebrows shot up. William smiled. "She said she was blessed beyond measure."

3

Harvey and William returned to the boat just as the heat of the day started to set in. Easy was still seated on the bench seat in the back of the boat with her legs stretched out far in front of her, her head tipped back. William thought she was asleep until he climbed into the boat and saw that her eyes were open. She was staring up at the sky, her gaze trained on the empty expanse of blue as though there was something written there.

She looked at him sidelong, not lifting her head. "How did it go?"

"Yes, Harvey, how do you think that went?" William asked as he guided the boat away from the shoreline, back toward home.

Harvey was making himself small as possible on the bench next to Easy. He knew he'd done badly, William thought. It radiated off him like a smell. "I didn't like that phone the researcher had," he ventured at last. "Or the chair. Why did that man think Salt Festival visitors join our community after the week's over?"

"How do you think you did?" William spoke a little more forcefully this time, cutting the careful out from under Harvey.

"I told the truth," Harvey replied.

William slapped the steering wheel and let out a short laugh. "You did at that. You told more truth than you meant to tell, I'd say."

"What do you mean?" Easy said. It sounded casual, but William caught something sharp underneath, and he understood that there had been a test happening here all along. He just didn't know whether it was a test for him or a test for Harvey.

That was fine. He knew how to make sure which of them wound up getting graded in the end.

"Harvey faltered," he said.

"I—"

William cut off Harvey's objection fast. "Don't pretend you didn't. Growth can't put down roots in dishonesty."

Something shaky entered Harvey's tone. "I was just surprised, is all. I've never talked about it with anyone. And that phone—"

William lifted a quelling finger. "You were upset. You were upset about losing someone, even though no one is ever lost. When that researcher said someone had 'passed away,' you agreed. Are you grieving?"

"No! No. It isn't that," Harvey hastened to reply. He was rushing, sweating. "It's something else." William waited. It took Harvey a long time to come up with an explanation. "I didn't know how to discuss it in a way that an outsider would understand. Their minds are so narrow, so dedicated to upholding the status quo. I didn't want Billings to come away with an idea that the miracle of the reef is something ugly."

William nodded thoughtfully. A decent effort, but not good enough. "I see. Easy, do you think that a miracle needs to be attractive? Do you think a miracle shouldn't be frightening? Awe-inspiring?"

Easy answered as though it was a real question. Her thoughtfulness—her genuine consideration—made William think that his instinct was right. He and Harvey were both being tested. "I think *they* think miracles need to be attractive. Because their version of consciousness is so . . . so muddied. So watered-down. They don't understand the way we do," she added, "so how could they be expected to see miracles the way we do?"

William half turned, measuring Easy out of the corner of one eye. "Hm. That's fair enough. Maybe I should have warned Harvey ahead of time, so he could have figured out how to frame the situation in a way outsiders would understand. I've interacted with them more than he has, in my handling of the business and all that. I'm sorry, Harvey. That was an oversight on my part."

"Oh, William. I hope you're not worried about that," Easy said. "These things happen."

William's knees creaked under him as the boat rocked. He was fine. The narrow margin by which he'd passed this test didn't matter nearly so much as the fact that he'd passed it at all. But he needed to be sure. He spoke again, his eyes fixed on the water in front of the boat. "I'm just relieved that no correction is going to be necessary, Harvey. Honestly, I've never had cause to worry about you before."

"Of course not," Easy laughed. "He's Harvey. He's the best we've got."

"I've always thought so too," William said. He wondered if Easy meant that, if she was letting him know that the test hadn't been for Harvey. It didn't matter. Nothing mattered. He could turn the situation to his favor; that's what he was best at. He glanced over his shoulder with his brow furrowed. "You know . . . it's the damnedest thing. I noticed that Caleb is fasting."

"That's odd," Easy said. A new thread of cool danger entered her voice. "I haven't heard anything about him struggling in his correction. Why would he need to fast, Harvey?"

"Ah." Harvey traced a crack in the leather seat cover. "No, it's nothing like that. Caleb just decided that he could use a reset. For the sake of his gut health."

"I see. And he decided this on his own?"

"We decided together," Harvey answered smoothly.

Easy shifted, the old leather seat creaking under her. William took it as a hint. He throttled the boat down to neutral and they slowed, the wind dying away around them, until they were left bobbing with the motion of the Vetiver.

"You decided together," Easy said. The water lapped at the sides of the boat as it came to an idle rest on the lake's surface. They were directly over the collapsed mine. It yawned wide and dark below the boat. "So you sat in judgment of Caleb, and his recent behavior and consumption. You decided, *together*, that you didn't need to fast—but that he did. And none of this was related to his ongoing correction?"

Harvey's fingers dug into that crack in the leather. He looked as though he wanted to climb into the seat and hide there. "It wasn't like that."

"Was it like something else?"

Harvey didn't—couldn't—answer. Beside him, Easy was terribly still. She radiated calm certainty. "Or maybe," she said, glancing to William, raising her brows reasonably, "you were planning to do something else to . . . how did you put it? To 'reset.' Maybe Caleb wanted to fast, and you wanted to choose a different way. Was that it, Harvey? Because, honestly, I can't make anything else make sense. Not without the conclusion being that you think you're better than Caleb."

Harvey looked caught. All three of them knew that what Easy had just said couldn't be so. That couldn't be the conclusion, because Harvey was Caleb's accountability partner, and his whole job was to keep Caleb on his level. To be better than Caleb would be to have failed in helping Caleb.

Harvey sucked in a sharp breath, blinking rapidly. "I wanted to ask your advice on that, actually," he said. "Both of your advice. I wasn't sure—I didn't think fasting would be enough for me. Because I denied Edith a chicken at Adelaide's welcome party. I've been reflecting, and—"

"Wasn't it Caleb who denied her the chicken?" Easy asked.

"No. It was me," Harvey insisted. "He was on the fence, but I said no. I denied everyone that experience of abundance. So I figured I should have a bigger reset than Caleb, but I didn't want to burden him with helping me decide on it. I'd hoped you would lead me."

William was about to speak, but Easy beat him to it. "Of course," she said. Her tone was gentle. "You denying Edith the chicken was an act of care for the community. You were thinking of our future. That's admirable."

Harvey's hopes rose. "Thank you," he whispered.

"And it's been a whole month since that party. Surely you've reflected and grown since then."

"I only think of our future."

"That's understandable for a man with your history. You want to plan ahead. But it leads you to lose track of the present," Easy said softly. She took Harvey's hand between hers. William watched as she stroked Harvey's palm with her fingertips. "And you can't contribute meaningfully to a community if you can't support it in expressing joy in the present, can you?"

"No." Harvey shook his head. "No. I'll do better."

"You won't just *do* better. You'll *be* better." Easy patted the back of his hand. You choose to live in intentional agreement with the community regarding your actions," she said as they rose to their feet together. Her voice carried as though everyone on the island was here listening to them.

William was awash in relief at the sound of those words. They were the beginning of a correction. Harvey hadn't been subject to a correction in a long time. He would be the sole focus of Easy's attention. He would be the one who had failed, and William would remain where he belonged: at the right hand of the leader he needed.

Harvey swallowed hard. "I do choose to live in intentional agreement with the community. And in my actions at the party, I demonstrated a lack of commitment to that agreement. In my heart and in my mind I demonstrated that I hold myself and my worldly desires over the needs of the community, and I am sorry."

Easy reached out and gave Harvey's shoulders a little shake. "Don't look so grim, kiddo," she said with a faint smile. "Chances for growth are a gift. Now, in the interest of growing and bettering yourself so as to better participate in intentional community"—she took a step forward, her foot landing squarely between Harvey's feet, her proximity forcing Harvey to take a step back, then another, until the lip of the boat pressed into the backs of Harvey's knees—"you will experience the present."

Easy gave a hard, sudden shove, and just like that, Harvey went over the side of the boat and into the water. He thrashed and flailed, snorting and coughing as water shot up his nostrils and climbed down into his throat. Below him, the shadow of the hole in the lakebed yawned wide. William thought he caught a flash of pink in the churning water.

"A drowning man can't form a plan, can he, William?" Easy called. She was leaning over the edge of the boat, watching as Harvey coughed and struggled to tread water.

"No," William answered. He felt the sunlight on his shoulders. This was good. This was right.

"Go on," Easy said, gesturing down to the water. "Tell Harvey what he's won."

William leaned over the edge of the boat beside Easy. He grinned down at Harvey. "It sounds like it's time for you to grow, my friend. You'll grow today by learning to respect the present moment. We'll see you back at the Cove. It's less than six miles from here. You should be able to find your way. Edith will be waiting for you at the pier with a change of clothes and a towel." He rapped the lip of the boat decisively. "We're going to head off. Enjoy your afternoon."

Easy took her seat. She didn't look back at William as they headed to the Cove. She had her head tipped back, the same way she had when Harvey and William got back to the boat, her eyes fixed on the sky. She only spoke once, when the Cove was in sight.

"I'm proud of you for seeking a leader in me today, William," she said warmly. "Every man needs one."

Two Years Ago

Jessie is collecting rags from around the island. It's laundry day, and the children are tasked with the work of cleaning whatever the residents of the Cove have soiled. Jessie is irritated that she's still being tasked with this work. She turned fifteen a few months ago, and she still has nearly a year left before she'll be allowed to do the work of adulthood.

Her age does give her one advantage: She gets to be the one to collect. It's not pleasant work, but it's better than sweating in the kitchen while the huge vinegary laundry kettles boil; better than hoisting smaller children onto her shoulders so they can string up the drying lines; better than cranking the wringer all day, until her shoulders burn and her hands are numb. She tells herself to be thankful to be where she is, hauling a basket of rags that really ought to be carried between two people.

She'll be making somewhere between fifteen and twenty trips to the canteen with that basket today. She's only been to the Old House and the chapel so far, but the thing is already half full. They all worked on cleaning out the chapel the night before. They scrubbed it the way they normally would for a birth or for the Salt Festival, even though it's February and nobody on the island is pregnant, which is all Adelaide's fault.

Jessie heads toward the garden. Her knees bump the basket as she walks. As she passes the garden, she can hear Nadine's breathy giggle. She rolls her eyes and picks up the pace toward the first cluster of houses in the trees. It's not that she doesn't approve of Nadine—she learned, in her most recent period of reflection, that she is not a person who disapproves of anyone.

But, if she's honest with herself, Jessie is sick of all the fucking that goes on around here. Someone is always doing it somewhere on the island. They're as bad as the cats. Half the time, William's office still has a thick, sweet fug of sex lingering in the air by the time she arrives there to sort donations. Leona's throat is eternally blooming with deep red bite marks. Harvey is always slipping into Edith's bed. Even around Caleb, it's oppressive—maybe even worse than with the others, Jessie thinks. Because he's so obviously, constantly trying not to think about it, ever since Sadie joined the reef and he got slapped with his celibacy correction. No babies for him, either, Jessie figures. Not until he can quit crying about his sister.

All of them are drowning each other in sex. Jessie has never cared about any of it. She's impatient to be with Marco, sure, but that isn't about desire. It's about a goal. Beyond that goal, she doesn't want to end up caught in the endless looping interminable conversation everyone's bodies seem determined to have with each other. It's mortifying, she privately thinks, to be so unfocused.

She knocks on the door of Ochre House, where Leona sleeps. "Laundry," she calls. Nobody answers her. This is normal—it's the time of day when pretty much everyone is off working on some chore or other—so she lets herself in.

Leona and William are tangled up in each other on the bed in the far corner. They're still clothed, but Jessie can tell it was a near miss that kept her from seeing more than she wants to. She heaves a sigh loud enough that she knows they'll be able to hear it. She stands in the doorway and repeats herself more emphatically. "Laundry?"

"None today," Leona says, her voice fat with held-back laughter. "Come back tomorrow!"

Jessie fumes. If Adelaide had come home on time, Jessie would have a Salt Year to look forward to. She'd have a break from the Cove. A year on her own out in the world, where she assumes people aren't like this. But Adelaide hasn't come home, so she's stuck here, with them. All these people who keep fucking but don't have any new babies to show for it. What, she wonders, is the point?

She slams the door of Leona's cabin on her way out. She hopes the noise ruins it for them.

SALT FESTIVAL

day three | morning

Celia dreamed of salt.

She was standing on a sandbank, staring out at an endless sea. She knew, the way one knows things in dreams, that the shore she stood on was the only land that hadn't been swallowed up yet. The waves lapped against the sand. They were not great violent crashing waves but the magnitude of even their gentle movements was driven home by the salt floes that rode them to shore. With each fresh ripple through the water, massive white sheets of salt crashed into each other, sending crystalline mists into the air.

Celia licked her lips and found them encrusted with a layer of grit that was so salty it almost seemed sweet.

She woke with her mouth pressed to her wrist. She'd been sucking sweat off her own skin in her sleep. It lingered metallic on her tongue. She allowed herself one last purse-lipped pull at the moisture before breaking contact.

It was pitch-dark in the little cabin. Easy was gone—there was no steady rhythm of breath coming from the top bunk over Celia's head. The island outside Grey House shivered with night-sounds, insects and wind and the soft distant noise that was simply the lake being a lake, moving constantly against the air and the land and itself.

Celia tried all her usual tricks to fall back asleep—counting backward from thirty, picturing herself walking down a flight of stairs, clenching and then relaxing every muscle in her body.

None of it worked.

None of it worked because she couldn't stop thinking about the lake. The way it had felt to fall into the water from the top of the cliff behind the Old House, to swim down toward those reaching fingers. The water sifting through her hair, cupping the planes of her body from every possible angle. The way the lake took hold of her as she walked into it. How it wrapped cold fingers around her calves, slid that grip up to her knees. The moment when she'd tipped backward into a float and the lapping movement of the Vetiver slipped past the skin of her stomach, around her breasts, over her thighs.

In the solitude of her bed, in the dark of the cabin, she couldn't separate thoughts of the lake from thoughts of Easy. The warmth of Easy's body against her as she sobbed had been the same as the pressure of the water around her ribcage when she dove. Easy had pressed Celia's back against the apple tree and the lake had slid a salt finger between her lips. She'd told Easy every secret she'd ever held in her heart, and she'd bled into the Vetiver.

The lake was there—undulating, sinuous, inviting. Easy was there—intense, languid, mercurial. Both were hers, if only in her mind. If only in the dark.

She slipped a hand down under the quilt, tugged at the hem of the borrowed red linen dress until it was up around her navel. Her fingers traveled down over the smooth skin of her belly. They dipped into the crease of her thigh, wandered until they met damp salt. *The water*, she thought, and a ghost of brine ribboned across her tongue, *Easy*, and she pressed the heel of her hand against the swell of her sex and rocked against herself like a rising tide, *the water*, she held her breath, *Easy*—

The door to the cabin opened.

Celia jerked, her eyes flying open, her hand whipping out from under the covers. Jessie stood in the doorway. Her eyes were locked onto Celia's hand. Her expression was knowing, but all she said was "You need to come with me."

Celia followed her out. Every inch of her skin felt raw with stifled need and fresh mortification. "What's going on?"

"Easy was supposed to wake you up and bring you," Jessie replied. She turned abruptly, walking around Grey House. She muttered as she went. "Some of us have our own morning chores to attend to." Celia followed her to the back of the cabin, where a tiny footpath led off into the trees.

There were no stars in the sky. Celia could just make out the dark outlines of the trees. "What time is it?" she asked as she hurried to keep up. How long had she been trying to get back to sleep, lost in thoughts of the water, sunk into her own pleasure?

Jessie glanced back at her. "It's late enough that I should be collecting laundry instead of fetching you. But that's what happens when you put someone like Easy in charge of a visitor. She went from being totally irresponsible to being responsible for everything. She isn't used to being in charge of one person."

Celia found it hard to imagine Easy—competent, confident Easy—being irresponsible. The footpath wound through the trees in tight switchbacks that seemed designed to turn Celia's ankles. She kept stepping on stones and needle-thin twigs. "Where are we going?" she asked, trying not to panic at the realization that she was wandering through the trees with a kid she didn't know. Was she in charge of Jessie here?

She asked herself what a mother would do in this situation. What she would do, if she was a mother the way Easy had explained it at Candle Hour. If Jessie was her child without being her child.

She could tell that she was asking the right question, but she couldn't come up with an answer.

"Easy decided you should be part of this group," Jessie replied briskly. "Personally, I don't know that I agree. But I guess she sees something special in you."

"Is this the other group? The one that Audrey joined?"

"Who?"

"Audrey? I met her on the way here, I think she joined the other group—"

She shook her head, pushed a low-hanging tree branch out of the way. "I don't know anyone named Audrey, sorry. Either way, this is the first time this particular group is getting together. And don't worry, you're not late this time, since I'm the one who came to get you. It's not that difficult to be on time. You can tell Easy I said so."

They got through the trees just as the horizon was starting to blush. The change was sudden. The dense foliage stopped short, like it'd been cut with pinking shears.

The land beyond the trees was a wide, flat expanse, sectioned off into a crooked grid. Celia counted twelve big rectangles, divided from each other by narrow ridges of sandy soil. A couple of them were filled with glassy water that reflected the lightening sky overhead. The grid went right up to the edge of the lake.

Celia didn't see another living soul besides Jessie.

"Where is everyone?" Celia asked. The breeze off the lake plucked at her hair, at her dress, at her bare arms.

"They're on the way." Jessie eyed her. "I thought it would take us longer to get through the trees. Easy told everyone your feet are tender."

She crossed her arms. "Well. They're not."

"Okay. Grab those buckets, we need to set them out." Jessie indicated a stack of tin buckets at the edge of the treeline.

Together, the two of them set the buckets out in a line. There were just a dozen of them. They didn't look impressive, all lined up like that. They looked small.

"Hey, Jessie—can I ask you something?"

"Are you going to ask me to take you to Adelaide? Because Easy told me you'd ask me that."

Celia toed one of the buckets. "I wasn't going to ask that." She hesitated. "Did Easy tell you to say no, if I asked?"

Jessie regarded her coolly. "Easy was just giving me a heads-up that you lose focus sometimes because you want to see a familiar face. She didn't tell me what to say to you. Why? Are you asking to see Adelaide?"

Before Celia could come up with an answer, the sound of Edith's voice cut through the morning.

". . . so glad you asked that," she was saying somewhere back in the trees. "I truly am. I think many people operate under the misconception that religious belief is the foundation of a strong community. And I appreciate why, I do. You may not believe this, but I used to have what I called 'beliefs,' too."

"Oh for fuck's sake," Jessie whispered to herself. She cut a quick glance at Celia. "Well. You heard me. I can't take that back, can I? Anyway, now's your last chance to run. Wanna?"

Celia covered her mouth to stifle a laugh, shook her head. "No."

"Good. Because even if she's annoying, Edith is a great teacher."

"I thought William was the teacher?"

Jessie scrunched her face up. "Okay, sure. Try telling Edith that." She said this last part with a wry smile. It made Celia feel like she'd done something right by laughing—like Jessie had temporarily forgiven her for being an outsider. "But she's wonderful. Really. You'll learn a lot from her. And . . . don't worry. Adelaide will be here when you're ready to see her. You've got time."

Edith stepped out from the trees a moment later, trailing a sleepy stripe of visitors behind her. It was a small group—Celia counted just five of them, six including herself. The others were all back in their own clothes. Crystal necklaces, patterned yoga pants, a stack of elastic bracelets. She looked down at yesterday's borrowed linen dress, and felt herself lifting away from the others like chipped polish being peeled off a fingernail.

She hadn't seen her duffel bag when she got back to the cabin the night before, and she hadn't noticed it on the way out, either. Which meant that she didn't know where all her clothes were. It didn't matter. She let the thought float away like debris on the surface of the water.

"Belief only exists," Edith was saying, "to divide feeling from action. You can tell yourself that you believe in things all day long. You can trick yourself into thinking that's the finish line, can't you?" A few scattered nods from among the group. "But what are you doing with all that belief? What's the work of your hands? We're only animals. We're driven by need. Belief is something you think about, something you tell people you possess—but what do you *need to do*? What can't you resist? Believe whatever you want. I mean it. Do what you want with your beliefs, but they can't define you, can they? Because we're defined by our actions. And in belief, there's no action."

Celia felt something cold nudge her foot. She looked down to see that she'd somehow drifted right up to the edge of the still water in one of those rectangular pools. She couldn't remember taking a single step, but ripples sang out from her toes all the way across the water's surface.

She watched as the water shifted, pulling sandy soil out from under her foot, causing her to sink just a little deeper into the place where she stood.

"That's why you're all here this morning," Edith continued, stepping neatly away from the water as she gestured to the lake.

"To learn how to trade in belief for action. Because that's what we've done here at Kindred Cove." She gestured to the divided-up land. "Look at the person next to you. Do you see the potential in them?"

Celia looked at Jessie, who rolled her eyes and raised her chin toward the other visitors, where Celia was supposed to be looking.

"If you're standing here this morning, that means someone at Kindred Cove recognized that same potential in you. You're ready to focus on action." Edith pointed to the water. "You're ready."

Rinna raised her hand. Celia noticed that her gold bangle was gone. She wondered if Rinna's husband had turned up yet, then had her question almost immediately answered when the woman asked, "Where's everyone else? It's been two days since I saw—"

"You're a noticer, Rinna." Edith nodded thoughtfully. "I think that's a beautiful thing about you. The others—those who weren't invited to join us this morning—are headed back to the mainland. They've all found what they came here for. They grew in their own ways," she said, "but the growth they were open to and prepared for was limited. And that's okay!" She looked around earnestly. "Not everyone is ready for everything at the same time. Maybe they'll come back another day, and maybe on that day, they'll be ready in the same way the six of you are now."

"My husband is going home?" Rinna said in a small voice.

Celia couldn't tell if she sounded worried or relieved. She wondered if the same thing had happened to Audrey—if she was headed home. Surely she wouldn't leave the island without answers about her daughter. But just as a question started to take shape in Celia's mind, Edith nodded to Jessie.

"Will you take it from here?" she asked.

Jessie sighed and breathed something that sounded like *I guess* before stepping forward. "This bucket," she said flatly as everyone else took up a bucket of their own, "is just like you. Not that you're empty," she added, knocking on the side of her bucket and drawing a laugh from the group. "But right now, you're full of beliefs. Which do just about as much for you as an empty bucket can, right? So let's go fill you up with action."

They each took two of the small buckets, and Jessie led them down to the water. Edith remained near the treeline, watching. Celia waded in up to her calves. As she walked into the lake, she nearly tripped over a sturdy ridge, and she realized that she was walking into a flooded flat like the ones on the shore. She remembered the submerged dock, and wondered how far the flats had sprawled before the lake rose to take bites out of them.

She dunked her buckets into the lake. The water rushed into them so fast and heavy that she nearly dropped them entirely. She was the first one into the water and the last one out of it, lingering until the last person in the group—one of the young women with the crystal necklaces, the remaining two of which didn't seem to be speaking to each other at this point—hauled her buckets out of the lake.

Celia lugged hers up onto the shore, spilling water on her legs and feet with every step.

"Okay, wow." Jessie looked around at them, her eyes wide. "You all really took the whole 'fill yourselves with action' thing seriously. Now you're going to get to participate in one of the most incredible things we do here at Kindred Cove—you're going to distill your action into something real. Edith, can you lead this part? I should probably head back up and take care of the—oh, come on," she muttered, her eyes on the trees, her friendly demeanor slipping. Edith was gone. "Well. Okay, look, I'll get you started and then I really do have to go."

She took them through the next step of the process, which didn't feel like it needed much explaining: emptying their buckets into the big rectangular flats, over and over again, hauling water up from the lake and adding it to the massive, shallow pools. It was a task that was simple enough for a child to understand. Jessie hurried through an explanation of how time and sunlight would pull the water out of the flats, allowing the salt—*the essence of your actions*, she called it—to crystallize.

Celia wasn't entirely sure that she needed this lesson. She had taken action by coming to Kindred Cove, hadn't she?

But every time she stepped into the water, her certainty ebbed. *If you could just admit to yourself that everything hurts, all the time*, Easy had said. Celia let the bucket handles dig into the meat of her fingers.

The answer to all that pain isn't inside your body right now, waiting to grow into a solution.

She carried the buckets up to the dry flats and she poured out water, and every time she did, the buckets got lighter, and her fingers hurt a little less.

Celia kept hauling water with all the other visitors long after Jessie disappeared up into the trees. They looked at each other from time to time—a classroom full of children left alone during a test, wondering if it was okay to tell each other the answers. Nobody spoke while Jessie was gone. It was just all them, and all that water, and all that salt.

Celia had lost track of how many times she'd walked into and out of the lake by the time Edith emerged from the treeline. She told them to set down their buckets. Celia had a hard time uncurling her fingers from the shape they'd made around the handle. Together, their little group walked toward the far end of the flat stripe of land they were on, beyond the pools they'd been filling.

The pools they approached were already full. Edith stood far from the water in them.

"Right now, you're filling yourself up with action," she said, her tones far more reverent than Jessie's had been. "And later on, with enough time and effort, you'll see the fruits of your labor." She bent and took up a small, short-tined rake from one of the strips of soil that separated the flats from each other. She stood carefully on dry land as she bent low and pulled the rake through one of the flats—one their group hadn't added any water to—and the shallow water broke into a web of wet white crystals.

One of the girls with the necklaces gasped. "Oh my god. Ice?"

Rinna rolled her eyes. "It's salt. Right?"

"Our very own," Edith said with a warm smile.

Celia wondered if this was the way to be a mother to a community, like Easy had said. If Edith was the one she should be paying attention to, as she tried to figure out how to be a new kind of person. A good kind of person.

Edith handed them all rakes. The rakes were small, just like the buckets. "To bring you closer to the work of your heart," Edith said.

Together, the six of them stooped over the water and raked up a mountain of salt. The work felt miraculous—the salt was waiting for them in the water, the outcomes waiting for them in their actions, and after another hour laboring in the brilliant sunlight, Celia understood. She understood it all. Only now did she see what was missing. Things that looked like nothing, the water told her, contain countless treasures for those who know to look.

She had to manifest the right outcome not only through focus and attention, not only through belief—but through action. She had to crystallize the family she deserved for herself, and then she had to rake that family up out of the water and pile its love up high around her, until the perfect sunlit sparkle of it was all she could see.

Believing wasn't enough. She had to make it so.

Sweat poured down her neck and she felt herself being the same as the lake. She was made of salt and water, too. She felt the deep well of possibility within her. She felt it aching to seep up out of her and become reality.

They hauled damp salt by the fistful into wide, shallow baskets. It crumbled and fell into the seams of their clothes, worked its way into the lines in their palms. It stung Celia's cut thumb at first, but then the sting died away, and she stopped noticing the moments when her open wound came into contact with the salt she was running her fingers through.

They left the baskets in the sun to dry. It felt like leaving bread dough to rise. Some part of her expected to come back the next day and find that the size of the salt piles had doubled. They licked salt off their own fingers as they walked back into the trees, crunched it between their back teeth. Celia looked down at her bare legs and saw that they were coated in a fine film of white powder.

She felt a million fingers of possibility reaching up from inside her.

They arrived at the canteen tired and parched and sun-baked. When Edith opened the doors wide, the visitors were met by a wall of applause. The noise was staggering. The tables were full. The walls were lined with children. Every face was bright with joy.

Celia walked to the back of the room and found her seat. Easy's chair next to her was empty. There was a plate of sliced cucumbers waiting for her. The applause was still going. William was saying something about potential, action, belief. She couldn't quite hear him over the noise.

She picked up a long oval cucumber slice and placed it flat on her tongue. It tasted green and growing and the quiet coolness of it soothed the red scream of her salt-scoured tongue. She closed her mouth around it the same way the water of the Vetiver closed over her head when she dove in. She let the slice of cucumber rest there until it was as warm as her own flesh.

She didn't swallow until the applause had died away.

"I'm so glad you were invited to stay for the second half of the Salt Festival," Leona said, reaching across the table to grasp Celia's hand. "I think there's so much potential in you."

"I better turn that potential into action," Celia replied with a grin. Leona burst into loud laughter. There was no food in front of her. There was no food anywhere, except for Celia's plate of cucumbers, and cucumbers in front of the other visitors, too. "Did everyone else eat already?"

Caleb slid into the empty seat next to her, the one Audrey had been sitting in their first night. "What did you think of the flats?" he asked, resting a hand on her arm.

Jessie leaned over her shoulder to fill her glass with water. "She did great. Sorry for being short with you this morning, by the way."

"Were you short with her?" Caleb asked.

Jessie nodded. "I was just stressed about my own work. Felt like I was leaving the children alone for too long. I shouldn't have taken it out on you, Celia. Besides, Easy was wrong about you—you held your own out there just fine."

Caleb reached up to take the pitcher of water from Jessie, filling his own glass. "Of course she did. Isn't it beautiful out there?"

Celia paused with a cucumber slice halfway to her mouth. What had Easy said about her? "It really is. Whose job is it to harvest the salt, usually?"

"Lots of people work on the flats," Caleb said vaguely. "When it's wet out, we use the distiller and pumps instead of buckets. It's, uh." He glanced up at Leona, who shook her head. "Lots of people," he repeated quietly.

"Do the children help with it at all?"

He glanced at Leona. "The children. Well. Leona?"

Leona was in the middle of telling Jessie something. She had the girl by the wrist, was holding her in place and whispering urgently into her ear. When Caleb interrupted, she froze. She hissed a few more words at Jessie and then let her go, pushing her gently by the arm. "I didn't catch that," she said with a smile that seemed to hold itself away from her teeth. "What about the children?"

Celia locked eyes with Leona, hauled a rake through herself, tongued the word *action*. "I was asking about how much the children help with the salt harvest. I noticed that the rakes and buckets are the perfect size for them. The work seems well-suited to little helpers. Do they get to participate at all?"

Leona looked at her hard. "You're asking if the children do labor for us at the salt flats?"

Caleb's laugh was small and sharp. "Leona, I don't think—"

"I don't think I'd call it that," Celia interrupted, leaning across the table. She could feel it, something new in the place that hard seed of pain usually rested. Something bright and sparking and somehow correct. "I mean, sure, it's hard work. But it's such an opportunity for them to learn about the potential in themselves. I'm thinking about how much I got out of doing it for just a few hours. If I'd gotten to do something like that when I was a kid—" She cut herself off, shook her head. The certainty in her flickered out. "Nevermind, this isn't my business. I'm sorry."

"I think what you said is really smart," Caleb said, his eyes darting between her and Leona. "Really smart."

Leona nodded slowly. "You know, Celia. Easy told me that you had a difficult childhood. I can see why you'd want to take part in building a brighter future for our children, here. It's a beautiful impulse."

Celia balked. "A difficult childhood?"

"Your parents died, right?" Caleb asked. The question was gentle, but it still struck Celia like a slap. She nodded, and Caleb nodded back, like they'd come to an agreement. "Were you sad?"

Celia remembered standing in the doorway of the house her parents left to her in their will, the house where she'd grown up, the only place she'd ever known them. She remembered standing in that doorway with rain falling behind her and a dark, empty house in front of her. The future had felt as thick as a wall of gelatin. She'd pressed herself right up against that impassible future, knowing that once she stepped into it, there would be no air, no movement, no escape. She'd be stuck in it for every waking moment of the rest of her life, and there was nothing for her to do but accept the suffocating reality of her grief.

"Yes. I was sad."

Caleb put his hand over hers. His touch was light, his skin barely coming into contact with hers. Leona's eyes were fixed on his hand. Her lips were pressed together tight. Caleb didn't seem to notice. "You know you don't have to be sad. Right?"

She nearly yanked her hand away. "What?"

"Nothing is ever lost," he said. "Your parents—"

"Caleb," Leona cut in. "I think Easy needs you in the kitchen."

He looked up at her, and then looked down at his hand and pulled it away from Celia. "I wasn't—okay. Yes. Thank you, Leona."

And then he was gone. Leona looked after him, shook her head. "Sorry about that. He gets a little carried away sometimes. To answer your question—yes, the children do help with the salt flats. Under adult supervision, of course. They learn so much from their experiences here."

Celia nodded. She couldn't feel her head moving, wasn't aware of the expression on her own face. She flexed the fingers of the hand that Caleb had touched. "What did he mean, nothing is ever lost?

People here keep saying that, and I don't . . . I don't think I know what it means."

Leona reached across the table. She put three fingertips on Celia's plate. The plate had a single cucumber slice left on it. Leona pushed it toward Celia. "You should eat this."

"What does it mean? What he said?"

Leona smiled a small, catlike smile. "Ask that question again after Candle Hour tonight. How about that?"

Celia didn't want to wait until after Candle Hour. She didn't want to have to wait at all. Because she remembered, now, the first time she'd ever heard that phrase.

It was at the first support group meeting Adelaide had joined.

Celia would never forget that day. Adelaide had floated in, late, wearing a pair of sneakers with a hole in each toe. She'd settled herself into the chair next to Celia, seeming almost to hover above the seat, the same way Caleb's hand had hovered over Celia's hand. She'd been so poised, so still, her hair falling down her back in a banner of bright brass, and she hadn't spoken until the end of the hour.

"You're all so sad," she'd said. Her voice had wonder and pity in it.

The social worker leading the group—a tiny woman who owned at least twenty cardigans of different colors, all in the same style—had cleared her throat and then said something about a range of different emotions showing up in the aftermath of loss.

Adelaide had beamed, shaking her head like the social worker was a child playing a senseless game. "But that doesn't make sense. Nothing is ever lost."

Adelaide had known something back then. Something Celia didn't know. And Caleb knew it, and Leona knew it. Easy, maybe, wherever she was—she knew it too.

You don't have to be sad.

Nothing is ever lost.

She lifted the final slice of cucumber from her plate and touched it to her lower lip. Candle Hour would come soon, she told herself. She'd learn what that phrase meant, and she'd get to see Adelaide and meet her baby, and she'd get to touch the curve at the nape of Easy's neck, and she'd get to swim in the lake and feel the salt on her skin.

And then she would understand everything.

Seventeen Years Ago

Caleb is standing in the alley behind the casino kitchen. It has a dedicated set of dumpsters, and there's a door between two of those dumpsters. Caleb has spent two days watching that door.

It took him four days to get here. He almost died, maybe should have died, but he didn't die. He made it. Four days of hiking through the desert, alone, with nothing but the clothes he was wearing and a compass he stole from the wilderness recovery counselor in charge of his group. Two thunderstorms rolled over the desert while he was making his way. They were terrifying—the wind whipping up sand to scour every inch of uncovered skin on his body, lightning splitting the sky open overhead, rivers appearing around him out of nowhere. Terrifying, but he figures they probably kept the heat from killing him.

He looks better now than he did when he made it into the Vegas suburbs. He managed to catch a ride to the Strip, and he's been sticking to the shade here, getting bottled water from the missionaries who litter the sidewalks, eating out of casino dumpsters. His face isn't blistered anymore. He knows he looks bad, but he doesn't look as bad as he did before, and he's pretty sure he can get a job from whoever walks out of that door next.

As he waits, a guy his age strolls into the alley with his hands in his pockets. His stride is purposeful. Too purposeful—Caleb's heart rockets for a moment, but then the guy sees him and slows down. Takes his hands out of his pockets, holds them up. "You work here?" he asks.

"I'm hoping to," Caleb answers. "You?"

"Same. Mind if I wait with you?"

They end up standing watch together for another hour. Caleb learns that the guy's name is Harvey, that their birthdays are only a week apart, that they both need a place to stay. Harvey has never been to a conversion therapy wilderness survival camp, but has spent time in the desert. He says he got stung by a scorpion once.

"That happened to a kid at my camp," Caleb says. "They had to medevac her. A helicopter came."

"Must have been a relief for her," Harvey says.

Before Caleb can say that yes, he thinks it really was a relief, the girl burst into laughter when she shook the scorpion from her sleeping bag—the kitchen door swings open. The guy who steps out, cigarette already hanging from his bottom lip, has the exhausted, fed-up look of a kitchen manager. They pounce on him immediately.

When they walk out of the alley, both of them are employed. Caleb asks Harvey if he wants to celebrate.

"Hell yeah, I want to celebrate," Harvey says, slapping Caleb on the shoulder, then wincing. "Sorry, are you still fried under there?"

"Not too bad," Caleb lies. "What do you want to do? How should we celebrate?"

Harvey grins at him. "By living, man. We celebrate by living."

FIVE MONTHS AGO

1

Edith could tell that Adelaide wasn't ready for labor. She'd been made soft by the world, the way meat can be made soft by honey, and she was completely unprepared for the way her body was about to rage and toil and transform.

But that was fine. She was pure once, and she could be made pure again.

Besides, Edith hadn't been prepared for her first one either. She'd spent most of that pregnancy in denial, refusing to believe that it was really happening, trying to support Dad and save the Cove's garden all at once. She'd spent her time arguing Dad into letting her visit a library on the mainland in order to learn more about growing food, and she hadn't spent any time at all getting ready for what was going to happen to her.

It wasn't the garden's fault that she hadn't prepared herself better. The baby came, as babies do. And it had hurt her—it had hurt her worse than she could have imagined—but she'd loved it.

She'd loved it too hard. That had come with consequences. But that was fine with Edith. *Consequences*, she remembered Dad saying, *are the way a community says I love you.*

Her community loved her very, very much.

She'd returned that love by committing herself to this community, to this garden, to Dad's leadership and guidance. She'd learned how to give up ownership over the things she loved. She ended up saving the garden, too. She'd learned about how the seasons in their part of the world didn't warm up and cool down in predictable patterns anymore. The growing zones had shifted. Their schedule of planting and ripening and harvesting happened on a whole different timeline than it had just a decade earlier. She'd learned to ignore the planting schedules in old almanacs, to read the unruly weather and taste the soil instead. She'd been the one to convince William to bring home a few cats to save their grain stores from the predations of the mice that proliferated in the undergrowth.

She'd learned to reap and share abundance.

No one had starved that year. Things could have been worse. Edith harmed her community by loving that baby so hard, yes—but she'd never once tried to dodge accountability for her actions, and she'd helped contribute to the greater good. She wanted to believe that meant something.

And now, she was determined to earn the trust of her community by doing everything right as often as she could for the rest of her life. Dad would say it was the least she could do.

This project—being good, and doing right—was what found Edith walking down the long road to the water's edge as the shadows of dusk started to weigh Kindred Cove down at the corners.

She gripped a towel that was knotted into a makeshift bundle. Clean, dry clothes were inside, along with a freshly cut aloe leaf wrapped in waxed cloth, just in case. William had told her that Harvey jumped out of the boat a long way off from shore, and Edith didn't know—none of them knew—how large the reef had grown. How close it might be to the surface these days. Sometimes, unpredictably, it would reach toward the island and then retreat, strange clouds of linked polyps drifting tantalizingly close to the land before ebbing away. He'd be in awful shape if he ran into a bloom like that on the long swim back to the island.

She was thinking of the girl as she walked. Adelaide simply wasn't ready to have that baby, but how to get her ready? The baby would come any day. Sunflower oil massages to start. Those were going to be important. Adelaide claimed to have been doing coconut oil massages before she came home, but that coconut oil could have come from anywhere. Sunflower oil from the island, though—that was pure, guaranteed. Edith herself handled the growing and the harvest. She ground the seeds into meal with big rollers, squeezed out the first pressing of oil with her hands, roasted the meal to coax it into giving up even more oil in the second pressing. The leftover meal, when she was done wringing oil out of it, went to Caleb and his chickens. Nothing wasted, nothing lost. Nothing tainted.

Leona, Edith knew, would insist on adding a few flakes of beeswax to the sunflower oil. She'd have things to say about purity of intention, purity of will, purity of effort. That was her style. She was practically religious about it. Edith wouldn't argue with her, though—if Adelaide's undercarriage ended up smelling like a candlestick, so be it. As long as the skin could stretch. That was all that mattered.

Edith made a mental note to check their stores of sunflower oil as she strode to the very end of the road, to where it met the water. The Vetiver was riding high on the island that day. The new pier was deep underwater, far enough down to render it unusable. The reef was growing fast. William's old boat was tied to a tree, since the dock was useless as a mooring point now. Edith could remember how that tree had looked a year ago, when it had been several meters above the waterline. Now, the water licked at the base of the trunk like an unschooled lover.

Edith stood beside the tree, her free hand resting on the taut rope, her eyes on the encroaching water, thinking the one thought that was forbidden to her.

She was thinking about walking in.

She and Dad had done that when they'd first seen the island twenty-five years earlier. He'd taken her by the hand and pulled her after him, laughing. The two of them had waded into the water with all their clothes on. It was still freshwater back then, just ten feet deep at its deepest point. The domes underneath were still dry and intact, supported by the huge white pillars that the mining company had carved out of the salt. The shore had been slick with algae. She could still feel the way the silty bottom of the lake had sucked on her heels as she took her first steps into it.

Dad had looked at her with the light of heaven in his eyes, and he'd said this was the place for them. He was freshly dropped out of seminary school back then, still talking about God and Jesus; he wouldn't leave those two behind for years yet. He'd said he could feel God in the water and a blessing on the land. He'd scooped water up out of the lake with his hands and let it fall onto the part in her hair, and if she hadn't already belonged to him, she would have wanted to belong to him after that day. Every single part of her, forever.

Edith didn't go into the water anymore, though. She hadn't gone into the water for fifteen years. It had started with an argument with Dad the day before the disaster. She'd been harping on and on about the most recent baby she'd birthed. About how much she missed the baby, how much she loved the baby, how she had a special individual claim to the baby. He'd invited her into the closet in the Old House for a period of reflection, and she'd refused. She hadn't wanted to grow.

She'd deserved the consequence he gave her. No bathing—no, he'd said, his face weary with disappointment. Even more than that. No touching the water of the Vetiver at all.

Not until she'd fixed her heart. He'd looked so sad when he said it.

And then, before he could give her permission to go back in, he was gone. The lake collapsed, and he disappeared into the deep dark gullet of the earth below the water. There was nothing for Edith to do—she couldn't get out from under her consequence, not without Dad there to verify that she had, indeed, fixed her heart. Everyone knew about it. They'd been there when he barred her from the water, and they all knew the edict hadn't been lifted. So, with their guidance—with the guidance of the community that loved her and needed her—she'd stayed on land ever since.

She didn't let the water touch her. Even when her feet were hot and she was coated in dust all the way up her calves. Even when her joints ached and her hands were tired from squeezing sunflower meal all afternoon. She didn't walk in, even though her soul itself was parched from fifteen years of bathing with damp rags soaked in captured rainwater, fifteen years of brushing baking soda through her hair, fifteen years of gazing at the lake without knowing the touch of it. She stared down at the glittering surface of the Vetiver, and just like every other day, she accepted that looking was all she'd ever do.

She watched for movement. She listened for a splash. Neither came—but then, from behind her, the sound of a voice.

"Edith! What are you doing down here?"

Edith whipped around to see Adelaide striding down the road, arms swinging, belly improbable. Her stride was confident in a way Edith couldn't pinpoint but couldn't stop noticing. Where had she learned that gait? When had she started tilting her head that way? She'd been home for over a month already and still wore the outside world like a second skin.

"Easy sent me down," Edith replied. She knew she sounded defensive, and that wasn't right, not with Adelaide just asking a simple question. But she didn't like the notion of this girl, with her newly cropped cap of strawberry blond hair and her nose just starting to freckle, being the one to call her to account.

"Anything I can help with?"

There it was—a glance at the towel, perfectly subtle, perfectly friendly, but a glance nonetheless. Everyone on the island, always trying to keep everyone else honest. It was a strength of the community, Edith reminded herself as she shook her head and gestured at the water. It wasn't something to be angry about. "Just waiting. Harvey took a swim, I guess. He's on the way in."

"So Easy sent you to get him?"

"Mm."

Adelaide had a little line between her eyebrows that looked just like the one Dad always used to get when he was listening carefully. "Does Easy seem . . . different to you? These days?"

Edith snorted. "You mean different from the girl who used to make moonshine under the dock and howl about hating it here? Yes, I'd say she's different."

"I don't know what happened," Adelaide murmured.

"She finally grew up while you were away. Must be tough, coming home expecting a mess only to find that your sister cleaned the place up."

"Did she? Clean the place up, I mean? I don't know what she's been doing while I'm gone. I've hardly talked to her. Hell, I feel like I've hardly seen her. She keeps having things to deal with."

"Oh, I'm sure she'll turn up." Edith shook her head. "She always does. Bad penny that way."

Adelaide cocked her head. "What?"

"It's a saying they have out there. You didn't run into it on your travels? A bad penny always turns up? Here I thought you were worldly now."

Adelaide hiked her skirt up past her knees and stepped into the water, letting out a sigh at what Edith imagined to be the cool kiss of it on her sore soles. "You all keep calling me that," she said softly. "Worldly. I suppose I must be. Anyway, nobody uses pennies anymore."

Edith's breath caught in her throat. She had to cough to find her voice. "What?"

"They got rid of them right after I got to the mainland. Some law, or something, I don't know. I guess they were more expensive to have in circulation than they were worth, so the government decided to stop minting them. Everyone was talking about it. They're not considered legal tender anymore."

Edith gripped the bundled-up towel with both hands, gripped it hard enough to feel her wrists groan. She couldn't make sense of why this was such a blow. She hadn't seen a penny in thirty years. She couldn't remember the last time she'd thought about money. *See a penny, pick it up, all day long you'll have good luck*, she thought, the words marching through her thoughts in a grade-school rhythm. *Take a penny, leave a penny. A penny saved is a penny earned.* She couldn't stop. *Pinch your pennies. Penny-wise and pound-foolish.* She could tell, from the sick slam of her heart, that these thoughts were wrong—that they were poison, toxins, microplastics that would embed themselves in her soul forever. She needed to squeeze them out of her mind like oil before they could set. *Penny for your thoughts.*

"The family I stayed with that first year, I guess they handle Kindred Salt nationwide distribution for William? Anyway, they had this huge old glass jug," Adelaide was saying, kicking water toward the horizon so it flew up in a huge glittering arc.

"And it was full of pennies?" Edith's voice sounded distant to her own ears.

Adelaide turned, her mouth an *O* of astonishment. Her hair fell into her eyes. Easy had cut it badly in the front. "Yes! How did you know? That can't be common practice! It's not—it's weird, right? I mean, even before they turned worthless, who wants that many pennies? What's the point?"

"You save them up," Edith said, as a flood of memory threatened to drown her. She found herself, all at once, dragged back to the living room of the apartment she and Leona and William and Dad had shared back before they'd found Kindred Cove, back when Dad was still a seminary student and William was picking pockets in the city center. The carpet was the kind of brown that had once been white, and they'd covered it with pillows because they couldn't afford a couch, and there'd been a big old glass jug in one corner.

She could recall the day they broke that jug with perfect clarity. Dad had been pacing the room talking about his vision for paradise, a perfect haven for people with shared values to labor in intentional community. Leona was sewing a patch onto one of the floor cushions. Edith had her head pillowed on Leona's thigh and was watching the movement of the needle, in and out of the fabric, moving in a half-time rhythm with William. He was rocking steadily on top of Edith, one of her legs slung over his shoulder like a rucksack. He was trying to put a baby into her because of a dream Dad had where she was pregnant and standing on top of a pile of coins. It was a vision, Dad said; as soon as Edith had a baby in her belly, they'd all be blessed with fortune.

She could still hear Dad's voice, the *pop pop pop* of Leona's needle, William's breath coming faster with every thrust. And then maybe she'd kicked out a leg, or maybe William had shoved, or maybe Dad had stumbled—and then the jar was toppling and cracking and there were pennies and glass everywhere.

William finished with a low grunt at the same moment that the jar broke, and Edith could remember thinking at first that the crunch of the glass was coming, somehow, from inside of her.

That jar of pennies wouldn't be worth anything now, she thought. It would just be so much trash.

"Anyway, I thought it was weird," Adelaide said, snapping Edith back into the present. "But Carl, the husband? He loved it. He was always finding pennies on the ground and dropping them in there at the end of the day. He called it art."

That girl sounded so young sometimes, Edith thought. "Well. Was it art?"

"How would I know?"

"Art should make you feel something. Did it make you feel something, looking at that jug full of pennies?"

Adelaide didn't answer. She was shading her eyes with a flat hand, pushing her hair up out of her eyes, squinting out at the water. She took a few steps deeper into the lake until it was up around her thighs, soaking the hem of her skirt. "Is that Harvey?"

"It'd be the right time for him." She could see what Adelaide saw—a dark shape splitting the surface of the water, headed toward the island. The splash of what must have been limbs.

"He's such a slow swimmer," Adelaide muttered. "Do you want help with him?"

"You'd best let me tend to him. I'll tell you if I run into Easy. Go on and see if there's dinner waiting for you anywhere," she added.

Adelaide stepped out of the Vetiver. She smelled of sun and saltwater. "Everyone is feeding me lately. I'm not even that hungry," she said with a soft smile. "No spare room."

Edith reached out and rested a palm low on Adelaide's belly, feeling the weight of the baby, the heft and solidity of it under the skin. "It's not you we're feeding. Nobody's thinking about you at all."

The smile faltered. "Edith. Can I ask you something? About your—you know. About why you don't go into the water?"

"Don't see how I can stop you," Edith said, withdrawing her hand.

"You always wanted your baby, right? That was the reason Dad kept you out of the water. Even all those years later, you wanted it all to yourself, instead of trusting it to the community."

Her, Edith thought, *the baby was a girl. I wanted* her *all to myself.* But aloud, she simply said, "I was selfish."

"That's the thing I'm wondering, though." She glanced out at the water. Harvey was still a long way out, and slowing with every stroke. "I wonder if it's actually wrong to want to be a mother to the baby. To want it to love you better than everyone else."

Edith took a half step back. She didn't do it on purpose. It happened on pure instinct. "Did Easy tell you to ask me that?"

"No. Please don't tell Easy I mentioned it—I just wondered. And I knew I could ask you, because you know so much more than everyone else. I thought you might understand how it feels." She reached out, caught Edith's hand, returned it to her belly. "Right now, this baby is all mine. It's just the two of us in here, you know? Nobody else can feel her move, not the way I can. Is it so wrong for me to love that?"

Edith had never been sure if Adelaide was an ally to her or not. The girl had always been quick to make sure everyone knew when Edith was doing things right—but she was equally quick to make sure everyone knew when Edith was doing things wrong. She'd changed out there in the world, but she couldn't have changed that much. Edith pushed her hand against Adelaide's belly hard, harder, so much harder, until the girl's eyes went wide, until the baby's skull was right up against Edith's palm.

"There," Edith said. "Now I can feel her move, too. Same as you."

"Edith—"

"What you have with her right now? It isn't so special. Your job is to let her grow on her own and then push her out. *Our* job is to make her into the person she's going to be. Together." She stared hard at Adelaide. "Together," she said again, more forcefully this time.

Adelaide pulled away slowly. She nodded, but her eyes were blank. Careful. "Together."

She floated back up the road and didn't look back.

Edith watched her until she was gone.

2

With Adelaide gone, Edith was left to the work of waiting for Harvey. He was taking a long time. She wished he would hurry up, because she could feel, even from where she was standing, the coolness rising off the water. She took a step back to keep herself from being tempted to take a step forward. Fifteen years since she'd been in that water. She wasn't about to break now. Not for anything. Because Edith was steadfast.

That's what Dad said to her on the day of the mine collapse. As the world ended around them, the clear water of the Vetiver vanishing into a bottomless abyss, he'd gripped her head tight, the heels of his hands digging into her temples, his forehead crushed against hers. His last instructions. To help her be good, she knew, even when her heart veered toward the bad. *Be always my steadfast companion.*

And then he stepped into the water, and none of them ever saw him again.

Edith was steadfast. That was why, when Harvey finally made it to the island, she didn't enter the water to help him to shore. She stayed on dry land while he dragged himself laboriously out of the lake with both arms and sprawled out in the dust, gasping. His breaths were coming hard and thick. He kept heaving as if he was about to sob, or maybe about to vomit. His outstretched hand bumped against Edith's ankle.

A drop of cool water trailed down the side of her foot.

She took a step back, then crouched down in front of him. "You made it." He didn't reply. He didn't even look up at her. His shirt clung to him, sodden, and through it she could see the muscles in his back working as he tried to catch his breath. "How do you feel?"

"Grateful," he replied, the word coming out on a ragged exhale.

Edith set down the bundled towel on his back, unfolded it, picked up the dry clothes and the aloe leaf. "There you go. Dry yourself off."

Harvey didn't move to take the towel. He turned his head to one side and laid his cheek on the ground. "I talked to a researcher," he panted.

Edith couldn't stop her eyes from going wide. "You what?"

Harvey's eyes were shut. "He told me to," he continued. "William brought me to shore and told me to tell the researcher about what happened to Sadie." He paused to cough. "I did my best. I think."

"Oh." She struggled to think of an explanation for this. Why would William choose Harvey, of all people? Why would Harvey get to go to shore and talk to an outsider? Why would Harvey be trusted with that kind of thing? Why not someone who had been there from the start, who had followed every single rule but one, who had been loyal and steadfast and earnest and good?

Her eyes landed on the damp hair at Harvey's temple as he coughed and coughed. Edith was gripped by an urge to drive her heel down onto that dip in his skull, to feel the thin bone shatter beneath her calloused skin, to crush the life out of him like pressing oil out of sunflower meal. She knew she could do it. The thought of the damp rich innards of him bathing her dry feet was so tempting that her mouth flooded with saliva. She could make wine out of this man and then throw what remained of him into the Vetiver and no one would ever know. They'd think he was lost to the lake and that would be that.

But if she did that, her feet would get wet. She'd be unable to avoid touching the water that sparkled in his hair, ran down his cheeks, collected in the dip of his philtrum. She'd have to compromise her steadfastness. And then she'd need to find a way to wash his blood away from her skin, and how could she do it without stepping into the cool clean water of the Vetiver?

He coughed one last time and spat thin white mucus onto the dust. The sight of the spreading dark patch it made in the dirt pulled Edith back to herself. She took a deep, slow breath, willing herself steady, and it worked. As the terrible desire to destroy Harvey receded, she found clarity.

The flaw in her thinking was obvious. William hadn't been granting special dispensation to Harvey. He couldn't have been. It would imply that talking to outsiders was something to yearn for, rather than something inherently detrimental to a person's soul.

William hadn't been giving Harvey a treat—he'd been letting Harvey come to harm. He'd been letting Harvey *taint* himself.

That had to mean Easy had very nearly given up on the boy. She wouldn't have let that happen otherwise. The swim, Edith could see now, had been a necessary cleansing—a last-ditch effort at correcting someone who was so rotten inside that he'd mentioned talking to an outsider as though it wasn't something to be ashamed of.

And here she'd come so close to pitying him.

Edith pursed her lips. "Dry yourself off. There might still be supper left by the time you get to the canteen. I'll tell Jessie she should expect you to come take charge of the children again soon. Whenever you decide you want to attend to your responsibilities." She turned away from Harvey, her eyes skipping away from him like pebbles bouncing down the side of the cliff behind the Old House.

"I'll be along shortly," he said. "Thank you, Edith."

She didn't reply. There was nothing to be said to a person like that. She just walked up the road, leaving him in the dust to cough up whatever foulness was in him.

She passed by the canteen without going inside, unable to imagine choking down dinner. Her failure was meal enough for her. How, she wondered, could she still be capable of such incorrect thinking?

She made her way up to the garden and wove her way across it, until she reached the blackberry patch. She stood in front of the thicket of vines, feeling the earth under her feet, willing the roil of shame in her belly to resolve itself into a decision.

She knew she'd been wrong to leave Harvey there, in one piece, a thorn wedging himself under the fingernail of the community. But it would be wrong, too, to break her commitments by touching him. By letting the water on his skin become the water on her skin. By letting his transgression become her own.

"Tell me what to do," she whispered, even though she had no one to ask.

And then she looked down at her feet. They were coated in dust from her walk up the road. She brushed one with the other, knocking the dirt loose to reveal a stripe of clean skin beneath. She'd need to walk through the grass behind the Old House, she thought idly, to get the rest off.

The shame within her crystallized. She remembered herself. She remembered her years of wisdom, of determination, of steadfastness.

She could make herself clean without the Vetiver touching her skin. There were always other ways.

She turned to walk back down the road, toward the shore. Toward Harvey. She was sure the water at his temples would be dry by the time she arrived.

Five Months Ago

William is eating a sandwich.

The wrapper lies on the floor of the passenger side of the car he's in. He will not pick it up before he leaves.

"Please," the researcher in the backseat says. The tarp underneath them crinkles as they try to roll over onto their back. "Don't do this. You don't have to do this."

The sandwich is from a chain restaurant. Their motto emphasizes the freshness of their ingredients. The ingredients aren't that fresh, but that's what William likes about them. Sometimes he gets tired of eating sun-ripened garden-grown hand-picked produce. Sometimes he wants lettuce that doesn't have a faint tack of saltwater clinging to the surface. Sometimes he wants wheat bread, and mustard. There's no mustard at Kindred Cove. Edith won't grow it because she doesn't like the taste. She says it's because she can't properly check for ripeness if she can't taste the produce she harvests, but William is sure that it's just a matter of her not wanting to have to avoid anything that comes out of the kitchen.

"I'll leave. I'll destroy all my research notes and go somewhere else. You'll never hear from me again. I can return the grant money, I—nobody cares about the lake, or about your, ah—"

"Community," William supplies thickly, his mouth full.

"Right. Nobody cares about your community; they won't look into the reef closely enough to find anything. Please, the zip ties are cutting off my circulation, I can't feel my hands, can you at least—"

"Doesn't matter who looks at the reef. Nothing to find," William replies.

There's no meat on the island either, except for chicken, when Caleb sees fit to give one of the old grizzled ones up so everyone can enjoy a stringy stew. William's sandwich has ham on it, and salami, and capicola. Three different kinds of pig. Harvey won't raise pigs on the island, says they're too smart to kill and too hungry to raise for any other reason. William only gets to eat pork when he takes an extended trip away from the island—Leona would be able to smell the meat on him if he came back without taking at least half a day to wash the taste of it away thoroughly enough that her tongue can't taste it on his.

He takes a swig of brown cola from a sweating glass bottle. It's been too long since he's had one of these. He thinks he ought to thank the researcher for reminding him to pick one up. The idea of thanking them leaves his mind as quickly as it enters. He reminds himself to stop and grab a little travel-sized mouthwash on the cab ride back to the island, after he's ditched this car wherever he winds up ditching it. No point getting into a fight with Leona. Not over a sandwich.

"Please," the researcher says again, their voice still muffled by the tarp. They haven't managed to roll over, then. Even babies, William thinks as he finishes the cola, learn how to roll over. "Please. I'll do anything. Please. I have a family."

"Everyone has a family," William replies. He takes the last bite of his sandwich, wipes his hands on the passenger seat, and starts the car.

SALT FESTIVAL

day three | evening

Celia was supposed to be at Candle Hour.

She could remember walking up the path to the chapel. She could remember the way the road had felt a little rougher under her feet than the night before. She'd mentioned it to Leona, who had laughed and said it was because of the salt Celia'd been walking on all day. *Your feet are sensitive because you rubbed them raw. Don't worry, though,* she'd added. *You'll toughen up.*

She remembered the Candle Hour talk, too, in bits and pieces. Caleb, who sat beside Celia at dinner again and refused to answer any questions about where Audrey had gone, had told them all about how True Accountability had changed his life. He'd talked about what it was like to have a community that was really, honestly, constantly invested in his well-being.

Celia had only been half listening, though. She'd been standing near the back of the group of visitors, distracted by the sound of the water against the cliffs. It didn't crash in huge waves, like it would if she were by the sea—but it was still in constant motion, lapping ceaselessly at the rocks, a great hand stroking the contours of the island. Celia felt that motion through her entire body. She'd wanted so badly to run and leap and fall and be consumed.

And now, here she was. At the water. Not at the base of the cliffs, but at the other end of the long road that spooled itself around the island—at the submerged dock. And she could not think of how she'd arrived here.

Celia looked over her shoulder and saw the island road behind her, curving up and away into the trees, the entirety of the Cove strung along its length. There was no clue along that road as to how she'd made it to the shore.

She couldn't remember. Normally, upon finding herself someplace without remembering how she'd gotten there, Celia would be gripped by panic. But there was no panic in her now. She felt the simple peace of finding herself right where she was supposed to be.

When she turned back, Lake Vetiver was stretched out in front of her, the moonlight on the water sparkling with cool invitation. Coming directly toward her, splitting the water down the middle like a blade gliding through the onionskin pages of a Bible, was a boat.

Someone stood at the helm, their hand on the steering wheel. It was too dark to see their face, but Celia thought she could make out Easy's silhouette. She cut the engine, and Celia watched as the little boat slowed until it was drifting. It was the first time she'd seen Easy all day.

Easy lifted a hand in greeting. There was a dull white light attached to it, like a flashlight but near her wrist. Celia waved back, but Easy'd already turned away from her and didn't see. She moved gracelessly, her long limbs stuttering as she bent to grab something from the floor of the boat. She only straightened halfway before tossing it over the side of the boat, where it unfolded into a billowing white tarp.

It caught the moonlight, stark and rippling as the lake itself. The tarp's arc through the air was arrested by a line Celia could just barely make out, which was tethered to the boat. The tarp caught in the air for a moment and then fell, landing on the surface of the water. A scant second later Easy followed it, hurling herself into the water in a dive that was nearly indistinguishable from a fall. The light on her wrist entered the water with her and glowed just below the surface like a distant candle.

Celia wondered if she was dreaming. Maybe she'd passed out at Candle Hour. Maybe nothing she did now had consequences or meaning. She took half a step forward into the water, trying to find certainty in the cool silk of it against her ankles. She gathered up the skirt of her dress in loose fistfuls. She stood with her feet in the water, feeling soft linen between her fingers and warm air on the backs of her knees, watching Easy surface next to the slowly sinking tarp.

She felt like she was floating six inches above the lakebed. Like she was an untethered balloon, drifting out with the current. She'd dreamed of this the night before, she now remembered—not Easy and the tarp, but the water, walking into it. In her dreams she'd stood here, right here, in this dress, with the silt slick beneath her and salt on her tongue.

The dream came back to her all at once, and she could not find anything to distinguish it from what she felt now. Nothing except Easy, whose presence created a kind of noise that couldn't be the product of Celia's dreaming mind.

Easy was, just that moment, flailing for the tarp, splashing and cursing loudly enough for Celia to faintly make out the sound of her voice, but not the specifics of her words. The light went out. She watched with one hand over her mouth, stifling a laugh as Easy shoved the tarp under the surface of the water, pulled it out, shoved it under again. In the darkness she merged with the tarp to form one thrashing creature. The battle went on for several minutes before she swam back to the boat and started the motor again, leaving the now fully submerged tarp in the water, dragging at the end of its tether.

Without consciously deciding to greet Easy, Celia found herself walking along the submerged dock toward where the boat was headed. She didn't know how she'd found her way to that dock, how she knew right where to find the waterlogged boards even without being able to see them.

The water met the middle of her thighs, wrapping around the backs of her knees and slipping between her legs. She dropped her dress and let the fabric float on the surface as she moved. She felt graceful, like she was walking on top of the water instead of cutting through it, until Easy cut the boat's engine again and she could hear the sound of her own splashing. She stopped then, suddenly embarrassed to be wading out to meet someone who hadn't invited her to come closer.

But then Easy called out a greeting. "What are you doing down here? Isn't everyone up at Candle Hour?" She sounded friendly enough, but there was strain in her voice.

"Sorry," Celia said reflexively. "I don't actually know what I'm doing down here. I sort of just . . . I'm just here." She nodded to the tarp, which she could just barely make out billowing underwater next to the boat like an attentive ghost. "I thought you said you all didn't go into the water at night? Isn't it too dangerous? What if you run into the reef?"

"I'm not going to run into the reef. I was just running an errand,"

Easy replied, her eyes on the road behind Celia. "And doing a little laundry." She grabbed a coil of rope from one side of the boat—the painter, Celia remembered from her arrival. She felt useful for remembering.

"Want me to take that?" She held out a hand, and Easy threw the rope to her. Celia barely caught it, her hands clumsy. They both laughed as she clutched the line to her chest to keep it from falling into the water. She eyed Easy's hands and wrists, but couldn't see the source of the light she'd had earlier. "Well, I suppose now that you've given this to me, I should do something with it."

Easy gestured down at the submerged dock below. "You could tie it to a cleat. There's one right next to your foot. I don't think it's a great idea to leave the line in the water for a long time, but this'll do for now."

Celia looked down into the water. She couldn't make out the dock through the dark, shifting water. "I would have to dive down in the dark," she said. "You said not to do that. Remember? At the first Candle Hour?" Part of her was afraid of the prospect. Another, larger, deeper part of her wanted it more than anything—to swim down into the dark water, to feel it close around her like cupped palms.

Easy stared at her for a long time, silent. A loud *crack* sounded from somewhere on the island, followed by distant laughter. Finally, she tilted her head and said, "Right. It would be hard to tie the knot underwater." She sounded disappointed.

"That wasn't—" Celia started to protest, but Easy cut her off.

"Help me haul the boat in," she said, grabbing the opposite line and jumping down out of the boat, onto the submerged dock. "What did you say you were doing down here?"

Together, Celia and Easy hauled the boat toward the shore. "I really don't know. This hasn't happened to me since just after my parents died. I used to find myself in different parts of my house. It's like sleepwalking, but—I'm not asleep. I just can't remember how I ended up where I am. I saw a doctor for it once and she tried to send me to therapy, but I couldn't afford to go."

"Sounds scary."

"Usually, yeah. But not this time. It just sort of felt . . . fine. I thought I was dreaming until I saw you in the water." Close to shore, the two of them stepped off the wood of the dock and onto the muddy bottom of the lake. They started making their way to the black gum tree where William had tied the boat up a few days earlier, their feet slipping in the silt. Celia noticed that the tree, which had previously been just above the water, was now partially submerged.

"So, that sleepwalking-not-sleepwalking thing—that's happening to you here?"

Celia wanted to stop and catch her breath, but Easy was still moving. "Just this one time. I didn't mean to wander off."

Easy made a noncommittal noise from somewhere low in her throat. "Can you untie the tarp? I couldn't get it earlier." She reached up to tie the boat to the gum. "Are you worried you'll get in trouble for leaving Candle Hour? Or are you worried about the fact that you don't remember leaving?"

"Both, I guess."

"Ah, well. Let that all go. You know, sometimes, something deeper than intention speaks through us. Ugh, fuck, I sound like Edith, sorry." Maybe she laughed, or maybe she just cleared her throat, Celia couldn't be sure. "But you know what I mean."

Celia didn't know what Easy meant. She didn't know how to ask. "I would have gone into the water, you know. To tie the boat up," Celia said, pulling at the rope, working on the knot.

"It's okay. Like you said, we don't encourage visitors to swim at night. I forgot that you're just a visitor, that's all."

Something thrilled in Celia's belly at the idea that she didn't seem like the other visitors. She clamped it down, reminded herself that visitors weren't allowed to stay. "If you'd told me to, I would have gone."

"You didn't, though," Easy insisted. Celia heard a splash, felt a tug on her arm. She turned to find Easy standing just behind her. She was close enough that Celia could smell her—sweat and saltwater and something muddy. "But you should have. You have to do things that scare you, Adelaide."

Celia frowned. "What?"

"I said you have to do things that scare you. You're braver than you realize."

"No, I heard that, but—you called me Adelaide."

This time, Easy's laughter was unmistakable. "What? No I didn't. I know your name, Celia." She leaned in so close that Celia could see reflection of moonlight on the water in her pupils. "Are you feeling okay?"

Celia wanted to argue, but she couldn't be sure that she'd heard right. And it didn't matter, did it? Easy thought she was brave. She hadn't acted brave tonight. She turned back to the tangle of rope that affixed the tarp to the cleat on the side of the boat. "Did you tie this knot?" she asked.

"Yeah. I'm . . . I don't really know much about knots, so I just kind of kept going until it seemed like it'd stay put."

"It's a sturdy one for sure." Celia worked at the knot until it finally came loose. She coiled the rope around her forearm, then slid the loops free and turned to hand them over. "What was the tarp for, anyway?"

"It just needed a wash."

"From what?"

Easy gave Celia a hard stare. Without answering, she started to reel the tarp in, dragging it up out of the water and bunching it up in her arms, heedless of the way it was drenching her shirt.

Celia looked down at her own dress and realized that she was soaked, too, the skirt plastered to her legs. She could remember dropping the fabric into the water, could remember the pleasing way it billowed around her as she walked, making her feel like something bigger than herself.

But that decision felt like it belonged to a different Celia, a Celia who hadn't been quite awake yet. She wondered if Easy was right—if something bigger than intention had pulled her down to the water's edge.

She wondered if she really was brave enough to swim down in the dark.

It was beyond late by the time Easy and Celia left the water behind. Celia's bones felt bloated with fatigue. She tried to tally up how much sleep she'd gotten over the previous two nights—or had she been here for three nights? It felt like longer than that, it felt like weeks. She found herself unable to think in hours and minutes. She'd had enough time to dream, at least.

But when they reached the bend in the road that led to their little cabin, Easy caught Celia by the elbow. "Wrong way," she said, guiding Celia straight.

"Oh, I was just going to go to bed," Celia said, but she didn't stop. She didn't turn around and walk away from Easy. It didn't occur to her that she could. "Candle Hour has to be over by now."

"Not tonight. Candle Hour tonight's important. You don't want to miss it." She was a few steps ahead of Celia now, but she looked over her shoulder and the night breeze ran fingers through her hair and the moonlight made a spark in her eye—and for a moment, she looked to Celia like something this island had made just so the land could feel what it was like to have a mouth and two legs. "I don't want you to miss it."

Celia jogged a few paces, caught up, and decided not to feel tired anymore.

The candles were burning low when they arrived at the top of the island. Residents of the island sat in twos and threes and fours on the grass and on the chapel steps. The murmur of their quiet conversations joined the night-sounds of the lake against the cliffs and the insects talking to each other, merging into a low, steady hum that enveloped Celia as she and Easy approached.

They passed Jessie and a clutch of children on the road.

"Off to bed?" Easy asked, not slowing down.

"They don't need to be here for this part. Nona, don't you dare," Jessie added, snapping at a little girl who immediately dropped the rock she was clutching. Jessie turned to walk backward, glaring at the little girl. "Have fun," she added, and Celia realized this was meant for her.

Celia whispered to Easy as they approached the chapel. "What did she mean? Easy?"

Easy steered the two of them around a couple in the grass—Leona, Celia realized, with her head pillowed on William's thigh. His fingers were tracing a line across Leona's collarbone.

As they passed, Leona caught Celia's eye and smiled up at her. "Oh, good. Everyone's been wondering where you are."

Celia couldn't remember the last time there'd been an *everyone* to wonder after her. It hadn't occurred to her that she might be missed, that she might be needed.

Easy gave her a knowing look. "That's community for you. No escaping the watchful eye, and all that. Scary, huh?" She wiggled her eyebrows when she said *scary*, her eyes crinkling with unsuppressed mirth.

She didn't wait for Celia to answer. Which was for the best, Celia thought—because she wasn't scared, not quite, but there was something enormous welling up inside of her that felt like a cousin to fear. She tried to identify it as the two of them walked up the chapel steps together.

By the time they reached the top, she recognized the feeling as desire.

She wanted that watchful eye on her.

She'd wanted it all her life, hadn't she? To be seen, noticed, looked after. For so many years, she'd rattled around inside her parents' empty house like a dry pea in a tin can. She'd lived an unseen life, and it had left her unmoored. Here, she was seen. Every moment, it felt like. She looked behind her, across the dark grass, and she saw a hundred eyes reflecting candlelight. They were looking at her, she felt. They *saw* her.

Inside the chapel, the visitors stood in a circle. Rinna, the reedy woman whose husband had returned to the mainland, was in the middle. She wore a faded cotton dress with large, clumsily stitched pockets, obviously a loan from the island. It was short on her, revealing the way the lowest few inches of her stick-straight thighs ended in sudden lollipop knees.

It occurred to Celia for the first time to worry about this woman, whose flesh stuck tight to her skull, whose husband had seemingly abandoned her, whose bony hands shook now in the center of the circle. She looked scared. She looked starved.

Caleb stood outside the circle of visitors. He spoke in slow, patient tones, his voice infinitely gentle. "Thank you for sharing with us, Rinna," he said. "You've told us what you see when you look at yourself. That took courage and trust. What did it take?"

All around Celia, the other visitors echoed Caleb's words. "Courage and trust."

Easy nudged Celia into the circle and stood beside her. "Courage and trust," she said, her husky voice a second behind the voices of the others. "I'm joining tonight, Caleb. Hope that's okay with you?"

"Of course." Caleb nodded, pacing behind the circle across from them, his face lit by the flickering glow of the candles in the chapel. "We heard you, Rinna. When you look at yourself, you see someone who is out of control. Ugly, cowardly, weak. Alone." He sounded sadder with every item he added to the list.

In the center of the circle, Rinna's shoulders shook. "D-did I say *alone*? I'm not alone. I have Hank."

"I heard *alone*," Caleb replied tenderly. "Because where is Hank now? And besides . . . how could you feel all the rest of that about yourself, if you were loved and supported the way you deserve to be? But we don't have to say you're alone, if you prefer not to."

Rinna wrapped her arms around her midsection. The candlelight cast heavy shadows across her face, sinking her cheeks in even further, hiding her eyes in darkness. Celia breathed in the beeswax-perfumed air in the chapel and wondered if Rinna was right about herself. Was she cowardly? Was she weak?

"No," Rinna said at last. She sounded more certain than Celia had heard her yet. "We should say *alone*. I think that's true. When I look at myself," she said, a little louder, her cadence measured like she was repeating a jump-rope rhyme, "I see someone who is alone."

Caleb spread his arms toward the circle. "Now it's our turn. Let's tell Rinna what we see."

A ripple of movement ran through the visitors in the circle as they joined hands. Celia looked away from Easy. That's what it was—not looking at the woman on her right, not picking a side at random. She was looking away from Easy. She was doing it to prove to herself that she didn't need to look toward her.

She looked away from Easy and took the hand of the woman in the crystal necklace who stood to her left—Celia thought her name started with a *C* or a *K*, and felt ashamed of not knowing for sure. Whatever her name was, she gave Celia a tight-lipped smile and kept her fingers cupped, holding space between their palms.

When Celia looked the other way, she found Easy already watching her, wearing a knowing half smile. She reached out and threaded her fingers between Celia's. They fit together perfectly. Her warm, dry, rough thumb traced a figure eight across Celia's knuckle.

And then, on the other side of the circle, the remaining of the two brothers spoke. "When I look at Rinna," he said slowly, "I see someone who is brave."

Caleb was nodding. "That's true, Mitchell. What's braver than sharing your truth with your community? Rinna gave us her truest self today. When I look at Rinna, I see someone who is brave."

"I see someone who is so brave," Easy said, pulling her gaze away from Celia a second after she started to speak. She squeezed Celia's fingers, just barely, just for a second. "Rinna, I remember how worried you were when Hank left. You told me you didn't know if you could do this alone. But when I look at you right now, I see someone who is brave. And strong."

The woman on Celia's other side spoke up. "So strong. I saw Rinna carry a basket of salt that I probably couldn't have lifted on my own, and she didn't even make it look hard."

Caleb cleared his throat. "That's wonderful, Kristen. Do you mind saying the whole thing?"

"Oh, right. Sorry." Kristen's hand was slack in Celia's. "When I look at Rinna, I see someone who is strong."

"I see someone who is beautiful," Celia said. The words floated up out of her like rising bubbles. She didn't know where they were coming from, what was making her say them. Did she think Rinna was beautiful? She wasn't sure. But Caleb had said that this woman saw herself as ugly, and Celia wanted to answer that. She wanted to fix it. "Rinna, you have such gorgeous hair, and your skin glows. You're elegant and striking. When I look at you, I see beauty." It became true to Celia as she said it. She saw it in her mind—Rinna walking into the lake, the sun on her shoulders, the breeze in her hair, the delicate flutter of her hands over the surface of the water. Rinna was beautiful. She was.

"I see someone who is beautiful," Easy echoed, and then it went around the circle—everyone agreeing that Rinna, whippet-thin Rinna, lonely, cowardly Rinna, was beautiful. Then they all agreed on her strength, and her courage. Finally, Caleb raised his arms again, like he was going to embrace the entire circle, and he said, "I see someone who is not alone."

Rinna was sobbing by now. She was curled over herself like a fiddlehead, her neck bowed, her shoulders heaving. She choked on every other breath.

"That's what I see. I see someone who is not alone," Caleb repeated. He was behind Celia now, and he reached between her and Kristen, lifting a hand toward Rinna. Easy dropped Celia's hand and copied him, stretching her fingers forward.

Celia reached, too. She was reaching for Rinna, and she was reaching for Easy's hand, and together, the two of them met Caleb at Rinna's bony shoulders. The circle closed in until all their overlapping hands rested on the weeping woman. Easy was pressed against Celia, the warm length of her body steady as an underwater tie beam. Celia leaned into her.

"I see someone who is not alone," Celia said.

And then, through her tears, Rinna spoke. "I am beautiful." The words came out thick and slow, like she was speaking around a swollen tongue. "I am strong. I am brave." She lifted her hands, finding the overlapping hands of the other visitors and pressing her shaking palms to them. "I am not alone."

Celia could not tell her hands from the others that supported Rinna. She couldn't feel herself as something separate from the tight press of limbs that the group had formed. She thought, *I am not alone*, and the thought was hers, and the thought was Rinna's, and the thought was Easy's, and the thought belonged to all of them at once. It belonged to the warmth of their bodies and the heat of their tears and the flicker of the candlelight that lit their faces as they pressed in around a woman who had, as they all watched, become beautiful.

The group melted apart again after several minutes. Caleb put an arm around Rinna's shoulders and suggested that everyone take a break. "We'll meet back here in ten minutes," he said. "Go get a little air. You're all doing amazing work tonight."

Celia walked out of the chapel, her whole body buzzing. As she passed the group under the apple tree, she thought she heard a soft sigh, a low murmur. She didn't look at the people there—didn't want to see the moment they were sharing, didn't want to feel the absence of warm skin against her own—but a slow heat climbed her throat. She flexed the fingers of her left hand, thought of Easy's palm flush against hers. She pressed her tongue against the inside of her lower lip and felt how soft her own flesh was.

There was a light inside the Old House.

Celia blinked at it, frozen. It grew brighter as she watched, then abruptly disappeared. She looked back toward the chapel and saw, clearly, the silhouette of Easy's lanky form next to Rinna's spindly one.

She remembered the light that had been in the house the night before, when she'd been trying so hard to listen to Easy. She remembered Easy, at some point, saying that she lived there with someone. The light could be that person, whoever they were. Or—she dared herself to think it—the light could be Adelaide.

Celia hesitated. She wasn't needed here, not now. Not while Rinna was still recovering from her time in the center of the circle. Nobody would miss Celia if she stepped away for a few minutes.

And if they did—well. Then she'd know she was missable.

It would be fine, she told herself as she slipped into the darkness between the chapel and the Old House. She'd just go and check. It would only take a moment.

The Old House looked smaller inside than it had the day before, when Easy had brought Celia into the kitchen. Then, the place had felt as enormous as the caverns of loneliness and longing where Celia had been living for all these years. She'd sobbed on the kitchen floor, and the Old House had seemed to grow around her, reflecting the way grief made her shrink into a small bead of pain.

Now, moonlight poured through the kitchen windows and marbled the shadowy hallway with streaks of gray. The dark door at the end of the hall was brightly outlined by the warm glow of whatever candles were burning on the other side. The house was a matchbox made of light and shadow. Celia felt that she would barely fit inside of it.

She shut the front door of the house behind her as quietly as she could. With that act—an attempt to remain silent, to pass unnoticed—she felt herself teeter on the brink of acknowledging that she was not here just to try to see Adelaide.

She was intruding into Easy's home. Into Easy's life. Seeing the world Easy inhabited every day.

Celia eyed the bright door at the opposite end of the hall. There was no sound from inside. It was a beacon. It was her obvious destination. She'd come to the house because of the light she'd seen in the window. She should follow the light now. If Adelaide was anywhere in this house, she'd be behind that door.

But there were other doors in the hall. Closed ones, hiding rooms Celia hadn't seen into when Easy brought her to the house before. Doors behind which Easy and Adelaide lived their lives.

Outside, Celia could hear the yowl of two cats fighting. Or maybe they were mating. She couldn't tell the difference.

She reminded herself that she did *want* to see Adelaide. That she would be glad if Adelaide was in the house to be seen. Besides, Celia had been in the house the day before, at Easy's invitation. She hadn't been told not to come back.

Celia kept the door at the end of the hall in her periphery as she carefully opened one of those closed white doors. She told herself that she was saving the bright door for last—not avoiding it, but holding it aside until she was sure that she was ready for it. She told herself this and she told herself that she believed it, and the belief nested inside of itself neatly enough that she felt it could be true.

Behind the closed white door, there was a bedroom with nearly the same layout as the cabin Celia shared with Easy. Instead of a single bunk bed, there were twin beds pushed to opposite walls. There was a writing desk, a small cedar chest, a closet with no doors on it. A uniquely human smell hung in the air—sleep-sweat and body oil. Celia slipped into the bedroom. She closed the door behind her, then shut her eyes tight, waiting for them to adjust to this new darkness. When she opened her eyes again, she could make out the shapes of the furniture, the contours of the space.

She stood at the foot of one of the beds and trailed her fingers across the bedsheets. Then she turned, reached into the closet, and grabbed the first thing she touched. It was a white linen dress, not very different from the one she was wearing, other than the color. The fabric was thin and soft with wear. It wasn't something Celia could picture Easy in—Celia had only ever seen her wearing wide-legged trousers with deep pockets, collared shirts with missing buttons, holey sweaters with patched elbows. This dress, Celia thought, must belong to Adelaide.

Celia pressed the fabric between her palms, feeling the warmth of her own skin through the weave.

A noise came from the hall—the sound of the front door opening, and then footsteps. It startled Celia enough that she dropped the dress. It fluttered across her feet. The footsteps in the hall passed the bedroom she was in. She bent quickly and scooped up the white dress, balling it in her fists. She looked to the closet, to the space beneath the beds.

Everywhere was too small. If she could hear the person in the hall moving, they'd be able to hear her trying to hide. There was nothing she could do.

She froze where she was and waited to get caught.

She heard a voice in the hall, on the other side of the bedroom door. It was soft and low and so close by. "Celia?" It was Easy. "Are you in here?"

Then came a few more footsteps, and the click of another door opening. Light poured through the crack under the bedroom door. Easy had opened the bright door at the end of the hall. Celia held her breath, watching her new, long shadow stretch across the bed in front of her.

"Has anyone been in here?" Easy said. A second voice answered her in words Celia couldn't make out. "Are you sure? You didn't see anyone?" Another muffled reply. "Okay. You're doing good work. Keep it up. I'll see you in the morning."

There was the click of the door closing, and the light from the hall vanished. Celia blinked hard in the sudden darkness, looked down at the wadded-up dress in her hands, gripped it a little tighter. Curled her toes and clenched her jaw. It would happen now, she thought. It would happen any moment.

But Easy didn't come into the bedroom. She walked right by it. She went into the kitchen, where she lingered for a minute, not saying anything, not doing anything Celia could hear. It was as though she was just standing there in the darkness, feeling the smallness of the house alongside Celia. Celia had her back to the bedroom door, and she wondered if Easy had her back to the kitchen doorway—if she was holding her breath too. Listening with the same intensity. Waiting.

And then there was movement again. The clear sound of Easy leaving the kitchen, then walking down the hall to the front door. Celia listened as the front door opened and then closed again. She heard the front steps creak in quick succession under Easy's footfalls.

That was it. Easy was gone. She hadn't come into the bedroom. Celia hadn't been discovered.

She pressed the dress to her mouth and inhaled deeply. It smelled like nothing. Her head swam. She should leave this house. Quit while she was still ahead.

But there was still that bright door. Easy had been talking to whoever was in there.

Adelaide. It had to be.

And if she didn't go and find out, then there would be no reason for her to have come into the house in the first place. She gripped the idea that she'd come here to find Adelaide even tighter, now that she'd escaped discovery. She needed to have been in the Old House for something other than the sight of Easy's bedroom, the feel of Easy's sheets, the smell of Easy's skin.

Celia stepped out into the hall. She still held the white dress. She didn't want to put it back. It felt like hers. The smell of beeswax was strong in the hall, almost oppressive. She opened her mouth and felt the sweetness of it coat her tongue as she made her way to the bright door.

The unpainted wood was warm under her touch.

She heard a shifting of weight inside. A rustling. Someone was on the other side.

Celia licked her lips. "Adelaide?" she whispered.

There was no reply.

She dropped the dress and then tried again, a little louder. "Adelaide, are you in here?" When there was still no answer, she decided that she was wasting time. She could find out the answer for herself. She let her hand fall to the doorknob.

"Don't." The answer came from behind the door. "Don't open the door. Please."

Celia froze. The voice was not Adelaide's, but it was familiar. She pressed her cheek to the warm, dark wood. ". . . Audrey?"

"Leave. I mean it. Go now."

"What are you doing? What's in there?" Celia couldn't imagine the room behind the door. She pictured a sprawling ballroom; she pictured a screened-in three-season room; she pictured a closet barely big enough to turn around in. "Are you . . . trapped?"

Audrey laughed. It sounded like she was right up against the other side of the door. Like her lips were against Celia's ear. "I'm going to see my daughter. Do you understand? Mackenzie is here and I'm going to see her. Do not fuck this up for me."

Celia recoiled from the door. Audrey's voice was as cold as a slap. "Where is she?"

"If I knew that, do you think I'd be doing their fucking exercises?" Another brittle laugh from the other side of the door. "They're going to take me to her. All I have to do is prove that I can stay here. Permanently."

Envy surged up in Celia, bright and hot and stinging. "But they don't let people—"

"You have to leave. If they catch you here, they'll think we're together somehow, and—"

"Is Adelaide in there with you?" She put her hand on the doorknob again. "Can I talk to her? Or see her? It's important."

"The only person in here with me is me. Now leave me alone so I can do the work. Go. I mean it."

Celia's fingers flexed around the doorknob. She wanted to open it—and then what? Her curiosity would be satisfied. But then she'd have to face Audrey's anger, and the dark house would fill up with the light from behind that door.

She could almost feel the wood flexing with the buildup of both, Audrey's determination and that bright warm fog of light. The two were inseparable in Celia's mind. Audrey bright and burning, the light furious.

"If you open that door," Audrey said slowly, "Easy will know."

Celia backed away from the door. She didn't have to think about it. Audrey's words pushed her as firmly as an open palm to the chest. "Okay," she said, lifting her fingers away from the knob. "I won't get in the way. I hope you get to see your daughter soon."

The only answer from behind the door was the creak of the floorboards settling.

Celia left. She passed the dark kitchen with its streaks of moonlight, and she made her way to the front door, and she eased it open and slid outside. She stood there for a moment, her back against the front door of the Old House, the salt air cold against her cheeks.

She heard voices at the chapel. A bright chime of laughter. She tripped down the front steps of the Old House fast, trying to distance herself from that bright door, from the hallway, from the bedroom. Only once she got to the lawn between the Old House and the chapel did she slow her pace. The grass was damp with fresh dew, slick underfoot. Celia looked up at the sky and saw fewer stars than before. She wondered how long it would be until dawn.

A bright call from the chapel—Rinna, standing on the broad steps, one skeletal arm raised high. "Celia! There you are! Come on, everyone's waiting!"

Celia jogged to the chapel, passing the flattened patches of grass where people had been sitting when she'd come this way before. Leona and William were gone. Everyone was gone, more or less, except for the visitors. The candles, burning low now, cast just enough light for Celia to see that Easy was still inside the chapel, watching her approach.

Their eyes caught. Celia met Easy's searching gaze with what she hoped was an open, relaxed smile. "Sorry to hold everyone up."

"There you are," Caleb said, his eyes crinkling with warm relief. "We've been looking for you. Is everything okay?"

Celia walked up the chapel steps. As she reached the top step, she realized that she'd left Adelaide's dress balled up on the floor in front of the closet. It was still there, lying where she'd dropped it, damp with the sweat of her palms. As obvious as a handprint on a pane of glass.

She stutter-stepped across the chapel threshold. The eyes of all the other visitors were on her. Easy was watching her. Caleb was watching her. The candles flickered at her feet, their warmth steaming the dew off her ankles.

It was too late to go back now. There was nothing she could do.

So she made a blank space in her mind where the dress should go, and she held that blankness steady as she entered the chapel.

She stepped into the center of the circle. "Sorry. I'm here now. I'm ready."

Caleb clapped his hands. “Let’s begin. Celia, tell us who you are.”

Celia didn’t know what to do with her hands. She didn’t want to cross her arms. She folded her fingers together in front of her, then caught Easy’s knowing smirk and let them fall to her sides instead. “I’m Celia. I live in Belleville, just outside St. Louis. I’m thirty-f—”

“None of that,” Caleb interrupted. “Those are all little details. Things you imagine define you. But they don’t, do they? If we took away your age, and the city you live in, and your name, you’d still be yourself. Wouldn’t you?”

“I think so,” she said. She realized that she couldn’t see everyone in the circle. No matter which way she turned, there would always be someone out of sight, looking at her. Seeing her fidget.

“What if we changed your name to, I don’t know. Linda. Or George. Or Pinecone.” A little ripple of laughter across the circle. “Who would that person be? Who would you see when you looked at them?” Celia forced herself to smile, as though there was nothing frightening about the idea of losing her own name.

She caught Easy’s eye again.

Easy’s eyes crinkled at the corners. She cocked her head. Then, with perfect clarity, while holding Celia’s gaze, she mouthed the name *Adelaide.*

It ran through Celia like an electric current. Her name peeled away from her like a bent-back fingernail—still attached, but suddenly searingly loose.

Because what if she was Adelaide, instead?

What if she wore taped-up shoes and wondered at other people’s sadness, and wore her hair long down her back and walked through the world with an ease and amazement that shouldn't belong together but somehow, inexplicably, did?

Then who would she be?

Would she be someone who could have the things Celia couldn't seem to manage?

She knew it wasn't true. A change of name wouldn't make her into a different person. That was the whole point of Caleb's question. Still, Easy's trick had worked. Now that the idea of *Celia* felt like something she could part with, she could see herself more clearly. She looked down at her hands, at the raw cut on her thumb. At her bare feet on the floor. A blade of grass was stuck to one of her ankles. She swallowed, cleared her throat, began.

"If I looked at that person, I'd see someone who has always been sad. Who is always sad," she said.

Caleb was walking behind Rinna. "Good. Keep it in the present, not the past. Who you are, not who you've been. Keep going."

Celia thought. "I'd see someone who can never seem to make anything work. I'd see someone who tries really hard, but who can't—sorry. I don't know how to say this without sounding negative."

"It's okay," Rinna said. "Keep going." Celia looked at her with surprise. She wore a glowing smile. It was the first time Celia had seen Rinna smile like that since their arrival on the island.

"I'd see someone who tries really hard but always seems to fail. If I looked at myself the way you're asking, I'd see a failure." The words boiled their way out of her, scalding. They felt clean. They felt true. She didn't meet anyone's eye. She didn't want to see them seeing her, didn't want to see them agreeing with her. "I'd see someone who doesn't know who she is, and doesn't know how to find out who she is."

"What else?" Caleb asked. "There's something you're holding back."

She clenched her hands into fists, then forced her fists open again. She wished she was still holding that white dress. "I don't, um. I don't think so. I can't think of more."

"No? If you looked at yourself as Pinecone, or George"—*Adelaide*, Celia thought, the name a whisper even inside her own mind—"all you'd see is someone who's sad, tries hard, is a failure, and doesn't know herself? That's it?"

"I'm thinking."

"You're holding back, Celia," Caleb said again. "Did you come here to keep holding yourself back? Is that why you sent that letter asking to be allowed to come to our island?"

Celia shook her head. "No, I—"

"The letter said you were lonely," Easy said softly.

Celia looked up then. She looked at Easy. The candlelight flickered in Easy's eyes like a question, and Celia wanted so badly to give the right answer. She shook her head, not to deny but because she felt lost and desperately wanted Easy to give her another clue.

"The letter said you had no one," Easy said. Celia heard someone behind her let out a little gasp. Kristen, maybe. "The letter said you needed our help."

"When I look at myself," Celia ventured. "When I see myself . . . I see someone with no real friends." Her eyes swam. She didn't want to have said that. She wanted to have said something different. Something less true.

Easy nodded encouragingly. On the other side of the circle, Caleb spoke again. "More. Tell us the rest. Come on, Celia. You can do this."

Celia closed her eyes, but she could still feel the heat of Easy's gaze on her. She lifted her hands to the back of her neck, stroked the fine hair there the way her mother had back when she was still alive and Celia was still a child who had a future ahead of her. She dropped her head forward and let the tears that pushed their way past her lashes fall to the floor at her feet. "I'd see someone with no family," she whispered.

"I didn't hear her," Kristen said. "We can't hear you."

"I'd see someone with no family," Celia said again, louder. "I'd see someone who doesn't have a family. I'd see someone who doesn't have a mother or a father or any siblings or aunts or uncles, or cousins or grandparents. I'd see someone whose family all died, who can't make a new family. I'd see someone who will never be a daughter to anyone, or a sister, or a mother. That's what I said, Kristen." She spat Kristen's name, like her aloneness was Kristen's doing. "I said I'd see someone with no fucking family, okay?"

"Okay," Kristen muttered. She sounded stung.

"That's good," Caleb said. His voice came from the same direction as Kristen's, and Celia could picture him resting a soothing hand on her shoulder, smiling at her. "That kind of emotion is healthy. It means you're getting to something real. Thank you for helping Celia pull that out of herself, Kristen."

Celia forced herself to open her eyes. Her skin felt as hot as a rash. She wanted to apologize. She wanted to claw Kristen's throat with her fingernails. She said nothing. She held herself perfectly still. Tears ran freely over her cheeks and down the front of her throat, soaking into the neckline of her borrowed dress.

"Thank you for sharing with us, Celia," he continued. "You've told us what you see when you look at yourself. That took courage and trust. What did it take?"

The entire circle echoed Caleb's words. "Courage and trust." It stung like antiseptic in a wound.

"Celia told us that when she looks at herself, she sees someone who is always sad. Grieving, maybe?" Caleb didn't wait for Celia to confirm this. "She said she sees someone who tries hard, so hard, but doesn't get results. She sees a failure who doesn't know herself. She sees someone who doesn't have friends or a family. She sees someone who is alone."

Celia couldn't seem to stop the tears. She was mortified to feel her chest heave, to hear herself gasp for breath on a sudden sob. Hearing Caleb repeat it all back made it feel even more true than when she'd said the words herself in the first place.

"Now, it's our turn. Let's tell Celia what we see."

Kristen spoke first. "I see someone who goes after what she wants."

Celia turned to face Kristen for the first time since stepping into the center of the circle. "What?"

"Now is a time to listen to your community," Caleb said gently. "Kristen is telling you what she sees."

"But—"

"I see someone," Kristen interrupted, her brow tight, "who goes after what she wants. I saw you getting in line to get on the boat, when we were coming here, and you looked like you'd clock anyone who tried to keep you away from the island."

Celia covered her mouth to hide her startled laughter. She didn't remember Kristen from the mainland. She didn't remember waiting in line. She just remembered thinking, over and over again, *This will work. This has to work.*

"I see someone who is joyful." This from Rinna. "You have a beautiful laugh, Celia."

"I see someone who is joyful," the remaining brother, Mitchell, echoed.

"I see someone who is joyful, too," Caleb said. "Anyone else?"

"I see a generous, thoughtful friend," Easy chimed in. "I've been spending a lot of time with Celia, and I've known her to be caring and kind, and hardworking, and honest. I can't imagine better qualities in a friend. Can any of you?"

A murmur of agreement from the circle. Celia slowly turned to look at all of them. The candles around the edge of the room were guttering now. Everyone's face was deep in shadow, so she couldn't read their expressions at all. She listened to their voices, though, and didn't hear a lie in any of them.

"I see a friend." The refrain traveled around the circle, one person at a time, until everyone had said it, even Caleb.

Celia had stopped crying for a moment when Kristen had startled her, but the tears were back in force now. She wrapped her arms around herself and bent her head, and she knew in some distant part of her mind that this was the same way Rinna had stood when it was her turn in the center, curled in on herself like there was something to protect in the middle of her chest. The place that Celia was curled around was the place where her grief lived—where that hard, awful seed of pain sometimes tried to push its way out of her, when she felt the most alone and the most hopeless. It hurt now, but the hurt felt different, like a wound being irrigated.

The pain doubled when Easy spoke again. "I see a mother."

This time, even Caleb slipped. "You see—a mother? I mean, yes, Easy sees a mother."

"Look at me. Hey." Easy's voice was low, a murmur that was as good as a fingertip under Celia's chin. "Come on. Adelaide, look at me."

Celia looked up then, her eyes filling with hot tears, her hands tightening into fists. She'd heard right, hadn't she? But when she met Easy's face, there was no hint that Easy had called her by any name at all, much less the wrong one.

"I see a mother," Easy said again, her eyes wide and brimming, her lips twitching up in a sweet smile. "I see someone who is made to nurture and care for others. I see someone who gives of herself tirelessly, even knowing that she might not get to see the results she's been dreaming of." She kept her hand low as she reached toward Celia. She extended her pinky finger, and gently, slowly, she nudged it into the curl of Celia's palm, until her smallest finger was snug inside the warm cave of Celia's fist. "I see someone who can be strong and gentle at the same time, who would die for the people she loves. I see someone who will sacrifice everything if she needs to. I see someone who doesn't get distracted by other people's toxic attachments to privacy and individuality. I see a mother," she said again, her voice thick with emotion. "Even if you never birth a child of your own, Celia. I see a mother in you."

Celia buckled. She folded forward, and her knees went loose beneath her. But before she could topple, Easy's hand was on her shoulder, holding her upright. Then another hand landed on her other shoulder. Then Kristen's hands on her back, and Rinna's, on her arms, and Caleb's, and so many other hands keeping her standing. She sobbed, her mouth falling open, an animal noise ripping its way out of her throat. *A mother*, Easy had said, and Celia thought she understood what Easy was telling her, but then Easy's lips were on her ear and Easy's voice was giving her even more.

"You are the opposite of alone. You never have to feel that way again. You're a mother, Adelaide. Be what you are. Be a mother." Then, for everyone, she raised her voice and said, "Together."

"Together," they repeated. "Together. Together. Together." The word ran through the circle, pulsed with the flicker of the guttering candles, vibrated through Celia in wave after wave. "Together."

Celia wept, leaning into the steady hands of the circle that supported her, and she didn't care that Easy had called her Adelaide again. It didn't matter. All that mattered was that Easy was right.

She was right.

She had to be right.

By the time the visitors were headed back to their cabins, the sky was beginning to lighten into predawn gray. Celia walked down the road beside Easy. She felt scoured clean inside.

"So," Easy said, her voice balancing on the edge of a laugh. "Told you that wasn't a night you'd want to miss. Was I right?"

Celia stepped around a camel cricket in the road. "I'm glad I went with you. It was a lot, though."

"It's an intense one, for sure. That was Caleb's first time leading it. I think he did a good job."

A laugh rang out from somewhere deep in the trees. Celia looked up at the sky, trying to find any remaining stars. "He did really good."

"So did you. I was really impressed by your honesty. A lot of people can't dig that deep, you know? You weren't there, but Kristen said that when she looks at herself, she sees a 'future entrepreneur.'"

"Seriously?"

"Seriously!" Easy cackled. "You missed it while you were snooping around in my house."

Celia's dress stuck fast to her skin. Her hair was cold against the back of her neck. It seemed impossible, but she'd forgotten about her trespass. It felt like a lifetime ago. She tried to sound playful and failed. "Am I in some kind of trouble?"

Easy reached up to tug on the end of a low-hanging branch. "Being in trouble is a made-up idea, Celia. That's punishment talking." She let the branch go and it snapped away from her, swinging up high, shaking loose a shower of leaves. "All we do here is care for each other. You demonstrated a lot of care tonight. Don't think I didn't notice. You cared for Adelaide enough to keep looking for her, even though you thought it could have gotten you in, as you put it, 'trouble.'"

Something inside of Celia uncurled. "I guess I just want to make sure she's okay. Is she okay?"

"What a question. What does 'being okay' mean? Are you asking if she's safe? Happy? Well loved?"

"All of it, I guess?"

"Mmm. I don't think that's what you mean. You're not worried about whether she's safe," Easy said. She stretched her arms high, then let them drop until her hands rested on the back of her head, her elbows splayed wide. She scrunched up her nose, like she was untangling a thorny question. "You didn't send police to come looking for her. You didn't bring anyone with you. I'd wager that you didn't even tell anyone you were coming here, did you? So you're not here on a rescue mission. Not to keep saying the same shit over and over, but—you're here because you care. Right?"

"Of course. I don't think she's in danger, I mean. I can't imagine you . . . hurting her," Celia said. She was mortified to even have to say this to Easy, to have to clarify. She tried to make it into a joke again. "It's not like you're some kind of monster."

Easy grinned. "Gee, thanks. But I don't think we're dealing with an 'of course' situation, here. You're unique, Celia. You handled this in a way nobody else would. People out there in the world don't care for each other the way you care. They make each other face life alone. You've seen it, haven't you? The way everyone has convinced themselves that they have no choice but to be selfish, to abandon each other."

Celia felt herself nodding. "Sure."

"You've never really felt like you fit in with that kind of life," Easy said. There was no question to it, no uncertainty at all—she said it like she might say *you have dark hair* or *there's something on your shirt*. "You care about people, and sometimes you worry that you care about them too much. You worry that you're obsessed with other people. You worry that you're crazy."

Celia glanced at Easy, startled. Had she really shared all that? She couldn't remember everything she'd said over the course of the past few days.

Easy slid her eyes sideways to meet Celia's. "It's not just you," she said. "Everyone here feels the same way."

Their cabin was just ahead of them. The door hung wide. Celia found herself slowing, reluctant to go inside just yet.

"We all care for each other," Easy went on, "in ways that I think the rest of the world would call strange. Because we put each other first." She stopped in front of the cabin, traced the letters on the sign with her fingertips. "We put the community first. I get the feeling you can relate to that mindset."

Celia nodded again. She could still feel the weight of what Easy had said inside the circle. *I see a mother.* "I can."

"I'm impressed by you," Easy said. "Most of the time, people like you are afraid of the thing they need most. But you—you seem brave enough to let it in."

She didn't know what to say to that. She didn't know what she was supposed to be letting in. They stood there in the first light of morning, in front of their cabin, staring at each other. Studying each other.

After a moment, Easy continued. "You came here for Adelaide," she mused. Her eyes dropped, following the movements of her fingers as they dipped and curled through the curves of the word *Grey*. "And you came here to try to have a baby. But you've been doing so much more than you thought you could. I've seen it in you. You've been growing."

Celia didn't know how to answer. After a long stretch of silence she simply said, "I think so. Yes."

Easy's index finger settled in the nock of the *s* in *House*. "Celia, may I risk overstepping?"

Celia nodded.

Easy stepped closer to her. Lifted a lock of her hair from her shoulder. "You came to Kindred Cove looking for one thing, but I think you've found something else entirely. I think you've found something greater than yourself. And that's saying something, because I don't think I've ever seen anyone who understands our work here at the Cove quite like you do."

She felt herself pulling in toward Easy. She only meant to exhale, but a word came out of her instead. "Really?"

"Really." Easy looked down at her with soft, serious eyes, then gave the sign a final, gentle tap. "I'll bet you're exhausted. Should we head inside?"

Celia walked into the cabin ahead of Easy on trembling legs. As she climbed into the lower bunk, she stuck her fingers in her mouth, tasted the lingering salt on her skin and the raw metallic flesh-taste of the healing wound on her thumb. Easy pulled herself up into the top bunk, and a moment later, her shirt and trousers fell to the floor beside the bed.

Celia only hesitated a moment before tugging her own dress off over her head. She wanted a clean one, she thought, in the morning. Not any of the clothes she'd brought with her. She would ask to borrow another. To borrow the white one she'd left on the floor of the Old House, maybe.

She could do that. She was brave. She was someone who went after what she wanted. Everyone said so.

With her eyes closed, Celia tried to go over the day in her mind. Starting when she'd woken alone in this same bed, with thoughts of Easy and the lake making her legs tremble. As she tried to remember what Edith had said about action and intention, she found her thoughts returning, over and over again, to the water. She wanted to hang on to everything she'd learned. But she couldn't make herself focus—not with the way the water rocked and rose against the island, relentless and all-consuming. She wanted to repeat Caleb's words like a mantra, but then there was the moonlight on the surface of the lake, and the smell of cold brine on the air. There was the sting of Audrey's fervent anger behind that door—but then there was the gentle tug of the water against her thighs when she'd walked out onto the dock in the dark. How it had pulled at her. How it had wanted her.

It was only when she woke with the warmth of a sunbeam falling across her pillow that she realized she'd fallen asleep in the first place. She could hear Easy softly breathing above her. She realized that the two of them had never bothered to close the door.

As she slid out of bed and stood with the sun on her bare skin, she found that she didn't mind the open door after all.

PART FOUR

trust is a choice

SALT FESTIVAL

day four | morning

Celia surprised herself by waking Easy up to ask about the white dress.

She had planned to wait—had planned to wear her own clothes, if a little reluctantly, until she worked up the courage to ask if the two of them could go back to the Old House and retrieve the dress from where Celia had left it balled up on the floor. But when she crouched next to her bunk, still nude, and reached under her bed to pull out her duffel, she realized that she didn't want to wait. She was only waiting because she thought she had to.

Everyone had seen courage in her. She decided to be the person they saw. She decided to be brave.

She stood and rose to her tiptoes so she could rest her chin on the edge of Easy's mattress. Easy slept in a tangle, the bedsheet crumpled into one long rope that snared around her long, loose limbs. Her lips were parted just enough that Celia could see the shell-white glint of her front teeth. Under the thin membrane of her eyelids, her pupils roamed, tracking something in a dream.

Celia stared for a few long seconds, trying to decide how to wake Easy up without startling her. But before she could make her decision, Easy's eyes snapped open. Her voice came out in a sleep-slurred rasp. "Were you watching me sleep?"

Celia shifted her weight between the balls of her feet. "Kind of. Only for a second though. I wanted to know—"

"Hang on. I just woke up, I'm not smart enough for questions yet." Easy pushed herself upright, shucking the coils of bedsheet like a snake shedding. Her shoulders were roped with muscle. A stark white scar ran down the center of her left breast, slicing across the nipple. A matching one scored her right flank, tracing a bright path all the way from her hipbone to the dark thatch of hair between her legs. There were three moles on the outside of her left thigh, all in a row.

Celia drank in this new knowledge of Easy's body. When she looked back up, Easy was watching her with an expression she couldn't read. "Sorry," Celia said automatically.

"For waking me up? Don't worry about it, I probably overslept anyway," Easy said, dismissing Celia's embarrassment with the generous ease of a landlord forgiving a renter's late fee. She swung her legs toward Celia and slithered down out of the bunk, letting her body stretch languidly as she went. Celia did not watch, and flushed at the knowledge that not-watching was difficult. "Do you want to get dressed and head to the canteen? We're not scheduled this morning, we can take our time."

Celia gathered her courage. "Actually, that's what I wanted to talk to you about." She told Easy about the dress and asked if she could wear it that day. She could feel her nakedness glowing between them as she confessed. She did not try to cover herself. She felt that she was proving something. Her self-conscious unselfconsciousness felt loud, and she decided that this was what courage felt like. Accepting exposure, making a demand, refusing to be embarrassed by either.

When she finished asking, Easy gave a single nod. "You have to wear something when we walk up the hill, though. Can you imagine what Kristen the Entrepreneur would say if she saw you? Don't tell anyone I said that," she added, rolling her eyes. "But seriously. You know she'd lose her mind." She bent and grabbed her shirt from the night before, then tossed it to Celia. "Here, you're small enough that this should cover you."

The shirt fell to the middle of Celia's thighs. As she buttoned it, Easy pulled another from beneath her pillow and pulled it on. They were essentially the same shirt in two different colors—Celia's was gray, while Easy's was the same faded red as the dress Celia'd been wearing the day before. As Easy pulled her rumpled trousers on, Celia closed her teeth around a small, secret thrill. It was the thrill of sameness. She could look at the buttons on Easy's shirt, and know what they felt like under her own fingertips. By the time the two of them got to the top of the island, her skin would smell like Easy's skin.

She ran out of the cabin and stood in the sunlight, waiting. Edith had been right. It was good to have a reason to leap out of bed in the morning.

The children were at the top of the island when the two of them arrived there. Small figures gathered in and around the chapel, generating a swarmlike hum of industry. Jessie stood outside, talking to a small boy who held a dripping rag. Celia couldn't make out what she was saying, but the boy was listening attentively, nodding hard, his face somber. When Jessie pointed at the chapel, the boy strode inside, radiating purpose.

"Cleaning crew," Easy said. "To get the place ready for tonight's Candle Hour. It'll be the last one, you know. Big festival night and all that."

Celia eyed the children as she passed. They were scrubbing the floors and walls with wet rags. Three older children—nearly teens, Celia guessed—sat on the front steps, carving candles with sharp pocketknives like the one Easy carried in her pocket. One of them had a bloodsoaked rag wrapped around her hand. It didn't seem to slow her carving at all.

"Hang on a second," Celia said. "Are they doing all the same things we did the other day? Did you have me in there doing—"

"Children's work, yeah," Easy answered. She grinned up at the crisp blue sky. "It's nice to reconnect with it sometimes, don't you think?"

Celia hadn't planned to call it *children's work*. She'd been about to ask if she'd been doing these kids' chores for them. But the way Easy said it made her think of it a different way—not as chores, but as labor. As something vital and useful.

She looked over her shoulder at the children. One of them carried a bucket of water down the chapel steps and lugged it to the apple tree to dump it out at the roots. The bucket was half the size of the child, but somehow, they managed to haul it without spilling a drop.

Easy saw her watching. "We don't believe in excluding children from the rhythms of working life. Come on, let's grab your dress and get some breakfast, I don't want to miss whatever Edith's got going this morning."

Inside, the house was filled with morning light. The white paint in the hallway gleamed with it. Celia felt that she was the same way—she felt open inside, bright and new. The white dress was near where she'd left it, pushed to one side of the floor. As she stooped to grab it, she caught sight of the shadow beneath the dark wooden door at the end of the hall.

Celia pulled on the dress, walked back out onto the front porch. "Is Audrey still in there?"

Easy was leaning against the rail. Her breath caught at Celia's question. Just a little—barely enough to notice—but Celia was standing so close to her, was watching her intently enough to see the skin at the nock of her throat twitch. "Audrey? In where?"

"In that room at the end of the hall. She was in there last night, right? I just wondered—"

In an instant, Easy became electrified. Her eyes were flashing, her pupils yawning wide. The tendons in her neck stood taut. "Did you see her?"

Celia took a half step back. Away from those eyes, back toward the safety of that long white hallway. "No."

"You didn't see Audrey? You can tell me the truth, Adelaide. I need to know."

Celia shook her head. "No, I didn't see her. Why do you keep calling me—"

Easy half collapsed with relief, her shoulders slumping into a dramatic parenthesis as the sudden strain in her body went slack. She ran her hands through her hair and blew out a hard sigh. "Okay. Sorry. That's just—it's really important to the process she was going through that you didn't open that door and interfere. Did you talk to her? It's okay if you did, I mean, it's not ideal, it'd be a setback, but. Did you? Celia, did you talk to her?"

Celia's answer didn't feel like a lie when she said it. "No. Just heard her voice, that's all." It felt like medicine, like a tonic she could spill down Easy's throat to dissolve away the tension that seemed to be vibrating through her at the mention of Audrey.

It worked. The rigidity in Easy's face drained away. She swayed briefly on her feet. "Good. That's good. She did such a—sorry if I was kind of—you know what? No," she said, giving her head a tight little shake. "I'm not sorry. I really want Audrey to be able to see her daughter, and it would have been a shame if something had happened to get in the way of that. I'm not sorry for being intense about it."

Relief surged through Celia like a wave of nausea. "She's here? Mackenzie?"

Easy gave Celia a quizzical smile. "Of course she is. You weren't worried, were you? She's not lost."

"I just didn't know. Audrey didn't tell me very much." She didn't want Easy to think she'd been worried. She didn't want to lose that feeling she'd had back in the cabin, like the two of them were on the same team. Like the two of them were the same. "But she's with her daughter now?"

Easy picked at a loose splinter on the porch rail. "Not yet. She's in the administrative office right now, signing some documents with William. Just asset transfers and stuff, to make sure she's not leaving any loose ends back home. I trust him to take things at the right pace, make sure she's ready. She came here with a lot of baggage, you know? But I think she's doing better now. A lot better. I'm glad she came." She looked Celia over, her eyes sprinting across the front of the white dress. A small, secret smile twitched around the corners of her mouth. "That looks good on you."

Celia looked down at herself. She could make out the shadows of her own body through the thin white fabric. It felt like something she'd been wearing all her life. With her eyes on the curve of her own belly, she heard herself ask, "Can I see it?"

"I think you're seeing it right now, aren't you?"

"No, I mean. The room." Celia paused as the air between her and Easy grew suddenly thick, the same way the future had felt thick on that night after her parents' death. There was something here now, something between the two of them that needed to be pushed into, inhaled, choked on if necessary. "I want to see the room Audrey was in."

Easy scrubbed her hands over her face hard, like she was trying to remove a layer of skin. "Oh. Oh man, Celia, I don't know. That's a big ask. That room is only for residents of the island. It's not that I don't trust you, it's just—you haven't made a commitment to stay here. To be part of this community."

"Did Audrey make that commitment?"

"That was the deal," Easy said on a sigh. She grimaced up at Celia, nakedly apologetic. "It's unorthodox—like I told you, we don't usually let visitors stay."

"It's so weird," Celia murmured. "On the mainland, everyone I talked to who knew about the Salt Festival said that at least half of the visitors who come here decide to stay. I wonder why—"

"I don't know what you all talk about on the mainland." Easy shrugged. "Anyway, I told Audrey that if she wanted to see her daughter, she had to agree not to leave. And we needed to be sure that she really wanted to make that commitment, so we asked her—I asked her, it was me, I should let you know that. I asked her to do the work we do here, on ourselves, to make sure she really wanted this."

Celia hated the distance this knowledge put between her and Easy. This community had secret places, places that Celia couldn't go, and those places stood between them, holding them apart with stiff outstretched arms. Keeping them separate. Making them different.

"I hate it too," Easy whispered, wrinkling her nose.

Celia laughed. "How did you know? That's exactly what I was thinking."

"Because I know you." Easy's eyes lingered on Celia's for long enough that she almost looked away. "And the thing is—fuck. Goddamn it. Okay, listen. The thing is, I know that you can handle seeing this. Even if you don't stay here," she said, her voice catching in a way that made Celia's tongue stick to her soft palate, "I know you'll understand what you're seeing. I think you'll appreciate it a lot, actually. But if I show you. Celia, if I show you this room, you can't tell anyone."

Celia's heart stuttered in her chest. "I won't."

"I mean *anyone*. You can't tell the other visitors, they won't get it. None of them are on your level. Rinna's close, but—I don't know, she needs more time away from that dipshit husband of hers."

"I won't tell them." Celia wanted to know more about Rinna's husband, wanted to hear Easy talk about him, but she also knew she wasn't supposed to focus on that. She tucked it away for later. All that mattered now was the room, was Easy trusting her, was the knowledge that Easy thought Celia was different from the others. *They won't get it,* Celia repeated to herself.

"And you can't tell any of the residents, either. They know that room is off-limits to visitors and I will never, I mean *never*, hear the end of it if they know I showed you. It's great here, I love everyone on this island, but the drama? Celia. You wouldn't believe the drama, and I am up to my neck as-is. I don't need people climbing down my throat about how I got too invested in this year's star visitor and showed her stuff I wasn't supposed to."

A shiver was rising through Celia. *Star visitor.* She felt like she was going to shake apart at the seams. She pressed her palms to her thighs to try to still her trembling fingers. "I won't tell anyone. I promise. I wouldn't."

Easy looked over at the chapel, then back at Celia. "Okay. If Jessie asks later, we went into the house so you could . . . I don't know, what, so you could wash your face at the sink? Let's go with that."

And then Easy had Celia by the hand. She led Celia inside, through the front door and down the hall, and stopped in front of that dark wooden door.

"I'm ready," Celia said.

Easy didn't let go of her hand. "I know."

Thirty Years Ago

William sits on the curb outside the Dog and Sparrow. It's been a bad night for business. Fridays should be profitable, but this one hasn't been—there was a shooting at an elementary school in the next town over, a failed gymnasium saferoom door that turned things into a bloodbath. Everyone at the bar is sad and angry, and nobody is looking to bet on pool or darts, which is the only way William has to make rent.

He's more than a little nervous about the lull. He lives in a Monday-through-Friday place, a so-called studio that's really just the main bedroom and en-suite bathroom of a local widow's house. She bolts the bedroom door so he can't get into the rest of the house, but she lets him have a hotplate in there so it's pretty nice, actually. Saturdays and Sundays, he's not allowed inside at all—apparently that's when her son comes home from college and needs the bed.

If William shows up on Monday morning and doesn't have the week's rent in hand, she'll find someone else to take the room, and he'll be spending more than just two nights a week sleeping on the floor of the Dog and Sparrow's storage closet. He sighs, scratches his chin. That's not really a reliable option, either, he thinks. Magda, who owns the Dog and Sparrow, only lets him sleep there over the weekend because he gives her a share of his nightly winnings.

Weekdays are out of the question. She's not going to let him crash for a cut of what he'll get on a Tuesday night. It'll never happen. He needs another solution, and he needs it now. Maybe, he considers, he could ask the widow to marry him. She'd have to let him into the rest of the house if they were married. He scans the gutter for dropped pennies. He needs the change, and he needs the luck.

Behind him, the front door of the bar swings open. A man in a silky button-down shirt stumbles out, half falls to the curb next to William. "Bum a smoke?"

"I was just gonna ask you that," William says. "It's dead in there, huh?"

"As a doornail. You ever heard of The Method? I usually get four or five phone numbers a night using the Steps, but tonight I'm coming up empty."

William eyes the man sitting next to him, decides to take pity, rummages in his jacket for the pack of smokes he was pretending not to have. "Here. You need this more than I do."

The man grins, then reaches into his own jacket pocket and pulls out a pack of the same brand. "Trade you."

They swap, each taking a cigarette from the other's crumpled pack. They stay on the curb for the rest of the night, bullshitting and smoking until they've identified each other as peers—not prey, like the rest of the people inside the Dog and Sparrow, but fellow predators nosing through the night for a hint of blood in the water. After that, the bullshit drops away and the conversation becomes something real. Something honest. Something strategic.

They don't go home until the bar and both packs of cigarettes are empty. By the time they part ways, they know that they're going to change the world together.

FIVE MONTHS AGO

1

Harvey was in Leona's way.

She found him stretched out in the middle of the road, halfway up the path from the water to Blue House, and the irritation she felt at the sight of him was so familiar to her that it was almost comfortable. In the entire thirty years she'd lived in this community, not a day had gone by that her efforts to contribute efficiently hadn't been thwarted somehow.

This morning was a perfect example. She was on her way to the canteen with a huge tin bucket of wax caps from the summer honey harvest. She'd drained the wax caps, washed them, left them out for the bees to finish cleaning, and stored them in William's office where they would stay cool. It was a huge amount of work, none of which was made easier by the distraction of Adelaide's return to the island. Today she would finally get to complete the task of processing the wax. The bucket was heavy, and the road between her apiary and the canteen was on the steep side. She needed to get to the canteen before Edith showed up with yesterday's immense radish harvest. Edith would be insistent on using every single surface and tool and heating element in the kitchen to clean and pickle them. There was no guarantee that she wasn't already on her way.

It was a tight timeline. Leona didn't have time to deal with whatever was going on with Harvey.

So of course here he was, sprawled out facedown in the dust in front of her.

He'd been gone all day the day before, leaving the children with Jessie at the salt flats, and now, through some kind of carelessness, he'd made himself into a problem she had to deal with before she could get on with the rest of the morning's work.

Her resentment unfurled big as a parachute.

She paused next to his feet. He didn't move. "Harvey," she said with undisguised impatience. When he didn't respond, she nudged his foot with her own. "Harvey. Get up."

She didn't have time for this. The metal bucket handle was digging into her palm. The sides of the bucket were sweating condensation. Her stomach let out a groan and she bit her lip hard. She didn't want to stop for breakfast until after she'd gone through at least one round of boiling and straining the wax. She bathed in a familiar wash of why-do-I-have-to-do-everything-for-everyone fury.

Harvey should know better than to block her path. He should know that she had things to get done.

She nudged him again. "Hey. Come on, get up." When he still didn't respond, she heaved a sigh. She set her bucket down hard, the metal rim thunking against the packed earth of the road, and then she set out trying to determine what Harvey's problem was.

The mystery resolved itself for her almost immediately. There was dirt inside his nostrils, cracked like it had become wet there and then dried in place. His lips were parted, like he had something to tell her and just needed to remember what it was. A dark puddle stained the ground beneath his head.

His temple was a stepped-on plum, overripe and rotten and bursting with soft wet red innards.

Leona straightened, wiping her hands on her skirt. She retrieved her bucket. Her stomach was still and her pulse was calm and her hands did not tremble. She walked the rest of the way up the hill to the canteen, her mind as blank as a freshly swept road.

2

She was not startled to find William standing in the kitchen. She was never startled to find William anywhere. He stood in front of a stainless steel prep table, separating an egg. He let the whites fall into an empty bowl before sliding the yolk onto a steaming dish of oats.

"I was just going to come find you," he said, his voice still husky with sleep. He stirred the egg yolk into the hot oats. Leona glanced bitterly at the whites, knowing he'd leave them there for someone else to deal with. "I think we're out of honey."

"We're not," she replied firmly, hauling her bucket onto the stainless steel countertop next to the stove. "Look again."

"I looked again."

"Well, look a third time," Leona snapped.

"Will you just help me find it?" William sounded impatient, as though her expectation that he'd survive on his own was unreasonable.

Leona didn't even respond. She stalked past him, hauled open the big door to the walk-in pantry, reached for the second-to-highest shelf, and pulled a jar of honey down. It wasn't hard to lay hands on—she could have grabbed any of the six other identical jars that were up there with it. But nothing happened around here if she wasn't the one handling it.

William thanked her and spooned the honey over the oats. "I figure she probably learned to like her oats sweet, while she was out in the world."

"She probably learned to like all kinds of things."

"She and the baby need to come first for a while," William replied, his eyes following her movements as she filled the lower pot of the double boiler with water.

Leona bristled, then told herself not to bristle, because shouldn't she be used to this by now?

Back in the day, it had been William's wife who came first. The widow, who had seemed so old back then, even though Leona was older now than the widow had been when she married William. The widow whose death had made the purchase of the island possible in the first place. Leona had understood why the widow had to come first—but still. It chafed. William had still been married to her when he met Leona, and their affair had made Leona *the other woman*, a position that acknowledged second-place status in the very name.

And then, after that wife died and William was finally free, Leona still hadn't gotten to come first. Because there had been Edith. Dad had decided that Edith was better for William. He'd taken Leona for himself. William had set himself to the task of loving Edith, and Dad had set himself to the task of loving his community and ignoring his wife.

And then they'd found the island with the old abandoned summer camp on it, and Dad had used William's now-late wife's life insurance payout to buy the island, and they'd created Kindred Cove together. Dad had promised her, had promised everyone, that the first baby born on the island would be called Adelaide after his own late mother. And when he'd said it, he'd pressed a hand to Leona's belly as though he already knew she'd be the one to birth that child. She thought she might finally, finally come out on top.

But Edith had stolen that from her. Edith had pushed the first Kindred Cove baby out onto the chapel floor. No one could be first after that. Leona was second again, second like always. She was sick to death of it.

She reminded herself to be reasonable. Adelaide and the baby had to come first, and that was just the way of things, and making a fuss wouldn't change it. "Fine with me."

"Don't be like that."

"I'm not being like anything. Do what you want."

William set the oats aside and walked across the kitchen to where she stood at the stove. He stood behind her, so close that she could feel his breath stirring the fine hairs at the back of her neck.

She turned on the stove under the double boiler, started scooping wax caps into the upper chamber with both hands. The wax had already started to soften in the warmth of the kitchen. It sank under her grip, holding the impression of her fingerprints.

"Don't be cranky at me for no reason," William murmured. He brushed her hip on one side, like he was dusting dirt off the fabric of her skirt.

Leona restrained a sigh—William was a human hammer, and every problem the two of them had with each other, he treated like a nail. What he had in mind wouldn't fix the fact that she had to take care of every damn thing for every damn one.

"Did I tell you I went with Easy and Harvey to the mainland yesterday?" he whispered into her hair. "Easy needed my help. So I helped."

Leona tilted her head to one side, let her hair fall away from her neck. She maintained a careful blankness in her mind around the walk to the canteen. "Is that right? You and Easy and Harvey?"

William didn't hesitate to take her invitation, his lips finding her skin before the water in the double boiler had even begun to bubble. "What can I say. I'm a helper. Do you need help?" And then he was dragging her skirt up, the fabric bunching in his fists on either side of her.

Leona held in a sigh. "I'm working."

"Mmm. Me too."

She gave the wax an idle stir to see if it was melting yet. It was, a little. She kept stirring as William found his way between her thighs. A slow stir, to keep it from getting too hot, trying not to help air bubbles find their way in. She stirred until the wax was liquid, which didn't take long, her feet braced shoulder-width apart to make room for the steady rocking of William's wrist. Once it was fully melted, she turned off the heat and shifted her center of gravity backward to sink down onto his crossed fingers.

This, she knew, was what he liked. He liked to watch her work while he was working her. It was no trouble to indulge him. "What happened with Easy and Harvey?" She made herself sound breathless when she asked.

He didn't answer. His teeth were on the nape of her neck, his fingers deep inside her, his movements earnest. William wasn't telling her what had happened—he was focused, trying to fix the thing that he'd decided was the problem.

So Leona moved the double boiler to a cool burner, and she gave William what he wanted. She threw her head back and emptied her lungs for him, buckled her knees for him, pulled her own hair. She clenched hard around him, and she made it sound as loud and frenzied and furious as a house collapsing so he'd have no reason to doubt that he'd done what he wanted to do. She invented an orgasm for him. She knew he'd believe it.

"Now you can't say you never come first," he breathed into her ear as he bent her over the stainless steel countertop.

He wasn't efficient with her the way he was with others. And Leona knew that for sure, because she had seen him with so many others. With them, he was concise, breathing deep and steady like a distance swimmer, touching them with the deft precision of a contractor laying tile, trying to make something out of nothing. With them, he was solving problems. Making little workers who would rake the salt and scrub the canteen and sweep the road, so everyone else could do the work that made them feel connected to purpose and intention. With the others, he was performing his responsibility to the community.

With her, he was messy. He kissed the place between her shoulderblades, wrapped her hair around his wrist, put a still-damp finger into her mouth to bite. He gripped her thighs, her stomach, her hips. He worked slow, and then fast, and then slow again.

He took his time with her and only her. He *appreciated* her. And she knew that she should be grateful for it—but there was that blankness in her mind in the shape of a burst plum, and there was the question of what had happened to Harvey and whether William had been involved, and there was the wax on the stove. It was probably setting up solid. It would need to be melted again so she could strain it. She'd melted it down for basically no reason, at this point.

But that was fine. She hadn't lost time on the chore. Nothing was ever lost.

Finally, William gathered her close, his arms flexing hard around her until she could hardly breathe. He drove into her in short, quick pulses, a strobe between her thighs, in and in and in. He gripped her tight, tighter, tightest—and then his body spasmed and he choked on her name and it was over.

As William panted and sagged against her, Leona stared at the bowl of oatmeal on the counter. A matte skin had congealed on the surface of it. By the time Adelaide got her breakfast, it would be cold.

She bit back a smile. There was some small satisfaction to be had here, after all.

3

He was still for a long time, holding Leona in place, holding himself in place as he softened inside of her. "Forty-eight's not too old, you know," he murmured. "Maybe lightning'll strike. You could have a baby right when Adelaide's ready to go again. Second over the finish line, just like last time."

She bit her tongue hard to keep from answering him, then shifted her hips forward a fraction. He was soft enough that he couldn't prevent himself from slipping out of her, flaccid and clammy against her thigh.

She wouldn't hold the comment against him. He wasn't capable of coherent enough thought to be cruel, not this soon after fucking her. She knew that. It stung to be reminded, though. The momentary satisfaction of Adelaide's breakfast being postponed wasn't enough to erase years of being put second. She didn't like that it still mattered, but it did.

Warmth trickled down the insides of her thighs. She straightened her skirt, shoving the fabric between her legs. "I should get back to the wax," she said softly. "And you'll want to bring that oatmeal to Adelaide. She's important."

"I didn't mean anything by it," William whispered, pressing a kiss to her shoulder. "You know I didn't."

"I know." She let out a long, slow breath, because he was right. She did know. For all her resentment, she never thought William would hurt her on purpose. He wanted her too much. Still. She turned the stove back on under the double boiler. The wax needed to be purified, and Adelaide needed breakfast. There was work to do.

She heard him draw breath as though to speak again—to say what, she couldn't imagine, because what was left to say?—when there was a noise from outside. It was a sudden squawk, a half-scream, like someone shrieking and stuffing a fist into their mouth at the same time.

"What in the world," William muttered, tucking himself back into his jeans with quick, practiced motions.

"Sounded like Jessie," Leona replied, giving the soft wax a gentle stir. "Probably found Harvey."

"Harvey?"

She looked at him with surprise. His cheeks still held a little flush. "Yes, Harvey. On the road. That wasn't—" She faltered, unsure how to finish the sentence. "I assumed you knew," she finished, the words coming slow and uncertain.

"Okay. Harvey." He tugged at the bottom of his shirt, then grabbed the cool oatmeal. "I'll take care of it." He pressed a kiss to her cheek and then he was gone.

Leona finished melting the beeswax and poured it through a straining cloth. She strained it four times, then five, until most of the visible impurities were gone. She took her time. When it was good enough for her purposes, she poured it into molds to harden, used the edge of a spatula to scrape away the drips that had dried. She cleaned up thoroughly, tossed William's abandoned egg whites into the scrap bin, scrubbed and wiped down the already-clean counters. She even set out the pickling crock for Edith.

Leona didn't want to leave the canteen. The longer she stayed, the stranger it was that no one else was coming in to join her, and the more certain she was that she wouldn't want to see what was happening outside.

Hunger no longer plucked at her middle. She ate anyway, cutting an apple into fat slices and drizzling honey over each one, licking her sticky fingers clean. She could have sliced the apple smaller, could have dipped it into the honey, but she found herself desperate for mess. She stuck a clean spoon into the jar William had left out on the counter and raised it to her mouth, letting the honey spill down her chin and chest. Sweetness flooded her throat.

She nearly choked on it, and there was no one to see, no one to witness the way she swallowed and swallowed and swallowed, the muscles of her tongue working to soothe the panicky spasm in her throat. She coughed, sour-sweet and sticky, forcing air through the bubble of honey that sat heavy across her soft palate, over her windpipe.

And then, heart pounding, she managed to draw a clear breath again. She stood there, hands braced on the counter exactly where they'd been braced when William was fucking her, and she sucked down air and waited to feel unafraid.

4

William stood outside, talking to Adelaide and Edith and Easy. Adelaide held an empty bowl, the oatmeal long gone. Edith carried an old laundry basket full of radishes. William had nothing in his hands. His fists clenched over and over, grasping at the air beside his thighs like his grip alone could anchor him to the road.

Harvey was on the ground just behind William. Nobody was looking at him. Leona didn't look at him, either. She already knew there was nothing to see.

Easy greeted Leona with a languid half smile. "Good morning. Were you finally dealing with that wax that's been sitting in William's office? I'm looking forward to a new batch of candles." Her voice was husky, like she'd just woken up, but her hair was wet as though she'd been swimming in the lake. "We were just discussing taking up a fast for the day."

"Easy was explaining it to us," Edith said, her mouth pinching irritably. "She was about to tell us why we need to fast right this minute, when some of us were on our way to eat breakfast."

"You all need to focus," Easy replied. "Adelaide's return has shaken everyone up. Lots of people are struggling with their commitments. Not your fault, Adelaide," she said warmly. "People are just excited that you're back."

"I've been back for a while. I can't imagine anyone's still all that excited," Adelaide said, frowning. Her eyes flicked down to the dark patch of soil under Harvey's head before returning to her empty bowl. She dropped her voice as though everyone couldn't hear her. "Easy, it's been weeks since the boat got fixed. When you asked me to come back, I really thought—"

"There's no rush, Del," Easy assured her. "You should focus on building your strength. And the rest of us should look inward," she added, aiming a significant look at everyone gathered there.

"A fast sounds like a great idea," Leona said. She rubbed the tip of her tongue against the roof of her mouth, seeking sweetness there.

Easy's gaze dropped to the front of Leona's skirt, to the still-damp wrinkles where she'd wadded it between her thighs. "Leona. I feel like I've barely seen you with Adelaide since she got home. Do you need an accountability partner for the fast? I'm sure she'd benefit from your help."

Adelaide ducked her head. Her eyes stayed blank.

"I'd love that. We'll be just fine together," Leona said smoothly.

"Good. I'm going to get Jessie—I need her to organize the children so the road can get cleaned up. If you see her, tell her to come find me?" Without another word, Easy headed down the path away from the rest of them, toward the office, her hands in her pockets, her stride long and loping.

William followed, chasing after Easy's heels like an eager terrier. Edith took Adelaide's bowl and vanished into the canteen with her radishes, humming softly to herself. Harvey stayed where he was, his face pressed into the dirt. His limbs were stiff with the weight of cold blood.

Leona threaded her arm through Adelaide's elbow and steered them both in the opposite direction, up the hill toward the Old House. "What's bothering you?" She watched Adelaide out of the corner of her eye, waiting to see if the girl would look back over her shoulder.

Adelaide kept herself pointed straight ahead. She fidgeted with that terrible new haircut of hers. "Oh, nothing. Just tired. How are you?"

Leona shook her head. "You're tired? I'm always tired. Too much work to do, not enough people willing to do it. And now the children will be at loose ends until Easy rounds up Jessie. You know who Jessie loves avoiding? Easy. The children's work will end up landing on me, you wait and see." The words flowed out of her freely, because who would Adelaide tell? Who would listen to the girl who'd stayed gone for so long? "Frankly, I'm looking forward to the moment you stop pretending you're not going to stay here, so we can finally get you to figure out what work you want to take up. Don't mind me, though, I'm used to doing everything myself while other people figure out what they feel like doing."

Adelaide frowned. "Leona, I don't think—"

"Oh, Caleb, good morning!" Leona waved, smiling brightly at the figure heading toward them. She stopped the flow of bitterness that had poured out of her, and she made her mind like the road. Freshly swept. Smooth. New.

"Morning!" He picked up his pace to meet them. "Adelaide! How's the day going?" His eyes didn't touch Adelaide.

"No news yet," Adelaide was saying. She stroked her stomach, gazing down at it with big wet cow-eyes. "And no news is a big relief, honestly. I'm not ready to say goodbye to the baby."

Leona pinched out a laugh. "Funny. When I was that far along, I couldn't wait to invite the community to share in what I was making. But I suppose some people like to keep things for themselves."

Caleb did look at Adelaide then. His gaze was just cold enough that Leona felt a hint of satisfaction. "Well, whenever you do want to share," he said. Adelaide looked like she was about to protest, but he cut her off. "Have either of you seen Harvey? I was hoping to eat with him. I finally get to break my fast today."

"Actually, everyone's fasting today. Easy said so." Leona said it without too much apology. A fast was a fast and nothing more. No reason to soften anything for Caleb.

"Really? Damn it. I mean, of course it's fine. It's fine," he said again. "It's just one more day. I'll tell Harvey when I see him. Is he at the salt flats with the kids already? Do you know?"

Leona only hesitated for a second. She saw Adelaide notice. But then, if Adelaide was noticing, that meant Adelaide was hesitating, too. Leona swallowed, remembering the honey that had coated her throat.

"Is who at the salt flats?" she said.

"Harvey?" Caleb cocked his head to one side.

Leona shook her head. "Easy said she was going to put Jessie in charge of the kids today."

Caleb's laugh was thin. "No way. Jessie? Come on, Easy wouldn't put her in charge of a litter of kittens." He glanced behind Leona as if she might be hiding Harvey behind one shoulder. "If you don't know where he is, that's fine, but if you do, will you just tell me? I don't want to spend half the morning looking for him."

"Caleb," Leona said, and it came out quieter than she wanted it to. Too quiet to be casual. "You can't go looking for him. There's no reason to look for something that isn't lost."

Caleb's face went slack. His lips lost their color. "No," he breathed. "What?"

Adelaide lifted a hand as though to reach for him. "I'm so—"

Leona pushed Adelaide's hand back down. "Don't," she whispered. "What's wrong with you?"

Caleb looked between them beseechingly. "This is a joke. Right? You're joking?"

"There's nothing to worry about," Leona said evenly. "We should go. I have things to do. I'm sure you do too, Caleb." Caleb sank to his knees as they passed, his face blanched, his eyes hollow. Leona tugged Adelaide along with her as she continued up the road, leaving him there with his fingers digging into the packed dirt.

5

They walked all the way up to the garden. The silence stretched between them like pulled sugar. Leona kept her eyes forward, not looking in at the bolted arugula that was swarming with her bees, the long twisting shadows of the pumpkin vines, the apple trees hanging heavy with the last of the harvest. The dust of the road ahead of her was smooth and settled and there was no stain on it anywhere.

Adelaide turned into the garden, grabbed an arugula blossom and lifted it to her mouth. She ran the petals across her bottom lip, shifting her weight from foot to foot. "I didn't mean to," she whispered. "Comfort him, I mean. It was an instinct."

"Instinct isn't an excuse."

"I know. It's just. I thought . . ." She paused again, far too long to be thinking of something honest to say. "I didn't want him to be alone with that feeling. After what happened with Sadie—"

"I thought he learned his lesson about that?"

Adelaide gave her an exasperated look. "He's been through a lot. We should support him. During my time off the island, I learned that lots of people—"

"Your time off the island," Leona interrupted tartly. "Do you really think anyone here wants to know what you learned during your 'time off the island'? Do you think you're doing anyone any good at all by bringing in all the ideas we've worked so hard to leave behind?"

Do you think you're doing yourself *any good*, she didn't add. There was a reason the Salt Year was supposed to last for a single year and no longer. The world had a way of sinking into people, turning their heads and their hearts, shaking their priorities. It was a dangerous place. And now here was Adelaide, trying to make this place dangerous, too. Looking at Harvey like something was the matter with him. Looking at Caleb like he'd suffered a loss.

Leona left Adelaide in the garden without bothering to slap the arugula blossom out of the girl's hand. Let her eat whatever she wanted and think whatever she wanted and feel whatever she wanted. It wasn't Leona's business. It wasn't her problem. She couldn't fix everyone and everything.

She walked down to her hives, which were set up halfway between the garden and the canteen, to do a last inspection before it was time to wrap them up for winter.

She wondered if Caleb was still on his knees.

It wasn't long before she got her answer. The hives were close to the road—not so close that they were easy to see through the trees, but close enough that Leona could listen to conversations as they passed her by. She heard it when Caleb met up with a couple of others. Una, from the sound of it, and Nadine, both of whom helped Edith in the garden and the kitchen.

"You all right, Caleb?" That was Una. She'd pushed Nona out nine years earlier, without even needing a Salt Year to make it happen. Nona was a good worker, but a problem Harvey often complained about over dinner.

Leona caught herself mid-thought: Harvey wouldn't be complaining about anything over dinner anymore. Jessie would have to take over the work of complaining about Nona.

Una was young, prone to crying. Sometimes, in her sleep, she still spoke the language she'd once shared with her parents—a worrying indication that she might miss them. She wasn't crying now, though. Improvement. Caleb, by contrast, let out a loud sniff.

His voice was thick. "Harvey is gone."

"What do you mean, gone?" Nadine was older than Una but younger than Leona. She kept her head shaved and used Edith's sunflower oil to make her dark skin shine. She had a tendency to ask questions that didn't need asking. William had a fondness for her long legs. Leona disliked her powerfully. "Like, you can't find him? I'm sure he'll turn up."

There had been dirt in Harvey's nostrils, Leona remembered. Like he'd inhaled the road. Maybe he'd lain there for some time, breathing in the soil deep enough that he could taste it on the back of his tongue before his breathing finally stopped. Maybe his lungs were full of brown powder like pollen stuck to a bee's legs.

"Yeah," Una echoed. "He'll turn up, Caleb. Why do you look so worried? This is Kindred Cove. Nothing that bad could happen to him. Not here."

Leona put the cover back on the hive. The count was healthy. The bees would have a good winter. She stalked through the trees, emerging just behind Nadine. Caleb's eyes went wide at the sight of her. "Caleb," she said, in the same voice she used when she found children sneaking food out of the pantry during a fast. "Did I hear you saying that Harvey is gone?"

"N-no," he stammered. "I wasn't—"

"No one is ever lost," she said firmly, looking from Caleb to Nadine to Una, meeting each of their eyes. "Harvey is still with us."

Nadine understood first. Her expression melted into glassy, smooth nothingness, perfect placidity, absolute calm. "Of course he is. He'll always be with us."

Una took longer to catch up, which Leona found unsurprising. "What are you two talking about? Harvey is—oh." She cut herself off at the sight of Nadine's blank face. "I mean, yeah. He's here."

"He's here."

Caleb seemed to shrink before them, his shoulders bending inward, his neck sinking down into his chest. Leona found it easy to picture Caleb as a child, curled around himself, trying with all his might to become invisible. "Please, can we just. Can one of you say that he's gone? I don't need anyone to be sad about it, but he was here, and that mattered, he mattered, if we could just—"

"I don't really understand how someone can be gone if they're right here with us," Una said, her hands twisting into a complicated little knot of fingers in front of her solar plexus. "But I can't stop you from saying what you want to say. That's a boundary concern, Caleb. It would be—I don't say this to be mean, okay? But I think you need to hear it. It would be toxic of you to ask us to police your actions by stopping you from saying these things. You should be trying to grow on your own."

"And it would be limiting of us to indulge you in that way," Nadine added, nodding earnestly. "I would never want to rob you of an opportunity to learn healthy coping skills."

Leona smiled at the girls. She promised herself that she'd be kinder to them in the future. They deserved it. They were good members of the community, and she was glad to see them growing.

6

That afternoon, a healthy breeze came up off the lake. Leona prepared the blankets she'd be using to wrap the beehives—quilts sewn from old shirts, the logos cut in half and distributed onto opposite sides of the patchwork. They needed to be aired out so as not to introduce pests to the hives. She hung them on lines outside the canteen, and everyone who passed by gave each quilt a hearty thwack to help knock dust and moth eggs loose. They all stepped around the mess that was still lying in the road, careful not to get blood on the soles of their feet.

Just before nightfall, Leona came to check on those blankets and found Caleb staring down at the body. Flies walked sticky-footed across the mess of Harvey's skull. The breeze was dying down and the smell was becoming apparent. Tears streamed down Caleb's face, his lips moving wordlessly.

For the second—or perhaps fifth—time that day, she was jolted by an electric pulse of resentment. Caleb wasn't in her way, but his tears were so useless to the community that they were basically an obstacle anyway. He should have been in the kitchen, helping Edith process radishes. Or, if Edith was done with that by now, Caleb could have been up at the chapel, sweeping and carving candles and preparing for the moment Adelaide gave birth. He'd been slouching around the island all day, staring into the water, collapsing to his knees, crying in the shadow of the canteen. It was too much to bear.

"Caleb," she snapped, loud enough to turn the heads of a few people who were headed into the canteen for water. "Can you help us keep our living space tidy, please?"

He looked up at her with red-rimmed eyes. "What?"

She sighed. It wasn't fair to her, having to point out everything that needed to be done. Having to manage other people's activities. But she was the one who could see which tasks were being neglected. She was the one who understood the rhythms of work and rest. According to Easy, William was in charge of logistics and finances, and Edith was in charge of the spiritual well-being and stomach of the community. Harvey had been in charge of managing the children. Leona supposed that stuck her with responsibilities like this one. She would do her duty to Kindred Cove, even if she resented it.

She looked down at the body in the road, raised her eyebrows, pursed her lips. When she looked back up at Caleb, she saw him understand.

"I can't," he whispered.

"I see. You expect the children to handle this, since maintaining the road is their job. But tell me this, Caleb: Do you intend to leave all your messes for your community to clean up? Do we need to update the distribution of responsibilities so we can plan for people to take care of your problems for you? This is Jessie's first day managing the children. Do you expect her to take on that much responsibility seamlessly?"

More residents had gathered. Adelaide was walking down the road toward them, her belly supported in the sling of her hands. It was good, Leona thought, to have an audience for this. Accountability mattered.

Caleb shook his head. "No, I just—"

"I can do it," Adelaide said as she approached.

Leona held up a hand without taking her eyes off Caleb. "Caleb is struggling in his commitment to this community, Adelaide. Do you care so little for him that you would let him abandon us completely?"

Caleb looked around. He seemed to realize all at once that he was being watched. The crowd had gravity to it. Close to one hundred people hovered, watching—in the shadow of the canteen, in the trees at the edge of the road, clustered in a crescent behind the place where Caleb stood.

"Do you know what I see when I look at you, Caleb?" Leona said softly.

He shook his head.

"I see a man who doesn't miss what isn't gone."

"I'll handle it." The words came out of him in a hoarse chop. He should have waited for someone else to speak for him—for someone else to tell him what he was. But he simply crouched next to Harvey. He drew a shuddering breath, then looped his forearms through Harvey's underarms. The flies that had been gathering rose up in alarm, startled but not enough to disappear. They circled, landed, and took off again as Caleb straightened.

"Pardon me," he whispered to Adelaide, who was standing too close for him to pass by.

"Caleb, let me help, it's—"

"I said, pardon me," he said again, more harshly this time. Either he was trying to stir up some anger within himself, or else he was choking on a sob. It sounded wet, and Leona's throat clenched around phantom honey at the sound. But the sob didn't matter—what mattered was that the job was getting done. It would do him good, Leona thought, to be productive. "I need to get by," he said. "Move out of the way, Adelaide."

She reached for his shoulder, but he was already moving past her—through her. He heaved the weight of Harvey's corpse backward and as he did, his shoulder met Adelaide's arm. He startled at the impact, nearly dropping his burden, stumbling into her even harder. She tripped backward a few steps and fell hard onto her backside, her legs splayed, the road unforgiving beneath her.

"Sorry," Caleb said, not looking at her. "Will someone check on her? I have to . . ." And he stopped there, the end of the sentence as far from him as Harvey's eyes were from opening.

Easy stood in the shadow of the canteen. Leona didn't know how long she'd been standing there near one of the hanging quilts, her arms crossed, her face still, watching all of this play out. As Leona watched, Easy walked over to Adelaide and knelt next to her, murmuring to her, brushing a stray tear off her cheek. She didn't smile at her sister.

Leona and everyone else followed Caleb to the water. He choked and coughed as he went, swallowing back tears and snot. Harvey's head bumped against his chest and the bottom of his chin, leaving stamps of muddy gore behind.

Progress was slow. Harvey's dragging heels left wobbling twin trails that were erased by the crowd that followed. Their feet shuffled through the packed dirt, knocking it loose, and eddies of dust swirled around their calves like churchyard mist.

When they made it to the water, the crowd stopped, but Caleb continued. He pulled Harvey into the lake and towed him through the shallows. Harvey's body was buoyant, but the water was difficult to wade through, and it was easy to hear the effortful labor of Caleb's breathing. He started to swim eventually, pulling Harvey out and out until he reached the part of the water where the reef came closest to the island.

Leona couldn't see the moment when those searching fingers of coral met the pulp of Harvey's temple. She couldn't see them reaching their way into him and transforming him, taking him for their own, making him into part of something bigger than himself. But she and the rest of the residents of Kindred Cove heard Caleb's yell, so it must have happened.

It was for the best. It was all for the best. Harvey had been one of them, had been part of their community, and now he'd be here forever. He'd become part of something that was better than he'd ever been, better than he'd ever failed to be.

This way, he could never be lost to them.

Caleb, Leona thought, *should be glad*.

Leona turned away from the water as Jessie started gathering the children. The girl was bossing all the little ones as though she hadn't been one of their number the day before. She was telling them that they'd need to clean up the mess of the road before anyone went to sleep. It was a task that should have been organized earlier in the day, but there was no fixing it now, and it was for the best, seeing as how Caleb had made such a mess anyway.

There was still plenty of work to be done. No time to lecture Jessie, no time to stand and stare and try to see what was happening beneath the surface of the Vetiver. Leona started to walk away just as the first ripple of the miracle tide washed up onto the shore.

Just as she made it to the gap in the treeline, Leona stumbled. The next thing she knew she was on her knees, hunched by the entrance to the road, vomit spilling up out of her like a pot boiling over. She couldn't recall exactly how much honey she'd eaten that morning, but what poured out of her mouth was sweet and viscous and slow and endless. It dripped up her throat, flowed over her tongue, coated the inside of her mouth, slid out of her, and pooled in the rocks at the roadside, golden and gleaming.

A cool breath of wind on the back of her neck, a lightness at her scalp—someone was holding her hair back. Leona gagged one more time, spat, sat back on her heels. She'd never felt quite so hollowed-out.

"Poor thing," Easy murmured, her fingers light on Leona's nape. "But look on the bright side. Could be a baby."

"What?" Leona panted, too aware of her sour-sweet breath. Children streamed around her, heading up toward the canteen to get the supplies they needed to smooth down the road.

"Oh, I'm only teasing you because William told me about your morning together." Easy's hand was light between Leona's shoulder-blades, rubbing in gentle circles. "I know you wouldn't be sick this soon. You two should keep trying, though. Adelaide's going to be the last to give birth this year, but you could be our second or third next year. Wouldn't that be something?"

Leona lifted her skirt and scrubbed at her tongue with the dusty hem, trying to erase the taste of honey and bile. A bright hot flush spread out under her skin at the sight of the redness that lingered around Adelaide's eyes.

Behind her, a few children still standing by the water screamed in delight as the lake rose up around their ankles.

"Wouldn't that be something."

Five Years Ago

Edith holds a stone in her palm. It is warm from the sun on one side, and cool on the other side, where it was sunk into the dirt near the back edge of the garden. She dug it up with her hands. Bent a fingernail back in the process. It throbs, but it can't hold a candle to the pain in her abdomen. She squeezes her thighs together tight around the wad of rags she's stuffed between her legs. Squeezes the rock in her hand.

This is the seventh pregnancy that's ended this way. This is the seventh smooth, round stone she's dug up from the edge of the garden.

She carefully kneels behind the blackberry patch. The blackberry patch is why Edith knows the garden is hers. Will always be hers, no matter what that boy Caleb wants for himself. She brushes mulch aside until she finds the long, knobbly stick she left here last time. Using the stick, she pushes through the brambles until she can see the six stones she's laid here.

She's placed them irregularly, so they don't look like gravestones. They aren't gravestones, she reminds herself. She's never buried anything here. If she was asked to articulate what the stones are for, she wouldn't be able to. She just knows that they're hers. They matter. They remember for her, when she needs to be able to stop remembering for a while.

She reaches into the brambles. They catch at her arm. She lets them. The torn skin will provide her with something that she needs: a wound. Something that will bleed where everyone can see it. Because tonight, she'll need to tell everyone what's happened, and as soon as she does, they'll all agree that she was never pregnant in the first place, and there will be nothing more to say. There's no special care to give to someone who hasn't lost anything, no sympathy to offer to someone who isn't suffering.

She pushes her arm into the blackberry patch up to the shoulder and sets the stone down where nobody will be able to see it. She can't see it, herself, not even with the blackberry vines pushed aside. But she knows it's there, and that's what matters.

She takes her time pulling her arm out of the thicket. She lets the thorns dig in deep as they can. Her arm will be chewed to ribbons. There will be blood to show, an injury to acknowledge. Someone will clean and bandage her. Someone will wrap her up and pack her pain away. They won't be able to help her with the sense of failure and loss that comes with every single stone she places in her garden, but she can carry all that on her own.

She has plenty of practice.

SALT FESTIVAL

day four | afternoon

Celia gripped Easy's hand, staring into the little room behind the door at the end of the hall in the Old House, trying to understand what she was seeing.

It was the size of a large closet. Maybe it had once been a walk-in pantry, or a canning cupboard. Whatever it used to be, it was something else now. A small wooden stool took up most of the floor space, with just enough room on all sides for whoever was seated there to reach out and touch the walls. Celia knew, though, without having to think about it, that she wouldn't want to touch the walls if she was the one sitting on that stool. Because every inch of the closet was covered in mirrors.

Not long mirrors. Not the full-length mirrors she'd covered with moving blankets in her parents' house, so she wouldn't have to watch herself crawl into their bed in the evenings. Not the massive wall-sized mirrors Celia used to see herself in every morning, at that gym where she'd spent a year showing up at dawn to get screamed at by a retired cop with Mickey Mouse tattoos covering both his legs. These mirrors were small. The biggest one was the size of a textbook. The smallest looked like they'd been pried out of pocket compacts. There were magnifying mirrors, cracked hiking mirrors still dangling their frayed lanyards, a hand mirror in an ornate metal frame.

All of them were affixed to the walls, forming an endless mosaic in which Celia saw a hundred different versions of her own startled face.

"I know," Easy said. Celia looked at her, as much to look away from the mirrors as anything else, and saw that Easy had turned so her back faced the little room full of mirrors. "It's a lot. You don't have to keep looking in there if you don't want to."

Celia didn't know if she wanted to look or not. She hadn't really looked at her reflection since the morning before her arrival on the island. She'd been enjoying the freedom from her own face, which always looked a little wrong to her—more tired around the eyes than she felt, disordered in ways she'd assumed would stay tidy, clumsily proportioned and hastily assembled.

But she missed it, too. Being able to see herself from all angles, being able to assess and analyze the version of her that the rest of the world could look at and judge and touch.

She wanted to know what Easy saw. She wanted to know how she'd changed in her time at the Cove. Surely everything was different now. Surely Easy could see it.

"What is this for?" she said, not looking back into the closet, but still able to see every small movement of her body in the reflections out of the corner of her eye.

"It's where we do an exercise that helps people break out of harmful behaviors and thought patterns. It's intense, but it's—honestly, Celia, it's transformative. I've seen it change lives." She paused, then added, softly, "I've seen it save lives."

Celia looked into the closet again. She caught her own eye in one of the mirrors, then another, her gaze bouncing from self to self. She realized that she wasn't just looking at her own reflection—she was looking at a reflection of a reflection of her reflection, a mirror image of a mirror image. She was seeing herself through so many layers of glass that she may as well have been underwater, looking up at the sun from the bottom of the lake.

She closed her eyes.

"How does it work?"

Beside her, close and quiet, Easy asked, "Do you want to try?"

Celia kept her eyes shut as Easy led her to the stool. Her hand in both of Easy's, her footfalls slow and careful, the soft rustle of Easy's clothing as she moved beside Celia, the rough plane of Easy's hand on her elbow. She lowered herself to the stool and sat with her knees apart, her palms resting on her thighs. "Okay," she said. "What do I do?"

"I'm going to be right outside the door," Easy whispered. She was right next to Celia's ear, her hands warm and steady on Celia's shoulders. "Normally I'd be standing outside the house, on the other side of that back wall, but I don't want to run into Jessie, so—it'll only be a short one, anyway. You don't need to do the whole thing. Just for a second, yeah?"

"Okay, but what do I—"

"Just trust me," Easy said. And then her hands were gone, leaving Celia's shoulders cold and light enough to float away. Celia heard the rustle of Easy's hands in her pockets, the strike of a match. Then she was pressing cool beeswax into Celia's hands. "Hold that. You're going to do great."

She pressed soft, dry lips against Celia's temple—Celia leaned into the kiss, shifting her weight sideways on the stool. Then she was gone, and Celia heard the click of the door closing.

"Open your eyes," Easy said from the other side of the wooden door.

Celia did as she was told. She was met by the sight of herself, illuminated by the shocking brightness of the little candle in her hands. Every mirror caught the light of the tiny flame and reflected it, hundreds of times over, filling the little room with light. Celia looked up and saw that there were mirrors on the ceiling as well as the walls, and the candlelight was in them, too. She could see herself with perfect illuminated clarity.

"What do you see?" Easy said. "Something simple, you don't have to go big with it."

Celia stared up at the version of herself that was reflected by the mirrors on the ceiling. "I see—oh god, my hair is a mess," she laughed. "I see the big tangle on the back of my head that nobody's been telling me about." It was true, there was a knot in the hair just behind the base of her skull. She focused on it, not wanting to look at the rest of herself. Not wanting to see the ways in which she still looked the same as she always had.

Outside, Easy laughed, too. "Sorry. I should have mentioned it, but there wasn't a good time. Okay, so, tell me about the knot in your hair. Why does it bother you?"

"Because—" Celia started, but then she stopped, because she didn't know how to explain why it bothered her.

"Don't do that. Don't think about it," Easy said urgently. "Don't try to come up with the right answer. Just say the first thing that comes to mind."

"I guess because it's messy," Celia ventured, reaching up to touch the snarl. "It makes me look like I don't take care of myself."

"Is that true? Is it true that you don't take care of yourself?"

Celia frowned, and all around her, a hundred Celias frowned. "No. I take care of myself. I guess I could take care of myself better, but—"

"But you do. You take care of yourself, I've seen you do it."

Celia held the candle in one hand, trying to comb her fingers through the tangle. "I try to take care of myself. I do my best, anyway. It's just that sometimes, I can't—"

Easy cut her off. "Stop there. We know what's true already, Celia. We know that you take care of yourself. So why are you so worried about that thing you think you see in your hair?"

Celia's fingers were stuck. She tugged them painfully loose. "Because it makes it seem like I don't take care of myself. Like I don't try." The words came easily. She didn't stop to think whether or not this was the deepest, truest thing she could say. She simply released the thought, giving it to Easy.

Easy would tell her if it was the truth. Celia knew she could trust her with that.

"You don't like the thing you see because you know it doesn't reflect the truth," Easy said. "It's a false image. It tells a lie to the people around you. What's the lie?"

Celia looked away from the ceiling and stared at her own face. There was nowhere in the room for her eyes to rest, no surface that didn't look back at her. She looked down into her own lap, but the candle was there, the flame so bright it made her eyes water. She returned her gaze to herself, to her many reflections, to the nervous pinch of her own mouth. Easy's words rang through her: *a false image.*

"What's the lie, Celia?" Easy said again.

Celia felt the slow burn of tears building. "I don't know. Um, sorry. This is a lot."

"I know," Easy said. "But I also know you can do it. Don't give up now."

She didn't want to let Easy down. She could hear the urgency, the *need* in Easy's voice. This was important. This was the key to everything.

If Celia couldn't do this, then she couldn't—she let herself think it for the first time, let herself feel how much she wanted it, let herself know the truth of what she wanted more than anything—she couldn't stay.

If she didn't do this, then she couldn't stay at Kindred Cove. So she pulled in a breath and looked at herself full-on, unblinking, determined. "The lie is that I don't take care of myself."

"Good," Easy breathed through the door. Celia pictured her standing there, eyes closed, forehead pressed to the dark wood. "The lie is that you don't take care of yourself. You're not unhappy with your hair, Celia. You're unhappy with the lie. You want to see a true reflection of yourself. You want to look with honest eyes. What would you see, if you were seeing the truth?"

Celia took in Easy's words. Around her, a hundred Celias nodded their agreement. "I'd see someone who takes care of herself."

"And if you were looking at someone who takes care of herself, you wouldn't see a tangle, would you?"

Searing heat fell across Celia's index finger. She sucked a breath in through her teeth, flinching hard enough that the candleflame flickered. By the time she looked down, the pain was gone, replaced by a gentle tightness across her skin. A long thin tongue of candlewax had dripped down the side of the beeswax pillar, draping itself across the back of her finger.

"Celia?" Easy prompted. "We're almost there. Are you still with me?"

Celia flexed her finger and felt the pull of the hardening wax on her skin. "I'm still with you. If I was looking at someone who takes care of herself, I wouldn't see a tangle."

"So look again, with honest eyes," Easy said. "When I look at you, I see someone who takes care of herself. Would I lie to you?"

Celia looked again. The features of her face floated apart from each other—wide brown eyes, small knob of a nose, jaw always a little off-center. In the space between them, she thought she saw a small pink mouth, a flash of strawberry blond hair. "You wouldn't lie to me," she said. "When you look at me—you see that. You see someone who takes care of herself."

"There's no tangle in your hair," Easy said. "There couldn't be. Because that would belong to someone who doesn't take care of herself.

That would belong to a fucking slob. And you're not that, are you, Celia? Everyone here knows that you take good care of yourself."

Celia flinched as violently as she had when the wax had dripped onto her hand. *A fucking slob.* Was that really what Easy thought? Was that what everyone thought? She looked at the back of her head in the reflections that surrounded her and tried to spot the tangle, but her eyes were swimming again.

"You take care of yourself. I see it, Celia. You can trust my eyes. You can trust me to tell you the truth of what I see. And I'm telling you, I see someone who takes care of herself. I don't see a tangle."

Celia reached up to touch the tangle again, but stopped before her fingers found the snarl of hair. She lowered her hand slowly to her lap. "There's no tangle," she whispered.

"There's no tangle," Easy said.

"I am a person who takes care of herself. My hair is—it's fine how it is."

A brushing sound, like Easy's hand stroking the wood of the door. "It's perfect how it is. You look perfect."

Celia looked at herself in the mirrors. She turned her head as far as she could, seeing herself from every angle. She saw herself truly, with honest eyes.

She saw the back of her head, and she saw nothing that needed fixing.

"There's no tangle," she said.

There was a brief, heavy silence from the other side of the door. "Say it again."

"There's no tangle," Celia said. "There's nothing wrong with my hair. I take care of myself. There's no tangle."

The door swung open wide. Easy stood there, beaming. She rushed into the closet and took the candle from Celia's hand, blew it out before dropping it to the floor. A spray of melted wax spattered across the floor, but there was no time to care because Easy was pulling Celia up off the stool and wrapping her in a sudden, tight embrace. "That was amazing," Easy said.

Celia buried her face in Easy's hair. "Did I do it right?"

"You did it perfectly. You were perfect." Easy pressed a hand to the back of Celia's head. Her palm was over the place where the tangle would be.

Celia tried to picture it in her mind, the thing she'd been looking at in the mirror, the back of her own head—but all she could picture was Easy's hand. "Thank you for showing me that," she said. "I get why you don't show visitors. It's . . . intense."

Easy pulled away. She was beaming. "I knew I was right to show it to you, though. I knew you'd get it. Now let's get out of here, before Jessie comes looking for us, yeah?"

Celia's head swam. "We'll need a better excuse for why we were in here. I could have washed my face twenty times, for how long that was."

Easy was already pulling her down the hall. "What are you talking about? We've only been inside a couple of minutes. Come on, let's get you some fresh air."

That felt impossible. Celia was sure she'd been in the mirror room for at least an hour. But when they stepped outside, the sky was the same bright clear blue; the air still held the crisp damp edge of the morning; Jessie and the children were still gathered at the chapel, scrubbing it clean.

"It felt like so much longer," she murmured.

Easy tripped down the front steps. "I know. But hey, you got through it, right? And now look at you. You're better than you were." She grinned up at Celia. "And I'll bet you're hungry."

Celia didn't know if she was hungry. She couldn't feel hunger, or the absence of hunger. Her hands tingled. She picked at the wax that still stuck to her index finger. "I'm starving."

Jessie and the children ended up joining Easy and Celia on the road down to the canteen. The kids streamed out of the chapel, dumping out buckets of dirty water, flinging wet rags up into the apple tree to dry. Jessie walked next to Celia, her arms swinging at her sides.

"What were you doing in the Old House for so long? I like this dress on you," she added, plucking at Celia's skirt.

Easy answered before Celia could say anything. "Celia needed to wash her face before breakfast. Any idea what Edith's making this morning?"

Jessie studied Celia's face. "You missed a spot. There." She poked Celia's temple with her middle finger. "And Edith left oats for everyone. Again. Hey!" She spun around, her voice suddenly sharp and authoritative. "Who are we leaving behind?"

The children ran then, tumbling down the road in a wave, their voices rising in a twenty-part chorus. "Anyone slow!"

"That's right! Ahead of me, now!" Jessie clapped her hands twice, and a flood of small, fast bodies darted around her and Celia and Easy as the children made their way up the road, toward the canteen.

"You've taken such good charge of them," Easy said. "I'm really impressed, Jessie."

Jessie pinked, ducking her chin. "It's not hard. They're good kids."

Celia watched as the children ran ahead on the road, chasing each other's heels. "You're in charge of all of them?"

"Oh, everyone is in charge of them," Jessie laughed. "I just supervise them while they're working. We're going to spend the rest of the day fixing up the road. Making it smooth for tonight. But everyone's together in it, you know? That's what communities are for. Nobody does anything alone."

"Jessie is being modest," Easy drawled. When she reached behind Celia to give Jessie's shoulder a push, her wrist brushed Celia's shoulder. "She manages the kids for most of the day. She gets them where they need to be, she makes sure they're acting right, she teaches them how to treat each other. She's raising them up right, and she's doing a damned good job."

Jessie stuck her fingers into her mouth and let out a high whistle. Celia thought she'd heard that whistle a few times before, carrying through the trees. The children, who were nearly all out of sight up the road, came trampling back. "No more running. Just walk, or you'll tear the road up worse than it already is," Jessie said, stepping around a divot in the packed dirt. "Go to the canteen and grab something to eat. I'll meet you all down at the shoreline. And Nona," she added, pointing to the little girl who Celia had noticed the night before, "if I catch you diving down under the old dock again, I'm telling Edith to feed you to the visitors for dinner. Got it?"

Nona's eyes went wide and fearful, flicking from Jessie to Celia. Celia raised her hands into claws and bared her teeth at the little girl, whose face opened into a sweet, sudden smile. She ran away, heedless of Jessie's instructions about walking, and the other children followed her, quick and vanishing and then gone around the bend.

"I love them. I do. But Nona's going to be the death of me," Jessie muttered. "That kid's favorite thing to do is test my patience. I don't know what she's gonna do next year."

Celia caught Easy's frown out of the corner of her eye. "What's next year?" she asked.

"Jessie's going to the mainland," Easy answered.

"It's going to be my Salt Year. Finally," Jessie said. She kicked one foot high to send her skirt swirling. "I get to go out there and bring back a baby."

Celia eyed her sidelong. "What do you mean, 'finally'? How long have you been waiting?"

Easy mouthed the words along with Jessie as she said them: "Oh, forever." Jessie spotted Easy's exaggerated expression of woe. "Quit it, she asked. Anyway, it doesn't matter how long I've been waiting. What matters is that I don't have to wait much longer. Tonight they're going to name me Salt Queen for the year, and then I'll be gone, and when

I come back everyone will be so excited because there will fucking finally be a new baby around here."

Celia stumbled over another divot in the road. "Wait," she blurted as Easy caught her elbow. "Didn't Adelaide have her baby here? I haven't seen them, but—"

"Oh, that was different," Jessie said breezily.

Easy kept her hand on Celia's elbow. "You know how it feels to have to wait, don't you, Celia? Jessie's been so patient, but it's time for her to have the experience you thought you wanted. A baby, at last."

The past tense snagged at Celia. *The experience you thought you wanted.* Didn't she still want it? When she searched herself, she couldn't find certainty. She thought she wanted to be a mother, but Easy had shown her, the whole community had shown her—Jessie was showing her even now—that she could have motherhood without needing to have a child of her own. Maybe it was time for her to want something different.

And before she could think about it more deeply, they were at the canteen. There were other people there, Leona and Caleb and a handful of children holding little squares of baked oats.

Celia found herself letting the question go.

Celia and Easy walked into the cool dark of the canteen, leaving Jessie outside to talk with Edith about which children would be helping in the kitchen that night. When they were alone, Easy gave Celia a soft, knowing smile. "Jessie likes you."

Celia blinked as her eyes adjusted. "She does?"

"Of course," Easy said. She reached across the long metal counter to grab two bars of baked oats, handed one over to Celia. "You're everything she wants to be. Just wait'll she comes back from her Salt Year. She'll be talking exactly like you do."

Celia twisted to look back through the open canteen doors. She couldn't see Jessie anymore. Couldn't imagine her with a different voice, different clothes, a swollen belly. "What will happen with the children? While she's gone, I mean?"

"Someone new will step up," Easy said, studying her oat bar closely and then setting it down. She reached over the counter again, rising onto her toes to reach far behind the metal surface, sending something clattering to the floor. Her voice grew strained as she rummaged for what she was seeking. "Someone who really loves the kids, who wants to do the work of caring for them. Someone who's excited about being a mother to a whole community." She grunted triumphantly and straightened, holding a heavy pair of kitchen shears. "It'll work out. I believe in us. Come over here for a second, will you?"

"What are those for?" Celia asked around a mouthful of oats.

Easy looked down at the scissors, then back up at Celia, her mouth tucking in at the corners in an almost-shy smile. "I want to celebrate what you did this morning. You connected with the reflection exercise in a way that takes most people a really long time. Will you let me?"

The smile—the near sheepishness of it, the way Easy's ears flushed pink at the tips—erased any hesitation Celia might otherwise have had. She crossed the short distance between them, brushing the last crumbs of her breakfast from her fingertips. Easy put a hand on her shoulder and pulled gently, turning Celia around.

"I'm so proud of you, Celia," Easy said softly. She gathered Celia's hair with one hand, her fingers brushing the nape of Celia's neck.

Celia let her head fall back as Easy closed one fist around her hair, holding it taut, her grip a firm and irresistible tug at Celia's scalp. Easy was behind her and she was pressure, she was control, she was gravity. And then Celia felt the molar-grinding shear of the scissors working their way through her gathered hair—and slowly, a little at a time, the pull on her scalp vanished, replaced by weightlessness.

It only took a few more minutes after that. Celia closed her eyes as Easy's fingers skated across her scalp, pulling sections of hair loose and then trimming them away. Her hair fell around her like rain sluicing off a rooftop. The scissors were huge. With every cut, they made a sound like swords crossing. The cold metal occasionally brushed against her skin, making her shiver. The air in the canteen kissed Celia's ears, her neck, the base of her skull. She could feel Easy's breath against her throat when she leaned in close to check her work.

When it was finished, Easy ran a hand through Celia's hair, brushed it out of her eyes. "There."

Celia raised her hands to feel what was left. It was short, shorter than it had ever been before. Still long enough to push out of her eyes, but too short to tie back. A strange, giddy laugh rose out of her and escaped before she could contain it. "Wow."

"Do you like it?"

"I can't see it. How does it look?"

Easy shook her head, echoed Celia's laugh. "Amazing. You look amazing. We should have done this sooner." She reached forward and ran her hand through Celia's hair again, slower this time. "It suits us."

Then she grinned and dove back over the counter, tossing the scissors back toward where she'd found them. She grabbed her oat bar and bit it in half, chewed hard around the too-large bite, started toward the door.

Celia looked down at the hair that littered the floor around her. "Shouldn't we clean this up?"

"Kids'll get it," Easy replied thickly around her mouthful of oats. "C'mon, there's something cool I want you to be part of."

Celia caught up to Easy and followed her out of the canteen, down the road toward the shoreline. She ran her hands across the back of her neck. She felt light. She felt free. "Hey, what you said before—"

"When?"

"The thing you said? About someone who's excited about being a mother to a whole community? About how that person would step up?"

"Mm?"

"What did you mean?" Most likely, she thought, Easy meant that she believed in the community at Kindred Cove. That she believed in their ability to work together to care for the children, to raise them well, to see them grow into the people they were meant to be.

But there was another *us* that Easy might believe in.

She didn't answer. She shoved the rest of the oat bar into her mouth and raised her eyebrows, shrugged, walked a little faster.

Celia let herself fall behind, trying to feel something other than the frantic hammering of her heartbeat. She stopped to examine the knobbly branch of a prickly ash, felt the skinlike softness of a jimsonweed blossom. She had a faint memory of being told about the flowers as a child, something about whether or not to eat them. She couldn't remember if they were poison or medicine.

She didn't know how to find out if she might be part of that *us* Easy had referenced. If she might be the person who was meant to be a mother to a community. She thought of the way the children looked at Jessie, followed her, trusted her. The way they needed her guidance. The way they'd be molded by her, shaped for the rest of their lives.

Celia wondered if they might look to her that way someday.

When she realized she'd been left behind, she picked up the pace. By the time she caught up with Easy at the shoreline, Jessie and the children were already there. The children were gathered around Jessie, who stood on the submerged dock. The water came up to her knees. She was saying something Celia couldn't quite make out, her voice low and stern. She looked deadly serious.

"Looks like someone's in trouble," Easy said.

Celia touched Easy's arm. "Bet you a hundred dollars it's Nona making her so mad. It sounded before like they had some serious beef to work out."

Easy raised her eyebrows. "A hundred dollars? I can't do shit with that. Make it a neckrub and you're on."

The thought of Easy's hands on her neck drew a strange, staccato laugh out of Celia. "Deal."

They wandered down toward the crowd at the water's edge. The children stood there, some holding buckets, others holding short, stiff-bristled brooms. Jessie was frowning down at the dock with her hands on her hips.

"Everything okay over here?" Easy called.

Jessie's head snapped up whip-fast. Her lips were white with anger. "It's Nona. She's under the dock."

Easy nudged Celia's arm with one sharp elbow. "Owe you one," she muttered. Then, louder: "She has to come up sometime, right?"

A poke-bellied girl with a long brown braid turned to look up over her shoulder at Easy. "She can hold her breath for a really long time," she said doubtfully.

Easy glanced between Jessie and the little girl. "How long has she been down there?"

The girl shrugged. "Since before I got here."

Celia frowned. She crouched down in front of the girl and looked into her bright, serious eyes. "How long ago did you get here?"

Easy touched Celia's shoulder. "They don't usually talk to outsiders," she whispered. "Don't be hurt if she—"

"A long time ago," the little girl said. She took a step closer to Celia, her chin wobbling with the threat of tears. "She ran ahead when Jessie stopped at the canteen for breakfast."

A sick sense of dread crept through Celia, winding around the base of her spine and scraping its way up to the base of her skull. Jessie's lips were still white, but now it looked more like panic than anger. Celia looked to Easy, hoping she'd misunderstood. "That must have been at least fifteen minutes ago. Remember, she stopped to talk to Edith . . . ?"

Easy's face had gone perfectly still. Her mouth was a straight, slack line. Her eyes passed over Celia like water sliding across plate glass. Her head turned a few degrees as though she was being rotated by a giant, steady hand, and she looked at Jessie.

Celia tried again. "Easy? That's too long. If Nona's really been in the water since we got to the canteen—"

"I'm sure it's fine," Easy said. Her voice came out half-flat, like the air had been let out of her. "I'm sure there's nothing to worry about. But if you want to go take a look, we can."

Celia swallowed. She felt exposed. The sun was hot on the newly bare skin of her neck. She didn't want to be the one to cause a fuss. She didn't want to create a problem. But she asked herself what a mother would do—what she would do, if she was the one in charge of the children. "I think we should at least check. Make sure everything's okay."

Easy gestured toward Jessie with one slow wave of an arm. "After you."

Ten Years Ago

Edith stands in William's office. She is between him and the door.

"I'm telling you, we have to try something different," she says. "It's been two years since the last birth."

"Communities go without new babies sometimes, Edith. It's fine. You should be enjoying the break from herding pregnant women through their deliveries. Why are you in my office instead, complaining about not having enough to do? Is Caleb running the whole garden on his own now? Is that it?"

She can remember a time when she was intimidated by William. He's always been a coiled spring of a man. There's a hum of withheld violence about him. He likes to break things with his hands. But somehow over the years since the lakebed opened up and drank down the Vetiver, that sense of restrained brutality has stopped being intimidating to her.

She's less afraid of pain than she used to be.

"I'm in your office because Dad's dead," she says flatly, "so I can't talk to him about it, can I? It's just you and me making the decisions."

"And Leona," he adds.

She gives him a weary look. "Oh? Are we inviting Leona in here? Does she enjoy weighing in on practical matters now, instead of making everything about spiritual purity? I'll go get her if you want her to be part of this conversation." She waits longer than necessary, letting his silence spool out until her point is past made. "I think you're well aware that we're not in a lull in terms of conception, only in terms of delivery."

"No one has ever lost a child at Kindred Cove," William says warningly.

"And we're going to keep not-losing our not-children until something changes," she snaps. "And then, a few years from now, we're not going to have anyone to do the work that makes it so you can sit on your ass in this office all day. Do you want to fix it or not?"

He pushes back from his desk, his chair scraping against the composite floor. "Fine. So there's a problem. You did it, you pointed it out. Look at your finger waving so bravely, Edith. What do you want me to do about it? Should I cork everyone up so the babies stay inside?"

She forces herself to take a deep, slow breath. She pulls William's words into herself and makes them part of herself, and when she breathes out again, she pushes her patience out into the world. She will make this place better by investing it with herself. She will make herself better by learning to tolerate the things she currently cannot bear.

"I think you can help with this issue the same way you help with all our other issues," she says slowly. "I think you can connect us with resources in the outside world. You take salt to the mainland once a month, don't you? So next time you go, take some extra cargo with you. Maybe if one of us gets pregnant out there," she adds, "it'll stick."

He stares at her hard. He doesn't like to feel cornered like this, she knows. He doesn't like to feel corrected. He's trying to think of a way to shut her down, to deny her. "I can't chaperone some fertile idiot through a sexual odyssey," he finally says. "I have too much work to do."

Triumph blazes inside her. He's not arguing anymore. He's negotiating. "Drop them off. Let them figure it out on their own and come back when they're knocked up."

"And if they don't come back?"

"Then they were never here. Take one of the young ones," she adds, inspired. "So if they don't come back, we don't have to rearrange anything."

"We have to give them a time limit," he says. "We can't just unclip the tether and let them run."

Now she's got him. "Six months," she suggests. "Long enough to get pregnant, but not long enough to have the baby away from the Cove."

"A year," he counters. "In case they lose the first one and have to try again."

Edith steps toward him and holds out her hand. He clasps it. A few years ago, he'd have taken the opportunity to pull her in for a kiss, but he hasn't done that since Leona found her way into his bed.

That's fine. Edith likes it better this way.

"A year," she confirms. "Next time you take salt to the mainland—"

He nods. "I'll bring extra."

FOUR AND A HALF MONTHS AGO

1

Edith looked up at the night sky and felt the ghost of Dad's palm on the top of her head.

Even after all these years on the island, she'd never stopped being stunned at the sight of the sky over Kindred Cove. The number of stars up there seemed reckless, like someone had tripped and spilled the whole batch all in one place. Sometimes wildfires on the mainland would throw a blanket of smoke into the sky, muting the intensity of the display—but even then, Edith could see more stars here than she ever had anywhere else.

It was never entirely dark on the island thanks to those stars. Tonight the moon was bright too, and it made Edith feel more awake than she did during the day, more alert. She walked between the trees, picking her way along the worn footpath that led from Violet House to the road. The moonlight scattered a frenzy of shadows before her.

She'd been checking in on everyone, as was her habit at the end of a day of fasting. People struggled in their hunger, she knew—it wasn't easy to set aside the complaints of the body, especially for those who thought they could get away with breaking the fast a little early. It also wasn't lost on her that today's hunger had been harder on folks than usual. It was the third last-minute fast Easy had called in just under a fortnight.

It came down to stress. She understood. Monitoring Adelaide's pregnancy was a strain on everyone. Shifting around responsibilities had been difficult, too—Jessie needed a lot of help stepping up into the role of leading the children. Caleb had made things right after his mortifying display two weeks earlier, spending an enormous amount of time reflecting in the room at the back of the Old House, but that had been yet another burden for everyone to manage. It wasn't too much to ask, a hungry day for everyone here and there, in the face of what Easy was taking on.

No part of Edith felt responsible for that stress. Harvey's death was his own responsibility. And now he was part of something greater than himself.

All was well.

Edith was comforted by what she found as she wandered between the little houses tucked back into the trees: dark doorways, silence, peace. Everyone was where they were supposed to be, doing what they were meant to do.

Except that there was someone on the road.

Edith frowned, not because there was anything wrong with someone being on the road, but because she didn't immediately recognize the shape of the person's back, the slope of their shoulders, the angle of their head. For all the brightness of the moon and stars, it was still impossible to make out specific features at this distance. Edith squinted, and then her frown deepened as she realized who it was she was failing to recognize.

"Adelaide?"

The figure turned and, in turning, became legible to Edith's eye at last. Adelaide's belly was a swelling wave, unmissable, unmistakable. She held her breasts in her hands, her elbows tucked neatly in against her sides. Edith ached with the memory of how swollen and tender her own breasts had been every time she'd been pregnant, how heavy. She wondered if Adelaide was even aware of holding herself, or if it was a private habit that had become second nature.

"What are you doing up?" Adelaide asked, her voice soft and a little raw, like she'd been crying.

"Keeping an eye on things. Couldn't sleep?"

Adelaide shook her head, lowered her hands to her sides. "My back is killing me. It's been hurting since Caleb knocked me down on that fast day two weeks ago. Walking usually helps, but tonight it just keeps getting worse."

Edith was close enough now to see the tight knot of Adelaide's mouth, the furrow in her brow. "How much does it hurt?" she asked.

"Pretty bad, on and off."

"On and off?"

"Yeah, like—in waves, kind of? It's fine, though. No part of me is comfortable right now anyway." She rubbed her lower back hard, pressing her knuckles into the muscles. "I just thought moving around a bit might help. Do you want to walk with me?"

The invitation was false, Edith could hear that easily enough. Adelaide didn't want company. She wanted to hide with her pain, like a sick cat dragging itself under a front porch.

But the way she was kneading her back, the clench in her jaw, the low swing of her belly—Edith couldn't ignore those, wasn't even going to try. She remembered how restless she'd been in the last few days of her own pregnancies, how in spite of her exhaustion she'd felt driven to pace the spiral road from the Old House to the water and back over and over again.

She looked into Adelaide's eyes and saw that familiar restlessness in them, and there was no way she was going to let the girl be on her own.

Looping an arm through Adelaide's elbow, Edith started leading them both down the slope of the road toward the water. Slow, leisurely—there was no reason to rush. "Did you know that I used to walk with Dad at night, just like this?"

Adelaide looked surprised. "No—what?"

Edith nodded. "We started doing it when the Cove was new. I wasn't that much older than you are now. William was trying hard as he could to get me pregnant, but he needed breaks, you know how it is. Dad had him meditating in between, to get his focus right. So I'd leave him to his breathing exercises, and I'd go and do chores or get snacks or even just look up at the sky for a little while before going back to him. And one night, I ran into Dad out here, pacing the road just like you were."

"What was he doing?"

"Just looking at different patches of dirt, trying to see their potential. He paused right there," Edith said, pointing at the edge of the section of road they were passing. It split off, right there, and led to Leona's apiary. "He paused right there and he said, *This is where the bees will do best.* Can you believe it?"

"Of course he did," Adelaide said softly. "He was always doing stuff like that."

"That's where I ran into him. He asked me to walk with him, and we ended up talking about everything that might happen here. We went all the way down to the water and back, and he dropped me off with William and said he knew we'd get it right soon. And when I came out to walk around the next night? There he was, waiting for me. We walked together like that the whole time I was pregnant with you," she added. "And after. When he took you in, and named you his own. When you and Easy were growing up. Right up until the day he disappeared, we had our evening walks."

Adelaide was quiet for a long time. When she finally spoke, her voice was soft and careful. "What do you think happened to him? I mean, I know he went into the water. But . . . what do you think happened to him after? What happened to his body?"

It was Edith's turn to be quiet. "I don't know," she said at last. "It's not for us to understand."

Adelaide drew a sharp breath. Was she overcome by emotion, Edith wondered, at the memory of her father? Or was she gulping down air to get herself through a fresh wave of pain? A glance at the girl's shuttered face offered no clarity.

"I should head back," Adelaide said as they approached the dark canteen. "I think maybe I need to lie down."

"Do you doubt your father's legacy?" She pressed a steadying hand to the small of Adelaide's back, pressing firmly, feeling for a pulse of tension in the muscle there. "Do you worry that his disappearance might mean he failed us?"

"Of course not." Adelaide was flinching away from the pressure of Edith's hand, but Edith didn't relent. "I just . . . I just wonder sometimes. It all happened at once, you know?"

"Mmm?"

"You remember. The mines collapsing, the lake changing, the miracle tides starting up, the reef. And him going away. It all happened at once. It feels connected." The muscle under Edith's hand knotted up tight. Adelaide's voice grew strained. "I know we're not supposed to talk about it, but I do think about it sometimes, and I wonder if he—Edith, I—" She cut herself short.

Edith dug into the flesh of the girl's back, feeling her pulse in her fingertips, waiting for the clenched muscle to release. "I know," she said. "You need to stay connected to your purpose. That's what'll get you through this."

Adelaide's steps slowed. Finally, she managed a reply. "Get me through what?"

"What's coming," Edith replied. "It's going to feel like you're being torn in half. You'll be scared that you're going to die. That's normal."

Adelaide opened her mouth to answer, then froze at a sound. It was the sound of the canteen door opening, followed by footsteps heading toward the main road. The rhythm of the footsteps was familiar. It was a rhythm that made irritation tug at the edges of Edith's practiced, hard-won patience.

"Well! It is a beautiful night," Leona called out. Adelaide and Edith turned as one to greet her. She strode toward them with her skirt in her hands, her movements purposeful and efficient until she reached a scuffed divot in the road, too deep for the children to sweep smooth. She paused there, her eyes lingering on that scuff as she greeted them. The sight of her staring down at it made Edith's heels itch. "What are you two doing out so late? Staying cool while you can?"

"We're going down to the water," Edith said. "Adelaide needs to get the weight of this baby off her back. What were you doing in the canteen?"

The accusation wasn't subtle, and Leona's reply was equally tart. "Checking on inventory. Good thing I ran into you, since you'll need someone to help our girl into the water." Leona tore her gaze off the road. It landed squarely on Adelaide's belly. "Is it time?"

Adelaide shook her head. "No. No, it's not time yet. I'm not that far along. I don't need to go into the water."

"She's having back pain." Edith didn't try to inject meaning into her words but she couldn't help herself. She saw Leona understand right away.

"Well," the other woman said, positioning herself on the opposite side of Adelaide from Edith and putting a firm hand on the girl's shoulder, "the water will be the best thing for that. I'm sorry to interrupt your dawdling, Edith, but we should really get going."

The irritation that had been tugging at Edith's patience yanked hard. She wanted to snap at Leona, to remind her that they'd been on their way already, that nobody had been *dawdling*. She smiled instead. "Thank you, yes. Let's go on down."

Adelaide stumbled as the two women urged her forward, Leona

pressing on her shoulder and Edith pressing on her hips. Their pace was quicker now, their earlier leisure replaced by Leona's possessive urgency.

"I really don't think this is necessary," Adelaide said, the smallest tremor in her voice. "I'm just tired."

"I remember that kind of tired. Like there could never be enough sleep in the world, right? But you can't sleep, either, can you?" Leona's certainty verged on smugness.

"I'm impressed that you still remember," Edith said smoothly. She let her hand rest in the dip at the base of Adelaide's spine, guiding the girl past the dark office, around the last bend in the road. "It's been such a long time for you."

"She's right. I can't sleep most nights," Adelaide agreed as though Edith hadn't spoken. "But I'm definitely tired right now. I should go to bed. Rest while I can so I'm ready for the work to come, right?"

She made as if to turn around, but Edith and Leona's hands were there on her, keeping her headed in the right direction. She balked, stopped in her tracks. They stood there at the top of the final slope down toward the water's edge. The slope was shorter than it had ever been.

"This will feel like rest," Edith promised. "The water will carry the baby for you for a little while. It will help."

"Have you bled at all today?" Leona asked, too sharp as always.

"A little. That's why I need to lie down, I had spotting early on and the doctor said—I was told that I should rest until it stopped."

Leona caught Edith's eye over Adelaide's shoulder. Edith knew they were having the same thought because it was the only thought possible in that moment: A conversation about "the doctor" could wait. That little bit of blood couldn't. Together with the back pain, that blood looked an awful lot like the first flags raised to signal the baby's readiness to join the community.

Below them, the water of the lake just barely kissed the trunks of the black gum trees. Adelaide looked at that dark water and pressed a hand to one side of her belly; Edith wondered if the baby was shifting inside of her, rolling, turning toward the call of the water.

Leona gave Adelaide an ungentle nudge. "Has anything else happened? Anything unusual?"

"No," Adelaide replied, stumbling forward. "What?"

"She's asking if your water broke," Edith finally said with a sigh. "It would feel like wetting yourself. It doesn't happen every time," she added.

"It might have happened while you were bathing."

"She hasn't gone into the water since that fasting day two weeks ago," Edith said, aiming a significant glance at Leona. She wasn't going to mention the other thing that happened that day. There was nothing to mention. But she wasn't willing to let it go unremarked upon—Adelaide had been avoiding the water since that day, and she wanted to know why.

Adelaide was insistent. "No, nothing like that has happened, my water didn't break. Listen—it's not time. It can't be time yet. I'm not ready. I'm not going in there." Adelaide took halting, reluctant steps forward, her feet shuffling across the packed dirt a few inches at a time. Edith pressed both hands into the back of Adelaide's hips once more, urging her on. Leona pushed on her shoulders. The water glinted in the moonlight like an open eye. "I don't want to go into the water. I don't want to be blessed. Not yet. Not tonight." She gasped, and under Edith's palms another muscle spasm rippled across her low back.

"What on earth are you so afraid of?" Leona snapped. "You know these waters. You know the Vetiver. Don't you want this baby to be born in community? Or are you waiting to find out what a *doctor* might say?"

"Please," Adelaide whimpered. The girl watched the water like it was an approaching knife. "I can't. I can't do this here. I'm not having my baby on this island, okay? Easy promised, we're going to leave, we're going to the mainland and we'll go live in St. Louis together, me and Easy and Celia. Easy promised we could move to the city together. I'm not going to have my baby in that water, the reef is still growing and I don't want it to touch me, I don't want it to touch my baby. Please just let me go to bed."

She kept babbling like that, on and on. She kept calling the baby hers. Leona looked at Edith again and there was something in her eyes that Edith rarely saw there: camaraderie. Kinship. Her eyes said *can you believe this child* and *what are we going to do about her* and *thank goodness we're in this together.*

Just like that, with one shared look between them, Leona and

Edith went from reluctant allies to steadfast ones. They were united in their kind and valiant efforts to help an intractable girl who didn't know what was good for her, who was resisting the very thing she needed most: a blessing from the lake, a moment without gravity, the warm tongue of saltwater on her skin.

"Please," she was saying, her voice buckling with needless tears. "Harvey just joined the reef two weeks ago. Don't make me get into the water with him."

Edith gave Leona a rueful smile, a *no I can't believe this child but we will handle it* smile, and then she braced one foot behind her and pressed the heels of her hands against either side of Adelaide's spine. "Harvey is part of this child's life too, Adelaide. We all are," Edith said. "And you should be thankful for that."

And then she pushed. She shoved hard. A grunt came from low in her throat and she heard Leona make the same noise, both of them together, one voice speaking one holy effort into being.

Adelaide let out a startled cry and tipped forward, tripping one foot past the other, her momentum carrying her down the slope too fast for balance. Edith and Leona stepped quickly after her but weren't close enough to catch her when she fell, her knees striking the packed earth with a hollow, resonant *thunk.*

The pain of impact seemed to knock the air out of the girl. She teetered forward, threw out a hand to catch herself. By the time Edith caught up to her, she was on all fours, a wet heft to her rapid breathing.

"What the fuck," she whispered. She didn't sound angry so much as removed from herself, far from the body that had just fallen a few meters from the water's edge.

That was good, Edith thought. That was perfect. The girl would want to be far from her body when it was time to let the lightning rip its way out of her. Best to start gaining that distance now.

"Almost there," Leona said, stooping to hook a hand under Adelaide's armpit. She looked up to Edith and gave a nod, and Edith copied her movements, slipping a hand into the damp pocket of skin where Adelaide's arm met her breast. "Just a little farther."

They hefted her, these two older women, these women who knew better than she did, these women who would get her through the ordeal to come. She went limp. She didn't fight them as they lifted her to her feet and propelled her to the edge of the Vetiver. But when the water touched her feet, she came to life, thrashing against them, tearing her arms from their respective grips with the force of a cat fighting to keep from being shoved into a sack. A sudden flash of white heat struck Edith as the girl's knuckles caught her ear and then she was loose, stumbling back up the slope backward, barely keeping her balance.

"I said no," she panted. "I said I don't want to. It isn't safe. I'm not going in. And I'm not staying here for one more fucking day."

Leona was looking at Adelaide like she was a stranger. Edith understood why. She couldn't remember a single other time the girl had acted so wrong. This was Easy's old way: ungrateful, ornery, selfish. Anyone might have expected this from her, back before she decided to get herself right with the community. That was why Easy hadn't been the one trusted with the work of enduring the world in order to bring a baby back to the Cove. Nobody would have extended her that trust. And nobody could have imagined sweet, intelligent Adelaide acting this way. Not back then.

Worse—worse than any of it—was the water that had splashed up onto Edith's legs. With all that thrashing and all that fight, Adelaide had managed to undo years of purposeful, careful obedience.

Adelaide, Edith thought through the ringing in her ear, was supposed to be the good one.

"What's gotten into you?" Edith hissed. "You're making this so complicated. It doesn't need to be complicated, Adelaide. Just get into the water and everything will feel better, I promise."

Adelaide shook her head. "I'm not going in that lake. Not tonight. I don't—" She palmed her stomach again, grimacing. "The baby doesn't want it. I can tell. She doesn't want to be in that water. I have to keep her safe."

Edith pursed her lips. She knew a lie when she heard one. Adelaide had never been skilled at deception—that, too, was Easy's area of expertise—and she was lying just as poorly now as she had when she was a child, her voice wavering and her eyes lifted to the stars so as not to risk meeting Leona's searching gaze. Edith watched as Adelaide's hands smoothed over the prow of her stomach over and over again.

Adelaide wasn't responding to what the baby wanted. She certainly wasn't thinking about what it needed. Edith didn't think Adelaide could feel that baby at all.

"Goodnight," Adelaide said resolutely. Then she turned on her heel and marched briskly up the hill, vanishing around the bend in the road before Leona or Edith could answer her.

2

Leona turned slowly to face Edith, the water sloshing gently around her ankles. "I cannot believe," she whispered.

"Me either," Edith replied, still standing on dry land just a few scant inches away from the lip of the lake. She knotted her fingers in her skirt. The fabric was damp. It felt incredible under her hands. A shiver ran through her. "Leona, I don't know if you saw, but—"

"I saw," Leona said. "Come on, then. You might as well fall down all the way before you get back up."

Edith shook her head. "It wouldn't be right."

"You're bleeding," Leona said. She touched Edith's neck with one hand, held it up to show off the blood that darkened her fingers. "Come on. Let me." She heard Leona's slow steps through the water. And then her hand was there, gentle pressure, tipping Edith's head to one side so her ear could rest fully in the palmful of water.

It stung badly enough that Edith thought the skin might have broken under Adelaide's swinging fist. She didn't care. It was bliss.

When Edith had first met Leona, she'd been instantly hypnotized. Leona had been nineteen years old then, with dark purple bruises on her collarbones that peeked out through the curtain of long black hair swinging around her shoulders. She'd known her way around Dad's apartment, hadn't seemed cowed by William's authoritative presence, thought cigarettes were boring. She'd seemed impossibly poised, impossibly mature. Sixteen-year-old Edith, who was dazzled by Dad's attention and had been trying to take up smoking for months, had looked into Leona's eyes and seen a knowledge there that she knew she'd do anything to obtain for herself.

But Leona had never liked her. Not since the day Dad had put Edith's hand into William's and named him the father of her future baby. Leona had ignored Edith, had rolled her eyes at Edith's questions, had left rooms when Edith entered them. When Edith and William had finally succeeded in making their own baby, Leona had given her the silent treatment for the duration of her pregnancy.

Edith didn't know why. She didn't know what she'd done to make Leona shut her out for so long, reflecting only cool indifference. She'd simply accepted it after a while. Over the years, as things at the Cove deteriorated, Leona seemed to forget to hate Edith—but still, theirs had remained a distant, strained relationship.

Until this: Leona's hand on Edith's hair, Leona's palm raising more water to Edith's ear, Leona's soft words encouraging Edith to take a few steps into the cool, dark shallows of the Vetiver. "You should keep soaking this for a little while," she was saying, "so it doesn't swell too badly. If anyone asks, you can tell them Tom got you." And she was walking deeper in, too, taking short shuffling steps through the silt, leaning on Edith so neither of them lost their balance.

"Thank you," Edith breathed. Somewhere inside of her, in a place she'd buried deep a long time ago, she was overcome with joy. Her feet in the water. Her ear in the water. The lake all around her. It made her feel new.

"Adelaide doesn't seem like herself," Leona murmured. "It's like she went out into the world and came back wrong."

Edith let out a sigh. "I don't like it," she answered. "Did you hear the way she kept saying *my baby*? She keeps bringing up doctors. And have you seen the way she moves now?"

"Oh, I've seen," Leona replied darkly. "She touches things like her hands are wet. Her feet are tender, she walks slow—"

"Too slow," Edith answered. She could hear the eagerness in her own voice, but she couldn't help that. Finally, *finally*, she and Leona had something to share beyond their commitment to the island. "And I haven't heard her say anything yet about what kind of work she plans on doing here after the baby is born."

"Probably thinks she won't have to do anything at all." Leona dipped her hand back into the water, lifted a fresh palmful to Edith's ear.

The sting was gone now, but Edith didn't want this to end, so she didn't say anything, didn't straighten. "She's got a surprise coming. And soon, by the sound of it."

The two of them stayed there for a long time, even after Leona grew tired of bending over Edith and straightened to dry her hands on her skirt. They talked about the girl, about the journey she'd been on and the strange way she was acting and the baby she'd brought home to them. After a while they walked out of the water, up the slope, to sit on the front step of Umber House, where Edith had slept since the day she and Dad and William had set up the little shed, right there where Dad had understood it needed to go.

It was only when the stars started to fade against the lightening sky that they realized they'd stayed up talking all night.

"I can't remember the last time I did that," Leona said with a startled laugh. "Well. Probably one of the nights with William, after Dad—" She caught herself, her tone pivoting hard to somber. "After what happened. He needed comfort, is all."

Edith let her head tilt to one side. She felt a little drunk with fatigue and something else, a kind of triumph at the idea of having finally won over the woman both Dad and William always seemed to have liked best. "He loves you so deeply," she said. "You must have been a great comfort to him."

Leona regarded her warily. "I think I was," she said. "I think I still am."

"Good. Now, we should both probably try to get a little sleep before dawn, shouldn't we?" Edith hauled herself to her feet, wincing at the ache in her back from a night spent sitting on wooden stairs. She extended a hand to Leona, and Leona accepted, pulling herself up gingerly.

"It's been good talking to you," Leona said. It sounded like she really meant it. There was something in her eyes, too—new, careful regard. "And listen, Edith—I don't think anyone needs to find out about what Adelaide did to you. She didn't mean to splash you, and you didn't mean to break your vow. We could probably just chalk that up to misfortune, don't you think?"

Something had been mended between them, or maybe forged, or maybe just acknowledged. Edith couldn't tell what it was and she was too tired to try to figure it out now. She simply trusted her arms to pull Leona into a tight hug, trusted her lungs to breathe in the smell of the other woman's skin. After a moment's hesitation, Leona returned the embrace.

"We'll keep an eye on Adelaide," Edith said. "We can get her on the right path. I know we can."

Leona pulled back and, for the first time since their first encounter twenty-nine years earlier, she looked at Edith with clear respect. "I know we can, too," she said, her voice warm with new trust. "We'll take care of her. Together."

Warmth spread through Edith's belly. "Together."

Eight Months Ago

Celia picks at her garden salad. The dressing has blue cheese in it. She read an article saying that the mold that defines blue cheese has antioxidants in it. That would make blue cheese a superfood. She thinks she is supposed to eat superfoods, to prevent cancer. Celia is afraid of cancer.

She is afraid of so many things.

"Is it bad?" Adelaide asks from across the table. It's their first time eating together. They both happened to be at the café near their fertility-and-child-loss support group, both of them wanting to get lunch before going into the community center basement to sit in a circle and try to heal.

"I'm not sure," Celia replies. "I never know if something is bad, or if I just think it's bad. How's yours?"

Adelaide has a bulgur bowl. Little pearls of wheat, bright pink shreds of salmon, dandelion greens. "Amazing. It's perfect. Did you know I never ate wheat until a few years ago? Never in my life," she says. She's glowing.

"You look so happy," Celia observes.

Adelaide nods. "I got a letter. From home."

Celia has never gotten a letter from anyone. "Is that good?"

"No. Not really," Adelaide admits. "It's from my sister, actually. I was supposed to—a couple of years ago, she was supposed to come join me. But she never did, and now she's asking me to come home. She said she needs me to come and see how well she's doing, but I know how to read between the lines." She's trying so hard not to smile. "She wants me to come get her. I'm going back in a few months, to rescue her from that place. The place we grew up. I'm going to bring her back here."

"Rescue? But you make it sound so idyllic when you talk about it in group." Celia forces herself to eat a wedge of beet. It's earthy and pungent with blue cheese. She hopes the antioxidants are working.

"Do I?" Adelaide raises her eyebrows. "I didn't think I talked about it very much."

"You talk about it all the time. You make it sound amazing. And now you're going back, right? So it can't be all that bad."

Adelaide gives her a small, tight smile. "Yeah, um. I guess it's not all bad."

The smile is enough for Celia to feel that she understands. To trust in her belief that the place where Adelaide grew up is probably, overall, pretty good. "So you're bringing your sister back here?"

"Oh, absolutely," Adelaide says. "I can't wait for you to meet her."

Celia wonders if maybe, in Adelaide, she's made a friend. Her heart beats hard, and she can feel the rhythm of it echoing through the unfillable hole in her sternum. "I can't wait either. I just know I'm going to love her."

SALT FESTIVAL

day four | afternoon

When Nona finally came out of the water, she did not seem alive.

Easy sent Jessie and the children away while the girl was still beneath the submerged dock. She told Jessie not to let the situation derail her day, emphasized that the road needed tending and that it would be good to give the children work to keep them from focusing on Nona.

"Go," she said. "I'll handle this."

Celia helped herd the children up toward the gap in the treeline, pulling them from the shallows and encouraging worried stragglers to follow their friends up into the trees. Jessie looked grateful for the help. She cast worried eyes toward the dock. "Do you think I should send for someone?" she asked, and Celia nodded without stopping to question whether she should be offering an opinion. Jessie caught two passing children by their shoulders. "Go find Caleb and William. Fast as you can." The children were gone before she finished the sentence. She watched them sprint up the road. "Fuck," she whispered. "This is going to throw everything off."

"Maybe she'll be okay," Celia offered, although she didn't see a way it could be so.

Jessie looked at her with a combination of understanding and disappointment. "You should go back and help Easy. Nice haircut, by the way."

But Easy didn't need help. She stood in the shallows, alone, and then, when Celia joined her, in silence. She didn't acknowledge that Celia was standing beside her, but when Celia stretched out her hand, Easy took it. They waited, fingers interlaced, while Caleb and William arrived, stripped, and dove down into the water.

Caleb came up first. William surfaced soon after, carrying the girl's limp body. Her arm dangled loose, fingers stretching toward the water. Her head hung at a sharp angle. Water streamed from the long ropes of hair that fell across her face.

Celia couldn't draw a full breath. Easy's grip on her other hand tightened once, so hard Celia felt her bones creak.

Then Easy let go.

After all that time in the water—there was no way the girl could be alive. Celia felt them both know it. She was sure that she and Easy were witnessing the kind of loss that would change them both forever. A distant part of her, like a half-numb limb, wondered if this would bring them closer together.

But then Nona's chest spasmed. She jackknifed in William's arms. The sudden shift in her weight made William stumble. He lost his footing on the submerged dock. Caleb lunged for him but was too far away, and William went down, surging forward and then falling into the water.

He landed hard. He dropped Nona.

She fell into the water so limp that she hardly made a splash.

He recovered fast, scooping her up into his arms again and hurrying the rest of the way to shore. Caleb tried to take her, but William brushed past him and set the girl down at the edge of the water.

She spasmed again, folded at the waist so her back rose off the dirt. Her head followed the arc of her chest, then swung forward. She convulsed, her spine rippling, her ribcage swelling under the soaked fabric of her thin dress. Water poured out of her mouth and down her front in a torrential, unceasing gout.

Celia was moving toward the girl when it happened. She saw the grayish cast of Nona's skin. She saw the sudden surge of water leave Nona's mouth. She saw Nona's fingers clench into fists around palmfuls of wet shoredirt.

And she thought she saw something else. Something livid and pink inside Nona's open mouth, behind the rushing water. Her tongue, Celia thought first, but it couldn't be her tongue because it was so bright, and it seemed to spread out to fill her entire gaping mouth—

Easy was pushing past Celia, rushing toward Nona, kneeling to push the little girl's hair away from her face. Caleb and William stepped forward, too, forming a close circle. Celia could see Easy's hand on the girl's heaving back, could hear the splash of water, could hear Easy murmuring something that sounded like *take care of her.*

And then Caleb was beside Celia, his arm around her shoulder, his fingertips floating just above her skin without touching it. "Come on. We should give them some space," he said. "She'll be okay."

"That's not possible," Celia said. "She was underwater for—what, twenty minutes? Half an hour? She can't be—"

"Time is funny when you're in a crisis," Caleb interrupted. The two of them were halfway to the treeline already. "It can feel like ages, I know. But honestly, you don't need to worry. The kids here get into scrapes all the time. We know how to take care of them."

Celia twisted to look back at Nona. William and Easy were in the way, blocking the girl from sight. "She can't have survived that. We need to call someone. The mainland, a hospital—"

Caleb pulled Celia into the trees and out of sight. He stepped around her neatly and gripped her by the arms. His touch shocked her. "Hey. Look at me." She was already looking at him, but the way he said it arrested her, pulled her mind away from the coughing girl on the shore and the strange pink mass inside her mouth. "I'm going to be honest with you, okay? Do you think you can handle that?"

Celia's arms ached under Caleb's fingers. She nodded.

"Here's the thing. Easy trusts you a lot. She's been letting you see and do things that we don't normally let visitors see and do. You know that, right?"

Celia blinked. This wasn't the honesty she'd been anticipating. She'd expected him to say something about how Nona was probably dead. She'd expected him to tell her how to be okay after witnessing the death of a girl who, less than an hour before, had laughed at the idea that Celia could be scary. It took her a moment to catch up to what he was saying. "Easy . . . trusts me?"

"Come on, Celia. You and I both know she's been giving you a lot of special treatment."

It was true. She knew it was. Caleb couldn't have known about Celia's time in the mirror room that morning, but she ran quickly through the other time she'd spent with Easy—swimming off the cliffs, carving candles, walking up the road late at night, staring at the stars, wearing this white dress.

Surely none of that mattered now. Not with Nona lying on the dirt, coughing up all that water.

"I feel uncomfortable with the way you've been presuming on that trust," Caleb continued. "It's not that you don't deserve it, okay? I'm sure you do. But trust is a two-way street, and I don't see you giving Easy back the trust she's been extending your way."

His words winded her. She wanted to know what was happening with Nona, and now that desire felt like a stone in her lung. It felt like she was betraying Easy. "I'm—I'm sorry, I didn't—"

"I know you didn't. That's why I'm telling you." He spoke quickly, like he was imparting a secret to her. "Trust is a choice you make, and so far, you're not choosing it. That's fucked-up. I'm sorry, I know this might not feel good to hear, but we value honest feedback here, and I think—I mean, I have to believe that you value it too. Otherwise I can't imagine that Easy would consider you such a strong candidate."

"A strong—?"

He glanced behind Celia briefly before returning his eyes to hers. "I'm just saying, you have to trust that Easy knows what she's doing with things. She's lived on this island since she was Nona's age. She knows how to handle a crisis, and she's going to handle this one just fine. The last thing she needs is you going around yelling about calling the mainland over a kid who's already sitting up on her own."

Celia nodded numbly. She hadn't thought she'd been yelling. Then again, she hadn't *thought* at all, she realized. She'd simply reacted. "I'm sorry."

Caleb's face split into a relieved grin. "Hey, don't worry about it. You didn't get far enough to cause a problem. And now"—he looked behind her again—"you know how to do better. Easy was right about you. You're growing fast."

Celia twisted to see what he was looking at. Behind her, through the trees, she caught a glimpse of Easy passing along the road. "Where is she going?"

"She and William are taking Nona to the office. To lie down, probably. I'm sure that whole situation was scary for her. She'll need a breather before she gets back to the other kids." Caleb let go of her at last. His grip had left vivid red imprints on Celia's skin. "Speaking of the kids—did you want to hang out with Jessie until Candle Hour?"

She rubbed her arms, thought of what he'd said about special treatment. About trusting Easy. She wanted to do the right thing, and she knew that all her instincts were wrong. Asking to go see Nona would mean she didn't trust Easy. Asking for answers would mean seeking out special treatment. She didn't know what to do. She didn't know what was right anymore. "What are the rest of the visitors doing?" she ventured. "Maybe I should join them."

He rolled his eyes. "They're with Edith up in the garden, harvesting for the big dinner tonight. She's telling them about how they need to treat their life as a garden and grow what they want to manifest. Honestly," he added, leaning close enough that she could smell the lake on him, "they might need to hear the lecture, but it's nothing you don't already know. You'd have a better time with Jessie. She and the kids are fixing up the road. Actually, now that I think of it, I don't think any visitor has ever participated in that before."

"Oh." She felt like she'd been spun around too fast to know which direction she was facing. Caleb was smiling at her. His eyes were warm.

Maybe she'd overreacted before, when he'd told her that she was—how had he put it? *Presuming on Easy's trust.* It had felt awful, but he didn't seem to think it was worth feeling awful about, and now he was offering her this. Yet another thing most visitors didn't get. Another opportunity to prove herself.

"Okay, yeah. Take me wherever I'm supposed to go."

"You're going to get a lot out of this," he said, turning back toward the road. Then he paused and looked back at her. "Love the hair, by the way. You look so much more like yourself."

She let Caleb lead her up the road. She could see the children ahead. William, Easy, and Nona were nowhere in sight.

Unease tugged at the inside of her navel. She pushed it down.

Trust was a choice, she told herself. And she was going to choose right this time.

PART FIVE

when you can’t trust yourself, trust your community

SALT FESTIVAL

day four | afternoon

The sun reached right through the thin white cotton of Celia's borrowed dress. It stroked her spine with warm fingers. There was a dark stripe down the center of the road, like a seam, and Celia wondered if it was where lakewater had spilled off Nona as she made her way to the office. Alive, Celia told herself again and again. As she'd made her way to the office *alive.*

Jessie greeted them with a too-bright smile at a break in the trees, past where the children were gathered. She held two rakes, just like the ones at the salt flats. Celia eyed the second rake. She wondered how Jessie had known to have it ready. Unease wormed its way through her again.

But then Jessie held out one of the rakes and said, "Finally! I was worried Easy might have changed the plan on account of the thing with Nona," and Celia realized that this had been what Easy wanted her to do all along. This was what she'd had planned for Celia from the beginning of the day.

Caleb had only been getting her back on track.

Celia was mortified at how right he'd been about her. She didn't give back the trust the people of Kindred Cove were extending her. She didn't choose trust when she had the opportunity. She had to do better than this.

She took the second rake.

Caleb left to join the visitors up in the garden, and Jessie showed Celia how to use the backside of the rake to loosen the dirt on the path. They worked a few meters at a time, scuffing the top layer of packed earth, then stooping to pick out small stones. "The kids'll come through behind us with water from the lake," Jessie said. "They'll sweep it, wet it down, and then walk over it to pack it smooth."

"Does that work?"

Jessie shrugged. "It's what we do."

"Right, but does it work?" Celia asked, tossing a stone into the trees.

"Don't throw rocks like that. There's stuff back there, people. You could hit something."

"What should we do with them, then? Is there a bucket or something?"

Jessie reached out and shoved two fingers into one of the hip pockets on Celia's dress. The pocket was deep enough for her to get her hand in there up to the wrist. "Stick them in your pockets. When we're done, we'll dump them off the cliff by the Old House."

Celia was skeptical. "I don't think my pockets will hold enough. There's a lot of road."

"You'll see. Your pockets are deeper than you think." Jessie shuffled through a patch of loosened dirt, making the dust cloud up around her ankles. "We've got a long way to go. You ready?"

Celia raked the dirt near the patch of jimsonweed she'd seen earlier. Or maybe it was a different patch, she couldn't tell. Dust settled in the trumpet-mouths of the blossoms. "Will the kids be okay without you there to watch them? Should we let them catch up with us?"

Jessie crouched, picked a series of stones out of the dirt, and shoved them into the wide front pocket that stretched across the stomach of her dress like a kangaroo's pouch. "I love how you're always trying to fix stuff that's not broken. Normally, I'd think it was annoying, but it works on you."

Celia looked down at the back of Jessie's head, the twist of her tied-up braid. She ran her hand across the hair on the back of her own head. It was prickly-short against her palm. "What do you mean?"

"You've only been here a few days," Jessie said lightly, working her fingernail under the edge of a stubborn pebble that was lodged hard in the dirt. "You showed up on a quest to make it so you could have a baby, but then when you figured out that you were broken, you put everything you had into trying to fix all the shit that's wrong inside you. And now you're trying to improve on my work with the kids." She kept shoving at the stone, her fingernail creaking against it. "You're relentless."

"I didn't mean to criticize," Celia said. She nudged Jessie's hand aside and chunked one corner of her rake down under the pebble, flipping it free of the dirt. "I was just asking how it works."

Jessie picked up the pebble and reached up to tuck it into Celia's pocket. It clicked against the others that were already in there. "No you weren't. But that's okay."

Celia stooped to pick up the last rock from the patch. She tossed it into the trees, then remembered what Jessie had said about how she shouldn't. It felt so natural to throw stones into the brush, she thought, but she was learning more and more here that the things that felt natural could hurt the people around her. She needed to do better. "You're going to have your, what's it called—your Salt Year, right? After tonight?"

Jessie scrubbed at the ground up ahead with her rake. "Right."

"Are you nervous? I can't imagine what it would be like to leave this place and end up in the world."

"You'd better figure out how to imagine it. You're leaving tomorrow, too."

It landed with Celia like a blow. She'd just started to allow herself to believe that she might get to stay. The thought of returning to her home made her tongue curl inside her mouth. All those empty rooms, all those low-slung power lines, all the boxes in the garage that had been intended to confer purpose into her purposeless life.

She didn't want any of it. It all felt like an inheritance she'd be taking up, from a life she'd lived and then sloughed off and forgotten.

The two of them worked their way up the road in taut silence. The work was rhythmic and difficult. Her arms ached, her hands stung. By the time they got to the canteen, Celia's dress was filmy with sweat, her legs coated in dust up to the calves, her pockets hanging heavy with stones that swung hard against her thighs every time she took a step.

"Do you want some water?" she asked.

Jessie nodded. Celia went inside and grabbed two cups from the kitchen, filled them with room-temperature water from the jugs in the pantry. There was no sign of the hair she and Easy had left on the floor. She wondered when the children had come up here to clean, which ones Jessie had sent to do the job.

When she came back out, Jessie was gone. Her rake lay by the side of the road, discarded.

Celia looked around. "Jessie?"

Jessie pushed her way out from between two dogwood trees. A shower of red berries rained down around her as the branches shook. "Here. Sorry. Had to pee."

The kangaroo pocket of Jessie's dress hung loose and baggy against her stomach, obviously empty. "What did you do with your stones?" Celia asked, handing over the water.

"What stones?"

Celia pointed to Jessie's pocket wordlessly as she drained her own cup. When Jessie didn't respond—didn't show any sign of comprehending—she indicated her own full pockets. "In your pockets. What did you do with them?"

Jessie looked down at her dress. "I never had any stones. Are you thinking of yours?"

"You did, I saw you. You put them into your dress pocket." Celia felt a strange, buzzing heat rising up in her throat. "Where are they?"

Jessie shrugged. "Sorry. I don't know what you mean. Do you want to run these back inside, or should I?"

Celia handed over her cup wordlessly. She waited until Jessie was walking into the canteen—then, she shoved her way between the dogwood trees where Jessie had emerged a minute earlier.

She walked quickly through the underbrush, her eyes on the ground, trying to spot a stash of dropped pebbles. She couldn't find them. She heard the sound of Jessie calling her name, of children's voices getting closer. She ignored both. She didn't turn back, not yet. She kept looking for the rocks, trying to find a pile or a pit—but there was nothing to find. The sound of the children grew loud. Jessie's voice became more urgent.

"Be right there," she called, and she turned back because there was nothing else to do. On her way back, she stuck her hands into her pockets. They were nearly full, the dense crush of rocks pulling the fabric taut, the weight of them swinging hard against her skin. She took out a fistful as she walked and dropped them like breadcrumbs, letting them rain down against the carpet of dead leaves underfoot.

When she looked behind her, she couldn't see any sign that she'd dropped anything at all. The pebbles had rattled down between the leaves and vanished.

By the time she returned to Jessie, her pockets were empty. The children stood there, clustered around Jessie, some of them holding dripping buckets. All of them were spattered with mud up to at least their knees. They stared at Celia with wide, serious eyes.

"Is Nona back yet?" Celia asked, surveying the children. She didn't see Nona's face among them. She tried to picture any of these children opening their mouths to reveal a bright yelp of pink behind a torrent of lakewater. The image came too easily.

"Come on," Jessie said, interrupting Celia's thoughts as she dropped a pebble into the loose-hanging pocket on the front of her dress. "The kids have work to do. Let's not keep them waiting."

It was late afternoon by the time they arrived at the chapel. Celia's hands were raw and red. Her healing thumb throbbed. She and Jessie had taken turns walking into the trees when their pockets were full, neither acknowledging the fact that they were dropping fistfuls of stones in the undergrowth. Now, with the end of their long task in sight, both of them were exhausted, bent, and breathless, and both their pockets were nearly full again.

Celia paused to sit on the chapel steps. She looked down the straight stretch of newly combed dirt that led from the cliffs to the turn in the road just before the garden. The kids had nearly caught up again. She watched them work. They were all different heights, presumably all different ages, but they looked the same somehow—skinny wrists and tangled hair and hard, determined eyes. All of them were soaked, muddy-footed. Silent.

Nona still wasn't among their number.

"Come on," Jessie said. "We're almost done. I want to be able to go for a swim before Candle Hour."

"Wait, I want to see how they do their part," Celia replied. Jessie sighed and slumped onto the chapel steps next to her.

They watched as the kids worked together to carry nesting buckets that looked heavy with water. When they reached a dry section of road, they pulled the nesting buckets apart. The interior buckets must have had holes drilled in the bottom, or maybe cracks cut into them—water seeped out in streams, and the bigger kids paced back and forth across the road in criss-crossing lines, holding the heavy buckets as high as their shaking arms could manage, soaking the loose dirt.

The smaller ones waited for a signal, and when they got it—when those heavy buckets were empty—they ran across the muddy patch, their small feet slapping the ground hard over and over again until it lay smooth. The littlest of them looked no older than three. She followed behind the others, her tiny soft legs pumping to keep up with them.

"When I was a kid," Celia said, "we'd churn up the ground by running on it like that. I remember we got into so much trouble at school one time because there was this patch of grass that was only supposed to be used for sports. And it rained, and we decided to play tag, and we ruined it. Tore it up. They had to replant."

Jessie snorted. "You were wearing shoes. And you didn't have a goal in mind. You were playing, not working. See how they're not chasing each other?"

She was right—the children weren't running after each other, weren't stretching their arms out and screaming in delight or pretend fear. They were quiet. Focused. Methodical.

"They also want to get this job done in time to wash up before Candle Hour." She put a little extra seasoning on *also*. "So they're doing it right. Even the ones who haven't done it before today—they've had the whole length of the road to figure it out. Kids love perfecting a method." She offered her own chapped hand to Celia. "Come on. Less watching, more doing. What do you say? Ready to get off your ass?"

Celia took Jessie's hand. Warm fluid seeped between her fingers as she stood. She couldn't tell if it was sweat or liquid from a broken blister, and she didn't know if it was hers or if it was Jessie's, but it didn't matter. They were nearly finished.

"I didn't see anyone in the garden. Where is everybody?" she said as she used her rake to scrape up stones in front of the Old House.

"Edith's got them in the kitchen by now. Visitors prep and serve dinner on the last night, it's a whole thing. 'You have to treat the potato like you treat your community,' or whatever," she said in an uncanny imitation of Edith's preaching cadence. "They'll love it. Speaking of the canteen—sorry, this is an awkward question, but. Was that your hair, on the floor in the kitchen? I had to send a couple of kids to clean it up earlier."

Celia ran a hand through her hair automatically. It was sleek with sweat. "Yeah, sorry. Easy said—"

"Wow. She really does think you're something special, huh? She doesn't give a haircut to just anyone."

"Really?"

Jessie turned away. "Let's finish this. I'm dying for a swim."

The two of them picked the last stones out of the road and tossed them over the edge of the cliff. They watched as the children soaked and flattened the dirt. Then they led the whole group down to the canteen together and left the children with Edith, who eyed their muddy feet with dismay but didn't turn them away.

The other visitors were in the canteen, washing and chopping vegetables. They seemed alien to Celia. They looked at her hair, her dress, her raw red hands, and she saw that they were envious of what she had. Of how she'd been transformed during her time here.

As the sun started to melt toward the horizon, Celia and Jessie walked down to the shore. They were too tired to talk, so they didn't. The road was smooth and solid underfoot. They passed the office, and the place where Caleb had told Celia she needed to trust, and the patch of shoredirt where hours before, a small girl had coughed up what looked like an impossible amount of water.

The surface of the lake was white with late-afternoon sun. The air was salt-damp and heavy. The water lapped at the black gum trees, at the island, at itself, and the cool promise of it sang out to Celia, pulling her toward an immersion that she knew would bring relief to every inch of her weary body.

Easy was already there. Her clothes were piled on the shore. She stood in the water, her back to the island, her hands skimming the surface of the lake.

"Come on, then," she called out without looking behind her. "It's perfect in here."

Celia swam out to where Easy was standing, leaving Jessie to float in the shallows. Easy was perfectly still, the water rising to just above her navel. When Celia tried to stand, too, her feet didn't touch anything but cool water. "I know you're taller than me," she called, "but this is ridiculous."

Easy turned slowly to face Celia. The sunlight caught the scar on her breast, making it gleam like the blades of the kitchen shears she'd held just a few hours earlier. She looked impossibly weary, but she still gave Celia that wide, sharp grin of hers. "I'm standing on a rock." She wobbled a little as she said it, stuck her arms out for balance. "It's big enough for two, if you want to join."

Celia swam over. She bumped into the rock sooner than she expected to, when she was still a meter or more away from Easy. It was wide but narrow, sticking up out of the lakebed like an incisor. She climbed up onto it slowly. "Ow. Fuck. How is this not killing your feet?"

"You get used to it." Easy scooped up water in one hand and poured it over the back of her own neck. "Did you have a good time with Jessie and the kids?"

"It was interesting."

Easy cackled. "I know, it's hard work and it sucks. But it's also something really special, right? You made it so everyone else can walk on that road more easily. You served your whole community all at once."

Celia rocked on her feet, trying to find a comfortable position. The rock in the water dug in deep, creasing her soles. It hurt enough that it took her a moment to hear what Easy had said. When she did, though, the pain faded. "I served my community," she repeated. "Yeah. That was really nice, actually. And the kids were great. They really show up, huh?"

"Under the right leadership, anyone will show up." Easy dipped her hands into the lake, then pressed them to her face. "Ugh. God, I'm exhausted."

"From the thing with Nona? How is she doing?"

"What? No. Just—it's just a lot, the Salt Festival. It's a lot to manage."

The water shifted around Celia, pushing at her hips. She nearly toppled off the rock, splashing wildly as she tried to regain her balance. She turned her feet out at a stark angle to try to keep them steady. As she stabilized, she snuck a peek at Easy. Her hands were still over her face. Water dripped down her wrists, toward her elbows. "That's it? Just the festival?"

Easy peeked between her fingers. "I'm not a good liar, am I?"

Celia laughed. "How should I know? You've only ever told me the truth, right?"

"Right." She sighed. "The thing with Nona. It's fine now, it was just tough for a minute there. These things are always hard. I mean, you saw, I don't have to tell you."

Celia nodded. "Can I ask you something?"

Easy looked at her for just one heartbeat before stepping off the rock and vanishing into the water. It happened so quickly that Celia could hardly understand what had happened. One moment, they were looking at each other, and the next, with barely a splash, Easy was gone.

She resurfaced a few meters away, pushing her saturated mop of dark hair away from her face. Her eyes were still shut tight against the water as she called out to Celia, "You should swim! Standing on that rock sucks!"

Looking down at herself, Celia could see that there was still cut hair stuck to her chest and shoulders. It had been there half the day, as she'd worked her way up the road, as she'd come back down, as she'd swum out to meet Easy in the water. She slid off the rock and scrubbed her hands over her skin, waiting for the loose pieces of herself to float away.

After a minute, Easy swam over to her. "Here, let me. Tilt your head back." She skimmed her palms over Celia's shoulders, over her neck, over her chest. She scooped water up over Celia's head, so it ran across her scalp and sluiced down behind her ears.

Celia squinted up at the bright sky. She let herself feel, just for a second, the nearness of Easy's body in the water—the way there was nothing but salt between them, the way they warmed the water together, the little currents beneath the surface stirred by Easy's kicking legs, the gentle brush of Easy's fingers wherever she helped to rinse away the hair and dirt and sweat from Celia's skin.

And then she forced herself to ask a question that she knew would ruin it.

"Easy, where's Nona? Is she okay?"

Easy's hands stilled. She pulled back from Celia, just enough to look her in the face. "Of course she's okay. Why are you so fixated on this?"

The water cooled around Celia's thighs, around her belly. "I'm not fixated."

"No, you're right, sorry. That sounded harsh. I just—" Easy blew out a long, irritated stream of air between pursed lips. "I feel like there's something else going on with you, here."

Celia dipped down into the water up to her chin. The lake touched her lower lip. "I don't think so," she said. "It just seemed really bad, before. I want to know if that little girl is, you know."

"Say it," Easy said. "Say what you're scared of."

"I want to know if she's dead," Celia whispered. The word *dead* skated across the surface of the water in front of her mouth.

Easy slid below the surface and came back up, closer to Celia than she'd been before. Water streamed down her face, rolling across the bridge of her nose, pooling in the nock of her cupid's bow. Her freckles swam in Celia's eyes. "Say the whole thing. Say it right. Say you're scared of it."

Celia swallowed. There was salt on her tongue. "I'm scared she's dead."

"Why are you scared of that? What scares you about it?"

"I don't—"

Easy's hands found Celia's hips under the water. Her grip was tight. Her eyes burned with urgent intensity. "Come on. Celia, you're doing so good today. Don't start fucking around now, not when you're so close to telling the truth. What scares you about the idea of Nona being dead?"

Celia shook her head. Her skin burned under Easy's fingers. The lake slid between the two of them like an eyelid closing, opening, closing, opening. "I don't—I don't know? It's scary, she might be—"

"It's not," Easy hissed. "You of all people should see what's really scaring you, here. It's not death, Celia. It's grief."

Celia's foot bumped Easy's under the water, both of them churning below to keep themselves afloat. "Grief," she repeated. "Does that mean—"

"It means you're scared she's dead. Because that would mean you'd have to grieve again," Easy interrupted. She pulled Celia closer, close enough that their knees knocked together as they kicked. "You're stuck on that feeling. Right here," she said, releasing Celia's hip to jab an index finger hard into her sternum. "That pain. You know it's hurting you but you're obsessed with it, aren't you? Isn't part of you clinging to it? Aren't you asking about Nona because you want to find out if you can keep that grief in your chest?"

Celia shook her head, tried to bob up a little higher out of the lake to keep the water out of her mouth. Easy's hand on her hip tugged her back down. "It's not like that. I don't want to feel that way. I want her to be okay."

"You want her to be okay, but you won't believe anyone that says she's okay. You didn't believe Caleb when he told you I could handle this, and you didn't believe Jessie when she said you didn't need to worry, and you don't believe me now, do you? You think that little girl needs to be grieved, and you think I'm hiding it from you, and you think you're going to find out about it and get to drill another little hole into your heart." Easy pulled down on Celia's hips again, dipping her deeper, sending water up over her top lip.

The water brushed Celia's nostrils and she panicked, flailed, but didn't pull away. She recovered and gasped. Saltwater ran between her parted lips. She swallowed it, let the bitter copper tang of it coat her tongue. There wasn't anything Easy had said that she could argue with. It felt so true that it made her feel sick, made her limbs feel heavy. She wanted to freeze in place and sink to the bottom of the lake. "I don't want that," she panted, and she didn't believe her own voice when she heard it, so she repeated herself to try to make it true. "I don't."

"You do," Easy insisted. "Some part of you keeps chasing grief, Celia. It's why you keep asking about Nona. It's why you keep asking about Adelaide. It's why you kept trying to get pregnant even after it was obvious that your body couldn't hang on to a fucking baby. Because you don't know how to exist without that pain in your chest." Easy's nose pinked and she looked at Celia with huge wet eyes and then tears were spilling down over her cheeks, falling freely into the water, Easy's salt joining the Vetiver's. "You can feel that the grief is hurting you. You know it's causing you harm. You have to let it go."

Celia reached up to touch Easy's tears. She touched her own cheeks next and found them wet, and she didn't know if she was crying too, or if this was just the lake on her cheeks. "I can't."

"You can. I told you, fuck's sake, don't you listen? You don't have to hang on to that anymore. Not here. Don't you remember?"

"Remember?" Celia's head was swimming. Easy's hands were on the small of her back now. Their legs kicked between each other. The lake dipped into her mouth.

"On the first night you were here. Candle Hour," Easy said. "At the shoreline. I told you that if you understand the truth, it can heal you. It can make everything okay. There is no grief or fear or loss or death if you know the truth. Do you remember?"

The first Candle Hour felt like a distant memory. It felt like another life. Celia remembered Easy looking into her eyes with such intensity, and that intensity was barely a single candleflame next to the blazing sunlight of her gaze now. "I remember," Celia said uncertainly.

"What's the truth I shared with you that night?"

Celia reached into her memory and saw Easy standing in front of the gathered visitors. "You said that nothing is ever lost."

"I'm telling you again now," Easy said, the plane of her belly pressing flush to Celia's, her forehead dropping forward to meet Celia's hairline, her fingers lacing behind Celia's back. "Nothing is ever lost, Celia. You can let go. Stop chasing grief. You don't have to feel it ever again. You can be more than that. You can be so much more."

There was a commotion at the shoreline, and they both looked up to see muddy-footed children streaming out from the trees. Celia felt Easy drift away from her like a held breath being released. Celia's hands clenched around nothing but water as Easy's breasts slipped across her own, as Easy's hips pulled away from hers, as Easy took her hands away to raise one in greeting.

Celia dove beneath the surface to try to clear her head. She kept her eyes closed and felt the lake slide cool fingers through her hair, across her scalp, behind her ears. She stayed under as long as she could.

When she came up again, Easy was still close by. The water was full of splashing children. Celia watched them, and she thought of what she would do if one of them went beneath the surface and didn't return.

She turned to Easy and felt the few feet of water between them, heavy with salt. "Okay," she said. "You're right. And I want to understand how nothing is ever lost. Easy, I do."

"I know you do," Easy murmured. "But?"

"But I need to know," Celia said. There was an apology in every word. She watched the disappointment fill Easy's face. "Where is Nona? Where is Adelaide? Where did everyone go?"

Easy sighed, then started swimming away from the shore. After a few strokes, she turned to look at Celia. "Come on," she said. "I'll take you."

Twenty-One Years Ago

Easy is watching the water with her hands in her pockets. Her pants are too big for her, and the rolled-up cuffs hang heavy around her ankles. She's trying hard not to cry.

She doesn't hear Dad coming up, doesn't look when he stops next to her. He stands with her for a while, silent, staring out at the lake. It's still freshwater, ten feet deep at the deepest point and shallow enough for wading in a lot of places. It's always a little warm from the sun.

"You know there's not a single part of the Vetiver where you can't see all the way to the bottom?" Dad says after a long time.

Easy shakes her head.

"Sure wish everything was as clear as the water is here," Dad says.

Easy nods. She knocks a tear off her cheek with one small knuckle.

After another long stretch of silence, Dad squats down next to Easy so he can look her in the eye. "You know growth can't put down roots in dishonesty," he says solemnly. "And silence is the exact same soil as lies. You want to tell me what you're feeling?"

"I don't want to say it," Easy whispers. Her voice is rough with held-back tears. "I'll get in trouble."

"Trouble is a made-up idea from where you used to live. We don't get in trouble here. We take care of each other, and we help each other grow. That's all," Dad says. "You won't get in trouble. If I break my word, you can toss me into the lake."

Easy looks up, startled. "Really?"

"Really. I'll even ask William to help you, in case I'm too heavy for you to pick up over your head."

That gets a small, tired laugh out of Easy. She's six, and she thinks of herself as too old for jokes like that one, but she's also alone and scared and sadder than she's ever been in her whole life, and that loneliness and fear and sorrow make her a little younger than her years. "Okay. Well. I guess—I'm feeling bad," she ventures.

"Mmm. Now we're getting somewhere. Any special kind of bad?" Dad looks into her face even as she looks at anything and everything that isn't him. "Maybe . . . guilty?"

She nods so minutely that it barely counts as movement. Still, Dad sees it, and that's enough. "I couldn't keep them from leaving," she whispers. "I did my best. I promise. But they said they didn't like it here anymore. They said stuff about you. Stuff that can't be true. They made it up, I think."

Dad considers this. "Did any of it worry you? The things they said about me?"

Easy shakes her head. "I told them they were wrong but they didn't believe me. I think it's like what you said to me before. I didn't tell them what you said," she adds, her eyes going wide with insistent sincerity. "I swear I didn't."

"I know. I'd know if you'd told them."

"But you were right. What you told me was right," Easy continues. "They love the conveniences of the world more than they love me. They tried to lure me with them by telling me about all the stuff we don't have here."

Dad stands, laying a hand on top of Easy's sun-warm hair. He looks down into her eyes. "And you feel guilty that you didn't do more to make them stay."

Easy can't nod because of Dad's hand. She has no choice but to say it out loud. "Yes."

The surface of the lake is as smooth as glass. Dad looks out over it and sighs. "I feel guilty, too," he confesses, shoving his hands into his pockets the same as Easy. "And I wish we'd both been able to make them stay. But, Easy, can I tell you a secret?" He waits for her to nod before confiding in her. "Sometimes, we're better off without our parents. Sometimes they hold us back."

Easy looks up at him warily. "Hold us back how?"

Dad shrugs. "I guess you'll have to show us all. You can do that, can't you? You're committed to doing the work. You want to grow."

"I am. And I do. I want to grow."

"Well, then," Dad says, smiling out at the still, sweet water of the Vetiver. "You will."

FOUR AND A HALF MONTHS AGO

1

Jessie frowned into the bucket of rosemary that rested between her knees. Her fingers were sticky with fragrant resin, her palms stung from the repetitive motion of stripping leaves off stems, and her nostrils were damn near numb from the smell that rose up out of the bucket like fog rolling across the lake. She had been sitting here working on the rosemary for hours, since Easy and William had come for Adelaide—and yet somehow, the bucket was only three inches or so full.

Jessie had watched that morning in the canteen, as Leona and Edith came to Easy and told her about Adelaide's refusal to touch the Vetiver. At midday, Easy had asked Jessie to send a couple of children into the mirror room to make sure it was clean. She'd sent Nona and Rhoda—those two were a good team for a simple job—and they'd scrubbed it from top to bottom, stocked it with Leona's candles, wiped down the mirrors with vinegar.

At dusk, when the room was ready and everyone had eaten dinner, the community had come for Adelaide. She'd been pacing in circles around the chapel, her hands braced at the small of her back, her face drawn with pain. Jessie had seen it all from her seat on the front steps of the Old House.

She'd had to stumble up onto the porch and get out of the way as Easy and William had half-carried a struggling, gasping Adelaide into the Old House, down the hall, and behind the unpainted door.

And then, when the door was locked behind Adelaide and Easy was busy talking about how her sister needed to see herself with honest eyes, Jessie had gotten back to work.

Edith had made Caleb trim the rosemary hedge the day before—everyone was working together to keep him busy, so he wouldn't backslide about Harvey—and today Jessie had to deal with the problem

Edith had created for her. The rosemary had to be dealt with, harvested and dried and packed up and put away. And it was Jessie who had to do it, even though it felt like children's work, because Easy had said so. *The kids are on laundry duty. I want you to sit on the front steps and get that rosemary processed*, she'd said, and she hadn't left any room for questions.

So here Jessie was, sitting right where she'd been all afternoon, working her way through the branches and listening to Adelaide's long, keening moans.

She reached back toward the pile, waved away a few of the fat bees that were circling the rosemary. Her palm landed on a bough the length of her entire arm. She hefted the thing and set it down on the step next to her. One of the bees followed.

Inside the house, Adelaide let out a low, guttural howl.

Jessie tsked, snapping a long stem off the bough. The bee landed on the branch at Jessie's side, examining one of the crepelike purple blossoms that dotted the mass of dark green. She gripped a rosemary stem in one fist and yanked it through with her other hand, letting the leaves rain down into the bucket.

The bee grew bored with the flowers on the bough and flew off toward the chapel. Jessie followed it with her eyes, wondering if it'd stop at the apple tree even though there were no blooms to speak of—and then her gaze landed on Easy, who was walking up the road.

She was headed right toward the house.

Jessie snapped another stem off the bough and stripped it into the bucket.

"Afternoon," Easy called as she approached the house. She had her hands in her pockets and a smile on her face.

Jessie was not inclined to smile back. "She's not doing great in there, I don't think."

Easy tried to peer around her as if the front door wasn't closed, as if she'd be able to see her sister making a fuss with her own eyes. "I heard. I'm gonna go check on her in a minute. Have you been back there at all?"

Jessie snapped another stem, the one that the bee had been walking on. "No chance. You gave me work to do and I'm doing it." Even to her own ears, she sounded snappish. She didn't care.

"Mm. So I did. But I think there are more important things," Easy said. She leaned on the porch rail and cocked her head at Jessie. "Tell you what. I'll make you a deal."

Jessie had never been one for bargaining. She liked to get what she wanted, or get nothing. "We'll see about that," she said.

Easy leaned forward and grabbed a rosemary bough with one long arm. "I'll finish this bough for you. Plus one more."

"And?"

"And you go around back and help Adelaide get through a little bit of this. You don't spend enough time helping other people reflect, Jessie." She shook the bough and a shower of rosemary leaves fell onto the steps. "I get why—you've barely spent any time in that room yourself. But I want to see you get good at it before you head off on your Salt Year."

Jessie's heart leapt. "My Salt Year? When?"

Easy's mouth melted into a wolfish grin. "We'll see. Maybe next year, after the Salt Festival. I said *maybe*," she emphasized. "But you have to show me that you're a little more community-minded, okay? We can't have you pulling an Adelaide and fucking off to who-knows-where for however long you feel like."

It was almost too much to consider. Her Salt Year. A chance to leave the island and come back with a baby and truly leave childhood behind. She jumped up from the porch and raced down the steps, crushing rosemary underfoot as she went. "Thank you," she said, "thank you thank you—"

"Hey." Easy grabbed her by the shoulder, stopping her short. She looked into Jessie's face and regarded her with a solemnity that made Jessie feel, for the first time, like they were peers. Like they were nearly equals. "Do a good job for her, okay? She really needs your help right now."

Jessie looked down at Easy's hand on her shoulder. "I will. And you do this rosemary right. No mess, no shortcuts. Or else Edith will blame it on me."

Easy took her hand away. "Deal. Thank you, Jessie."

Jessie walked around the side of the house. She passed under the open kitchen window just as Adelaide made another of those low, wrenching moans. This one ended in half a sob. Jessie stumbled, caught herself. On instinct, she rose onto her toes and peered into the kitchen, as though she'd be able to see through to where Adelaide was waiting.

The white paint inside the Old House needed a touch-up. Jessie had done the task every fall with the children for years. This year, she'd be the one to direct them in the daylong chore. They were still working their way through the original tubs of paint that Dad and William had brought to the island with them—it was in huge plastic tubs labeled *not for resale*, and it was only ever used for the Old House and the chapel. They had to open every window and door in the place to keep from choking on the fumes when it was time to cover up the chips and scuffs, but it was always worth the effort.

The place gleamed inside, the same pristine high-gloss white covering the floor and the ceiling and the walls, every surface exactly the same.

A job well done, Harvey used to say every year.

But not this year. They'd skipped the touch-ups on account of all the fuss over Adelaide being home. It showed. A scuff down low near the floorboards, a flaking patch of paint halfway between the front door and the open archway that led into the kitchen. A new long scrape near one of the bedroom doors, probably from Adelaide fighting as she was carried down the hall. A mess.

The whole house would need to be sanded and scrubbed and fixed up, except for the door at the end of the hall. That one was bare wood. *Unfinished, just like you.* That's what Edith said the first time she sent Jessie into that room to become a better version of herself. And it had worked, hadn't it? She was as good as a person could be. Except for the brief slip she'd made in William's office, with the shoes and the compact mirror and the pressed powder.

But that was behind her now. So far behind her, she could barely even remember it. Those mistakes belonged to someone she could no longer imagine being.

She looked away from the scuffs and chips in the paint and continued toward the back of the Old House. Easy had given her a job, and she was going to do it.

She didn't stop until she came to the peephole that looked into the mirrored room. She flicked the painted flap of tarp that covered the hole and pressed her cheek to the wall.

Inside, Adelaide was still screaming.

2

Adelaide was breathing heavily on the other side of the wall, every breath trailing off into a soft whimper. Jessie paused, listening. She didn't press her eye to the peephole. Not yet. Inside, Adelaide went quiet for a moment before speaking, this time in a higher, more timid voice than Jessie had ever heard from her.

"Edith? Is that you?"

Jessie froze. She didn't say anything.

"Edith. Please, please just—could I have a glass of water? I'm so thirsty. Please, Edith, I promise I won't try to get out again. I promise."

Jessie knew she should probably start in on Adelaide. She should put her eye to the hole in the wall and say what she saw. But she'd never heard Adelaide sound this way before. Young, scared. Vulnerable.

"I didn't mean what I said about going back to the mainland. I really didn't. I just felt so scared, and it hurt so much, and I needed—please," she finished weakly, her voice breaking over what sounded like a sob.

There was a smell. With her nose right next to the hole in the wall, Jessie couldn't miss it. It wasn't the usual fug of beeswax that hung around the back half of the Old House when someone was in the mirror room. It was something else, something overpowering enough that the beeswax couldn't cover it. Old blood, like menstrual blood but with a strange bready sweetness to it, and sweat and vomit and sour milk, and under it all, the potent stink of meat.

"Please please please," Adelaide sobbed. There was a string of small wet noises.

"I'm not Edith," Jessie whispered at last.

The pause from inside the closet was impossibly heavy. ". . . Jessie. What are you doing here?"

Jessie hated that Adelaide had been able to recognize her voice. She wanted to be unrecognizable, authoritative, mysterious. She was on the outside of the wall. She was supposed to be in control. "I came to help you," she finished. "Easy sent me," she added, immediately regretting it.

"Is Easy coming?"

Jessie looked over her shoulder at the front door. "No," she answered at last. "Are you ready to start? Tell me what you see when you look at yourself."

"No." Adelaide's voice turned fast and desperate. "No, I'm not ready for that. I need your help. Me and the baby need your help."

"Is it a boy or a girl?" Jessie asked.

"I don't know yet. Listen, you have to get me out of here. William put a lock on the door. I can't get out of here. Can you help?"

Jessie leaned her back against the wall, frowning down at the rosemary sap that was stuck between her fingers. "Adelaide. Stop."

"I need you to come inside and undo the lock, Jessie. Please. Do you think you can do that?"

Jessie bit her lip. She could undo the lock. She could do anything. "What is it like?" Silence from the other side of the wall. She tapped on the still-covered peephole with a fingertip. "Adelaide?"

"What is what like?" Adelaide was very quiet, so quiet that Jessie thought maybe she already understood the question and just didn't want to answer.

"Being pregnant. What is it like?"

"I'll tell you if you let me out."

A tiny laugh hiccuped its way out of Jessie's throat before she could stop it. She couldn't believe Adelaide had said it out loud, just like that. Had forgotten that Jessie didn't bargain. "I'll let you out if you tell me," she retorted.

More heavy whimpers. They took a long time to die down and Jessie was about to ask again, to remind Adelaide of what she had to do—but then Adelaide got ahold of herself.

"It's a lot."

"A lot what?"

"Just a lot," Adelaide snapped.

"That's not good enough," Jessie retorted. She glanced at the corner of the house—had she been loud? Loud enough for Easy to hear?

Then she put her lips right up to the peephole and whispered, "I want to know what it's like. I want to know what it feels like."

She could hear Adelaide's uneven breathing. Finally, after what felt like forever, she got her answer.

"It feels like becoming a different kind of creature. Everything changes. It's like all your bones are breaking, and your muscles are rearranging, and your skin is stretching, all so you can be—I don't know, a bird."

"A bird?"

"It feels like that."

Jessie wasn't satisfied, not even remotely. She didn't know what else she wanted out of Adelaide—something sensational, something harrowing. Something to make it feel less unfair. She stared at the peephole, chewing her lip, trying to figure out what would soothe the vivid sense of frustration that was burning its way through her.

"I'll be right back," she whispered. "I'm going to get you that water you asked for."

She raced away, running up the road on light feet, all the way to the salt flats. She scooped up a half-full bucket of lakewater, then ran back up the road, skirting her way behind the chapel so Easy wouldn't see her. She was only gone for ten minutes, maybe fifteen. It was simple enough to climb through the kitchen window, fill a cup from the bucket, and tiptoe it down the hall.

She pressed her lips to the crack in the closet door. "I have water for you. But you have to promise not to try to come out, if I give it to you."

"I promise," Adelaide replied right away.

Jessie undid the lock on the outside of the door. She opened it just a few inches.

Just enough to pass the cup inside.

Just enough to see.

The little room was more spacious than it'd been when Jessie had last been in there. It had been three and a half years since she'd done anything bad enough to get sent for a period of reflection. Back then there had been shelves lining the walls, and the mirrors Dad pulled out of every cabin had been propped up on them, just waiting to fall and break.

While Adelaide was gone, though, Easy had been hard at work. She'd fixed the place up herself. Sometime during that period, those shelves had been removed. The mirrors were fixed directly to the walls now. There were no frames, no gaps in the seams—glass covered every inch of the walls. Adelaide was reflected over and over, into infinity.

When Jessie had been in the closet all those years ago, there had been places where she could rest her eyes without seeing herself. Adelaide couldn't do that. There was no part of this closet that didn't show her who she was. Her own face and body surrounded her. No matter where she looked she would be confronted with the sight of herself. In every direction, from every angle, inescapable. Unignorable.

And it was a sight to behold. The stool was off in a corner, perched on top of the mirrors on the floor. The candle burned blindingly bright. The mirrored walls were smeared with streaks of viscous red fluid. Adelaide was on the floor, facing the peephole, on her knees with her hands braced against the glass to either side of her. She wasn't holding her candle—she'd used melted wax to fix it to one of the mirrors on the ground. She looked like she was about to throw up. Her head was low, her shoulders hunched, her hair sweat-damp and matted. She was wild-eyed, drenched in sweat. Her belly looked overripe, like it was ready to split down some invisible seam.

Jessie felt the world slipping out from beneath her, the ground rotating away from her, the days passing, her body transforming in the absence of her attention to it. She felt her own Salt Year looming ahead of her. She imagined the way she'd stretch and shift and tilt and *change* in the time between this moment and this time next year.

It was a lot, Adelaide had said, and for just one instant, Jessie almost understood what that meant.

Her vision mercifully blurred with tears and she was finally able to look away from that vision of herself, blinking hard and fast to try to escape the violent rush of longing that had threatened to overcome her. When she opened her eyes again, she did not look into the mirrors.

She looked directly and only at Adelaide.

"Here," she said, crouching to tuck the cup of water just inside the door. "I think this will help a lot."

Adelaide crept forward. She took the cup. She drank greedily at first, then gagged, choked, and spat up a stream of watery bile. "Is this saltwater? Jessie, please—"

"You need it," Jessie said. "You've been too far from the lake for too long. It'll help, I promise. Did you spill it all?" She looked down briefly at the floor, then flinched away from the sight of the wet mess surrounding Adelaide. "I can get more."

"Please," Adelaide said thickly. "Please."

Jessie shook her head. "I tried." She eased the door shut and locked it again from the outside. Then she climbed back out through the kitchen window, and crept around to the peephole in the back wall of the house.

She didn't want to do this. Adelaide was surely beyond help. But she'd promised Easy that she'd try.

"So," Jessie said, lifting the flap and pressing her eye to the hole in the wall. Adelaide hadn't moved. "Take a look at yourself. What do you see?"

Adelaide didn't look up. As Jessie watched, a drop of sweat rolled down Adelaide's nose and fell to the mirror beneath her bowed head. "Please let me out," she said. Her voice was hoarse. "I'll leave the island, me and the baby. That's what you want, isn't it? You wish I hadn't come back. Let me out of here and you'll never have to see us again."

Jessie's heart pounded. Was that what she wanted? She wasn't sure. She couldn't think. If Adelaide left and took her new outside-world personality with her, maybe everything that felt so wrong at the Cove would be right again.

But then again, if Adelaide was gone, maybe the blame would land with Jessie. Easy had sent her back here to help, and if she didn't help enough and Adelaide left, would she get to have her Salt Year at all? Would she get her chance to have a baby? She needed to get her chance, she needed to have the baby so that—

Her mind froze there. Jessie frowned, trying to think. So that what?

William had always said that they needed to bring new life to the island. It was important to have babies, to raise children up in community, to give them the kinds of lives they could never get in the outside world. It was important to build the kind of community that would raise the children right. It would be a disaster, not having children to raise in community.

But as she stood there in the dark, her face pressed hard against the back wall of the house, the smell of blood filling her nose and mouth, she couldn't quite remember *why* it would be a disaster.

She clenched her fists, dug her nails into her palms hard. Shame flooded her. She should know the answer to this. Her heart was, as Edith liked to say, beating in the right direction—she knew what was important, she knew what mattered. Knowing all that should have told her what was the right thing to do. But she couldn't figure it out. The phrase *intentional participation in growing community* kept cycling through her mind and she couldn't seem to think past it.

Adelaide whimpered again inside the closet, breaking Jessie out of her thoughts. She didn't know how long she'd been standing there, trying to figure out what to do next. From inside the closet, Adelaide whispered again, might have been whispering all along. "Jessie. Please—"

Jessie came to her senses. "Stop it. Stop it, stop it, stop it, Adelaide. You went out into the world. You went out there and you came back rotten. Look at yourself." Her fingernails were deep in her palms, and the pain kept her mind clear. She wouldn't let Adelaide get the better of her. She wouldn't. "Look how you're behaving. Don't you want better for your baby?"

"I'll do better," Adelaide whispered. "I promise I'll do better. Just please, please let me out."

"I know you don't want that. Come on, Adelaide. Look at yourself and tell me what you see."

Adelaide doubled over, her hands slapping the floor, cracking one of the mirrors under her palm. She let out a long moan.

"You're struggling right now," Jessie said, trying hard to keep her voice even. "I can see that. You're having a hard time readjusting to life at home. I want to help you. Let me help you. Drink a little water."

Adelaide's moan continued unbroken, rising in pitch and in volume until it blistered up into a full-throated scream.

Jessie decided to try another tactic. She treated Adelaide the way she treated the children. Harvey had taught her, over the years, by example—how to calm down a sobbing child with a broken arm or a screaming-red coral burn or an eye full of salt. Adelaide didn't sound different from those children. Maybe, Jessie thought, she needed the same thing.

So she brought her voice up loud enough to cut across Adelaide's screaming, and she said, "I see someone who isn't in pain."

The screaming stopped. Adelaide panted, stared up at Jessie through ropy hanks of sweat-soaked hair. "What?"

"I see someone who is not wounded," Jessie continued. "I see someone who is not injured. I see someone who is not in pain."

Adelaide panted hard, her face twisting. She said, "No," but the sound didn't stop, and the *o* stretched out into an agonizing howl.

"I see someone who is not in pain. I see someone who doesn't hurt," she said again. She pressed her hands against the wall. She watched the candleflame flickering. "I see someone whose mind is calm. I see someone whose body is calm. What do you see, Adelaide?"

Adelaide looked down at the mirror between her hands. "I see," she gasped. "I see myself."

Jessie slammed her palm against the wall. "That's not how it works! God, what's wrong with you?" This was hopeless, she thought. Adelaide had been gone for too long. She'd forgotten everything important. "Tell me what you see!"

"I see. My eye. It has blood in it." She lifted her chin and pointed her face at the peephole, opened her eyes wide. One of them was red from the iris to the tear duct. "Look at that."

Jessie frowned. "I don't see any blood in this room. I see someone who is not bleeding."

Adelaide let out a strange, strangled laugh that ended in a pained gasp. "It's—fuck, Jessie, it hurts so much, you have no idea—"

"I see someone who is not in pain," Jessie interrupted. Adelaide collapsed onto her elbows, her body tilted forward at a steep angle.

"I am," Adelaide panted, "in pain."

A surge of energy raced through Jessie. This was it. She was getting somewhere. "Is that what you see?"

Adelaide shook her head. "Can't see. Eyes closed."

"You can't—Adelaide, come on. Your baby needs you. You can't close your eyes. Is that what you see? Do you see someone who's in pain?"

Adelaide screamed again. It was a grating, impossible sound, like stones falling from the cliffs, like the way Leona always described the world opening up to swallow the lake. She lifted her head and roared, and in that moment, Jessie saw, her eyes were open.

When she stopped, Jessie tried again. "Do you see someone who's in pain? Because I see someone—" She stopped, wet her lips. "I see someone who is powerful."

Adelaide blinked blearily. "Wha?"

"I see someone who is strong." Jessie pressed her whole body up against the wall. The smell of blood and ammonia was so powerful that she could taste it down to the bottom of her throat. "I see someone who can do this."

Adelaide shook her head. "I see . . . tired. I'm so, so tired, Jessie. I can't."

"I see someone who can. I see someone who always told me we can do the things we intend to do, if we trust that nothing is ever lost. I see someone who isn't tired at all."

Inside the little room, Adelaide's body shifted, and it looked like she was going to scream again. But she bit down hard on her arm instead, and the only noise that came out of her was strangled by her own flesh between her teeth.

"Good," Jessie whispered. "Tell me what you see, Adelaide."

Adelaide looked up at the mirrors on the wall across from her. "I see someone who is strong," she said. She didn't sound like she meant it. "I see someone who is not going to die from this."

Jessie's lips brushed the wall. "Yes yes yes. I see someone who is going to live through this, and I see someone who is strong, and I see someone who isn't going to scream anymore. What do you see?"

"I see someone who is going to live through this, and I see someone who is strong," Adelaide said, and then her back hunched and her shoulders rippled and she dug her teeth into her arm again.

"And someone who isn't going to scream," Jessie said, loud as she dared.

Inside the little room, Adelaide didn't scream. A guttural growl surged out of her, but she didn't scream. When she was finished, she pushed herself up to her knees and sat with her hands braced on her thighs. Dark blood seeped from between her legs and pooled on the glass beneath her. "I need help. I need a doctor. This can't be right. It hurts so much."

"If you were in pain," Jessie said firmly, "you wouldn't be sitting up. I see someone who is sitting up."

Adelaide slowly straightened. She stood with her eyes closed, her back pressed to the mirrors, her feet slipping on the blood-smeared glass of the floor. "Jessie, please."

"You're standing. You're standing like someone who's strong, who isn't in pain. And I see someone who's strong, who isn't in pain." In desperation, she added, "Tell me what you see and I'll ask Easy if you can come out of there."

Adelaide's eyes flashed open. She was looking right at the peephole, right into Jessie's eye. "I see someone who isn't in pain," she said at once.

"You didn't even look. Come on. Just—really look. Look at yourself, Adelaide."

After a long moment, Adelaide's eyes slid to the wall across from her. She drew a slow, shuddering breath. "I see sweat. I see blood. I see—fuck, my dress is ruined," she added, plucking at the sodden once-white linen. "I see someone who is—" She cut off, clenching her teeth, buckling around her swollen belly.

"Come on," Jessie hissed. "Say it."

"I see someone who is not in pain," Adelaide groaned. "I see someone who is not in pain, I see someone who is not in pain, I see—please, fuck, Jessie—"

"Keep going," Jessie said urgently.

And she did. Adelaide said it over and over again, her eyes fixed on herself in the hundred mirrors of the room at the back of the Old House. Jessie promised to let her out over and over, if she'd just say the words a few more times, if she'd just mean them more.

By the time Jessie left, Adelaide was saying it on her own. She wasn't screaming anymore. She was on the floor again, blood puddling beneath her, blood streaming from the places on her arms where she'd bitten hard and harder. But she was saying, without prompting, that when she looked in those mirrors, she saw someone who wasn't in pain.

She finished all the lakewater in the cup, and she kept it down.

Jessie walked back to the front of the house without telling Adelaide that she was leaving. As she rounded the corner and walked under the still-open kitchen window, she felt the warmth of well-earned pride spreading through her.

She had helped. She had made a difference.

When she got to the front porch, she was surprised to find Easy still sitting there. She was still stripping rosemary stems, using her fists now. An impressive dent had been made in the pile on the tarp. She looked up at Jessie and waited.

"Get up," Jessie said. "You're in my seat."

"You're the boss," Easy said. She stood up and looked Jessie over. She smiled like she saw something there that she'd been waiting for. "How is she doing in there?"

Jessie took her seat on the porch and picked up a rosemary stem. "Better every minute."

Two Weeks Ago

Celia has made up her mind.

She isn't going to Kindred Cove.

Her duffel sits in the middle of her bed, unzipped, empty. Next to it, her things for the week are stacked up—jeans and shirts and underwear and socks, sturdy hiking boots and flip-flops, toiletries, vitamins, tiny jewel-like bottles of skincare serums. She gathered everything this morning, and since then, she's been wandering guiltily around her house.

She spent half an hour standing in the empty nursery, tonguing the painful quiet of the little pink room. Adelaide had helped her paint it months and months ago. After she got the letter telling her to come back to the island, but before she'd admitted to being pregnant. She didn't help a lot—she arrived late and left early, and mostly she'd just wanted to talk about what they'd do when she got back from the island.

But she'd done the corners, and the parts around the light switch and the power outlet. The tricky little edges. She'd been so slow and patient, so careful. Not a drop of paint was out of place.

Celia isn't going to Kindred Cove, she's decided, because it's possible that Adelaide is happy there. If Celia arrives, and finds Adelaide, and Adelaide is glowing with motherly fulfillment, loving her baby and her community, perfectly content without Celia in her life—it will be too much.

Because Adelaide was here once. She'd painted those corners. She'd laughed with Celia at the absurdity of painting the nursery even though there wasn't a living baby to occupy it, and then she'd pulled Celia into a tight hug and whispered the word *yet* into her hair. She'd talked about a future where they could put both their babies into the faux-birch crib and watch them fall asleep together.

That Adelaide was real. And if she went to Kindred Cove and decided she liked life there more than she liked that potential future of theirs—Celia doesn't think she could stand seeing it.

She's about to put the duffel back into the closet when the other possibility occurs to her.

That Adelaide might be miserable at the Cove. That she might be there with a baby she doesn't actually love, realizing that she's not cut out to be a mother. Or, Celia thinks slowly, the idea white-hot—or, she might be there with no baby at all. She might be grieving. She might be clenching her entire heart around a tight knot of pain and loss. She might, like Celia, have no idea how to let go of it.

Celia turns slowly back toward the bed. If Adelaide is happy at the Cove, she thinks, it will feel like a betrayal. It will hurt. But if not—if Adelaide is living in the room of sorrow that has been Celia's whole life for nearly as long as she can remember—Celia wants to see it. Because it will mean she's not alone, after all.

She tries to spit out the thought. The yearning for Adelaide's pain. She tries to push it away. It's a wrong thought, a cruel thought, a vicious hungry thought. But she can't. This is what her grief has turned her into, she realizes with slow-dawning horror: someone who hopes life has jammed a corkscrew into Adelaide's sternum, spiraling through the bone to leave a cold yawning hole of grief that can never be filled or fixed or solved.

All so Celia can feel a little less alone.

She hurls her clothes into the duffel. At the last moment, she grabs the sonogram that's been on her bedside table since the last time she found out she was pregnant. She shoves it all the way down to the bottom of the bag, under the clothes.

She has to go to Kindred Cove. She has to find out if they can take the thought from her. The pain behind the thought. The loneliness behind the pain.

She needs their help.

She needs them to make her better.

SALT FESTIVAL

day four | afternoon

Celia followed Easy through the water. She didn't know where they were going, but Easy had said this was the way to see Nona, and Celia trusted her. That was enough. It had to be enough.

She followed the pull of Easy's current away from the island. The water was still warm, the sun still well above the horizon. Celia felt that she had fallen outside of time. She lost herself in the feeling of pushing through the water, in the rhythm of her own breath, in the occasional flashes of livid pink and deep red below the surface.

They stopped twice so Easy could get her bearings, and each time, Celia looked back at the dark mass of the island and understood that there were parts of Kindred Cove she hadn't seen yet. Parts she would never see, if she left.

The third time they stopped, Easy made them both tread water for a long time, so they could catch their breath. "We're almost there. Stay with me," she said. "Promise you'll stay with me."

Celia promised.

She wasn't sure if they were talking about the same thing, but she meant it either way. She wanted Easy to mean it, too.

When they were far enough out that Celia's arms were starting to go numb and Kindred Cove looked like a dark coin balanced on the surface of the water, Easy dove straight down, pulling Celia with her a short way before letting go of her wrist. Celia followed the sinuous rhythm of Easy's legs kicking, the undulations of the muscles between her shoulderblades. She followed the shadow of Easy's movements, and keeping her eyes on that shadow meant they arrived at their destination before she realized what she was swimming toward.

The reef.

She already knew it was enormous. It reached long arms around the east half of the island, and one of those arms continued in a bridge that was growing toward the mainland. The beginning of that bridge was what they were above now, she realized—the place where the arc of the reef turned away from the Cove.

Now, with the reef in front of her, the vastness of it felt real in a way it hadn't before. It wasn't just that the reef was huge. It was alive, too, more alive than anything Celia had ever seen before. *The reef is connection*, that's what William and Edith and Jessie and Caleb and Leona and Easy had all been saying. Celia saw now what they meant. The reef was connected endlessly to itself. It lived alongside itself and within itself. It was eternal.

Easy and Celia surfaced, sucked down air, and dove again. They swam down close enough to see the fingers of the reef shifting with the current of the water. Celia's jaw cracked, and then she could feel the warm tongue of the lake in her ear canals, sliding in and settling, becoming familiar so quickly that she forgot it wasn't part of her. She wasn't thinking about needing air, not yet, because she wasn't thinking about anything—there was only the flash of Easy's thighs scissoring across each other as she kicked her way through the water, and the pink and red fingers below that didn't look like any kind of coral Celia had ever seen before. They were reaching into the water, toward the pale palm of her hand, if she could just get a little closer—

Easy pulled her hand back. She shook her head, raised her arms, and crossed her wrists into an *X. Don't touch*, Celia understood, and she withdrew her hand even though she ached to feel those deep pink fingers intertwined with her own. She had no idea how long they'd been under the water—thirty seconds? a minute?—but already, Easy was pointing to the surface, trying to tug her up for air.

She pulled away.

She just wanted to stay a little longer.

Easy grabbed her wrist. She shook her head. Celia held up a single finger—*just one more look*, she thought, but Easy didn't see or didn't understand, and then the two of them were breaking the surface again, into the awful noise of the too-thin, too-cool air.

"I know," Easy panted before she could say anything. "I know you want to look closer. But this isn't what I wanted to show you, and there's not that much time before we should get back for Candle Hour. Still with me? Not too tired?"

"Still with you," Celia said. She didn't feel tired at all. She didn't feel cold or out of breath. She felt perfect.

Easy led her down again, but this time, she turned sharply and swam along the length of the reef. Celia watched the pinks blend into reds and oranges. She could live down here, in the perfect rhythm of the water. She never wanted to leave.

And then Easy pointed up ahead, and Celia saw the first body.

Five and a Half Years Ago

Easy is standing at the dock with her hands in her pockets. She's supposed to be helping Edith at the salt flats—the Salt Festival visitors are having their day of toil, learning about potential and action, sweating their way to some kind of epiphany. Easy's not trusted around visitors, but she's supposed to linger in the trees, listening for anyone who might sound like a potential keeper.

Right now, she's more than a little drunk, and the last thing she wants is to watch mainlanders sweat while they do children's work.

Adelaide comes up behind her and drapes herself over her sister's shoulders, looping her arms around Easy's chest. "Are you moping?"

"Of course I'm moping," she answers, leaning her head back to thunk it against Adelaide's. She wants to slam her skull into Adelaide's nose. She wants to make her sister sputter and bleed. She wants to scream. "You're leaving. I don't want you to go."

"I have to," she says. "It's my year. I'm late as it is."

"I know. But what if you didn't? What if you just said, *No, I'm not leaving, make your own babies?*"

Adelaide laughs. It's her fake laugh. Too musical, too tinkling. "Who knows. Maybe one of the visitors will catch my eye tonight, and I'll end up staying here with them forever. Which one should I go for? The guy with the *Fish Fear Me* hat or the kid who keeps trying to sneak into the Old House?"

Easy turns to face her. "Don't. Don't joke. You and I both know what'll happen if that kid—"

"I'm sure they'll be fine," she says, rolling her eyes. "William likes this group. He'll take them home after Candle Hour. Nobody will have to suffer any consequences for anything."

Easy looks around. She's thorough. She makes sure nobody is around to hear what she says next. She leans in and whispers directly into Adelaide's ear. "When you go, I don't think you should come back."

She rears back. "What? I thought you didn't want me to leave!"

"I don't," Easy whispers urgently. "But that's selfish, okay? I just don't want to be here by myself. But it's not good here, Adelaide. Since Dad died—"

"Changed," Adelaide corrects. "He just changed."

"Whatever. It's been getting worse here. You feel it, right? And the Salt Festival visitors—William takes some of them back to the mainland, but not all of them. You and I—don't interrupt me this time—you and I both know where they are. The ones that we all say never came here." Her head swims. "Why would he do that?"

"He has reasons for everything he does," Adelaide counters. "Forgive me if you not understanding doesn't make me think there's nothing to understand."

Easy steps toward her. Adelaide steps away. The lake is still, the air quiet. Easy whispers again. "Once you get out there, into the world. Just . . . promise me that if it's better out there, you'll stay. Okay? If you haven't come back by, let's say two Salt Festivals from now, I'll find a way to come join you. Just promise me that much."

Adelaide sighs. "Yeah. Okay. If it's better, I'll stay out there, and I'll wait for you to come find me. But while I'm gone, you have to promise me you'll try to figure your shit out. I mean it. It's good here if you just let it be good. You could be part of something greater than yourself. Will you try? For me?"

Easy wraps her long arms around Adelaide. She buries her face in Adelaide's neck and breathes her in. She is dizzy with moonshine and relief. She would do anything for her sister. "I'll do everything I can to really appreciate this place. I'll clean up my act. For you."

"Do you promise?"

Easy nods into Adelaide's shoulder. "I promise."

FOUR AND A HALF MONTHS AGO

1

Caleb sat on the bench at his usual table in the canteen. His plate was in front of him, untouched. He couldn't bring himself to pick up his fork.

Easy regarded him coolly, a spoonful of grits balanced in her hand. "Are you fasting, Caleb?"

"No." He wanted to say more, hunted through his mind for an explanation as to why he couldn't make himself break the yolk of the egg in his bowl. It stared back up at him like a milky yellow eye.

Easy's leg was twitching fast under the table. "You'd better eat, then. You're going to want to head up and help Adelaide before too long here. I think she's really struggling with her period of reflection."

He nodded and forced himself to shove his spoon into his bowl. He began the work of rearranging the contents, trying to make the volume appear smaller. Adelaide had been in the mirror room for the better part of a day now, and everyone but him had been up there to see her. To help her see herself more clearly. Caleb knew he should find his way up there too, but he couldn't imagine looking at Adelaide and telling her anything that would be useful. Not when he, himself, was so broken.

Everyone else in the canteen seemed fine. A little tired, maybe, but that was to be expected, what with the effort of the past few days. They'd all been working hard to get ready for the arrival of the new baby. Everyone was airing out linens and harvesting extra food. The kids had cleaned up the road and scrubbed out the chapel. There really wasn't much that needed doing, but everyone wanted to lay their hands on the work of preparing, and so everyone found ways to exhaust themselves.

As Caleb watched Easy, who was listening to Leona tell some story about one of her hives, he wondered what Easy had been doing all day. What work had busied her hands? She'd spent a good amount of time counseling him in the weeks after what had happened with Harvey. He'd spent some time intermittently crying and vomiting and staring at the lake after all that mess, but he was doing better lately. Thinner than usual, and slower, and half the time he came to the end of his day without knowing how he'd gotten there—but he was doing better. Everyone said so.

Easy had helped him get here, and now, he didn't need nearly as much of her attention. So what, he wondered, was she doing with her time? She seemed beyond tired. She kept glancing at the door, biting her thumbnail, drawing sharp breaths like she wanted to speak but didn't know how to say the thing she was thinking. But Caleb didn't see a single other person paying attention to the fact that Easy was acting strange.

Caleb finished moving his grits around and lifted his nearly empty spoon to his mouth. He left it there for a moment, the salt stuck to the metal dissolving on his tongue as he watched Easy. She was worried. He could tell.

He'd never seen Easy look worried before.

After a minute, she seemed to feel his gaze on her. Her eyes flicked to him, and her brows lifted in a silent question.

"What's the matter?" Caleb asked.

Easy gave her head a quick shake. "Nothing. Nothing's the matter."

He frowned. "Okay, then . . . what are you thinking about?"

Easy spun her fork between her fingers. "I'm thinking about Adelaide. I'm wondering how she's doing."

"I'm sure she's fine. Do you want me to go check on her now? I'm happy to do it."

Her mouth gave a sudden twitch. "I don't know about *fine*. You know she only went in that room twice in her life before this past couple of months, right?"

Caleb nearly dropped his spoon. "That can't be right," he said. "Everyone takes periods of reflection. It's—it's accountability."

"Not Adelaide," Easy said. The words came out soft as warm butter. "She only got sent a couple of times, when we were kids. The first time, she was only in there for a few hours. The second time, she didn't even actually do it."

Caleb looked around to see if anyone else was hearing this. On Easy's other side, Leona was still deep in her hive conversation. The children leaned against the walls, their eyes heavy-lidded with boredom. It was just the two of them. He was the only one learning these secrets. "How did she get out of it?" he whispered.

"It was the day Dad died," Easy replied. "And everyone forgot. Maybe this is awful, but . . . I'm kind of glad Adelaide's getting to find out what it's like in that room," Easy said. She whispered it, her eyes fixed on her plate. "My whole life, ever since Dad took me in, she's been telling me how it's not that hard to do the work we do in there. I always thought . . . like, *how would you know?*" She pushed her spoon across the center of her bowl, dividing the remainder of her grits down the middle. "But now she's doing her work. And part of me is glad that she understands what it's like, now. To actually try to grow."

Caleb nodded slowly. "Of course you're glad. You want her to be better." Everything made sense now, he thought. Of course everything had gone wrong after Adelaide came home.

She'd never even bothered trying to improve herself. She'd never taken accountability for anything.

Something threatened him from within, then. A hot, sudden rage that boiled up like milk foaming up in a saucepan. The phrase *it all makes sense* roiled in his stomach, scalded his throat. He clenched a fist around his spoon. He wanted it to bend. He wanted it to break.

He bit down on his tongue hard and told himself that he was a calm person. He told himself over and over until the anger subsided.

Easy glanced at the door again. "When do you think you're heading up?"

"Do you want me to go now?" Caleb set his spoon down in his bowl. The corner of it nicked the yolk, releasing an ooze of yellow.

"I just don't know who's with her right now." She looked around the canteen. "I thought it was supposed to be Edith, but she's here."

"I can go now."

"I need some air," Easy said suddenly, pushing her chair back from the table. She strode to the door, her hands in her hair. Caleb followed her without thinking. The two of them headed toward the double doors that led outside, Caleb so close behind Easy that he almost stepped on her heels.

"Where are you going?"

She pushed her hands through her hair. "I need to check on her. I need to let her know that she's okay. I'm the reason she came back, and—look, it's complicated." She pressed a shoulder against the heavy canteen door and pushed, leaning her entire body into the movement as the door swung open. The deep gold light of predusk streamed in around the shadow of her body.

"I get it," Caleb said. "You feel guilty that you're happy she's in there, right?"

Easy froze. Behind Caleb, the canteen door swung shut, sealing the soft sounds of dinner inside. "Guilty?" She turned slowly to face him. "Why would I feel guilty?"

He shrugged. "Because you always took care of her back in the day. I remember the two of you always looking out for each other, and now she's growing, and it hurts. Harvey used to—back when he'd look out for me by making me grow, he used to feel guilty about it, too."

Easy studied Caleb. She wasn't quite frowning. She opened her mouth, then closed it again and gave a minute nod. "Maybe that's it."

Behind her, a shadow melted out of the trees. Caleb looked, and Easy turned to see what he was looking at, and together, the two of them saw her.

Adelaide had broken free.

She swayed slightly on her feet. Her short hair hung in lank wet ropes around a face the color of milkfat. The skin around her eyes was mottled with purple. One eye had a bright bloom of red next to the tear duct where a vessel had burst. The bottom half of her dress was so wet it looked black. Slick, ropy gore streaked her calves. As Caleb watched, a few heavy drops of blood fell between Adelaide's thighs, splattering onto the dust.

Adelaide's arms were clutched close to her chest. With one hand, she gripped a mass of flesh that was a deep, rich, livery purple. A thick white rope of tissue snaked from that mass of flesh all the way to the impossibly small, blood-streaked infant in her arms.

When Adelaide spoke, her voice had splinters in it.

"Easy," she said, tears spilling from her wide, exhausted eyes. "I'm not in pain."

2

In what felt like an impossibly short amount of time, the entire population of Kindred Cove was mobilized to mark the arrival of a new member of their community.

They waited at the top of the island, filling the road and the patch of grass between the chapel and the Old House, crowded between the trees, pushing right up to the edge of the cliffs. The crowd was so dense that their shared excitement stepped between them, walking from shoulder to shoulder, never touching the ground.

Later, they all anticipated, the chapel would throb with triumph. Later, the glow of the celebration would be a warm beacon against the dark of the night—every window open, every candle lit. But for now, they waited.

Caleb couldn't make himself feel the sense of celebration that everyone else seemed to be experiencing. Easy had left him behind so quickly. The two of them had seen Adelaide together and then Edith had come outside, and she and Easy had taken Adelaide up the hill and out of sight. Caleb knew they were inside the Old House, but he didn't know what was happening in there. He was stuck here, mashed between the railing of the front steps of the Old House and three other people, bare rosemary stems crushed beneath his feet.

On the chapel steps, Jessie led the children in a clapping game. She was good with them. Good at keeping them busy when they might have gotten impatient; good at tending to their hurts; good at helping them grow.

That heat boiled up in him again. His heart was pounding. He swallowed the anger down. There was no good reason for things to be any other way. There was no reason for anyone but Jessie to be in charge of the children. There was no reason for him to be invited inside the Old House. Not when he'd spent so much of his time here hurting himself and his community, attaching himself to grief for Sadie and Harvey when they hadn't gone anywhere. When there was no reason to miss anyone. When nothing was ever lost.

He wondered if he should be allowed anywhere near Adelaide and that baby. He wanted to ask Easy what she thought. If she thought he'd poison them just by being too close.

They hadn't been gathered long when the front door of the Old House opened. A ripple ran through the crowd—a wave of surprise followed immediately by a dip of silence. Easy stepped out onto the front porch, followed by William. Edith was behind them, supporting a woozy-looking Adelaide. Their faces were grave.

"Friends," Easy said, adjusting a cloth bundle that she gripped with both hands, "thank you for gathering. You were told to come here to welcome a new member of our community. I'm sorry to say that you were misinformed."

Caleb watched Edith's face. It was as still as glass.

"Although we all thought that our beloved Adelaide was pregnant, she wasn't," Easy said. She said it as firm as a planted foot, as firm as a dropped stone. "As you can see, there is no baby here. Adelaide did not give birth. Nothing has been lost."

Behind her, Adelaide slumped. Edith braced an arm around her, then gently nudged her a few steps forward.

"William, you'll help Adelaide on the way down to the water?" Easy asked softly enough that only those closest to the porch could hear. "She may not be able to walk on her own."

"Don't help me," Adelaide sighed. "I'm not going."

"Make a path," William called out, walking down the front steps, splitting the crowd in half down the middle. "Down to the water."

Every eye except Caleb's followed William. Caleb was still watching Easy. She looked sharp as broken glass. A flush rode high on her cheekbones.

"I'm not going," Adelaide said again. Her voice creaked with exhaustion. "I'm too tired."

Easy held the bundle out to Adelaide, who didn't acknowledge it at all. "You wouldn't be so tired if you'd had the support of your community. We all wanted to help you with this, Adelaide. But you chose—"

"I didn't choose—"

"You chose," Easy said again, still quiet but loud enough that Caleb blinked in surprise, "to do this on your own, at every step. You went out into the world and stayed there rather than coming home on time. You refused our advice. You wouldn't listen when we told you what your body needed. You didn't wait for us to be gathered around you in the chapel before you started to push. You did it all on your own, Adelaide, and this community doesn't work that way."

Adelaide stared hard at Easy. She looked like a bruise. "I'm sorry," she said at last. Her voice broke across the words. "I'm sorry I did it all wrong. I meant to do things right. I understand that this is my fault. But I can't do what you're asking me to do. I can't."

"Clear the road," William was saying. He walked through the crowd with his arms wide, cutting a path through the close-pressed bodies of everyone who had come to see the baby that had never been. "You can stand on either side, but keep the middle path clear."

Easy shoved the bundle against Adelaide's chest. "You can, and you will. Walk down to the water. Go."

Adelaide didn't lift her arms. She tried to take a step back, but Edith was right behind her.

Caleb tried to speak, but his voice wouldn't come. He cleared his throat and tried again. "You don't look tired," he said.

Adelaide looked down at him. Her eyes were huge. She looked like an animal caught in a hole. "What?"

"You don't look tired. If you were tired . . ." He considered her face. Her eyes were ringed with deep shadows. Her mouth sagged. Her eye was half red with blood. "If you were tired, you'd be ugly," he said. "And you're not ugly. You're beautiful. I don't see a tired person, when I look at you."

Easy shoved the bundle at her again. This time Adelaide took it. Her eyes flashed with something cold and furious as she staggered forward, toward the steps, toward the waiting crowd.

Behind her, Edith reached out a hand as if to grab her. It stayed there, half raised, Edith's intention cut off before it could become real.

That's what Caleb was looking at as Adelaide walked down onto the steps that led to the front porch of the Old House. Edith's hand. That's where Caleb's attention was when Adelaide turned to look down at him.

That's why Caleb was startled when Adelaide said his name.

He turned in surprise—just in time to see the bundle of cloth dropping over the rail.

He caught it by pure instinct, his arms shooting out just in time for the bundle to fall into them. It was bigger than he'd expected, heavier. It looked like a wad of bedsheets but there was a solidity to it, and a stillness. He held it for a moment, frozen. He remembered how it had felt to hold Sadie when she was just a baby, when his mother had made him sit on the couch surrounded by pillows and said, *Meet your new sister.*

All he could think, back then the same as now, was *I'm not supposed to have this.*

Adelaide was already gone. The front steps shook with the reverberations of the front door of the Old House slamming behind her.

"I'll handle her," Easy said, following her into the house.

Caleb turned to the crowd. Every eye was on him. He shifted his grip, grabbing the bundle by the knot on top. He didn't know what to do. He couldn't keep this. He wasn't sure if it was even okay for him to be touching it. But he couldn't walk it down to the water and swim it out to the reef, either—that was Adelaide's job, just like Harvey had been his job.

He panicked. "Here," he said, passing the bundle to the person next to him, desperate to stop doing the wrong thing.

But then the person next to him turned and handed the bundle to the person next to them. That person repeated the action, handing the bundle to Leona. She pursed her lips in distaste, but she took it, pressed it to her chest, and then passed it on.

William came up the porch, but Caleb didn't watch him go inside. He drifted with the crowd, following that cloth bundle as it was passed toward the road and then down. They moved, filling in the gap William had carved, filtering between each other, nudging their way forward. Moving along the winding path that connected one end of the island to the other, moving past the Old House, past the chapel, past the garden. Moving toward the shoreline at the end of the road as one.

Caleb allowed pressure at his back to nudge him forward. He couldn't even turn to see who was shoving up against him—he just traveled with the group, which was moving like one enormous breathing heaving creature to retreat from the place where Adelaide hadn't had a baby after all. He found himself drifting to the front of the crowd and that was how he realized that they were all cycling past each other.

As he watched, Jessie handed the bundle to that little girl, Nona. She had come to him to hold a baby chicken, and now she reached for the bundle with the same tender reverence. Once it was safely in the younger girl's arms, Jessie found her way to the outer edge of the group to make room for someone else to step forward.

And then, when they emerged from the trees and onto the shoreline, it was Caleb's turn again. He took the bundle as it was passed to him. The knot had come undone, or someone had pulled it loose, and in his arms, the fabric fell away to reveal a single radiantly pink foot.

Caleb blinked down at it only once before wrapping it tightly in the loose hank of fabric. He retied the knot himself, tight and secure, before turning to see who should take the bundle next.

The person behind him jostled him hard. He turned instinctively and there was Easy—but before Caleb could ask why she'd shoved him, she moved aside to make way for William and Edith.

They had Adelaide between them again. Each gripped her by one elbow as they hauled her toward the spot where Caleb stood. Adelaide's feet skimmed the dirt, her toes skipping over buried stones in painful stutters.

They stopped in front of Caleb.

"Take it," Easy murmured. "You have a responsibility to see through. Take it now, Adelaide, and walk it down to the water."

Adelaide turned her head to one side. "I can't," she whispered. "Please don't make me."

Caleb held the bundle toward her. "I care about you so much, Adelaide. And—and when I look at you. I see someone who can be better than you're being right now."

Adelaide's eyes flashed. "Stop that," she growled. "Stop trying to be Harvey. Stop trying to be Easy. You don't see anything. Do you have any idea what I just went through? Have you ever felt your organs move to make room for someone's skull? Have you ever felt another person rolling over inside you? Have you ever listened to the sound of your own body tearing itself apart," she added, her eyes shining, "to make room for someone else's body to pass through you? Have you, Caleb? Have you felt anything like that in your small, sad life?"

Everyone at Kindred Cove was there to hear it. Everyone Caleb had ever known stood there, listening, not making the slightest sound. It was quiet enough that he could hear Adelaide's weight shifting on the dirt. That was the only sound, besides the lapping of the water just a few meters away.

He thought of the way Sadie's body had rippled when it bloomed. He thought of Harvey asleep on the mattress next to him in their Las Vegas apartment, the way he'd turned over and over in the night unless Caleb's arms were tight around him. He thought of the sound of Harvey's skin tearing open in the water when the coral had finally taken him.

He clutched the bundle tight in his fists and realized that the searing rage he'd been fighting had been replaced by cool, still water.

"Maybe I've never felt any of that," Caleb said crisply. "But neither have you."

Adelaide froze. "Don't," she whispered.

But Caleb did, because he finally felt what he knew he was supposed to feel. He felt the total absence of grief. The total absence of sorrow. The total absence of loss. He touched, in his mind, all his memories of Sadie and Harvey, and none of those memories hurt him, because he understood at last that they weren't lost any more than Adelaide's baby was lost. They'd been born, in pain and in blood, into a new existence. That was all.

He finally understood what everyone meant when they said that those who went into the water became part of something greater than themselves, and he wanted Adelaide to understand it, too.

He would do his best to do right by her. He would, as Edith had once told him, earn the trust of his community by doing everything right as often as he could for the rest of his life. It was the least he could do, and he was going to start here.

"There was never a baby, Adelaide," Caleb said. "And that means you didn't feel any of those things. I'm sorry, but you can't have. That's just how it is."

The red glare of her bloodied eye sang at him like the coral that had reached up to take Harvey out of his arms in the water. She gave up on him, turning instead to her sister. "Easy. Stop this. Tell them to stop this."

"I—"

"You're the only person who ever understood me," she whispered, straining toward her sister now. "Please. You're the only one who ever really cared about me."

Caleb glanced between her and Easy. Everyone was watching them. He wanted Adelaide to stop this. He wanted her to get away from Easy.

"Of course I care about you," Easy started.

"Then help me," she begged, her voice still shredded from her hours of screaming. She twisted between William and Edith, her eyes wide, her legs trembling. "You don't have to do this. You don't have to do any of this. Just let me go."

"I know I don't have to do this," Easy answered. "I don't have to do anything I don't want to do. And neither do you." She stepped forward and pressed her forehead to Adelaide's. "But you could be part of something. You could be part of this community, if you'd only try. When I look at you—"

"Don't fucking say it," Adelaide spat. "Don't say what you see when you look at me. Why did you send me that letter, Easy? Why did you ask me to come back home? I could have stayed where I was. I could have had a life out there. Me and the baby could have had a *life*."

Easy closed her eyes, her forehead still pressed to her sister's. "That's exactly what I was afraid of. I sent that letter asking you to come back because I want better things for you, Adelaide. We've made better things here. I've made myself better, just like you asked. I got my shit together. I've done everything I could to make this place into a home for you." Her voice broke. "You have no idea how much it hurts to see you rejecting it. I've worked so hard. For you. For us."

"Easy has been working so hard, for so long," Leona said, stepping up next to Edith.

"So long," Edith added. "I don't think Adelaide even noticed how hard Easy's been working."

"I don't think she did," Leona agreed.

Adelaide shook her head, rearing back, away from Easy. She broke free of William and Edith and stood there, her shoulders slumped, her blood-filled eye scanning the faces around her as though she didn't recognize any of them. "You didn't do this for me. None of this is for me."

Caleb felt the cloth of the bundle in his hands stretching under the intensity of his grip. "Of course it's for you," he said. It came out hoarse, but he still felt the attention of the crowd turning to him. He cleared his throat. "You could have everything, Adelaide. Easy's transformed this place, and we've all worked together to make it perfect. I've done everything I can to let that perfection shape me, and look how well I'm doing! You could do it, too. We all believe in the person you can be if you just try. All you have to do is let this one thing go."

Jessie stepped up next to Caleb. She regarded Adelaide with true and honest pity. "You tried to make us all worse," Jessie said. "We welcomed you home and tried to support you, and you undermined us. I have to take responsibility for the fact that I let my jealousy prevent me from seeing what you were really like. Who you really were. How you were trying to sow doubt." Tears brimmed in Jessie's eyes as she turned to look at the people around her. "I'm sorry, everyone. I'm sorry I didn't do better."

"It's okay," William said, coming over to put an arm around Jessie and rubbing her shoulder briskly. "You did your best with her. We all did. And we all failed." He spoke in carrying tones, a preaching voice that was meant for everyone. "This is what it means to be a community. We celebrate together, and we process our failures together. We share victories and we share defeat. We were too optimistic about Adelaide's return." He shook his head. "I, more than anyone, take responsibility for letting her come back in the first place. I could have turned her away before she got onto the boat to come back. I exposed us all to her deception, and I didn't protect you from her. I'm sorry."

Adelaide staggered backward, away from Caleb and the bundle he held. Leona was nearby and caught her by the shoulders, turning her toward the water. "I should have said something about it sooner," Leona said. Edith, who stood just behind her, let out a loud wet sniff. "I knew she was acting different, but I didn't speak up. She's been wrong ever since she came home, and I kept trying to make her better instead of just accepting that she'd changed. I'm sorry."

Caleb bowed his head, wrung the linen in his hands, kept it

folded over that tiny foot. The weight of the bundle made his entire body feel heavy. "I should have known right away. She made me feel tempted to break my promise to this community. I fasted, in secret, to cope with it. I should have told you all, but I didn't want to admit how much she hurt me. How much she set me back."

"You couldn't have known," William said, his eyes fixed firmly on Adelaide. "You did your best."

"I brought her into our community in the first place," Edith said, so softly that the words were almost lost to the sound of the water lapping at the shore. "I carried her. I birthed her, right here on this island. It's all my fault. If I'd tried harder—if I'd done better—" She let out a low, ugly sob that swallowed up her apology.

Easy stepped close to Caleb and put a hand on his shoulder. "Will you give me that?" she murmured. He nodded, letting her take the thing he held, the thing that was not and had never been and thus could never be lost. Easy closed her eyes briefly before lifting her chin and fixing her gaze on her sister. Adelaide stared back, her breath coming fast, her eyes wide and disbelieving.

"When Dad took me in," Easy said, a tremor in her voice, "he told me that it was my job to be there for Adelaide. He told me that even though my parents had been so broken that they had to leave the island—even though I came from something rotten, he said I could be fixed. He tried so hard to fix me. All of you tried so hard to fix me," she said, tears spilling down her cheeks. "And I think I know now why I couldn't get better until Adelaide left for her Salt Year."

"She influenced you," William said gently. "She hobbled you. You couldn't grow while she was there, keeping you broken."

"I'm sorry I didn't see it sooner," Easy said.

"No," Adelaide breathed. "No, no, no, Easy—"

"It's not your fault," Leona said.

"You did your best," Edith agreed.

Adelaide's gaze darted from Easy to the bundle to Caleb to the crowd. She looked around at everyone she'd ever known and she seemed to find nothing familiar, nothing comforting. Whatever she was hoping to see was absent, and in the absence of it her fear melted into visible, naked panic.

She ran.

She ducked past Caleb and scrambled up toward the road. Her progress was painful to watch—she was slow and sore, and it was obvious that she wouldn't make it far on her own power. But no one wanted to give chase, and for a moment, it seemed like a genuine possibility that she'd escape.

She was just a few steps up the road when she stumbled. One of her legs buckled under her and she went down hard, her elbow hitting the ground with an audible crack. She didn't get up right away. She stayed on the ground, gasping, the wind evidently knocked out of her. After a long minute of struggle, she finally tried to push herself upright—but she put her weight on the arm that had hit the ground. She cried out in pain as it, too, buckled under her.

Caleb walked up the road toward her. Easy handed the bundle to Jessie, then followed him. They each took one of Adelaide's arms and helped her to her feet.

"Please," Adelaide begged, trying to jerk away from them, too depleted to succeed. "Please don't."

"It's okay," Easy said, nudging her way under one of Adelaide's arms to help hold her upright. "You're not alone."

"We've got you," Caleb said, doing the same.

Together, they walked her the rest of the way down to the water. Their community joined them, and soon they were all supporting Adelaide together, making sure no single person was carrying too much of her. She let out a ragged scream as they lifted her ankles, cupped the backs of her knees, supported the weight of her head with their outstretched palms. Jessie placed the bundle on her chest, tucking it into the front of her dress to hold it secure.

"You don't need to be scared," Easy said, sliding a hand over Adelaide's mouth to silence her. "Nothing bad is going to happen to you."

The water that evening was sweet and gentle. It caressed the shore in a sweeping wave, lapped at the calves of the gathered crowd as they walked into the shallows. Adelaide's increasingly frantic screams, already muffled by Easy's palm, were swallowed by the sound of their legs splashing through the water.

Edith hesitated at the water's edge, but then Easy nodded to her and said, "You've more than proven yourself, Edith. It's time to come into the water." And so she did, in front of the community that loved her. She stepped into the water and she put her rough hands on one of Adelaide's arms, her grip firm and certain as the tender correction of her family at the Cove.

"Look," Caleb said, his lips against Adelaide's ear. He knew, even as he said it, that Adelaide could only see the sky—his hands were in her hair, holding her head so firmly that she wouldn't be able to turn and see what he saw. So he told her. "The reef is here. It came for you, just like it came for Harvey."

Because it was. He could see it from where he stood—the coral blooming into a vast swathe of writhing scarlet tendrils. They were reaching toward the shore, those thousand convulsing fingers of vibrant connection. They were reaching for the island. They were reaching for Adelaide.

The entire community reached back.

Leona's hands were soft, the way they always were from the hours she spent shaping and smoothing beeswax. She took Adelaide's free arm, and with that, she and Edith finally knew true fellowship with each other, in spite of their long years of resentment and competition.

Jessie's hands were small and urgent on her ribs.

William's hands, which had done so much work over the years fixing everything on the island that needed to be fixed and breaking everything on the island that needed to be broken for whoever proved themself to be his leader, were strong under Adelaide's hips.

Caleb's hands were weak but deft, slipping through Adelaide's hair as easily as they would through the feathers of a loose chicken that needed to be returned to the coop.

Easy's hands were cool and gentle. One cupped the back of Adelaide's neck; the other was pressed tight across her mouth.

Adelaide tried to twist, tried to thrash, tried to fight—but the people who had loved her best for all her life held her tight. There was nowhere for her to go.

The hands that supported Adelaide lowered in unison, bringing her down to meet the rising water. All those hands moved from below to above once the Vetiver had hold of her. They pressed down on her hips, her shoulders, the slack swell of her belly, the tops of her thighs. Easy, still holding the back of Adelaide's neck, gazed down at her with beatific certainty.

"Don't be afraid," Easy said again as the water rose up around her hips, possessive and insistent. "You are always changing. Sometimes it hurts to grow," she added. "But it's always worth it."

Adelaide opened her mouth, to answer or to beg or to scream. Before any sound could leave her throat, Easy lifted her hands up out of the water and pressed them to Adelaide's forehead, pushing her face below the surface.

They all held Adelaide down together. There were enough hands working together, enough churn from the ongoing rush of the miracle tide, that they didn't even feel her fight. She may as well have been part of the reef already. Those reaching fingers of coral brushed against their heels, leaving burning welts that would linger for weeks, but no one felt the pain, not really. Or if they did, they knew that the pain was worth it. The pain would always be worth it.

They didn't take their hands away from Adelaide's body until she herself began to bloom. At long last, her skin pulsed, rippling and clenching, writhing under the palms of the people who loved her best—until it finally erupted into a violent spray of branching red coral. It stretched down into the water. It reached for the reef and the crowd parted for it, letting it pass so Adelaide could become part of something greater than herself.

The community at Kindred Cove stood together in the rising water. They watched Adelaide grow, and they knew they had done what was best for her.

They had done it together.

Always

Beneath the surface of the Vetiver, the reef is growing.

It grows like breathing. It grows like aging. It grows like dying. Growth, to the reef, is an expression of existence. The act of growing is no more or less decisive than the act of digestion—both are a function of living, unconscious and inexorable.

Every mature polyp reaches soft fingers up into the water, combing the gentle shifting currents of the lake for whatever might drift or swim by. Taking what is given, eating when fed.

None of them will ever find a reason to stop reaching. None of them will ever find a reason to stop growing.

The polyps are building places for themselves to rest—massive shelves of calcium, dimpled to cup their basal plates, sturdy enough to hold them fast even when the water is in storm-swept turmoil. These shelves form a branching skeleton that lofts high above the cratered and cavernous bottom of the lake, like a single enormous hand hefting the hungry polyps toward the sun.

Building that skeleton is the work of the entire colony and all its ancestors. Each polyp will build on whatever it must, on stone or old plate or brother or new dead flesh. The growth of the reef is fast. There's no time to waste. The polyps are committed to the work of survival and expansion.

They thrive in all their budding branching reaching glory in the warm belt of water close to the surface, where little fish swim and die and rot away. The bones of those little fish rain down onto the soft mouths of the polyps like calcium-rich manna.

There is coral near the surface, and there is coral down deep, where the skeleton the colony has built vanishes into the hole that gave the lake a new bottom. Down there in the caverns, the world was once held up by great white pillars of salt; now, water pushes up against the weight of the ceiling, and massive lacelike fans of coral whisper their lives into the abyssal deep. They don't know how to reach for the warmer waters, how to catch a flurry of treasure from the shallows. They grow and grow in the cold depths and don't even know they're reaching for each other.

The reef above knows what it is reaching for. The polyps up there live shoulder to shoulder, their soft stinging fingers brushing against each other in constant silent conversation. They move as individuals, but they grow as one. They bud on their own, and then their buds join the community, and together they become greater each day—spreading, splitting, feasting, building. One polyp on its own can only grow so much, but no polyp will ever know the lonely limitation of solitude.

They are born into fellowship. They create an abundance of unanimity as a simple extension of the existence they can never—will never—stop sharing with every single one of their fellows.

Thousands of fingers blanketing a single calcified hand, reaching as one toward the growth and light that sustain them. They will never stop reaching.

They will never stop growing.

Together.

SALT FESTIVAL

day four | evening

Celia knew right away what she was looking at. She saw an arm first—there was no mistaking it for anything else. The skin was still intact, pale and whole. The elbow bent slightly, like the person the arm belonged to was reaching out to shake Easy's hand. But Celia couldn't see who the arm belonged to, because the flesh of it was only whole up to the shoulder.

That's where the skin ended, and the coral began.

Branching red polyps erupted out of the chest of the body like taste buds on a tongue. Little bumps toward the shoulder, and long, waving tendrils over the heart. Something in the center of the mass of coral glinted, and it wasn't until they were closer that Celia realized what was catching the light.

It was a small crystal suspended on a silver chain.

They swam parallel to the reef. They surfaced for air and then dove again—ten, twelve times. Celia saw, and kept seeing. Some of the bodies were more complete than others; some were mostly gone. The irregular contour of the reef registered differently to her eye now, the long stretching sections resolving into shapes that she could recognize as former arms and legs.

Before the burning in her lungs could no longer be ignored, Celia saw one final corpse. It was an impossibly small one. Shreds of fabric hung in the water all around it. The coral that emerged from the rotted linen was a soft, sweet pink, similar to the color she'd painted her nursery at home. It spread out into delicate lacy fans that swayed with the motion of the water, gently rocking themselves in a heartbeat rhythm.

The tiny body was clutched by two thick branches of coral. Above those arms, Celia saw the only thing she'd been able to recognize as a face during her time in the water.

The eyes were gone, replaced by small, gently pulsating orange polyps. The mouth was still intact, though, and it was familiar to Celia. She knew those small, perfectly pink rosebud lips that always looked like they were braced for a kiss.

She glanced over at Easy, the turning of her head slow and dream-like against the drag of the water. Easy nodded.

She took it as the only thing it could be. Confirmation. She was seeing what she thought she was seeing.

She looked for a very long time.

After that, it didn't feel like there was any reason to keep diving back down. Celia had seen what Easy wanted her to see. They returned to the island instead. They didn't speak as they went, swimming in silence until the lakebed rose up beneath them. Once it was shallow enough to walk, Celia waded onto dry land, feeling the unwelcome weight of gravity settling over her as she went.

Easy stayed in the water still, submerged up to her knees. "Do you know where you are?"

Celia looked around her. "Here?"

It was so quiet, except for the water and the trees. The sky was just growing dark. Easy pointed to the land behind Celia. "Those are the salt flats. That's how far we swam. Wild, huh? We went nearly half a mile out, and a quarter of the way around the island. You're a good swimmer."

"Those bodies," Celia said. She slid her arms around her bare stomach, drummed her fingers across her ribs. "That's where Adelaide's been this whole time. She's not on the island at all."

Easy nodded. "Not on the island. But here, with us. Part of everything. Always."

"But I've seen her. Around the island. I've heard her voice, I've—"

Easy splashed up out of the shallows. "That's how I knew, Celia. That's how I knew you belonged here." She was grinning wildly, her eyes bright. There was a livid red welt on her calf. "I thought you might, from your letter, but that day when you said you saw Adelaide—that told me everything I needed to know. You belong here. Because you see her. You know, deep in a place that nothing could ever touch, that she's with us. She's right here, always. Forever."

Celia shook her head. Her entire body was starting to hum. She wanted to float away from that hum. She wanted to detach herself from it. "But she and Nona are gone. They're not here."

Easy stood so close that the water from her skin dripped onto Celia's. "I thought you understood. They're not gone. Nona isn't gone. She's in the reef, and the reef is all around us."

Celia blinked fast. She shook her head. "I didn't see Nona down there." Goose bumps rose across the surface of her skin as the warm lakewater dried, leaving her skin cool in its absence.

"I'm telling you, though. That's where she is. Do you trust me?"

Celia didn't think. She didn't have to. She knew the right answer. "Of course."

"I took her down today. Me and William. To a spot farther out than where you and I were swimming. She grew into the reef so fast, it's like she was born for it. She's perfect exactly where she is." She searched Celia's eyes with her own. "So now you've seen it. You don't have to wonder anymore, you don't have to worry. She's part of something greater than herself. There's nothing to be scared of."

"Does it hurt?" she whispered. "When they . . . change?"

Easy smiled. "Probably. Doesn't everything?"

"Then how are you not scared?"

"I'm scared all the time." Easy's fingers found Celia's. They tangled together like branching fronds of coral finding each other in the water. "But that's okay. I'm okay, because I put in the work to be okay. That's what I've been trying to get you to see about Kindred Cove. We're not holy or chosen or blessed. We just want to be okay, so we make it happen. That's the difference between us and the mainlanders. That's the difference between you and the other visitors." She pressed her lips to Celia's hairline, her hand gently cupping the back of Celia's head before she pulled away. "You want it enough."

"What if I'm still scared?"

"Of what?"

Celia swallowed. Her throat was so dry, which felt impossible because she'd just spent so long in the water. She looked up at the sky and saw the first star of the evening. "Of losing people. Of the way it hurts when they go."

"That question is why I had to show you. Because I think—Celia,

I think you belong here. The Cove has so much to teach you, and you have so much to teach us."

The hum had risen to a strident buzz that reverberated all the way through Celia's bones. She'd lost track of herself in the water—she'd felt like she was part of the lake, part of everything. But now she could feel herself, could feel the rush of her own blood, could feel the reverse-shiver of her skin warming.

She squeezed her eyes shut tight and reminded herself of what Caleb had said when he pulled her into the trees, what Jessie had said while they were scraping up stones, what everyone had said to her by candlelight. She tried to picture herself in the mirror room, her face looking back at her a thousand times over. She wanted to be able to see herself in those mirrors, unafraid just like Easy was, certain just like Jessie was, trusting just like Caleb was. She wanted to be the person they saw in her.

When she opened her eyes again, she couldn't feel the buzzing anymore. She couldn't feel her body at all. She was floating inside herself, her blood a gently rippling ocean, her skin a vast bubble that stretched around her like the dome of the sky. She had seen Adelaide on the island, and she had seen Adelaide in the water, and it was just like Easy had said. She didn't have to worry.

"I used to feel the same way you feel right now," Easy continued. "I was scared of loss. I wanted answers that made sense to me. I wanted to feel like I understood things, like things were fair and just, like everything was happening the way I thought it was supposed to." She gripped Celia's arms, then let go and took Celia's hands, then let go of those and grabbed Celia by the hips. It felt like she wanted to grab on everywhere, all at once, with all of herself. "You don't know how to let go of those ideas right now. I get it. All you have to do is trust us. You have to accept that there are some things you don't need to know right away, because they'll take time to learn. Like letting go of grief, and understanding that nothing is ever lost—I know it all feels too big to take in right now. But it's all true, I promise, and you'll see it someday. Not everyone can trust in that, Celia, do you understand? Not everyone can handle it. But I know you can. I see so much of her in you."

"Who?"

Easy looked down at Celia and the corners of her mouth lifted into the softest smile. She brushed a strand of hair away from Celia's temple. "Adelaide."

"I'm not her," Celia whispered, her stinging tongue clumsy in her mouth.

Easy sighed out a laugh. "Of course not. You understand everything she couldn't."

And Celia knew that Easy was right, because she did understand. She understood exactly. She knew how not to see the things that needed to stay unseen. She'd been doing it her whole life—not knowing things, and trusting that it was fine to not know.

Back home, she'd perfected it. She'd thrown her batteries in the trash, and she'd sold cheap leggings that were sewn by exhausted children to people who didn't want them, and she'd fallen in love over and over again with people who didn't remember they'd ever met her in the first place. She hadn't asked why Adelaide didn't have a birth certificate, and she hadn't asked why IVF cost so much money, and she hadn't asked whether it was fair that her parents had died because a bridge wasn't rated correctly by a regulatory commission that barely existed anymore. She'd read an article that said the ocean currents were shifting, she'd heard a podcast about the way demand for fish oil capsules was depleting the global krill population and collapsing the food chain. She'd watched a documentary about whales diving deep enough to kill themselves to try to escape the awful noise of ships.

And then she'd forgotten it all

She'd turned away from the part of her mind that knew any of it. She abandoned the part of her that knew she often hurt people she cared about, the part of her that knew her parents should still be alive, the part of her that knew everything, everywhere, was dying. She stopped knowing. She stopped being someone who *could* know. She sold essential oils to friends of friends who also needed to stop being people who could know. She handed them tiny bottles that smelled like lavender, and she told them *this will help you sleep*, and in some ways it was true, wasn't it? It helped them all sleep, the idea that the only problems in the world were ones that were small enough to be seen, comprehended, solved by little bottles of what ultimately amounted to nothing more than strong perfume.

There were hundreds of things, thousands of things, a whole

world of things in the life she was used to that were absolutely vital to look away from, because seeing was drowning.

Here, she didn't need to see everything. She didn't need to know everything. And here, it wouldn't be so scary to drown. She could close her eyes and lean back into the water, not knowing what would happen to her—and she could trust that no matter what happened to her, nothing would ever be bad again.

Celia looked up into Easy's eyes. The sky above them was filling with stars, and the water was full of people who would never be lost or hurt or sad again, and they mattered the exact same amount.

Celia couldn't touch either one.

"I do think I can do it," she whispered, and tears as warm as lake-water flooded down her cheeks. "I want to put in the work."

"Good," Easy said, pulling Celia into a tight embrace. Her skin was cold. Celia imagined hers was, too. It didn't matter. None of it mattered. "Let's go to Candle Hour. Everyone will be so happy when we tell them."

"Tell them what?"

Easy smiled down at her. "That you're going to stay."

Three Years Ago

"Are you sure this is okay? I thought we weren't supposed to go into the water at night."

Mackenzie's assigned Salt Festival companion, Edith, doesn't slow down. "Of course it's okay. I'll be with you." She leads Mackenzie around the last curve of the road, and the two of them spill out onto the shore. Edith points to the water, which glitters in the moonlight. "Go on. It'll help with those swollen ankles."

Mackenzie hesitates. Her borrowed linen dress doesn't quite fit her six-months-along belly, and it flutters around her knees, shortened by the swell of her baby. "You're not coming in with me?"

"You need to do this part on your own," Edith says. "Isn't that what you're scared of? Having to do things on your own?"

It stings because it's true, and because she's not sure how Edith can tell. Mackenzie takes a few steps into the cool water of Lake Vetiver. Lets the chill suck the embarrassed heat out of her.

That fear—the fear she thought was a secret—is what brought her to Kindred Cove for the Salt Festival. She only has a few months left, she knows, to figure out what to do when the baby arrives. How to explain to her boyfriend that she doesn't want him involved, not because he's a bad person but because he's useless and she can't be responsible for both him and an infant. How to raise it, all by herself, to be someone who thinks and says and does all the right things.

Since she got here, she's realized that she needs to ask her mom for help getting through the first year. The prospect is almost as scary as going it alone. Things have been so tense between them for so long. Audrey has always looked at her like she's waiting for something to slip into place, like she's waiting for some missing personality trait to sprout up out of the depths of her inadequate daughter. Going to her for help is going to feel like confirming that inadequacy.

"Edith?" Mackenzie whispers, wading a little deeper into the water, letting it slip across the sensitive creases at the backs of her knees. "What if I don't want the baby?"

Edith doesn't answer right away. When she does, her voice is blank, and in the blankness Mackenzie hears fathomless depths of judgment. "Seems like a decision that's past making. You're, what, six months along now? It's been a while since I was on the mainland, but back in my day, they didn't let you change your mind this late."

Mackenzie hikes her dress up around her hips and wades deeper. Edith was right—the water is helping. "That's not what I meant," she says, although that hasn't always been true. For a month after she found out about the baby, she'd vacillated, and then the choice had been made for her by a bombing at the only clinic in her state, and that was that. "What I mean is, what if I give birth to it, and I look at it, and I think, *I don't want this*, and I'm just . . . stuck?"

Under Mackenzie's feet, the silt of the lakebed sinks and shifts. She curls her toes down into it. Watches the surface of the water. Waits for Edith to answer.

But Edith doesn't. Mackenzie turns around and realizes that the shore is much farther than she thought. She's waded out far enough into the lake that Edith surely can't hear her anymore. The older woman is just a shadow against the treeline.

A childlike, lost-in-public panic flutters in Mackenzie. It feels like the baby rolling over. She rubs her belly and finds it wet with lakewater—when, she wonders, did she go into the water deep enough for her stomach to be submerged? And how did she fail to feel it?

She plucks at her dress. It's soaked through, cold, clinging to her heavy breasts. She tries to strip it off over her head and gets tangled up in the wet linen, loses her footing, falls into the water. It fills her ears and mouth. Her tongue swells with salt. She surfaces, spitting and choking, her dress hanging in a lank coil of streaming linen around her neck.

"Edith?" she calls out hoarsely, trying to push wet hanks of hair out of her eyes, spinning in place to find the shore.

"You're all right," Edith calls back. Mackenzie whips toward the sound of her voice. "It's not so deep. Come on back, if you're done for tonight."

Mackenzie is already wading back toward where she thinks the shore is, blinking hard. It feels like the water is pulling at her calves and ankles, trying to keep her in the lake. It feels like the water is rising around her. It feels like the lake wants her.

She shakes her head. One of her ears gives a soft pop and skin-warm water dribbles out of it, down the side of her neck.

"I fell," she calls nonsensically, just to apply her voice to the vastness of the night.

"I saw," Edith replies.

She sounds a little closer. Mackenzie thinks she must be headed in the right direction. She wades forward a few more steps—and her foot lands on something that is not lakebed silt.

It's firm, but not entirely hard. It feels like skin. Like treading on someone else's bare foot. She pulls back—and that's when the pain begins. The arch of her foot burns, a burn that spreads up her ankle with every heartbeat. A half-strangled swear slips out of Mackenzie before she can stop herself.

"Mackenzie?" Edith calls. There's a faint note of concern in her voice.

"I'm fine," Mackenzie replies. It comes out on a sob of pain. "I just stepped on something. Some kind of . . . animal, I think. It stung me, maybe."

Edith hesitates. Again, when she replies, her voice is blank—curiously flat. The note of concern has evaporated, replaced by total remove. "Come on, then. I'll take a look. Nothing a good night's rest won't fix."

Mackenzie shivers with pain as she stumbles out of the water toward Edith. Her calf and thigh are gripped by pink lightning. "Are you sure?" she chokes out. "It feels—"

"I'm sure," Edith replies, wrapping Mackenzie in a rough linen towel, not touching her damp skin anywhere. "You're at Kindred Cove, Mackenzie. We'll take care of you here."

SALT FESTIVAL

day four | evening

They stood at the back of the crowd at Candle Hour. Celia wore a dress that Easy had grabbed from a cabin on their way up the road. It wasn't hers, but it was hers, because everything at the Cove was hers now.

She touched her lips, then caught Easy seeing her touch her lips. At the front of the crowd, Jessie wore a crown of flowers and cried what looked to be ecstatic tears at the promise of her Salt Year.

"She's going to have a great time," Easy murmured.

"She's going to hate it out there," Celia replied.

Easy covered her mouth to stifle a shotgun blast of a laugh. "She's going to have a great time hating it," she said, and Celia couldn't disagree. "I should help her prepare. She has to put the kids to bed and then get ready to leave in the morning. It's going to be a lot for her to handle. And you should go enjoy the party," she said, winking at Celia. "The final night of the Salt Festival is—well. You'll see. Have fun. You deserve to celebrate."

And with that she was gone, pushing her way forward through the crowd to embrace Jessie and lead her away into the night. William said a few final words to the crowd about finding community in each other, and turning purpose into meaning.

And then it was over. The last Candle Hour of the Salt Festival. Rinna clung to Kristen, both of them weeping. Edith and William spoke softly to Audrey, who looked exhausted and somber. And then there was a hand on Celia's shoulder, and she turned to find a resident of the Cove she hadn't met yet—a young woman with long, dark hair and a gummy smile.

"I just wanted to say I'm so happy you're staying," she said, beaming at Celia. "I've been hoping you would."

"Oh—how did you—that means so much to me," Celia said, and

then she was embracing this woman she'd never seen before, this woman who had somehow known her and wanted her to stay.

"When I look at you," the young woman said, pulling back just enough to look Celia in the eye, "I see one of us."

From behind Celia, an unfamiliar voice called out. "Is that Celia? I'm so excited she's staying!"

And then there was a man she hadn't seen before either, half his face pink with branching burns. He pulled her in close and she could smell salt on his skin, and he was saying the same thing—"I'd hoped you would stay"—and then he was telling her that when he looked at her, he saw family.

It happened so many times that Celia lost count of the people who appeared to embrace her. All of them said that they'd wanted her to stick around. One person with tangled blond curls said they'd been intimidated by her, that they hadn't wanted to come say anything, that they'd been hoping to learn from her. And every single person told her in some way that when they looked at her, they saw someone who belonged.

It left Celia dizzy. She could feel the full fatigue of the day sinking deep into her—the morning she'd spent with Easy in the room at the back of the Old House, and the long, arduous work of cleaning up the road with Jessie, and the swim and the dive and the haircut and the reef and Nona. And now this, the arms of so many strangers who were going to become her family.

Her heart felt as swollen as a kissed mouth.

When she realized she hadn't eaten since the oat bar in the canteen before Easy cut her hair, she finally pulled herself away. She made her way toward the chapel, passing residents and visitors who stood in twos and threes, talking and laughing—some of them embracing, clinging tightly to each other, moving together. Celia moved between the groups, her head swimming from the way she'd been pulled through the crowd, from arms to open arms, from person to loving person.

She needed to eat something. She knew she did. But when she ascended the chapel steps, she found a picked-over table of food, with only an untouched mountain of honeycomb in the center. Leona stood over it, staring at the honeycomb with a frown.

She looked up as Celia approached. "I'm surprised things are taking so long," she said mildly. "I'd have thought you'd all be out rolling around on the lawn by now."

"What do you mean?"

"Oh, you'll see," Leona replied, her mouth curling up at the corners. "I heard you're staying. How was your conversation with Easy? Did she help you understand some things?"

Celia didn't know how to summarize the experience of swimming alongside Easy, of falling into the arms of this crowd of people who were becoming her family. She felt alive to the point of overflowing.

In the past when she'd felt this way, she hadn't been able to tell anyone, because the feeling had been the result of a one-sided fixation. This time, the feeling came from the work of her hands and body, the sweet oblivion of the lake, the knowledge that all she had to do was let happiness flood into her like a miracle tide rising over the island of her soul.

This time, maybe it wouldn't hurt to share how she felt.

"It was amazing," she told Leona. "She helped me understand everything."

Leona laughed. There was real warmth in it. "Really? Everything, huh? That was fast."

"Really!" An answering laugh bubbled up in Celia, not because she was startled or surprised but because Leona was laughing and it felt good to mirror her, to become a reflection of her emotions and reactions, to blend into her. And then the crowd outside the chapel picked up the laughter, too, and the two of them were in an empty chapel surrounded by contagious, reasonless joy.

After the noise died down, Celia pointed at the honeycomb. "How do you eat this?"

Leona was still watching her thoughtfully, but her gaze had softened. She carved off a hunk of comb with a knife that still had some wax on it from candle carving. She handed it over without explanation, looking Celia up and down one more time. "You'll figure it out," she said. "You're one of the good ones. I can tell. Easy wouldn't have picked you if you weren't," she added thoughtfully. "She really has come a long way. I'll see you outside." She left, but slowly, looking over her shoulder at Celia the entire way.

Celia didn't know what to do with the chunk of honeycomb. It was large enough that she needed both hands to hold it, and it was dripping with a shocking amount of honey. She looked around for help, but there was no one to meet her gaze. She lifted her wrists to try to prevent it from spilling onto the floor; honey ran down the heels of her hands, oozing onto her forearms. Instinct took over, and before she could think of a better solution she lifted the comb to her mouth and took a bite.

Honey immediately spilled into her mouth, down her throat, onto her chest. She understood her mistake instantly: There was no way she could eat this entire honeycomb, and wasn't it made of beeswax? She wasn't even sure if beeswax was edible. She rolled the mouthful of wax around with her tongue and in her uncertainty it registered firmly as *not-food, do not swallow.*

She sped toward the wide-open chapel doors, slightly frantic, in need of a place to set the comb down and spit it out. But when she got to the chapel steps, she froze. She forgot the wax in her mouth, the dripping comb in her hands, the honey that coated her hands and chin. For just a moment, she forgot everything that wasn't the scene before her.

When she'd walked into the chapel, the crowd outside had been fluid, filled with laughter and conversation and the soft sound of skin just starting to touch skin. There was still laughter now—but the conversation had changed. The clover between the chapel and the Old House was carpeted with discarded clothes. There were still candles on the chapel steps, on the outer ledges of the windows and in the low branches of the apple tree, and their flickering light fell on a sea of skin. The air was heavy with the competing smells of beeswax and peppermint oil and sweat and sex.

They were still clustered in their twos and threes, but now, the residents and visitors moved together as one.

As Celia watched, the disjointed rhythms of each group began to fall into harmony. A hand extended from one couple to find purchase in a group of four; an outstretched foot braced against a nearby hip for leverage; a pair became a quartet, then subsumed a nearby trio. She spotted one of the remaining crystal-necklace women, her mouth locked around Mitchell's index finger. Two men she recognized from the canteen were churning and sweating on opposite sides of a pair of women who'd told Celia they were excited to be her new sisters. The women leaned against each other's backs, bracing each other against the ceaseless rhythmic thrusting. As Celia watched, Leona stepped down the chapel steps and out of her dress, then walked into the crowd and allowed herself to be pulled down by the first pair of hands that reached for her.

It was like watching individual loops of thread braiding themselves into a tapestry; before long, the small groups scattered across the lawn had formed one vast undulating wave of flesh. It was a single great and glorious body, and that body was touching itself for the sheer pleasure of knowing its own skin, as entangled as held hands, as self-connected as the reef.

A sigh began at the apple tree and rippled out through the crowd, heading toward the chapel. Celia shivered at the sound of all those voices raised in the same ecstatic song, calling out together, calling out to something greater than themselves, something familiar, something deep within her that ached to answer—

She stumbled down the steps, tripping over a dozen outstretched arms and legs, pulling away from a reaching hand before the fingers could find purchase on her ankle. She dropped the uneaten section of honeycomb and it was caught before it hit the ground, crushed in a pair of fists to release a waterfall of honey onto an expanse of writhing flesh.

Celia didn't stop to see how many mouths would meet that sweet spill—she kept moving. She wasn't quite running, didn't have a destination in mind, her teeth were sinking into the soft warm wax on her tongue and she couldn't breathe around it—couldn't breathe through that collective moan, the single rising note of shared ecstasy that kept passing through the crowd.

She found herself at the treeline and slipped into the shadows, hoping to take a moment to get her bearings. But she wasn't alone. Caleb was there, leaning against a mockernut hickory, his hands in his pockets.

Celia stared at him for a long moment, unable to find words, her mouth full of sweet wax.

"Hey there," Caleb said at last. "You okay?"

"I'm—" Celia spat the wax into her sticky palm. "I'm fine. What are you doing here?"

"Just checking in. I like to know how things are progressing up here."

"So . . . this happens a lot?"

"Depends on the occasion," he said. "It's not every time."

Celia couldn't make out his expression. His voice was totally devoid of emotion, perfectly calm. "And you didn't want to, um." She gestured over her shoulder. "You didn't want to celebrate?"

"I'm not really invited to this part of the festivities," he replied.

"Oh. I'm sorry." The wax sat cold and heavy in her hand.

"No, no, it's for my own good. It's in my best interest. I need to not get, you know, distracted. And it's not a big deal to miss it. I mean, nobody has to join if they don't want to. Like Jessie, she never stuck around this late even before she had the kids to deal with. They do a slumber party down in the canteen on nights like tonight, and I think she's always been happy to join them down there. And Easy only comes to these things sometimes. Really, the only people who participate are the ones who feel comfortable taking on the responsibility."

"The responsibility?"

He eyed her. "Of helping bring new energy into the community. We only have so many people here, you know? We can't all go around getting each other pregnant all the time, especially given how many people here aren't sure who they're related to. But there's new people at the Salt Festival, so it's a good opportunity for anyone who's looking to get knocked up." He shrugged. "Anyway, like I said, lots of people don't stay for this part. It's not mandatory or anything. It's not a big deal. I don't feel like I'm missing out."

"Of course. That makes sense," Celia said, even though she wasn't sure she understood.

She took comfort from the knowledge that the children were safe. The thought crossed her mind that Jessie seemed young, too young to have a history of opting out of this part of the celebration—but then, she snuffed that thought out with logic. *He wouldn't have said the children don't stay for this part if Jessie, a child, had ever been invited to stay for this part*, she told herself firmly.

The logic was thin, but it was enough to smooth over any concerns she might have been having. Any thoughts that might not have fit quite right.

There was no need to struggle with dissonance, because she'd eliminated the dissonance within herself.

She'd committed to doing the work, and she'd done it.

All was well, and she could stay here and be happy forever. She was electric. She was invincible.

Celia glanced over her shoulder at the party without thinking, then quickly turned away, flinching away from the yawning, urgent hunger that opened inside her at the sight of the crowd.

"I heard you're staying?"

She sucked honey off her bottom lip. She flexed her hands, felt the stickiness on them. She could feel the movement of the crowd behind her. She wondered if Easy would join in. "I think so. I mean, yes."

"Which is it? You think so, or yes?"

"Yes. It's yes," she breathed. "I'm just not used to saying that. But I will be, soon. I'm staying."

He lifted a hand toward her. His palm hovered a millimeter from the bare skin of her shoulder. "Good," he said. "I was hoping you would. After we talked today, I felt such confidence in you. I think you'll do really good things here, Celia. It can be tricky—there's paperwork to move your assets around, to make sure nothing gets messed up when you move. William will help with that, though. He's got a whole system for processing the transfers. He knows how to handle this stuff; don't let it stress you out. It's all worth it."

"I have faith that everything will work out," she said. The words felt like a new kind of truth, the kind she'd never thought was real. *I have faith.*

She'd said things like that before. She'd said that she trusted the universe, that she believed in destiny, that she knew she could manifest the future she was intended for. But she'd never meant any of that the way she meant this. She'd never felt it the way she did now. She'd always thought of her belief as being about trust, about clinging to something hard enough that it might squeeze her hand back someday.

But this faith felt like inevitability. This was new and all-encompassing. It didn't feel like this faith was a part of her—it felt like *she* was part of *it.*

Things would work out whether she believed in them or not. It wasn't the belief itself that she needed to work for. It was everything else. And she was ready to work.

Caleb was still watching her. His eyes caught the candlelight. "Faith, huh?"

Celia nodded. "Yeah. I guess so."

"It never felt that simple to me," he said. "Maybe you can help me understand."

Celia smiled up at the sky, at the handful of stars that were already out. "You know what I think?"

"No, but I hope you're going to tell me."

"I think it's in you already. You wouldn't be here if you didn't have enough faith to commit to the work. Maybe you just need someone to help hold you to it."

"Like an accountability partner?" he whispered. The words sounded heavy, the way he said them.

"Yeah. Like an accountability partner. I could do that, if you want," she offered. "I mean, I don't really know how, but—"

"Yes. Yes, I'd like that. Would you?" His voice was soft and Celia could tell that the curiosity in it was genuine and she thought, in that moment, that she might love him. Not a romantic love, not the kind of love that made her obsess and fantasize and think in terms of access and control. This was a love that encompassed the entire island, a love that needed nothing but her commitment to confirm it or anchor it.

She loved everyone in that moment. Every single person on the island. Every person off the island, too. They were here with her, and she loved them, and the love that flooded through her was boundless and limitless and she felt like she was going to burst with it.

"Of course," she said. "Can we talk about it more tomorrow? I think I need to—I think I need to go."

He reached up again, and this time, he let his palm come into contact with her bare arm. His hand was trembling. His eyes were glassy with tears. "Of course. Thank you, Celia. Thank you for deciding to stay."

She walked away from him and she couldn't feel the earth beneath her feet, couldn't feel the raw patches on her palms. She was water sliding through water, she was wind brushing past wind, she was skin on skin. She approached the mass of bodies that sprawled across the lawn. There was honey on her lips, on her throat, in her hair. She let her palms skim the surface of the crowd and felt the stickiness dissolve away in the saltwater slick of their commingled sweat; she sweetened the party just by being in it, and in return it pulled her in deeper. She parted her lips and dipped her chin to taste the skin of a person whose face she could not see, and she let salt flood the sweet film of honey off her tongue.

I have faith, she thought as her knees buckled, her head dropping backward in a bright flash of ecstasy, every hand within reaching distance reaching for her and her alone. She felt no fear. She felt no worry. She felt nothing but the touch of her community.

We have faith. Together.

PART SIX

you can be made pure again

home | day one

When Celia woke on Sunday morning, there was a layer of dew on her belly. She traced a fingertip through it. It had condensed on the invisibly fine hairs that covered the skin of her stomach. The sun wasn't up yet, but it was just light out enough that she could see the way the tiny dewdrops combined to fill the pool of her navel.

When she sat up, that pool spilled, releasing the faintest trickle of water. She braced herself against the apple tree as she got her bearings. She hadn't noticed, the night before, the way she'd traveled from the edge of the crowd to the center of it. As her palm met the solidity of the tree, and the water traced a trail down to the raw, aching center of her, she stared at the Old House.

She wanted to spend more time in that room. She wanted to learn how to see with the eyes of the community.

She couldn't wait for this place to make every broken part of her better.

She picked her way across the sleeping figures on the lawn, heading toward the Old House. None of them stirred. She looked into their faces as she moved, and didn't see a single visitor among them. When she looked back and scanned the crowd, she couldn't spot anyone whose face she had looked into across the candlelit circle in the chapel. It sent a thrill through her—the thought that maybe the visitors had been woken up, escorted back to their cabins by their chaperones, invited to prepare to leave. It sent a thrill through her because she had been allowed to sleep here, among the residents.

She wasn't an outsider anymore. She belonged here.

A whisper caught her. "Do you want your dress?" Celia turned to see Jessie tiptoeing around the edge of the sleeping group. She had a length of white cloth draped over one arm. She moved with practiced silence.

"Thanks," Celia whispered back, taking the dress and slipping it over her head. It was a little damp with dew, too. "Do you know who this belongs to? Easy and I just sort of grabbed it on our way up here."

"Everything belongs to everyone," Jessie replied. She smiled, an easier smile than Celia had seen on her the entire week.

"Big day," Celia said. "Are you busy? Getting ready to leave with the visitors later?"

Jessie shook her head. "I'm ready. Everything is ready. But the visitors are already gone. They left right after Candle Hour last night," she said.

"They did? How—"

And then she stopped herself. She decided that William had gently gathered the other visitors once they were spent and sated. That he'd taken them on a midnight trip across the water, sworn them to secrecy about everything they'd witnessed, and sent them home. She decided to believe that, and deciding to believe it made it true.

If those Salt Festival visitors decided not to return to their homes from there—if their friends and family thought they'd stayed at Kindred Cove—that wasn't her business. She wasn't part of that world anymore.

Nothing bad had happened to the rest of the Salt Festival visitors. That idea agreed with what her community told her was true, so she knew it was right.

"Anyway," Jessie was saying, "I'm not leaving until after your acceptance into the community. I decided I wanted to be here for it." A few of the sleepers at the edge of the crowd nearest to them began to stir. Jessie glanced over. "I should probably take care of everyone. Get them awake and down to the canteen. I always try to help out, the morning after. Everyone's tired."

"Where are the kids?"

"Making breakfast for everyone. You're going to be such a natural with them, Celia. I really think that."

"A natural?" Celia could feel the ballast of fatigue pulling down on her own body. There was weight in her shoulders that hadn't been there the day before, a throb in her joints that she didn't recognize from anywhere else.

"It'll only be for a little while, but you'll be great at it. I won't be gone long. I'm going to do a better job than Adelaide did. It's not hard, right? Getting pregnant, I mean? You just have to want it enough. Adelaide must not have wanted it very much at all."

Celia was still thinking about the truth, and how she could create it. A week earlier, she would have been stung by Jessie's words. Hurt at the implication that she just hadn't wanted it enough. Now, she felt nothing, and the nothing-feeling was bliss. "I'm sure you'll do great," she said.

Jessie left to go wake the others, leaving Celia behind. She touched the fabric of her white dress where it lay over her stomach. It was dry now. It wasn't borrowed, because it belonged to everyone, and she was part of everyone. It was hers, and it was theirs, and she was theirs, and they were hers.

Easy was sitting on the porch steps at the Old House. A pregnant gray tabby cat lounged on the porch behind her, swollen and exhausted with the weight of her litter. They both watched Celia approach. Easy's chin was in her hand, her elbow on her knee. She gave Celia a lazy smile. "You had a good time last night?" she asked when they were close enough for conversation.

"I'm exhausted."

"That's a 'yes.'"

Celia sat on the step below Easy's loose-limbed sprawl. The wood was damp with dew. "Jessie said everyone else left?"

A little cloud of condensation puffed out between Easy's lips as she answered. It didn't feel cold enough for that, but the air was heavy and damp enough that Celia supposed maybe the temperature didn't make a difference. "What do you mean? Everyone's still here. They're sleeping, but they're right over there."

Celia looked at the residents, who were stirring as Jessie stepped between them, speaking to them softly, touching their legs and arms. "I meant the visitors."

"There aren't any visitors here. It's just us. It's just family now."

Celia felt like she'd been scraped clean. She touched the bare skin on the back of her neck. "Where's Audrey?"

"She's inside. Spending a little more time reflecting," Easy said. There was a wry twist in her voice.

Celia shifted to look at her. "She's still staying, then?"

Easy looked down at Celia with surprise. "Do you think it's a good idea to add two new people to a community at once? We haven't done that since Caleb and Harvey, and look how that turned out."

"How did it—"

"No, Audrey won't be staying with us. Not the same way you are. She lacks focus." She frowned. "You look unhappy."

"I didn't know I'd be taking her place." Celia dug a fingernail into the woodgrain of the porch step. Dark concentric rings stained the wood near her thigh. Guilt twisted in her gut.

The look Easy gave her was flatly curious. Her chin still rested in her palm. She drummed her fingers against the curve of her jaw. "Would you change it? Would you go so she could stay?"

The house Celia grew up in pulsed in her mind. The garage full of boxes of things nobody wanted to buy. The street outside the front door with the cracked, uneven sidewalk. Her lonely trips to the grocery store where she stared at produce and tried to figure out if she'd actually eat it or if it would just rot in her fridge until she got fed up enough to throw it away. The embryos that would either sit in cold storage forever or sit in her body until they fell out in an unspooling of blood and pain.

"No."

"That's what I thought," Easy said, leaning forward and kissing the crown of Celia's head. Then she cupped Celia's chin, tilted her face up to catch a slanting beam of early sunlight. "Are you hungry?"

"Starving," Celia whispered, feeling the way her jawbone moved against Easy's fingers. She hadn't eaten anything other than honey since the previous afternoon. She'd cleaned up the road, she'd swum for miles, she'd given her body over to the community for what must have been hours.

Easy studied her mouth for a moment before looking back up into her eyes. "Stay that way. Don't eat breakfast today. We're going to celebrate you joining the community. One last button on the Salt Festival."

"I thought it was over?"

"For visitors, yes," Easy said, turning toward the front door. "But this year, I decided to add a little something extra for residents. To remind us what we're building here, together." She looked over her shoulder and her eyes traced Celia's entire body in one smooth sweep, and Celia felt it in her skin and in her blood: She was part of that "together."

Celia couldn't nod without breaking Easy's grip, so she didn't. She just stared up into Easy's eyes, knowing that she didn't need to say yes. She just needed to do as she was told.

"Come inside with me. We need to get Audrey."

"Lead the way," she said, and Easy did, and following her felt perfect.

Inside the house, down the hall, the plain wood of the door waited for them. Easy glanced at Celia one last time before opening it. Her glance said *stay with me.*

"Are you ready?" she asked.

Audrey's voice was hoarse. "I'm ready. Could I have a little water, first? It's been—"

"You'll get some water, yes. And you'll see who you want to see. Let's go." Easy turned around, a smile twisting one corner of her mouth. She looked at Celia with an expression halfway between exasperation and amusement. *Can you believe this?*

Celia shook her head and rolled her eyes, even though she didn't know what was funny. Whether she understood the joke didn't matter. All that mattered was being in on it.

Audrey stumbled out of the closet, blinking. She looked ragged, limp. Wilted. She tripped over her own feet as she made her way to the front door.

"Where is Mackenzie?" she asked, not looking back at Easy and Celia. "Does she know I'm staying?"

Easy gave Celia another wry glance. Her answer sounded like a held-back laugh. "Come with me and ask her yourself."

The entire population of Kindred Cove stood at the shoreline. They lined the road and filled the water, leaning on each other and standing alone, all of them patiently waiting. Breakfast was over, and the work of the day would wait.

It was time for them to close the Salt Festival.

Celia, Easy, and Audrey walked out of the treeline and joined them. They touched Celia as she passed, a gentle brush of reverent fingers like branching polyps meeting each other in the water. Encouraging smiles came from the sea of faces that, a week earlier, had been completely unfamiliar to Celia. Now, she could see herself in all of them, even the ones she didn't know well. When she looked at those faces, she understood who she was.

She could check the truth she found inside herself against the truth they all shared. They would do it with her. They would do it for her.

The miracle tide came in as they stood there. It came in and it kept coming, washing the shoredirt with clean saltwater, meeting the gathered crowd. She thought she felt herself rising with the tide. As she looked out toward the sparkling expanse of the Vetiver, she saw a bloom of vibrant, luscious pink and red reaching up toward the island.

"Where is she?" Audrey asked. She stood beside Celia, water up to her calves, peering into every face in the crowd. Her hands were shaking at her sides. "Where's my daughter?"

Easy waded over to Audrey and took the older woman's face in her hands. "This community welcomed you to the Salt Festival in a spirit of trust and growth." She looked as if she was going to kiss Audrey. Celia was close enough to see the soft line of her mouth twitch. "But you came here under false pretenses, Audrey. You presumed upon our trust, and you betrayed it."

William appeared behind Audrey. He moved through the water so quietly. And then his hands were resting on her shoulders. She tried to turn to see who was touching her, but Easy's hands were firm on her face, holding her in place.

"Here at Kindred Cove," Easy continued, "we don't believe in punishment. So in spite of your betrayal, we are still going to let you stay here, and we are going to offer you the gift of growth."

Leona and Edith flanked Audrey, taking her hands—no, Celia realized. Taking her *wrists*. They held her tight. Audrey flinched away from them, her eyes starting to flash with fear.

"You are going," Easy said, as Caleb reached down into the water to take Audrey's calves in his hands, "to be part of something so much greater than yourself."

Audrey began to thrash. A high animal noise came out of her throat. Jessie braced her hands against Audrey's hips and lifted, and together, they bore her up out of the water.

Easy turned and looked at Celia.

Celia didn't know what was causing the reef to grow that morning. She didn't know what had happened overnight to make it expand enough to send the water reaching up toward the treeline at the Cove. There were some things that didn't need to be known. She knew she was correct in her not-knowing, and she allowed it to keep her safe and happy and perfectly at home

And the not-knowing left enough space in her mind for her to understand what Easy wanted from her.

She was ready to be the person her community knew she could be. She had everything to gain, and nothing could ever be lost to her again.

She moved through the water until she reached Audrey. The crowd around the older woman parted for her, leaving a path that guided her toward Audrey's head. She stood beside Easy. Together, the community bore Audrey down onto her back, holding her just above the surface of the water.

Easy's hands moved to cup the back of Audrey's head, her fingers tangled in Audrey's hair. The water licked at Celia's thighs.

She looked down into Audrey's face. "When I look at you," she said, "I see someone who is not afraid."

"Please," Audrey said. "Don't do this. Please. I'll leave. I won't tell anyone—"

Celia put her palm over Audrey's mouth. She felt Easy's leg pressing against hers, and a sharp sting against her heel. Out of the corner of her eye, she saw something pink and livid moving under the surface of the water. Growing. Reaching. Coming.

"You were pure once," Celia said, smiling down into Audrey's eyes. She used the pad of her thumb to wipe away the tears that were spilling down across Audrey's temples. All around them, the community moved as one, deeper into the water, bearing Audrey forward.

"Good," Easy whispered, her lips brushing the shell of Celia's ear.

Celia felt another sharp sting against her calf. She glanced down and saw that a single soft pink finger of the reef was brushing her leg. Tasting her. It had stretched so close to the shore. It was a miracle.

Her hand was still tight over Audrey's mouth. She raised her other hand, and she rested it gently over Audrey's wide, wet eyes.

"You were pure once," she repeated. "And you can be made pure again."

And then—with all her strength and with all the strength of the community that loved her and would fix her and would help her grow into the person she was meant to be—she pushed Audrey's head under the surface of the Vetiver.

Their hands were steady. Their hearts were calm. Their minds were free of doubt. Their work was effortless, because there were so many of them, and because they were all working in concert. Together, the community held Audrey in place as the reef reached up to meet her.

As Audrey's frantic struggling slowed, Celia felt a kind of certainty she'd never known before. Here at Kindred Cove, she knew her future could only be beautiful. She was ready for that beautiful future to begin. There was nothing else in the world that she could think to want.

Nothing else mattered, as long as they were all here together.

ACKNOWLEDGMENTS

In stories, hungry demons tantalize their prey with compelling offers. Wealth, power, knowledge, sex, music, love, beauty. Earthly pleasures in exchange for the silly little shred of gossamer we call a "soul."

In researching this book, I came to realize that there is a much simpler offer one can make to reap unfathomable profit from even the most selfless of people. Indeed, the selfless are the most vulnerable to this bait—which is perhaps why predatory communities around the world use it to lure in thousands of people. Those people routinely put their money and resources and community connections and corporate leverage into the hands of high-control groups, not just willingly, but eagerly, and it's all because of one simple promise:

You can be good, and I can tell you how.

So many of us want, more than anything, to be good. We want to do right by others, and we want to help those who need it, and we want to fix the seemingly endless problems we see in the world. But life is a complicated creature, and the world is a perplexing machine, and there are many, many systems in place to ensure that no matter how good one person is—no matter how hard one person works—it will never feel like *enough*.

This is where the promise steps in. Have you ever felt hopeless? Have you ever felt lonely? Have you ever felt guilty? All that can be wiped away if you simply follow the rules of the community. If you follow the rules, you will be loved. If you follow the rules, you will know you have done right, and you won't have to ask questions. If you follow the rules, you will be clean and pure, and you will know the satisfaction of correct alignment with the way things ought to be.

What an overwhelming relief it is, to know that one is *good*. To know that one is *loved*. To know that there is a right way and a wrong way, and that the right way can be pursued with enough focus to add up to absolution.

All one must do to pursue the right way hard enough is: Want it the most. Practice total devotion. Prove loyalty.

This pattern echoes far beyond the clasped hands of religion. Motivational speakers, finance gurus, fitness programs, diet plans, multi-level marketing schemes, corporate "families"—even small, insular friend groups with particular attachment systems—fall into this dynamic. Anyone who is hungry for community, purpose, or clarity is susceptible to the pitch. That includes you, reader. That includes me. It is too, too tempting to say that we know better—but that temptation leaves us vulnerable. Vulnerable to financial exploitation; to the extraction of our labor; to the dissolution of our boundaries and self-worth. Vulnerable to the loss of communities who really *do* love us, but who aren't part of the groups approved of by the rules that promise to cleanse our souls.

If you want to learn a little more about how high-control groups operate across various sectors of our society, start with the book *Cultish: The Language of Fanaticism* by linguist Amanda Montell. If you want to dive deeper and learn more about how high-control groups manipulate our desire to connect to something larger than ourselves, I highly recommend *Terror, Love and Brainwashing: Attachment in Cults and Totalitarian Systems* by totalitarianism expert Alexandra Stein.

And if you recognized yourself in this book, and you want to find a way to heal the wounds caused by the community that was supposed to love you, there are resources available:

- Immediate free, confidential referrals for mental health support at 1-800-662-HELP (4357)
- Recovery, intervention, and counseling resources at https://www.peopleleavecults.com
- Support for former high-control group members, families, and loved ones, as well as research and reading material, at https://www.icsahome.com
- Reading and research material, as well as support resources, at https://www.forensiccounselor.org/?Topics_of_Interest__Cults_and_Support_for_Former_Cult_Members

Thank you so, so much to everyone who supported the creation of this book. To the friends and family who were there for me over the incredibly long and challenging journey of writing it; to my wonderful agent and editor; to the colleagues and professional team who supported it from its conception to final iteration; to the team who created the package, the cover, the interiors; to the team who got it into the hands of booksellers and readers everywhere; to the booksellers themselves (my heroes).

To you, my friend, who is reading this now. Thank you. There is nothing you need to memorize in order to become good, and worthy, and loved. There is nothing you need to abandon in order to become pure. There are no rules you must follow, nor creeds to which you must adhere.

It is in you already. It always has been. No one can take it from you.

—Gailey

ABOUT THE AUTHOR

Kate Dollarhyde 2023

SARAH GAILEY is a Hugo Award and British Fantasy Award–winning and bestselling author of speculative fiction, short stories, and essays. Their nonfiction has been published by dozens of venues internationally. Their fiction has been published in more than seven different languages. They have written comics for Marvel, EC, and BOOM! Studios, including multiple original series. They are the editor and publisher of *Stone Soup* and *Love Letters: Reasons to Be Alive.*

sarahgailey.com
Instagram: @gaileyfrey
TikTok: @gaileyfrey
Facebook: Sarah Gailey
Bluesky: @sarahgailey.bsky.social